THE CAIN CONSPIRACY

THE CAIN CONSPIRACY

NICK THACKER

The Cain Conspiracy: Harvey Bennett Thrillers, Book #9
Copyright © 2022 by Nick Thacker
Published by Conundrum Publishing

PROLOGUE
GARZA

TWENTY-ONE YEARS **Ago**

He screamed.

He'd tried his best to stay silent, to not give in to the pressure, the pain.

He'd failed.

Vicente Garza's head hung loosely on his neck. He felt no more need to fight. No more need to pretend that he was strong.

He felt a tear descending from the corner of his eye, the same corner in which he saw the man working on his wife. In vain. He'd heard the flatline half an hour ago, and only because one of the assistants had turned off the noise had the sinister sin wave stopped.

The man worked, frantically moving around the bed and touching, tapping, doing whatever he thought might work. A 'doctor,' but Vicente was unsure anyone in the United States would call him that.

The treatment plan had been simple: extract the tumor using traditional surgical methods, then use the new experimental laser therapy to seal off the area, creating a cancer-free cavity. The laser would effectively kill the tissue in that location, but — more importantly — the medication inside would attract the cancerous cells

1

toward it, at which point they would apply more of the laser-extraction technique.

It was a treatment Vicente didn't understand. One that wasn't even close to being an approved treatment back home. But what he did understand is that his wife was dying.

None of the doctors would help him. The military wanted him to accept the fact that she was going to be taken from him; even his priest wished for him to begin the grief journey. Begin fighting the battle of grief, they had said.

He wasn't ready for any of it. His wife was still breathing, still walking and talking and loving. She was still taking care of him and their young daughter, Victoria. His wife was still... alive.

Why fight a battle that has not begun?

Grief can wait, he told himself. We will find the solution.

And then he met the man who'd offered that solution.

The family had been visiting Guadalajara, Mexico, the city Garza's parents had been from. His wife was beginning to lose her hair from the chemotherapy treatments that weren't having any other positive effects, and they were staying in a hotel for a short vacation before they had to be back home for more doctor visits and treatments.

Garza, after helping his wife into bed and kissing his daughter on the forehead, had snuck down to the bar and overheard a conversation between two men from Mexico City.

One was some sort of pharmaceutical representative that came across more like a drug dealer, the other some sort of doctor. They were discussing, in low tones, how many more shipments of a special new drug they would need to prove to the doctor's staff that the treatment was effective. The doctor was sure a positive result would be replicable within a month , the dealer more skeptical — and therefore wanting to artificially boost the price of his drug.

Garza was listening in without paying much attention until the doctor leaned in close to his friend and said, "I believe the cancer is completely gone. The side effects are minimal, but we can treat for those."

The second man nodded, then grunted. "Price is still going up. It has been taking too long, and my suppliers are having more trouble sourcing the ingredients."

The doctor put his palms up, feigning retreat. "Okay, okay, I understand. I can... possibly increase the payment by fifteen percent. But if —"

"Excuse me," Garza had said. "I — I am terribly sorry to butt in. May I ask what you are talking about?"

The two men weren't pleased that a stranger had suddenly entered the conversation, but Garza had quickly learned that the drug was not illegal, merely untested. When he pried a little further, he discovered that "untested" simply meant the treatment had not been sufficiently and authoritatively studied and analyzed by the requisite cadre of doctors.

In other words, the doctor scoffed, it had not been through the ten-year-long process of being stripped apart only to discover what the doctor already knew: this drug and treatment plan *worked*. He had the human trials to prove it.

PROLOGUE
GARZA

TWENTY-ONE YEARS **Ago**

Garza wanted in. He knew he would do *anything* to save his wife's life, but he wanted to see these results first. The doctor and his supplier agreed to meet in Mexico City the next week, and Garza would have the first half of the required cash in hand: $250,000, in US bills. The entirety of their remaining savings.

The treatments worked... at first. His wife's strength increased, and her pain had reduced by at least a quarter. Garza was elated, and he sold their home and wired the cash to Mexico, gladly handing it over to the doctor and his team.

And then, after about six months of regular laser treatment, his wife's heath failed. She grew weaker than she'd ever been, and her waking hours were filled with screams of agony. The doctor was unsure what the cause was, assuring Garza that the treatment would kick in at any moment.

Those moments had long passed, and Garza now sat in a chair against a dingy, dimly lit wall in the doctor's private operating room. His wife lay motionless on a gurney while the doctor and his two assistants worked.

A fourth man stood in the corner, barely visible in the shadows.

If not for his bright-white clerical collar, Garza would have forgotten he was there. The man was furiously working his way through the beads on his rosary.

In vain, no doubt. Garza sneered in his direction. *Useless body,* he thought. *And I am paying for his presence.* It was a mandatory expense on the office's list of "general hospitality" fees to have a professional clergyman in attendance. A strange, antiquated ritual, shoving the religion of the masses down the throats of the few. Garza was disgusted by the egregious force-feeding of religion, but he was more disgusted by the logistics: during his time in this place he had noticed that the only rooms that featured these on-call clergy were the rooms of patients who had the money to put up for the luxury.

He knew it was over. He knew there was nothing they could do, nothing the priest could pray that would bring her back. Perhaps the cancer had already metastasized too far throughout her body before the new treatment, perhaps there was a side effect that the doctor hadn't yet uncovered.

Whatever the reason, Garza screamed.

The doctor turned around, shock on his face, while the priest slunk back even further. "Mr. — Mr. Garza, please," he said. "You must calm down."

"You *killed* her!"

"Sir, we — I did no such thing. She — she simply... the treatment did not..."

The two assistants left the room, citing the need to refill some medication or another. But Garza had seen their eyes — they were scared of him. *Terrified.*

And rightfully so. Garza's temper had worsened the last few months, mostly because he was no longer sleeping, and his daughter, merely six years old, was unable to fend for herself. He had no time to rest, no time to not be a parent, and he felt guilty whenever he took even a moment for himself.

I sit, while she's dying, he would tell himself.

But they weren't just afraid of his personality. Besides his building temper and deteriorating attitude, he was built like a tank. Years of special forces service and a post-military career in private security had chiseled his body into a powerful, functional piece of weaponry. He'd killed many men — and some women — and it had long ago ceased to affect him.

He stood, calming himself down, and approached the doctor. Besides his dead wife, they were alone in the room. Garza and the doctor and his well-paid priest. He knew his wife would wait — he could say goodbye later. Right now the only thing he could see was his own rage. He had been duped, fooled by this idiot doctor and his money-grabbing business partner.

In a moment of weakness he had agreed to a no-win situation, a con. He could see it all clearly now. The doctor had no intention — or even the means — to save his wife. It was a money grab. Even the local church was in on it. He wondered how much money would be funneled into the coffers of the parish church.

"How much of the money do you get?" Garza growled.

The doctor's eyes widened, two little beady disks behind equally round eyeglasses. "I — I do not know what you are talking —"

"How much?" he roared.

"I... I get 60 percent," he stammered.

Garza seethed, his fists clenching and unclenching by his sides. *Victoria is out there*, he reminded himself. She had been coming to every treatment, waiting in the lobby. There was nowhere else for her, but Garza hadn't wanted her inside the room. *She can hear you.*

He shook his head. *No, she can't.*

"60 percent of *my* money, to kill my wife."

"It's not... it's not like that," the doctor said. "I swear!"

Garza attacked before the doctor even knew it was coming. A quick flat-fingered jab to the man's throat, and he stumbled backward and hit the bed. Garza pounced, grabbing the man's shoulders and sending a knee to the doctor's groin.

The priest darted for the door. Garza reached out to stop him, to catch him and make him pay for his taking advantage of his family as well, but the thinner man slid through his grasp. Garza let him run, turning his attention back to the doctor.

The doctor gasped, the sound coming out like a throaty growl, and Garza let him fall. He sat there on the floor, on his knees, watching Garza with pleading eyes.

Garza reached for the first thing he could find: the tiny handheld laser. He examined it for a moment. A single button turned the device on and off, and a knob on the side increased the power. It was running through a power adaptor that was plugged into the nearby wall.

The doctor's eyes once again widened and he tried to get back to his feet, but Garza was there first.

He grabbed the man's arms and fed his own behind them, locking the smaller doctor in place. Garza easily held his weight as he struggled and kicked. He started to call for help.

Garza stuffed the laser into the man's open mouth, then hit the button.

At first, nothing happened.

Garza used his thumb and forefinger to turn the laser's power up to the maximum amount, and he felt the doctor beginning to choke. Smoke poured from his mouth, and Garza was suddenly hit by a disgusting wave of odor.

Burning flesh.

Vicente Garza stood there, crying, the doctor silently screaming into the laser that was protruding out of his mouth.

He would stand here as long as it took. He was done feeling out of control. He was done feeling like he had failed.

He would do anything for his wife in life, and now, in her death, he was doing something.

PART ONE
ACT 1

"PULL OVER."

The soldier, dressed in black, complete with a black skullcap, looked over at his commanding officer.

"Sir?"

"Pull over," the man said again. His eyes were hidden behind dark sunglasses, his own head sporting a similar black skullcap. The driver hadn't even realized the man had seen the police lights. He was stoic, unmoving, and the driver was almost sorry he'd volunteered to drive under his command.

Some of the other privates would have at least talked, he thought. *Or at least let us listen to music.*

But Briggs was a statue, a singular piece of muscle that, to Private Jerrick Derrick, was incapable of human emotion. Jerrick Derrick, the man who had spent his life running from slights poking fun at his name, had found a relatively peaceful fit in the ranks of Ravenshadow, a private military contractor run by a man he looked up to as a mentor.

But he felt he had a long way to go before he understood the inner workings of the group — what was appropriate, what was not, and just how far they would go to achieve their goals. It was a new form of politics Jerrick hadn't experienced before.

"But sir, if they see the —"

"That's an order, private."

The young driver nodded once, gritted his teeth, and slowed the vehicle. The brakes squealed a bit, the humid, damp air no doubt a factor. The massive troop transport truck veered right, its passenger-side tires finding a dip just off the side of the asphalt and melting into it. The truck's frame creaked in protest, and he felt some of their payload shifting in the back.

They came to a complete stop, a hiss emanating from somewhere in the depths of the engine compartment, and the driver looked again at his commanding officer. *Now what?* Derrick wondered.

The police cruiser kept its siren lights on as the officer stepped out. He was doughy, fat around the waist, and looked as though he'd be better served driving a desk chair than a police cruiser.

Derrick watched the man from his side mirror. He checked his belt, pushed in a bit of shirt that had popped free, then sauntered toward the truck. He had his hand on his pistol.

The officer strode up to the side of the massive truck, squinting in the noonday sun, and made a motion to roll the window down.

"Si?" Derrick asked. He hoped the policeman knew English — 'si' was about the extent of his Spanish.

The officer mumbled something in Spanish. Derrick shook his head.

"Get out," Briggs mumbled.

"What?"

"He said get out. So get out."

Derrick was confused. "But we can't —"

"Get out, private. Take him around back. He wants to see what we're hauling."

Derrick flashed a glance down at the assault rifle leaning against the truck's front seat between him and Briggs. Briggs' own rifle was in his hand. Neither was visible to the police officer.

Derrick flicked the handle open and put a leg down on the rail. "Should I show him?"

He watched Briggs' face for a sign of any emotion. *Is he nervous? Scared? Ignorant?* Instead, Briggs just nodded. "Show him."

Derrick, wide-eyed, got out of the truck and hopped to the hot asphalt road. The officer was short, about four inches shorter than Derrick, and he looked up at the soldier with a suspicious eye.

"American?" the officer asked. Of course, there was nothing overtly 'American' about Derrick's uniform — all-black said nothing but soldier — but the officer obviously suspected something.

Derrick nodded.

The officer asked something else. He caught "donde" — *where* — and "porque" — *why*. Something else about military something or other. Derrick shrugged.

"Su troca," the officer said. More words. *He wants to see what's in the truck.*

Derrick couldn't see Briggs from this angle. He hoped he wasn't about to let him get arrested. Derrick motioned with a dipped neck toward the back of the truck. The officer put a hand out and Derrick led the way.

There was a canvas drape covering the back of the truck. It looked like a modernized wagon, the kind used in the old west. This one, however, was dirty green and about three times the size.

The officer stepped up to the back of the truck and Derrick could see Spanish insignia and the man's city of origin on a badge on his shoulder. He didn't recognize the name of the town, but he assumed it was one of the smaller cities they'd passed by on the way out here.

And 'here,' to Derrick, seemed like 'nowhere.' Born and raised in Detroit, Derrick was used to sprawling city blocks, industrial complexes, and suburban houses as far as he could see. He was used to people.

Being out here in the rainforest, crawling over pothole-studded roads that hadn't been maintained since they'd been laid down thirty years ago, was like driving through a whole different world.

He took a sharp breath, watching the officer. The man still had his hand on his weapon, but it was holstered. Derrick did the mental calculus. One-half second to get it unclipped, another to get it out, then between one and three to actually flick the safety off and aim it.

Derrick's sidearm was under the seat in the truck's cab, but he knew he still had the upper hand. The cop wouldn't expect the young man to be so fast, so quick to the draw. Derrick knew he could have the officer completely subdued in under two seconds flat, as long as he kept the distance between them under four feet.

The officer went for the back of the truck. Derrick closed the distance. The officer lifted a hand up and began pulling back the drape.

Briggs appeared from the other side of the vehicle. He hadn't heard him get out; perhaps his door was still open.

The drape was pulled to the side fully now, and the officer tossed it up and over the edge of the truck's frame, where it stayed. He looked into the trailer.

Seconds passed. The officer didn't move, both Briggs and Derrick now standing behind him. The policeman still had his hand on his pistol, but he didn't try to unholster it.

He took a slow step back. Derrick watched him carefully. He was no doubt surprised, to say the least. *Confused? Appalled?*

The officer finally turned, also slowly and methodically, and faced Derrick. He saw Briggs had joined them. He swallowed, then lifted the pistol out of its holster.

Briggs was there, fast — too fast to be real — and he had his hand lifted already. Derrick would have missed it if he'd blinked. The older soldier didn't hesitate. He fired.

The officer went down, a crumpled heap on the side of the road. Blood, pooling out around his head. His mouth, moving but not talking. His eyes, wide and surprised and still trying to comprehend.

Briggs watched the man die, then looked up at Derrick. "Let's go."

He turned and walked back toward the front seat.

Derrick nodded to no one in particular, his eyes moving from the police officer to the back of the truck.

Eyes met his. Twenty pairs of them. Men, women, and children. All tied, all gagged. Their brown, sun-beaten faces were silent, their bodies unmoving.

They watched him as he watched them. Waiting for something. They didn't know what, and, to be honest, he didn't either.

So there was nothing to say. He was doing his job, that was it.

He pulled the canvas flap back down over the rear-end of the transport truck and walked back to the driver's seat. He pulled himself up and in, put the truck in drive, then pulled away from the dead policeman and his squad car.

Briggs was looking out the front window, silent and stoic.

CHAPTER 2

BEN

"JULES!" Ben yelled. Then he laughed. *I'm yelling for someone inside a log cabin.*

The space they were in was small, just a living room and kitchen and attached bedroom. But it was the *other* section, the new section, that he was yelling through. The Civilian Special Operations had contracted a new wing to the cabin, attached through the kitchen, where Ben was standing. The wing had bedrooms that could sleep 10, a full-sized commercial kitchen, and an office complex on the second floor. There was even a makeshift lounge, which was really just another bedroom they'd added a television, couch, and a few board games to.

A woman appeared in the hallway, but it wasn't Julie.

"You know," she said. "We used to call her 'Jelly.' She ever tell you that?

Ben's mouth was a hard line. "No. No, she didn't."

"Well, anyway," the woman said. "'Jules' never seemed... right. Just didn't fit, you know?" Alexis Richardson stepped up to Ben and reached up to fix his bowtie. "Don't worry, Harvey," she said. "I'll fix this. No reason to bother Julie with it."

Ben sidestepped and ducked out of her reach. "No, I can tie my own tie. I wasn't... that's not what I needed."

"Well, what is it you need, dear?" Alexis asked. "I'm sure I can help with it."

You're not a professionally trained psychologist, Ben thought. *And I highly doubt you've had experience with trauma-induced anxiety.*

"It's fine," he said. "I'll just wait."

Alexis huffed and shrugged, but thankfully turned to leave. He saw her dart back into her bedroom, no doubt looking for another place to insert herself.

Their time here had been strained, to say the least. To Ben, his cabin was his place of solitude. It was a retreat. Somewhere he could *hide.* The past week had been a blur — getting the wedding planned, the logistics taken care of, and the invites out to the small group of attendees.

Ben's parents were dead, but Julie's had immediately flown out to Anchorage and driven to the cabin when they'd heard the wedding was happening. Both retired, Alexis a high-school teacher and Warren a regional pilot, they'd dropped everything to be there for their daughter and her soon-to-be-husband.

They were nice enough, too. Warren was placid and docile, easy to be around, and he enjoyed sampling Ben's growing whiskey and rum collection. Alexis was pleasant, but Ben wasn't sure she knew how to relax. She was either cleaning, folding clothes — he was amazed at how many outfits one woman needed for a week-long trip — or cooking. The cooking part he liked, but altogether it made him feel like he wasn't working hard enough. He and Julie couldn't sit down in the evening to talk without Alexis butting in and asking about something or other.

But Julie was happy. She had a great relationship with her parents, and no matter how strange it was to be in the close presence of another couple like this, he wanted a relationship with them as well. They were nice, kind people, and Ben felt like he'd been given another chance to have an adult relationship with his parents through them.

He walked back through the kitchen and dining room into the bedroom. There were clothes everywhere, Julie's of course. What she would wear before the wedding, what she would wear during the wedding — she hated the idea of a huge, flowing white dress — and what she would wear after. Still, Ben didn't understand why he was seeing at least seven different dresses on the bed.

He flopped onto the chair and opened the laptop on the desk. Mindlessly clicking through websites and news updates, finding nothing of intrigue, he was about to close it again when he heard a knock on the door.

"Hey, brother," Reggie's voice said. "How you doing?"

Ben smiled. "Which hand did you use to knock?"

Reggie looked confused for a brief moment then laughed. "It hurts a bit, but not in the way you'd expect." He held up his prosthetic arm for examination. The wound had nearly healed, but there was still some serious physical therapy and training he was undergoing to get used the new prosthetic.

He'd lost his arm in Peru, just over a month ago. Thanks to a full-time doctor and nurse paid for by the CSO, his recovery had been quick and mostly worry-free, and Ben knew he was excited to start working with the more advanced prosthetics.

He walked to the bed and roughly slid the dresses to the side, then sat on the edge of the bed and turned to Ben.

"Anyway," Ben said, "I'm fine. It's... hard."

"Yeah, Alexis can be a handful, huh? Last night she cornered me and Sarah and asked us about when we were going to have kids. *Kids.* Who asks that?"

Ben laughed. "No, that's fine. I mean, you're right. That's hard. But I'm talking about Julie. How do I know she's ready?"

Reggie grinned. "I think you mean, how do you know *you're* ready."

"I'm ready," Ben said. "Never been more ready."

"Than what's the problem? You can only know yourself. Can't worry about her, my man."

"But... I *do* worry about her."

Reggie paused, then stepped into the room. "Ah, I see. Well, I guess you just have to trust that she's telling you the truth."

"Of course I trust her."

"Than you have to trust *yourself* to know there's nothing more you can do. Ben — look. I've been there. I know how you're feeling right now. It's... weird. Trying to balance it all and make a good impression and juggle your feelings with what you *think* she's feel-ing... let me just give you some advice: you will *never* truly know what she's feeling."

Ben cocked an eyebrow.

"I'm serious. I mean, you'll know her better than anyone — better than her parents. But you'll never really know *exactly* what she's feeling at any given time."

"Why?"

"Well, because. Women are..." he stopped. "Ben, how many emotions can you name? Off the top fo your head?"

"Uh, anger. Happiness. Joy — is that happiness? Yeah. Okay, confusion? Is that an emotion?"

"Sure."

"What's the point?"

"So you named like three-and-a-half emotions. Julie *might* be angry about something, but chances are she's actually *ambivalent,* or pissed, or perturbed, or annoyed, or —"

"Got it."

"So you're wondering if she's confused, or scared, or trying to figure herself out with this... memory stuff."

"Yeah, exactly."

"Yeah, she is. One-hundred percent, man. Of *course* she's trying to figure it out. But that doesn't at all mean she's not *ready*. You're talking about getting married, man. You've *been* talking about it, for like years now. You *know* she's ready. But that doesn't mean she's not feeling all sorts of weird stuff."

"Gotcha. So you're saying that she's ready, but she's just feeling all those things women feel, and that's normal?"

"Ben," Reggie said. "You're a smart guy. Real sharp. But sometimes you can be a bit one-speed, you know?"

"Uh..."

"No, I'm *not* saying those are things 'women' feel. *I'm* saying they're things *all* of us feel. We — dudes — just aren't used to processing them all. So we make it *their* problem instead."

Reggie stood up before Ben could answer, walked to Ben's chair, and started fixing his tie. "Come on, man, don't you know how to tie one of these? You're such a barbarian."

CHAPTER 3

JULIE

JULIE WAS FRANTIC. She'd long ago taken off the smartwatch, after the third time it told her that her heart rate was elevated and that it would 'be helpful to take a minute to breathe.'

Take a minute to breathe, my —

"Jelly!"

She whipped her head around, even more frantic, until she remembered that her mother and father were here, too. It was weird, having them stay in the same house — a house she shared with the man she was about to marry.

"Jelly, you in here?" Her mom's head popped around the corner, looking into the lounge. "Why are you hiding in here?" she asked.

"I'm not *hiding*, Mom," Julie said. "This is the only room that has a full-length mirror.

"Oh," her mother said, not even trying to hide her concern. "Are — are you okay?"

"I'm fine, Mom. Doing my hair. Want to help?"

Alexis Richardson's eyes lit up like Julie had just told her she was her most favorite person on the planet. "I would do anything, Jelly. What do you need?"

"Wine. Lots of it. Just... grab whatever you can carry, and a glass — two glasses, sorry — and bring it here."

"Oh," Alexis said again, this time downtrodden. She sulked away, and Julie heard her flats smacking against the floor of the add-on wing's hallway.

She shook her head. *Why does she have to be so* there *all the time?* Julie knew she was overreacting, but her mother always seemed to have everything together — everything figured out, in its place, ready. She never stopped. She wondered how her father put up with it.

And where's Ben?

She had less than an hour, and she hadn't even put on her dress. She wanted to get her hair just right — it was the only characteristic of herself she felt any vanity toward, and it was important that it looked exactly the way she'd pictured it. The trouble was, she hadn't really *pictured* anything more than "perfect." *What was perfect? What does that even mean?*

She felt scared suddenly, as if she needed someone to just tell her to sit down and relax, and that they — whoever they were — would just start messing with her hair until *they* thought it was perfect.

But she had no one, at least not in that way. Her maid of honor would be Dr. Sarah Lindgren, the woman whom she had come to know very well over the last months, and a woman she now trusted with her life. But *trusting* someone with her life was far different from *spending* that life together.

Her grade school friends and college acquaintances were all gone, spread around the world as they'd moved into their adult lives. None of them had been particularly close with her, but it was as much her fault as theirs. She'd spent her school years focused on mathematics and computer science, turning her brilliance and intelligence into experience with programming and data systems. That had turned into a career working for the Biological Threat Research division of the CDC, then into a new career at the newly formed CSO.

Her job was... vague. She was part of a team that worked to solve mysteries, find hidden treasures, and generally work between the gaps in the system. Things that were too off-limits for their own government yet too large to tackle by local law enforcement were the sort of missions the CSO took on.

Julie fumbled with a quiff of hair near the back of her head before deciding it was pointless. *I'll just watch a YouTube video later or something,* she thought. She stood up, turned to leave, and was met at the door by her mother, holding two bottles of wine — a red and a white — and two glasses.

Julie started to cry. Her mother walked into the room, took her hand, and sat her down again in front of the mirror. She poured two glasses of red wine, tall enough that the glasses nearly spilled as she carried them, and handed one to Julie. She then put hers down, turned Julie's head to face the mirror, and began working on her hair.

"Thanks, Mom," Julie whispered.

Her mother smiled, a sweet, knowing thing. "Did you know that I almost didn't marry your father?"

Julie's eyes grew and she took a long, deep sip of wine.

"It's true."

"I thought — I thought he was the 'only one.' You always said that."

"Oh, he was — and is — the only one for me. That's never changed. But when I was getting ready for my wedding, months out, he was constantly asking if I was okay. So sweet, so kind. Just... always making sure I was okay."

"That's... why you almost called it off?"

"Well, I don't think I ever would have called it off, but I struggled with it, sure. I mean, how was I supposed to know that he was the right one for me?"

"Yeah, but you just *knew*, right?"

"I knew, but that didn't mean there weren't any doubts."

"I'm not doubting anything about Ben, Mom."

"I am not saying you are," Alexis said. "What I *am* saying is that I see so much of myself in you."

"And so much of Dad in Ben?"

"No, not at all. I'm saying that I know you — I know how you are, and how stubborn you can be."

Julie rolled her eyes. *Not a great pep talk, Mom.*

"But that's a good thing. And you've found a man who respects that, and understands that. He knows that *you* want to make your own decisions. He knows that *you* need a voice, and he gives you that."

"He... yeah, he does," Julie said. "That's exactly how he is."

"Well, then there's no reason to doubt anything. You two will be fine."

She smiled again, and Julie took another sip. She caught a glance at her hair in the mirror as she did. A French braid fell from one side on the top of her head to the other, a diagonal design that fell just behind her left shoulder.

She swallowed, choking up. She reached up and grabbed Alexis' hand. "Mom, it's perfect."

CHAPTER 4
CISCO

CISCO CABRERA STEPPED DOWN from the back of the huge truck and was immediately shuffled into a line. His mouth and neck hurt from the gag they'd tied around his head, but he felt nothing in the way of his own pain. Instead, he felt for the others — his mother and father, and his young sister with her baby. He wanted to do something, but these men, the white men wearing all black uniforms, were powerful.

They had come into the village at night, when everyone was sleeping. They were a small, close-knit community, many of whom had been in the same village all their lives, going back generations. They fished, grew corn and yucca, and the village had a reasonably profitable enterprise turning some of their product into beer and distillates.

They had no defenses of any kind, and by the time Cisco realized what was happening it was too late. His was the last home the men had entered, and they had quickly tied and gagged all of his family, including his two-year old niece. No one fought back — what would be the point?

After a two-hour journey, they were pulled off the truck and were now walking through a large doorway. It stood on the side of a mountain, the gaping maw of the door disappearing into black noth-ingness. It was into this hole where they were led.

At the end of a long, wide tunnel, more men appeared and pulled them apart. Cisco and his father were led one direction, his mother and sister with her child another. Into a room, dark and damp. The air smelled of earth, the same soil he had tilled every year for just about all of his thirty-three years.

A man came up to him. Taller than Cisco, wearing the black uniform. "Nombre?" he barked.

Cisco told him his name.

"Años?

He told him. Asked where they were, and what they were going to do with them. The man ignored him, or didn't understand, and wrote down Cisco's name on a piece of paper and then moved to Cisco's father and started again.

It took half an hour to question all of the men in the room, and then they were taken into another room, three at a time. Cisco was the last man of a set of three into this room, so he was split up from his father. He was weighed on a scale, his chest and torso measured, then asked a rapid set of questions. He tried to answer as many as he could, but he didn't understand a few. They didn't seem to care.

When they were done in this room, they were once again split — three doorways, one for each of them. Cisco stepped through his and found a bed and chair, and some medical instruments on a tray in a small built-in cabinet. A single, dim bulb hung from the ceiling. He walked over and sat in the chair. His hands were still tied, so it was uncomfortable. He tried to move around, to keep focused, but found that he was exhausted. He hadn't eaten in hours, nor had he had any water. He sat back down.

He was unsure how long he waited in the small room. Five minutes or five hours. Time had stood still in here. He wanted to know how his father was doing, and what they had done with his mother and sister. Were they taking care of his niece. He felt cold, but didn't shiver; he knew it was from within, not the temperature of the room.

Finally the door opened. Cisco shot to his feet, both scared and excited that something was happening. A man walked in, wearing a white coat, followed by two more black-clad men. The white coated man looked at Cisco, examining him from the opposite side of the room, and said something under his breath to the other men. These two men stepped forward, grabbed Cisco's arms, and pushed him down onto the bed.

He tried fighting back — knowing it was in vain, but no longer hoping there would be a positive outcome for all this trouble. They hardly worked to keep him pinned, holding his already-bound arms down on the bed. He kicked his legs, but there was no one near enough for him to contact.

The man in white stepped forward and held up a long, sharp needle. Liquid squirted from the end of it. Cisco had always hated needles. He'd had shots as a boy, only once, in the big city nearby, but hardly anyone in his village thought modern medicine a necessity, and his parents dropped the issue after he complained incessantly for weeks.

The man — a doctor, he guessed — plunged the needle into Cisco's arm. He felt the cold steel, the pulsating warmth of the liquid, the empty void of feeling as it coursed through him. It was moving, *replacing* him. He felt raw, as if devoid of any emotion, then... nothing.

He could still see the three men, but there was no attachment or detachment related to them. They were apparitions. Wraiths. Floating above his head.

They were no longer holding his arms, but it didn't matter. He couldn't move them even if they weren't still tied behind his back. He watched them leave, thinking nothing of it. Or thinking of it in a acknowledgement sort of way but not with any purpose. They were gone, he was alone.

He didn't think to leave — didn't want to. He didn't want to do anything. But he was alive. Was that good? Was the shot supposed to kill him?

No. Why would they go through all that trouble?

And then, as if stopping his own thoughts in mid-sentence, he realized he didn't care. He was totally complacent, totally apathetic.

He lay his head back down on the bed, hard and flat and no pillow to rest it on. He closed his eyes, but he didn't want to sleep. He didn't want to do anything.

He looked up at the ceiling, the tiny gray squares staring back down at him.

He stayed this way until they came for him the next day.

CHAPTER 5

BEN

ARCHIBALD QUINONES, a Jesuit priest, administered the wedding. The setting was idyllic: the cabin's front 'yard' had been converted into a beautiful, picturesque wedding venue, by way of white folding chairs, ribbons, and what must have been a metric ton of flowers.

The trees lined the area just beyond where Archie stood beneath the lattice, where Ben had waited for Julie to walk down the aisle arm in arm with her father.

She was stunning, and Ben could hardly focus on the vows as Archie led them through them. When it was time for the exchanging of rings, Reggie and Sarah, themselves a beautiful couple, handed them to their friends with a smile.

Then they kissed, and the assembled crowd of people cheered. Mrs. E stood next to her husband on a mounted television screen. Mr. E, who was dressed to the nines and seated behind his own desk at his home, clapped along with everyone else.

Ben and Julie walked up the aisle and disappeared into their cabin, where they changed clothes and reemerged a few minutes later, ready to celebrate. The wedding area in front of the cabin would also serve as a banquet hall, and hired teams were already erecting a white tent over the area.

Ben, walking with Julie, made his way around the tent and shook hands with everyone in attendance. It didn't take long, as there were fewer than fifteen people there. When they got to the end of the line, Ben saw the final person waiting to congratulate them.

"Victoria," he said. "Thank you for coming."

Victoria Reyes smiled. "I wouldn't miss it for the world. Thank you for having me."

Ben was about to turn away when he felt her hand on his arm.

"Ben," she said, her voice low.

Oh, no. He didn't need to know her very well to know that tone was not something she used for exciting news.

"Are you going back to Peru?"

Ben's breath caught in his throat. He took a step back, and Julie put her hand on his back. Victoria stepped forward, staying in front of them.

"I... hadn't really thought about it," Ben said.

Victoria smiled, but she had a distant look in her eyes. "I'm not sure I believe that."

Ben sighed. "Okay, fine. Yes. We've talked about it. Garza — your father — whatever he was planning there isn't over."

"I know," she said.

Julie stepped in. "But we don't have any details yet. It's still... well, the wedding sort of took over this last month, and Reggie's healing and everything."

Victoria nodded. From somewhere behind him Ben heard strains of music piping through the PA system that had been erected at the edge of the tent.

"He has to be stopped."

Ben looked up at the tent, then down at the ground. "Listen, Victoria. I know how you feel. And I think —"

"You do *not* know how I feel," she said, her voice suddenly shaky. Alexis and Warren Richardson, who were talking to Mrs. E, looked over. "He's *my father*. He *must* be stopped."

"Vic," Julie said, taking the woman's hand. "He *will* be stopped. I promise you. But... these things take time. We have to plan, and we have to —"

"I figured it out," Victoria said. "The Temple of Solomon. It's the Hall of Records, the repository for the collected wisdom of the ancients. It's in —"

"Peru," Ben said. "Between the two pillars. The mountain."

Victoria seemed shocked, then impressed. "Yes, exactly."

When they had been in Peru the last time, there had been two temples — two identical ancient stone temples, each with a raised dais inside it and round stone table — a 'pillar' — on it. The pillars were representations of the pillars that stood outside the first Temple of Solomon, built by one of the early Freemasons named Hiram Abiff.

Reggie and Sarah had been kidnapped, strapped down to one of the pillars, and a guillotine had been placed above their wrists.

Ben and his team had found the pillar — but it was the wrong one.

Reggie had lost his entire arm protecting Sarah, and Ben had been at the wrong pillar. The memory haunted him, but he knew it was nothing compared to the haunting memories Julie was facing.

Memories that involved Victoria's father, Vicente "The Hawk" Garza.

"I figured it out, too. When we left Peru the last time. It makes sense, geographically, and I bet the proportions line up, too. The '33' multiplier and all that."

"They do. Everything points to the mountain — at least somewhere inside of it — being the final resting place of the Hall of Records. And I want to go there."

"Victoria," Ben said softly. "That entire area is going to be crawling with Ravenshadow forces. Your father's going to still be there — he *won* that battle, remember? We barely made it out alive, but he took out one of our team and a whole bunch of the Guild

Rite guys. There's no chance he's leaving it undefended, and I'd bet he's even moved all operations to Peru — he'll have an army there, if he doesn't already."

"But he may not know about the mountain, and what's inside it. Which is why we need to go. I'm fluent in Spanish, and if we go now I can —"

"We *will*. Just... give it time."

"We might not *have* time," Victoria said, clearly frustrated. But she didn't push it further. She turned on a heel and walked away. Ben saw her enter the cabin and turn left. They'd established the cabin's kitchen and tiny dining table as the de facto bar — self-serve and open all the time. He wasn't sure if Victoria Reyes drank, but she didn't reappear in the doorway.

Ben and Julie stayed there for a moment, looking into the cabin, until Alexis corralled them over to her conversation with Mrs. E.

"Mrs. E tells me you two have been to Antarctica? Jelly, you didn't tell me you've been there. What an amazing trip! Was it a cruise?"

CHAPTER 6
BEN

BEN SAT on the bed in the room. The lights were out, but there was plenty of it spilling in from outside. The party was raging, if twenty people dancing to oldies and disco could be considered "raging."

Ben was alone, and he sipped from a glass of bourbon Reggie had gotten him. It was good — a bit briny, but smooth and full of caramel. He watched the legs of the whiskey as they snaked down the inside edges of the rocks glass, also a gift. The pumping strains of music wafted in, but it was otherwise quiet. Peaceful, almost.

I'm married.

It was weird. Surreal. He'd never had any doubt that Juliette Richardson was the woman he wanted to spend the rest of his life with, it was just he didn't really know what *the rest of his life* meant. How could he imagine the next years of his life when he could hardly have imagined the *last* few years?

He took another sip, and a dark shape appeared in the doorway of his room.

Ben was immediately on high alert, and he slid sideways on the bed, depositing his drink onto the desk and grabbing the loaded Glock from underneath it. He was standing now, facing the doorway, the Glock perfectly balanced in his grasp and pointed at the door.

"Christ, man, sorry." The shape put its arms up and backed up a step. The voice was young, a man's, probably somewhere in his twenties. Ben was breathing rapidly, but he did nothing to try to slow it.

"Who the hell are you?"

"Can we... talk?"

"We're talking now."

"Man, you *are* on edge. They told me you would be. It's... still weird, though."

The man stopped talking and his face caught a bit of the light bouncing off the walls. Ben saw a bit of it. He dropped the pistol to his side, but didn't set it down. "You look familiar."

"I look — Harvey, are you serious? *Familiar*?"

The man backed up into the living room, finally putting his arms down. "Come on, man. Let's talk. Oh, and congratulations."

Ben followed him out into the living room, where there was enough light to see the kid's face. Ben stopped, stared. Did a double-take.

"Zach?"

The kid grinned. "In the flesh. How you been, Harvey?"

"I — I uh, go by 'Ben' now."

"Well, I go by Pete now. Sort of. I'm still deciding."

"Pete."

"Yeah... long story."

"Well, *Pete*. It's uh, good to see you." Ben's eyes flicked downward. He now wished he were holding the glass of bourbon instead of the pistol. He'd get more use of it. "I... uh, sorry I didn't invite you."

Pete or Zach waved it off. "Don't worry about it. Wouldn't have been able to find me, anyway."

"Working for the government or something?" Ben asked.

"I wish it was that cool," Zach said. "But no. Just needed a change. I was working for a place, and... now I'm not. Working somewhere else now, doing chemistry stuff."

"You — were pretty good at that sorta thing, right?"

Zach scoffed. "I was *nine*, Ben. I don't think anyone's good at anything when they're nine."

The last time they'd seen each other, Ben had been nineteen, his little brother nine. They were on a camping trip, just the Bennett men. Johnson Bennett, their father, wanted a little time in nature with his boys while their mother was out of town.

That trip had ended in devastating horror. Zach had been hospitalized and their father had died. A grizzly attack, a freak accident. Ben hadn't thought about it in years. He'd opened up to Julie about it, but he'd told the story in a staccato, detached way. Just the facts. He'd given Reggie and the others even less.

"Fair enough. So, you like the new life?"

"It's... different. Good a life as any, I guess. The job's good pay. You?"

"What about me?"

"Your *job*. They — the weird guy on the TV out there said you were part of something called the CSO?"

"Yeah. That's Mr. E."

"Is he as weird as he seems?"

"Weirder. Never even met him in person."

Zach laughed. "I met your wife, too."

Ben raised an eyebrow.

"You're batting out of your league. She's perfect, Har — Ben. Well done."

"Thanks. Zach, what are you doing here?"

Zach took a breath. He'd caught him off-guard. Ben immediately felt bad.

"Sorry, I mean... I'm not used to — this is weird."

"Yeah," Zach said.

"Can I get you a drink?"

"I don't drink."

"I have water. Do you drink that?"

Zach smiled. "I saw a seltzer water out front. I'll grab one on the way out."

"You're leaving?"

"I didn't expect to stay. I've got a room in Anchorage for the night. No big deal."

"We have room here. More than enough space, and more than enough food. Plenty of seltzer water, too."

"Thanks, Ben. I appreciate it. It would be good to catch up, but I don't want to impose."

"You're not. We just built a wing that can sleep ten, and we've got a couch here. Stay, at least a night. I want you to meet everyone."

Zach walked over and hugged Ben. Ben wasn't quite sure what to do with the pistol in his hand, so he held it tightly and patted his little brother on the back with the butt of it.

CHAPTER 7

GARZA

VICENTE GARZA PACED OUTSIDE the makeshift hospital room. They were inside an abandoned mine, but Garza wouldn't have known it by just looking around. The walls were pristine white, sprayed with two coats of interior paint. The hallways were bright, lit by fluorescent hanging fixtures that were all wired in sequence and driven by the massive generators he'd had his team set up in a nearby room.

As the founder and president of Ravenshadow Security, LLC, Garza had been looking for an offshore location to move his growing army of security professionals. Taxes and government scrutiny in the United States had only gotten worse over the past decade, and Garza wanted out. He still worked for many US companies, but his business location was far from important to his clients. They wanted anonymity and subtlety, and they respected his desire for the same.

The mine he'd purchased in Peru was structurally sound, needing little architectural support. His team had put in the infrastructure they'd needed, slapped a few coats of paint on the new walls, and called it home. The place had been remarkably clean — no sign of mining equipment or coal or anything. Now the new Ravenshadow headquarters boasted living quarters for up to two-hundred men, complete with a commercial kitchen and two recreation halls. His work building the Ravenshadow crew had slowly paid off, and he would now be able to reap the benefits.

Purchasing land in Peru had been a struggle at first, but the price was incomparable to anything he might be able to find elsewhere. The international company who had owned the mine and rights to the surrounding land was about to file for bankruptcy in Peruvian court, and he had saved them a lot of money and grief by making a lowball offer on all of it. His bank hadn't even batted an eye at the purchase of the property, knowing that Garza was more than good for the amount — he had always made it a point to never miss a payment that was rightfully owed.

His long-term goal was to move the entirety of his operations out of the United States, from Philadelphia, and into Peru. It had, so far, proven to be a tax haven for his company, and he was already beginning to make side deals with some of the military officials in the area — a feat which was far easier in the less-stable economic environment of South America.

He stopped pacing and looked through the rectangular window in the door. Dr. Prichard was still examining something on the monitors, his face masked in an expression of confusion and shaded blue by the LED display. Garza knocked twice in rapid succession, didn't wait for Prichard's response, and barged in.

"Well?" he asked.

Dr. Prichard's eyebrows rose, then fell, as he looked up. "Oh, right... sorry. The... administration is complete."

"*And?*"

"It was successful."

Garza sighed. "You *successfully* administered the drug, or the drug's effects when you administered it was successful?"

"Oh, right. Uh, well, I'm checking into that now. You know, without Dr. —"

"I don't have the time to onboard another doctor, Prichard,"

Garza said. He knew the complaint well. Dr. Prichard had been advocating for hiring another doctor for the past month, after the brutal death of his colleague Dr. Ruth Jenner. "It will take weeks to even *find* someone willing to make the trip, not to mention the months of training you and I will need to provide."

"Yes, but —"

"I understand the reasoning, Dr. Prichard," Garza said. "But I am working against a much different set of pressures than you. Please do not ask again."

Prichard's eyebrows danced again, but he nodded quickly and stood up. The chair bounced backward as he rose, and he fumbled around for his footing. At some point in the past month, Garza thought, the man had descended into a *mad scientist* routine. It was annoying, but Prichard was the best he had.

"Right," Prichard said, continuing a conversation that had apparently been developing only in his mind, "so when I administered the treatment an hour ago, the subject had quite adverse effects at first."

"At first?"

"Yes."

Garza pinched his forefinger between his thumb and ring finger, trying to distract himself from his annoyance by causing himself physical pain. "*How long* were these adverse effects?"

"Oh — right. Well, uh, five minutes?"

"And then?"

"And then the dosage's side effects faded away and led to a more stable condition in the subject."

"I see. Results?"

"Well," Dr. Prichard said, "I believe the results are promising. Uh, here." He shifted to the corner of the room, next to the bed where the patient, an elderly Peruvian woman, was asleep. He stood at the head of the bed and tapped the woman's arm.

Her eyes opened slowly, flickering, then they focused on Garza and Prichard. When they met the doctor's gaze, they widened, a look of fear coming over them. She stiffened, her wrists jerking upward, but the vinyl bindings holding them in place at her sides did their job. After a few seconds of fighting in vain, she fell back to the bed, defeated.

"The effects are subtle, as you have no doubt noticed. She is still very much the same person — her personality remains unchanged."

"And we will be able to create a version of the drug that can be successfully airborne-dispersed?"

"Yes, I believe so, but it will take —"

"But it worked?" Garza asked.

"Oh, yes," Prichard replied. "Very much so. She is *far* more willing to accept outside persuasion than she would without the medication."

"I see. Prove it."

Dr. Prichard flicked his eyes to Garza, then back at the patient. "Well... uh, you see... the dosage is but a single portion of the overall treatment plan that I have —"

"Prove it," Garza said again.

"Right. Okay." Prichard cleared his throat, then sniffed. The staff Garza had hired were required to speak and understand Spanish, and he and Dr. Prichard were no exception. With a fluent, smooth voice, Prichard gently called out to the subject in the bed. "Ms., uh, Patient 84, do you know who I am?"

Patient 84 nodded.

"Good. Now, if you would, please lift your right arm."

The elderly woman's right arm rose into the air a few inches until it was caught by the strap.

"Fine, thank you. Now, Patient 84, please lift your left arm."

She did.

Garza stepped forward. "Will she respond to me?"

"Dr. Prichard shook his head. "I — I don't believe so, sir. The treatment — the remaining portion of the drug, at least, it's — meant to be administered over the course of —"

"Patient 84," Garza said in Spanish, "do you know who I am?"

The woman frowned, but didn't take her eyes off Garza. She shook her head.

"Okay, that's fine," Garza said. "Patient 84, please nod your head."

The subject seemed confused at first, but she eventually nodded.

"Very good. Now, I would like Dr. Prichard to remove your straps."

Prichard began to argue, but Garza held up a hand. Prichard complied, leaning over the woman and removing the straps holding her to the bed.

"Patient 84, please take the scalpel from Dr. Prichard."

Dr. Prichard balked. "But I'm not even *holding* a —"

"Enough," Garza said. He reached into his pocket and retrieved a medical scalpel, its metal razor-sharp edge gleaming. He handed it to Prichard. "Patient 84, please take the scalpel."

With a shaking hand, patient 84 took the knife from Prichard's hand. She held it out in front of her, over her chest, the tip pointing upward. If there was any idea in her eyes that she knew what she was holding, Garza couldn't see it.

"Patient 84," Garza continued, "please sit up."

The woman complied immediately.

"Dr. Prichard, this is remarkable."

"Y — yes, sir. The serum is from your own discovery, the borrachero."

Garza nodded. The Columbian plant borrachero, which, when processed a certain way, produced a drug similar to scopolamine called "buradanga." It caused short-term amnesia, hallucinations, and — if a high enough dosage was administered — a loss of free will. By mixing in a few additives as well, including the plant *datura stramo-nium,* or "Jimson weed," Garza's team had created a serum that he was hoping could produce an almost zombie-like state of robotic compliance in his subjects.

"Very good. Patient 84," Garza said, "please turn the scalpel around and place the tip of it on your wrist."

"Garza," Prichard said. "The complete dosage is not —"

"Do it."

The woman's eyes seemed to grow, a fiery rage behind them, but she did as she was told. He watched the tip of the blade descend onto the tired, weathered flesh of the old woman's wrist, and she naturally turned her palms over as it fell. The blade landed on her forearm, between the radius and ulna bones.

Garza did not hesitate. "Patient 84, please use the scalpel to cut a line from the bottom of your palm to your elbow. Do it now."

The patient looked up at Garza, her eyes pleading. But her hand was already in motion, the scalpel ripping through flesh as if it were a chef's knife falling through a piece of fresh meat. Blood seeped out the newly formed crack, at first slowly, then increasing in volume until the woman's arm was completely covered in crimson.

Garza watched, fascinated. He had always had an interest in medical procedures and human anatomy, but he had never spent the time to learn either craft. Still, he was riveted to the scene.

"Garza?"

Garza held a finger up to his lips, silencing his employee.

The woman began breathing heavily, her internal emotions fighting against the chemical brain damage that had consumed her consciousness. Her eyes fell to her arm, and Garza could see she was unable to process what was happening. Her environment was completely foreign to her, and her facial expression now reflected that.

Garza watched, in a trance, as Patient 84 slowly and painfully bled out, her rising heart rate and internal temperature swing causing Dr. Prichard's monitor to beep. The incessant noise finally got the best of Garza and he turned, exiting the room.

"Get a janitorial crew out here that can clean this up," Garza said, over his shoulder as he reentered the pristine-white hallway.

"WHAT DO YOU THINK?" She asked Ben. Julie was sitting across from him on one of the white folding chairs that was still under the wedding tent. She was fidgeting, trying to get the short dress to lay properly across her legs. *This is why I don't dress up,* she thought.

"I don't want to think about it at all," Ben said, lifting his glass to his mouth and taking a sip. "We just got *married*, Jules. Can't we just enjoy the evening?"

Reggie and Sarah walked over, and Julie could tell they were going to sit near them.

She smiled. "Yeah, I know. It's just — " she leaned in close to Ben and whispered. "This could be our *chance*, Ben."

"We had a chance to kill him, four times already. We failed."

"No, I'm talking about the Hall of Records."

"You really think it's there?"

"I think *something's* there," she said. Reggie pulled up a chair for Sarah, then another for himself. His prosthetic arm was in a cast, apparently offering him a bit of relief from the strain. "Garza may not know about it, but you and Victoria came to the same conclusion — the Temple of Solomon, the pillars — it's all right there."

Ben nodded. "Still, it's in the heart of Ravenshadow's base. If they're still there, they'll kill us. And you remember the —"

"The giants," Reggie said. "Yeah, those assholes were something else."

When they had been in Peru, they'd discovered that Garza had been working on something sinister: recreating the Biblical Nephilim, ancient giants that once roamed the earth. By severing a bone, then healing it and resetting it with the addition of a strain of yeast, the bone would grow far more rapidly than previously possible.

It had led to the creation of a small army of grotesque, massive soldiers — men from the Ravenshadow group that had volunteered.

Or, like Reggie, had *been* volunteered.

"They were sick and dying," Julie said. "Their bone structure couldn't handle their own weight. Garza said so himself, remember? There's a good chance they'll all be gone when we get there."

"Or there's a chance he's got a hundred of them now."

Sarah was quiet, but she looked at Reggie. They locked eyes for a moment, then Reggie turned back to Ben and Julie. "I don't think it's smart, Julie," he said.

Julie felt her stomach drop. Reggie was a trained soldier, an ex-Army sniper who had seen his fair share of fighting and bloodshed. There was no one besides Ben she trusted her life to more, and if he felt the mission was dangerous, she knew she would be wise to heed his advice.

"With my arm," he continued, "and our... history, it seems like we'd be better off waiting it out. See if he surfaces again."

"We may not have time," Julie said, realizing that her voice had risen and was carrying throughout the tent. People were mingling about — a handful of workers they'd hired for waiting tables and cleaning, her parents, Mrs. E, wheeling her husband around on the television screen. Her mom looked over with a concerned look on her face. Julie gave her a thumbs-up sign and turned back to the conversation.

"I get it," she said. "He's stronger than us. More prepared. But isn't this *exactly* what we're supposed to be doing? Isn't the Civilian Special Operations a group that's supposed to take on the projects that are deemed too dangerous for small-time law enforcement and too risky or politically driven for government?"

"Julie," Ben said, "this is different. We're talking about a guy who's been building an *army*. Possibly one with dudes who are *twice our size*. And he's well-funded. The Catholic Church backs him, and I wouldn't be surprised if he's got the governments of a few third-world countries in the palm of his hand, too." He paused. Took a drink. "I just don't see how we'd be able to do anything. Not by ourselves."

"We've got four, maybe four-and-a-half people willing to fight," Reggie said.

She and Ben looked at Reggie, who just shrugged and held up his prosthetic.

"So what do we do?" Julie asked. "You told Victoria that we were definitely going to do something."

"I did," Ben sighed. "But it was partly because I wanted to enjoy *this* — the wedding. And partly because, in my book, calling someone else to handle it *is* doing something."

"Who would you call?" Julie asked.

"I don't know — Mr. E's got connections with the Joint Chiefs. Maybe they'll be able to pull some strings with the different branches, and —"

"You know damn well the US military isn't going to fly to Peru to rout out a mercenary-for-hire. Not for no reason."

"So we give them a reason," Ben said. "We tell them, uh, the Hall of Records is there, but we're afraid it's being guarded."

"...and they'll call the Peruvian government, who'll just send out a small team to investigate. Do you think for a minute Garza hasn't already prepared for that outcome?"

Ben stood up. "Jules, what you're talking about — what you're recommending... it's *insane*. We went down there once already, to get these guys back. We almost got killed six ways to Sunday. Going back? It's a death sentence."

Reggie nodded. "I'm sorry, Julie," he said. "I'd have to agree."

"What are we agreeing about?" Julie heard a voice say. She looked up and saw Archibald Quinones, walking over from behind Ben.

Reggie quickly filled him in. The older man, still wearing his Jesuit priest's robe and collar, nodded along. When he finished, he leaned in to the group.

"Well, if it helps one way or another, I may have some information."

They all stared at Archie.

"Victoria Reyes pulled me aside about an hour ago. She said she had already spoken with you, Harvey."

Ben nodded.

"She said you would not join her."

"Join her?"

Archie nodded. "Yes. She told me she is going back to Peru. To find her father, and to try to talk him into letting her examine the mountain where she believes the Hall of Records lies. She invited me along, for my 'historic expertise' of the area."

Julie's mouth fell open.

"And she said she is leaving tomorrow morning, first thing, with or without me."

CHAPTER 9

BEN

"SHE'S *LEAVING*?" Ben asked. "For Peru?"

"Tomorrow, yes," Archie said.

"Is she serious?"

"She seemed quite serious, Harvey."

Reggie stood up as well and faced Archie. "She'll get killed, man. Why didn't you try to stop her?"

"I do not think that is true," he said. "Perhaps, but I find it more likely her father will have mercy."

"Mercy?" Julie asked. "For Vicente Garza? He'll *torture* her."

The group sat in silence for a moment, until Ben spoke again. "We can't go," he said. "It's still a suicide mission."

"We went for Reggie and Sarah last time," Julie said. "Are you saying we —"

"*She* made her decision!" Ben said, nearly shouting. "If she dies, my hands are clean."

Julie glared at him, but Ben didn't back down. *It's the truth,* he told himself. *It's not my fault.*

"Harvey," Archie said. "There is more."

Ben rolled his eyes. "You've got to be kidding me."

"I was sent this article — it pertains to a Peruvian village situated very closely to our land, the land Garza was on."

He pulled up the article on his phone and held it out for Ben and the others to see. Ben read the headline silently, then waited for Archie to translate it from Spanish.

"It says '20 Villagers Missing Near Chachapoyas Valley,'"

"And that's related to Garza or Ravenshadow?" Ben asked.

"The article says that a farmer who often traded with this village, visited them to find that they had all mysteriously vanished. There was food left on tables, smoking fire pits, even a laptop open with a half-charged battery.

"The farmer told the police, claiming it was *El Muki*, due to the close proximity of the mountain range, and —"

"*El Muki?*" Reggie asked.

"It is a Peruvian legend, a superstition. A light-skinned man with reddish features and a white beard that lives in the mines of the Andes. He lures people into his mine to work for him, promising great riches. They never reappear."

"Well," Julie said. "That sounds realistic."

"However it may *sound*," Archie said, "the farmer who believed it died the following day."

"Seriously?" Reggie asked.

"He complained of heart pain, went to a friend who was a doctor, and died in the doctor's arms."

"Poison?" Ben asked.

"Most likely, though the authorities in that region are not releasing any other details. It does seem likely that whatever this man knew, someone did not want him telling anyone about it."

Ben stretched, then swirled his drink. "It's an interesting story, but it's still just a legend. We don't know that —"

"We know Garza's there," Julie said. "Why can't this be his doing?"

"Because we *don't know*," Ben said. "We're not just going to assume he's behind every crime in Peru. Kidnapping a whole village, killing an old farmer? Come on, Jules. It's ridiculous."

"What if it's not?"

Ben didn't have an answer for that. In truth, he wanted it to be true. He wanted a reason to go back, to finish what they'd started in Philadelphia. They'd crossed paths with "The Hawk" in The Bahamas, then again in Egypt, and finally in Peru, where they'd nearly all been killed. Ben wanted nothing more than to put a bullet through the man's skull for what he'd done to him, but mostly for what he'd done to Julie.

He looked at her, his bride. Juliette Alexandria Bennett. It sounded weird in his mind. He was sure it would get easier with time, but for now it seemed foreign. She met his eyes, and he suddenly realized something.

Oh, Julie.

"You okay?" he asked. He felt the gazes of Reggie, Sarah, and Archie on him. It was a strange question to ask, but it was important.

"I'm fine, why?"

"I just — I want to make sure you're —"

"I'm *fine*, Ben."

"Okay." He put his hands up. "Sorry. It's been a crazy few days, and with all this — it's just a lot, that's all."

"No," she said. "I'm sorry. I shouldn't have snapped. What... what did you mean? Why'd you ask me that?"

Ben looked around at his friends, his team. Reggie had been there. Archie and Sarah had gotten the stories from either him or Ben. Together it was a shared memory, one they'd all tried to suppress.

But they knew there would come a time. They knew Julie would eventually remember, too.

"Jules," Ben said. "Why do you want to go to Peru? Why do you need to finish this with Garza?"

She bit her lip.

"Julie, you can say it." He saw a tear forming in her eye, but his own eyes were beginning to blur. He wiped them, then grabbed her hands in his. "I love you. I — *we're* — all here for you."

She looked at him, then took a deep breath. "I remember. I remember what he did to me."

CHAPTER 10
EDMUND

FATHER EDMUND CANISIUS tightened his collar and examined himself in the mirror. His nose and cheeks were liver-spotted, but he brushed a respectable amount of base from the tiny makeup kit over them and reexamined. He needed to look the part — confident, young, expert.

He was confident, and quite an expert, but his youth had left him around thirty years ago. It didn't matter. The dealers at this convention preferred experience, wisdom, and mutual respect far more than they did youthful zealousness. He would make an impact, if for no other reason than his name.

It was true: he had already heard of a few online news sources claiming that he would be in attendance at the *Conferencia Episcopal Peruana Internacional* — the Peruvian International Episcopal Conference. A week-long celebration of Peruvian Catholicism, the latest in Church thinking, and a gathering of some of the top South American Catholic voices. It was a yearly convention, and usually brought together the most vocal and popular speakers and Catholics from around the continent.

But it rarely brought attendees all the way from the Vatican. Father Edmund Canisius was an Italian-born Jesuit who had climbed the ranks of the Catholic Church and found himself a part of the Holy See's administrative and legislative team. He was an authoritative figure, both respected and feared, but his brethren often sought him out for his experience and knowledge of both worldly and sacred matters.

His job in Peru was simple: meet with the head of Orland Group, a private defense contractor that would be exhibiting in the country for another convention that coincided with the CEPI. Hand over the offer to purchase their latest development, as soon as it was ready.

The problem was that he had no idea what he was buying. No one from his office had felt it necessary to brief him on what exactly they were purchasing.

He practiced his pitch: introduce himself, shake hands, smile in a way that was confident yet not arrogant. Hold his head high, chin up, but not condescendingly.

His task was not the difficult part; the challenge would be in negotiating with Orland without knowing exactly what it was on offer. Worse, the Orland Group was a secretive bunch. They tended to be quite cloak-and-dagger; certainly when it came to new contacts.

Canisius was concerned that their relationship might begin on the wrong foot. He hoped his superiors had called ahead and made the initial contacts and exchanges. Things would be much easier if they had, but there was no telling what his office would do; the Church was about as secretive about their work as Orland Group.

He knew this deal was massive, he could see that much in the amount of money they were allowing him to move around. What he *didn't* know — what he would never know — is what the actual exchange would be. Money for... what? His research into the Orland Group had turned up only vague answers, corporate speak and language geared toward shareholders. It was the typical canned information he could expect from any major conglomeration's public-facing page: total dollars' worth of revenue, general R&D amounts, technical roadblocks.

But his job wasn't to know. It was to broker the deal and come home. They needed him because it fit the narrative: a Vatican priest on a work-related vacation in Peru, attending a Catholic convention. It would be sensationalized, of course: many locals would have a hard time understanding why a high-level priest such as he would spend his time at a regional conference. Those cover stories had already been written and prepared.

No, he was the perfect candidate for his team for another reason: his intuition and ability to read a person. He had a proven track-record for determining the trustworthiness of another person, after only a few minutes speaking with them. It was both a talent, given to him by God, as well as a honed skill. An art he cherished and practiced.

They needed Father Canisius to determine whether or not their investment here, with Orland Group, would pan out.

They needed him to secure their assets.

He wiggled his clerical collar again and checked his makeup once more. Finding everything satisfactory, he flipped off the light switch and stepped out of the hotel bathroom.

CHAPTER 11

BEN

"BEN, A WORD?"

Ben's mind was moving a hundred miles an hour. First, Victoria Reyes' news that she would be heading to Peru. Second, the news about the disappeared villagers and the dead farmer. Then, as if that weren't enough, Julie's revelation that she remembered what had happened. That she remembered what Vicente Garza had done to her.

"Yeah, buddy, what's up?" he asked. He stepped over to where Reggie was waiting, just inside the cabin's front door. While there hadn't been very many people at the wedding, it still felt to Ben like too many. Too many conversations to juggle, too many hands to shake.

"About Julie," Reggie said. "She gonna be okay?"

Ben shrugged. "Yeah. I mean, I guess. I'm not a, you know..."

"A shrink?"

"Right, I'm not a shrink."

"You think she should see one?"

"No idea. Probably. Hard to say. I never have, and God knows I could use one."

"I have," Reggie said. "They're not all bad. Usually pretty good, actually. Might be worth going, just to see."

Ben sniffed. Looked down at his drink, which was dwindling. Reggie reached for it, and Ben gave it to him. "Yeah," he said. "I might do that."

Reggie topped off their drinks with the bourbon he'd gotten Ben for the wedding, and added a huge cube-shaped piece of ice into the top of it.

"Sorry it's not a proper build," Reggie said.

"Huh?"

"The drink — it's supposed to be ice-first. Then liquor."

Ben chuckled. "Yeah, like I care about that."

Reggie grinned. "Well, you know... that's sorta the way we do things here. In this little group."

"What's that supposed to mean?"

"You know," Reggie said. "There's a right way and a wrong way to do things. You wanna find your friends who've been kidnapped, you call the police. That's the *right* way."

"I liked my way better."

"Oh, trust me," Reggie said. "Me too." His grin extended all the way around his face. Ben hadn't seen that smile for a long time — it was a characteristic of Reggie's, and he'd had a hard time showing it of late.

"What's your point?"

"Well, just that I think the CSO, by *definition*, does things... a little differently. We put the drink in, *then* stick the cube on top."

"Okay..."

"So I'm saying that the 'right' way to handle this situation with Garza... the way we *should* do it, is to ignore it. Peru's not exactly close, and Garza's pretty well-protected down there. Hell, whoever we call wouldn't even have *jurisdiction*."

"Right, that's my point," Ben said. "That's what I was trying to tell —"

"*Unless* we didn't call someone by-the-book."

Ben looked at him quizzically.

"Look, Ben. I got kicked out of the Army, but I was good. *Real* good. I turned some heads, and those heads have now risen through the ranks. They've kept an eye on me, and I think — I'm not *sure*, but I *think* — I could call in a favor or two."

"What's that mean?"

"Well, *we* can't go to Peru. Not alone. The CSO, it's — like you said — a suicide mission. We're trained better now than we ever have been, but we're still a handful of people. Not even a squad. Against Garza, who's got an army of Ravenshadow grunts who'll do whatever he says, and —"

"Giants. Possibly."

"Right. But if we had a *team*, a group of soldiers, a surgical force..."

"You know people who would do that?"

"I know people who *might* be able to put something together. Mr. E might as well, but at least his word would help us out. There's a guy I worked for way back when — Sturdivant. Career army guy. He's in charge of a lot more now, including stuff like this."

"You think they'd be up for it? Whoever these soldiers are?"

"I know they would be, Ben. It's what they do — Rangers, 75th. They're trained, the ones I know went through Ranger School, too. I think we could get a fireteam or squad down with us."

"Reggie..."

"You're scared?"

"Of course I'm scared!" Ben said. "I just got married. I feel like a *kid*, Reggie. I wasn't trained like you, like Mrs. E."

"You know my arm got chopped off last time I went, Ben?"

Ben looked at him, seething.

"You know what kept me going?"

"Adrenaline?" Ben asked.

"Yeah, sure," Reggie said. "That was part of it. Adrenaline gets the good press, but when something like that happens, when your *arm gets chopped off by an eccentric lunatic,* you're *scared.* Fear, Ben, increases blood flow, gets you moving. It heats up lactic acid, which helps us focus. And it produces *cortisol.* That helps with clotting blood. It helps you keep going. The human body builds in chemicals that help us fight when we're *terrified out of our minds.*"

Ben swallowed a sip of the bourbon. It tasted warm now, even though the ice cube had settled and already chilled the drink.

"I'm saying that we should go *because* we're scared. We know this guy better than *anyone.* We know his strengths, his weaknesses, we've fought him before."

"Yeah, but we haven't killed him yet."

"And he hasn't killed *us* yet, either."

Good point, Ben thought. Still, he wasn't sure. Messing around with a guy like Vicente Garza, in an unfamiliar country, still seemed like a suicide mission. With or without the Army Rangers.

"I need to think about it, man," Ben said.

"Well think fast. Victoria said she's leaving tomorrow."

"SOLDIER 147, PLEASE STAND."

The high-pitched whine seemed to fade as Vicente Garza focused on the machine standing in front of him.

Garza waited, the operator watching him for the next order. Garza nodded, and the operator repeated the instruction.

"Soldier 147 — Cisco Cabrera — please stand."

Through the glass, Garza saw the open warehouse laid out in front of and slightly below him. Its walls were piled high with wooden crates, boxes of gear, and cast-aside bits and pieces of suits and technical apparatus. The center, the "demonstration floor" as they called it, was empty, save for a single man, wrapped in a cacophony of tech. His head swiveled and his body followed suit, the whining sound returning to Garza's attention.

He stood. It appeared to be difficult, as the motion had taken four whole seconds. But 147 now stood on the other side of the glass, staring blankly at Garza and the operator, as well as the three men behind them.

"Don't use their names," Garza said. "It reattaches them to their unrequited memories." That was the theory, anyway. Vicente Garza wasn't entirely sure *what* it would cause in their minds, but he didn't want to take the chance that his subjects would all suddenly have a change of heart and decide to spurn his experiments.

"Got it. Yessir. Orders?"

"Tell him to walk forward."

"Soldier 147, please walk toward the booth."

The man's expression stayed blank, his eyes stoic and unmoving, and he stepped forward. The tech around him clinked and rattled, but the bodysuit moved, slowly at least.

"It's working, sir."

Garza stared, silent.

Two more steps, and the bodysuit fell sideways. The quarter-ton apparatus around 147 bounced on the concrete floor of the warehouse, then settled. 147 was still staring out in the space between the suit's armored "shoulders," his eyes still expressionless and dead.

Three engineers ran out to the main floor and began pulling the suit back up. Garza heard the report through the tiny wall speakers. "— balance gyro might be out, or at least malfunctioning." "Could be just a support weld. Something snapped, maybe?"

Garza turned to the other men in the room with him. "How long?"

"To repair the suit? Well, it depends on whether it's —"

"How long until we're fully operational?" he barked.

"Sir, it really is a matter of how many subjects are prepared for —"

"Days? Months?"

The man shrugged, and his colleague jumped in. "My estimate is two weeks."

The other two men, a mechanical engineer and a robotics specialist, turned to their colleague with open jaws. They began to argue.

"Fine," Garza said. "I want fully operational prototypes within a week. After that, we double down on production. Hire as many people as you need to get this done. I lost one *very* lucrative contract, and I am not about to lose another."

The men nodded in tandem, then left the room. He assumed they were going to get to work immediately — two weeks was a tall order, and even Garza was pessimistic that it could be accomplished.

It has to be, he thought. *Two years and twenty-million dollars, and I've got nothing to show for it.*

He had intended to bring another project to light long before this one. A project that would have changed the world, and human history. A project that, he now realized, was doomed to failure from the start. He hadn't realized just how many other factions had been vying for control of his research, and when it had come down to his project or his life, he'd chosen the latter.

So this was it. His best bet at landing a permanent place in the annals of history. Not that it was about fame, or even fortune. He had a bit of both, at least in some circles. But he wanted the *achievement.* To know he'd done it. To know he'd created something miraculous.

"Ready for round four, sir," the operator muttered.

"Same thing, run it back."

The operator nodded, then spoke into the mic. "Soldier 147, please stand up."

147 stood, this time in three seconds.

"147, please walk toward the booth."

The exoskeleton suit and the man inside slowly marched toward the booth. He stopped a few feet in front of the glass. Due to the suit's height and size, 147 and Garza were now at eye level. Garza looked at the young man inside the suit and watched his eyes. *Does he know?* he wondered. *Does he care?*

His doctors had explained that the subjects should do neither, but Garza had always been skeptical of doctors.

"Orders, sir?"

"Tell him to walk a circle around the warehouse, steady at five miles per hour."

The operator pressed the transmit button on the mic and was

about to speak, when Garza saw something flicker in 147's eyes. They... came to life. As if the man had suddenly woken up from a dream. Nothing else moved or changed.

"Hold that," Garza said. He watched. The young man's face registered nothing. Blank, empty expression, as always. "Vital monitoring?" Garza asked.

"Heart rate elevated, blood pressure within normal range, nothing else —"

"Give the order again," Garza said.

"Yessir." The operator did, and Garza waited. Nothing happened.

For three seconds, Garza locked eyes with the kid.

"Again, Soldier 147, please —"

147's arm rose, the exoskeleton's pistons and hydraulic fittings firing and pushing like artificial muscles. The gigantic arm extended nearly to the glass, a parallel line with the floor.

"Sir..."

"Hold that."

147's face was still empty, and Garza watched. Three more seconds passed, and then... *there.*

The kid's eyes flickered again, this time with an unmistakable fury. Garza's own eyes widened and he reached down for the emergency killswitch mounted on the control panel in front of him. It was too late.

Soldier 147's arm flew backwards, propelled by the opposite thrust of the launch. The tiny wrist-mounted rocket slammed into the glass and through it, into the control room.

Garza fell to the floor, almost getting there before the blast enveloped him. He covered his head with his arms and felt the searing heat of fire and glass scraping away his clothes and hair.

And then, within half a second, it was over.

He rose, carefully holding onto the edge of the control panel desk for support. The back of his shirt and pants had been burned off, a few areas of second-degree burning on his skin already starting to swell and rash. He looked to where the operator had been. Nothing but a charred husk remained, a piece of the chair, and a section of window that had somehow survived the blast intact.

Garza turned to the warehouse floor. Smoke billowed from somewhere below the window, partially blocking his view. He saw the suit, lying on the floor on its back about halfway across the room. His men surrounded the subject, rifles pointed and awaiting his order. They closed in, shrinking the circle around the suit and preparing to blast it with enough rounds to decimate a solid block of concrete in a half-minute.

And then Garza saw 147's eyes. He was lying on the floor, partially crushed beneath the weight of his own suit.

Still staring at him. Blank, lifeless eyes.

Still seeing him.

Garza held up a hand, and the men on the floor relaxed.

He had no mic, but there was no need for it anymore; he shouted through the smoke.

"Repair the suit, and send 147 back to the ward. Fix him up."

"Sir?" one of his men shouted back.

"We will use him as a model. Take an MRI and run the battery of tests. I want to know what he's made of."

CHAPTER 13
JULIE

I'M MARRIED, she thought. *Juliette Alexandria Bennett. JAB.* She smiled into the mirror, pushing her hair around and then a strand of it over her ear. *Married to Ben.*

She was alone in the cabin, as the rest of the party was still outside, chatting with one another and dancing. Ben and Reggie had been arguing about something when she'd snuck away. She examined her face in the mirror, trying to see if it physically expressed how she felt inside.

Am I old? she wondered. It had been two years and ten months since she'd met Ben, and those nearly three years had been an absolute whirlwind. From their time at Yellowstone, to trekking through the Amazon Rainforest and a research station in Antarctica to their time in Alaska, they'd been together. They'd never questioned whether or not they *should* be together. Being with Ben felt *right*.

Still, she had nothing to compare him to. She had no experience with long-term relationships — when she'd met Ben, she was thirty-three years old, but she might as well have been a teenager. Her entire knowledge of relationships had come from her high school and early college years, before she'd gotten serious with her computer science and cryptography courses. She'd gone on a few dates, but nothing stuck. Her experience of men was mostly garnered from the pages of the rare *Cosmopolitan* magazine she'd pick up at the supermarket.

Not that she was unhappy with Ben — she couldn't have lucked into a stronger, kinder man if she'd tried. He was stubborn, but it wasn't even close to her own stubbornness, and he often let her win. He didn't need her approval to feel confident about himself, though he often sought it anyway. She loved that about him.

So she couldn't figure out what it was she was feeling. *Ben's perfect, you're fine,* she kept telling herself. *Your friends are here, and they're here for you.*

Yet... something about their conversation had jolted her into awareness of how she was truly feeling. There was something calling to her, deep inside her. It had started a few months ago as a simple hollow anxiety, not something she was used to but not something she wasn't able to handle. When that anxiety grew into a hardened ball of depression, then fear, she sensed her subconscious trying to tell her something.

That something had been repeated to her in her dreams for the past month. Waking up with cold sweats more nights than she could count, she knew she needed to address the issue: *what was causing this?*

It was a memory, she knew, but she couldn't quite place exactly *which* memory. Something to do with Ben? The CSO team?

It eventually became clear to her a few nights ago, after she and Ben debriefed about their trip to Peru. Something about the way Ben had said Vicente Garza's name — something about the way he *looked* at her when he'd said it — clued her in.

It had taken the next day to unravel, but she eventually knew: Garza was the man in the dream. The man in her nightmare. She was the woman, coerced by him, to kill her friend.

Joshua Jefferson died because of me.

No. She wouldn't let herself believe that. *He died because of him. Because of Garza.*

Her wedding day had been filled with joy and life, but there was death inside of her. She knew that now, and she couldn't *not* feel it. It trickled down over the entirety of her core emotions, tainting her joy and happiness and love for Ben with a blackened, terrifying realization.

A realization that this wasn't going to end.

She wasn't going to just *get over it*.

She couldn't talk or reason or believe her way out of it — something had to be *done*. Physically, by her.

She looked into the mirror and her reflection told her more about what she needed than her own subconscious. She needed to *act*.

She wiped away the tear that had been collecting on her cheek and flicked it down into the sink, then started washing her hands. Julie's face was still pristine, the makeup she rarely wore still hiding all her imperfections, all the vain flaws she loved to hate.

None of those mattered now — she was dealing with an imperfection inside of her, something that had been *put* there. Something that didn't belong.

She needed to get rid of it, and in the last hour, she'd finally found a way to do just that.

She hoped Ben could forgive her.

CHAPTER 14

BEN

BEN WAS UP EARLY the next day. The alarm hadn't gone off yet, and he surprised himself by feeling rested, even though he and Reggie had stayed up far too late and had a bit too much to drink. And then Ben had stumbled into the bedroom, waited for Julie, and fallen asleep.

She was gone now, too, her spot in the bed empty. He saw that the bathroom door was closed and opted for the hallway bathroom in the new CSO suite. He rose, stretched, and headed around the cabin and into the hallway.

After showering and shaving, Ben decided to check in with someone he hadn't spoken with at all the previous day. He turned into the small conference room and pressed a button on the device sitting on the table. About a minute later, the television screen faded on, a rail-thin man appearing in front of him.

"Mr. E," Ben said. "We didn't get a chance to chat yesterday."

The man smiled back at him. "No, I am afraid we did not. My apologies — but congratulations, Harvey. I am thoroughly glad for you and Juliette."

Ben nodded. "Thanks. I, uh, wanted to ask about something else, though."

"Vicente Garza?"

He nodded again. "He needs to be stopped, but —"

"But you do not believe you are the man to do it?"

"Yeah," Ben said. "Something like that."

Mr. E, the founder of the Civilian Special Operations, and the team's benefactor, stared back at Ben. For a moment Ben felt as though they were sharing the same room, as if Mr. E was there in the flesh. He had never met the man in person — Mr. E was reclusive and sickly, and he preferred his own study in his home in Michigan. To Ben's knowledge, the man never left his house. He had plenty of money, thanks to an ownership in one of the largest global communications companies and other related investments, so it was quite possible he simply hired help to shop, clean, and cook for him.

His wife, Mrs. E, was equally enigmatic, and all Ben knew of her was that she was a well-trained fighter, specializing in hand-to-hand combat, and that she was — he thought — of Russian descent. They made an odd pair, but they were both likable and loyal.

"Harvey," Mr. E said. "I understand your fear. You were not trained for this. You were a park ranger, a man solely wanting to find solace in the world around him, and nothing else."

"Yeah…"

"But now you are here. Look around you, Harvey. *You* helped create this. Sure, I paid for it, but I would not have had anything to invest in if not for you. You believe that there are organizations specializing in this sort of work, and you are wrong. There are, certainly, organizations — governments, police forces, private militaries — that specialize in finding evil and corrupt powers and removing them. But they are either too large or too small, too overt or covert, too politically minded or answering to no one. There is little in-between. There are *no* forces that work for the *common* good and do not have to answer to a politically driven narrow-minded entity.

"Think about Agent Etienne Sharpe at Interpol. He was serving with the Guild Rite while working for Interpol. Neither had any idea of what the other was doing. Police forces are understaffed, militaries are bloated with bureaucracy, private security is untrustworthy. Add to that the fact that most organizations will only work to right a wrong if there is a large payoff for them. Harvey, these are the reasons that an organization of *civilians*, men and women who are interested only in discovering the ancient truths and mysteries that may cause others to resort to evil, needed to be created. It is why the CSO exists, why you were recruited and now lead it."

Ben nodded along. He'd heard the arguments before, that governments were too bloated and corrupt to achieve anything philanthropic, and he'd heard the same from Agent Sharpe at Interpol. He'd joined the Guild Rite, a Masonic-like fraternity that claimed to have an ancient lineage, because of his interest in righting wrongs in the world. Many of his brethren were now just charred remains in the Chachapoyas Valley in Peru. Though there were many more members around the world, Sharpe claimed that they were mostly scattered, their ideals and goals not always overlapping.

So it was with many other organizations that had grown too large to maneuver.

"But... it still doesn't seem to be the right fit for *me*."

"Why? Because you are not a soldier? A brilliant tactician? No, Harvey, that is not why you are the perfect fit for this role. You are where you are because you are *here*."

"Because I was in the right place at the right time?"

Mr. E shook his head. "No, because you kept coming back. You have seen your friends killed, innocent people murdered and tortured, and you rushed in to help. You fought back, where most would recoil and hide."

"But... I want to hide now. I *don't* want to 'rush in and help.'"

"And that is precisely why you are the right man for the job."

Ben sighed. He squeezed his eyes shut. He didn't want to think about this right now, but at the same time he wondered what had led him to walking into this room in the first place? What had urged him to press that button, to hail their friend and ally?

He had a feeling Mr. E was right — the man usually was.

"Why don't you ever come here?" Ben blurted out. "Why not come see what you've been building?"

Mr. E paused. Gripped the back of the chair he was standing behind. "I wish I could, Harvey. I truly do. I miss my wife, and it would bring me great joy to meet you all in person. But, as you probably know, my health is... failing. It has been for quite some time. My house is actually more of a hospital now, and I believe that is the only reason I am still alive."

"Cancer?" Ben asked.

"Yes, some. But the cause of that cancer is something else. Something doctors are not as familiar with. It is a disease, a debilitating one, and they are unsure how it developed. For that reason, they are unsure whether my life will end in a year or in ten. They have more questions than answers."

Ben felt a pang of regret for the man. He must live in fear that every day might be his last.

"My illness is the reason I gave up running my company — not because my health prevented it, but because I realized that running a business was not what I was put on this planet to do. No, Harvey, it was something else — something bigger."

"The CSO?"

"Perhaps. Only time will tell. But I believe it is a step in the right direction. If I can do only a little good, root out only a little evil, then I have done what I need to do."

"I see," Ben said.

"Do you?"

"What does that mean?"

"I am asking if you *truly* see what I am talking about."

"I... I guess." Ben suddenly felt like he was a kid again, a nineteen-year-old running through the woods on a camping trip, trying to understand something profound about life but coming up short.

"Ben," Mr. E said, surprising him with the use of his nickname. "Now is the time to decide what it is you are fighting for."

"Okay..." he said. He still didn't grasp what it was Mr. E was trying to tell him. He was about to open his mouth and protest when Reggie burst into the room.

"Ben," Reggie said, gasping. "Julie's gone."

PART TWO

ACT 2

THE MORNING SUN seemed to press down, and that combined with the high humidity made it feel as though Garza had a hot, damp washcloth on the back of his neck. The tunnel's gently increasing temperature that led from his base in the mountain to the wide-open valley hadn't fully prepared him for the late summer heat. And even though it was October, he still couldn't bring himself to admit that it was fall.

In this portion of Peru, summer seemed to be the constant, broken only by a few weeks at a time by the rest of the "seasons." There hadn't been a day so far during his time here that he would have preferred being outside.

He wiped a growing collection of sweat from his brow using the sleeve of his fatigues. For these field exercises, Garza always wanted to look like his men. He might be set back a bit, off the field of play, but it helped him feel connected with his team. Today, however, he questioned his desire to fit in, wondering how much more comfortable he'd feel wearing a t-shirt and shorts.

"Move into position," he said, his voice carrying easily through the throat mic he wore around his neck. The dual-sensor mic and earpiece kit was a new addition for his team. They had helped design the product, and some of his men were currently testing the new waterproof underwater send-and-receive technology. So far the frequency hadn't interfered with the other all-important frequency: the one that accompanied Garza's main line of experimentation, and the one they were testing out here today.

"Affirmative, sir," his team leader said. *"TTE?"*

Garza wasn't sure about the exact time-to-engagement. He wanted to create the element of surprise, so he'd told the men manning the computers back inside the base to wait fifteen minutes for him to get topside, then an arbitrary amount of time after before starting the test.

"Unknown. Heels up. Shouldn't be long."

"Confirming paint rounds only?" another man asked.

"Correct."

Garza strode over to the tall metal tower the construction crew had put up. It had been fabricated atop one of the ancient stone buildings that had been left here by the valley's previous inhabitants. Most of the building had disappeared — the heavy stones having either settled into the earth or fallen away completely — and what was left was a triangle-shaped stone wall. He climbed the ladder and walked out to the edge of the lookout station, the entire valley open below him. His tower was on the edge of the valley itself, tucked between a few trees that backed up to the base of the mountain.

"In position," he said.

It only took three-and-a-half minutes. The techs inside the mountain sounded the alarm, then Garza caught sight of the metal box opening up in the field in front of him, about a football field away. Two Ravenshadow units, wearing full tactical gear and protective goggles, converged on the box from opposite sides, their rifles pointed at the swinging door.

They stopped short, about fifty feet away, and he saw each unit's leader issuing orders.

The door on the box opened fully and the machine inside

stepped out. An exoskeleton with a subject inside, guiding it forward on its two reinforced legs.

"Engage," he heard a tech's voice say in his ear. The machine immediately turned to its left and began firing a blistering amount of Simunition paint rounds toward its target. Six rotating turrets on the machine's shoulder-mounted modified M134 minigun fired tactical paint rounds at a rate of 5,000 rounds per minute. In less than a second three of the unit's men were "dead," clutching very painful, very brightly colored "wounds" on their chests.

"Hold," the tech said. The subject inside the exoskeleton halted the machine, awaiting further orders.

"Okay," Garza said, trying to hide his excitement. "That didn't take long. Teams One and Two, fall back to cover and regroup. We'll hit him again in exactly one minute."

The teams dispersed, finding cover behind trees and boulders that lined the edges of the valley. The subject waiting in the exoskeleton watched Garza with cold, dead eyes.

When one minute had expired, the tech in Garza's ear delivered the next set of orders to the subject and the exoskeleton. *"Initiate heat tracking, engage all hostiles."*

The men's weapons exploded to life, hoping the long-range attack would be devastating enough to confuse the exoskeleton. But the suit reacted immediately, dropping to its knees and crouching, turning into a smaller target. At the same time, miniaturized reflectors all across the suit triangulated and immediately pinpointed the locations of the shooters. That data was sent at the speed of light to the suit's central processing unit, which relayed targeting orders to the seventeen individual guns across the suit's armor. Those guns began shooting less than a quarter-second after the units' own firing began.

The Ravenshadow men had not been briefed as to the devastating accuracy of the tracking and defense technology Garza had built into the exoskeleton. His tests of the suit's effectiveness against unsuspecting enemies needed to be as accurate as possible, so he often rotated his testing units in the field, giving all of his men their own first-time experience with new builds. He knew his men talked, swapped stories of what they were building here, but he also remembered what it was like to be a young soldier. Lots of speculation, plenty of hyperbole, and a great deal of skepticism.

They were professionals, and he wasn't concerned about what they knew of the project. Keeping them in the dark was simply a way to keep his experiments as clean and streamlined as possible.

And this experiment was certainly impressive. Still, he needed to know one final piece of data.

"Switch to live rounds," he said into his throat mic.

"Sir?" the technician asked. *"Live rounds will most likely impact the subject inside the —"*

"I'm well aware of the effect live ammunition will have, soldier," he said. "Do you know of any other way to test the suit's structural stamina?"

He already knew the answer. The exoskeleton was just that — it was nothing but a heap of metal and electrical components without a living human being inside. Robotics technology had advanced rapidly over the past decades, but armies around the world were still years away from bringing to battle fully functional robotic weapons that did *not* need direct human guidance.

Garza hoped that he could build not just the exoskeleton suit, but an army of soldiers who were willing to wear them, as well.

"Exchange magazines," he said. "And engage immediately. Note that the subject will be firing returns with Simunition rounds, but please act as though you are engaging with an actual hostile force."

He needed the experiment to be clean; he needed to know how long the suit would hold up against two hostile infantry units approaching from opposite fronts, but he wasn't about to sacrifice his own Ravenshadow forces for a test.

He watched the subject inside the suit, flicking a magnification switch on the side of his tactical sunglasses that digitally zoomed his field of view. The subject's face came into focus, the eyes and cold stare betraying nothing of her internal emotions. Garza knew well the effects of the anti-stimulant; he knew that the subject was still feeling everything, still processing, still *thinking*. They just... couldn't act on those thoughts. Their mind had been overtaken, turned into a compliant computer processor, ready to receive external input.

This subject, a young woman, had responded well to the dosing and had shown that she was capable of managing the suit's appendages easily while drugged. The younger, more agile subjects tended to be that way — not a surprise to Garza or his doctors.

He flicked the magnification back off again and removed his glasses. He wanted to see the battle with his own, unaltered eyes.

"Engage when ready," he said.

CHAPTER 16

EDMUND

FATHER EDMUND CANISIUS wished he could lose the collar and tight-fitting robe. He wanted to relax, to forget this whole thing. He was tired of the charade, the appearance, and wanted nothing more than to head back to his luxury accommodations and soak in the massive tub for an hour, catching up on his reading.

He shifted in his chair. *No, there is a job to do.* He pushed away the thoughts of laziness and reminded himself why he was here. He believed in the mission of his church, *the* church. He believed in his team back at the Vatican, and he believed in himself. He knew he was the best person for this job, even if he had not been informed of exactly *why* he was the best for it.

Canisius pushed a cold, hard pad of butter around an equally cold and hard piece of bread. He had torn the bread violently from the loaf, prepared to shove it into his mouth — he often overate when he felt impatient or anxious — but quickly recovered and set it back down on his plate. He sniffed, then looked around.

No one is watching me, he reminded himself. *No one cares that I am here.*

For the entirety of his time in Peru, from the moment he had disembarked from the jet and was met on the tarmac with Peruvian journalists and reporters, to the moment he had left his hotel to be driven to this restaurant, he had been inundated with people. Requests for autographs from the celebrity-seekers, blessings from the devout, and quotes for those whose careers were based on nothing but the vapidity of chasing another lede.

Until he'd settled into his booth. At this restaurant, the *premier* Peruvian upscale restaurant within driving distance from the hotel district, he finally felt alone. The other men and women here were like him — important, wealthy. They didn't need his blessings or attention, and they were more than happy to leave him to his own business.

He sighed a breath of relief. *Relax,* he told himself again. *You are the right man for this job. Whatever it may be, they have chosen you for a reason.*

He cleared his throat as a party of three men and two women neared his table, all wearing elegant gowns and tuxedos. *Have I underdressed?* he wondered.

No matter. In his line of work, there was no such thing as underdressing. Wearing the cloth of the clergy was always en vogue, and he wore it proudly, smartly.

But the party turned at the last minute and headed toward another table, near the back of the restaurant. He saw the lead man wave at a couple that had already been seated at the large banquet table.

He turned back to his bread, fiddled with the cold steel knife on the unforgiving piece of butter, and was about to take a bite when someone said his name.

"Father Canisius?" a woman's voice asked.

He looked up, sucked in a breath. He had to steady his nerves as well as his reaction as he took in the sight of a *very* attractive woman, perhaps fifteen or twenty years his junior. Another characteristic of his line of work was not often interacting with women dressed as she was.

The woman wore what he could only describe as a "ballroom dress," a sequined emerald-green dress that clung to her curved body. A single strap carried the dress up and over a shoulder; the other was bare. Her hair was wavy, dark-brown with streaks of red that he wasn't sure was natural or dyed. Her eyes were quick, sharp and alert, and her entire presence screamed control.

He sat up straighter in his chair, inadvertently clearing his throat and wiping his hands on his legs.

"I — uh, pardon me," he said, rising to his feet. "I apologize, I am waiting for someone."

He reached out a hand, expecting her to place hers within it, daintily, as the proper women of his generation had been taught. Instead, she gripped his tightly and shook it, once, never releasing eye contact. Her smile leaned out of the side of her mouth, a corner of her lip creeping upward.

"Father Canisius," she said again. "My name is Rebecca St. Clair. I'm with the Orland Group."

He couldn't hide his surprise. *They sent a woman?* "Oh," he said. "I *do* apologize, then. I believed I was waiting for, uh..." he stopped when he realized his folly.

"For a man?" St. Clair said, pulling the chair across from Canisius' out and taking a seat.

"Well, uh, I —"

She smiled, but he could see the fire in her eyes. "Please," she said. "No problem. It wouldn't be the first time."

He put the bread back on the table — he hadn't realized he'd been holding it the entire time — and then sat once again. "Well, I mean no disrespect. In my particular business, it is, well, somewhat of a fraternity."

She smiled again, and this time it seemed she actually believed it. "Never mind. I am sorry I'm late," she continued. "This entire trip has been a whirlwind of logistical nightmares. I'm supposed to be at a gala across town after our meeting — I do hope we don't have to cut things short."

He tapped at the corners of his mouth with his heavy cloth napkin before speaking. "Well, I have to admit that in my own logistical excitement, I was unable to read the brief detailing our meeting here."

She waved it off. "You weren't supposed to know. Think nothing of it — it does not speak to your intelligence or capability, Father. It is merely a precaution. These meetings can be rather delicate."

He nodded, but knew the confusion was showing on his face. *Am I truly the right man for this job?* He had been given hardly any information. Mostly numbers, at what price they were hoping to close the deal, a few pointers, and then he had been told to get ready. That everything else would become clear during the meeting.

"Anyway," St. Clair said, reaching into a small clutch she'd been holding. "If you don't mind, I won't be eating. Please do not let it stop you, and please know that my company will graciously accept the tab."

"Thank you for that," he said. "Can you... tell me a bit about what we are negotiating?"

She looked at him inquisitively, as if contemplating something. "Father, this will not be much of a negotiation. The price has all but been set."

"Then why —"

"We are here to sign the papers and shake hands, and those two events will take place over the course of two separate meetings. As we've already shaken hands, I believe our meeting is now adjourned."

"Then why did they —"

"Deals like this often have the side effect of 'leaking,' as I like to say. Either from one party or the other. My organization is public, which implies a certain sense of openness. Transparency." She cocked an eyebrow, as if saying, *just like yours.* "But these deals always lean more to the *private* side of things, and I have a lot of employees working very hard to keep the details on that side. As such, it is of the utmost importance that we both conduct our business with discretion, brevity, and clarity. And, it goes without saying, our agreement is fully binding and oral in nature."

"A contract that will not be signed?" he asked.

"Oral does not preclude a signature — it will simply happen virtually, through an encrypted digital connection that records our verbal acceptance as the signature itself once we are both satisfied with the final terms." She pulled her hand out of the clutch and revealed a single sheet of paper, about the size of an index card. She didn't offer it to Father Canisius. "Now, I believe the agreement our stakeholders came to was an exchange of thirty-two point two three million dollars upon successful negotiation here, and an additional amount of exactly three times that upon successful delivery of the first prototypes."

Prototypes? Delivery? He wished he had not left his antacid medication back at the hotel. "Uh, yes," he mumbled. "That is the number — price — my associates have prepared."

"Very well."

He waited.

"I believe we are done here."

This time he didn't even try to hide his shock. "I — I am sorry, Ms. St. Clair. This, all of this — whatever we are to call it — does not make sense to me. I traveled halfway around the world to meet with a —"

"You traveled here to do business with the Orland Group, and you are."

"May I ask what the nature of *your* work is with the Orland Group, Ms. St. Clair?" He was tired of feeling beaten down — getting interrupted — by this woman.

"Of course," she said. "I should have given you a card before I sat down. I am not used to being unrecognized, a feeling I'm sure you know well."

He nodded, feeling slightly sated for the moment.

The woman reached back into her clutch and withdrew another piece of paper, this one cardstock and in the unmistakable shape of a business card. She handed it to him. The front had the Orland Group logo and nothing else, and turned it over to the back.

He could feel the smug grin he knew she was pointing in his direction as he read the opposite side.

It had her name, Rebecca St. Clair, in all capital letters on one line, then an email address.

Below that, separated by a blank line, was a single word.

President.

CHAPTER 17

BEN

THE MORNING FLEW BY. In less than an hour Ben had packed a change of clothes, some bathroom essentials, and Julie's laptop. He wasn't sure he'd even get a chance to use the clothes or hygiene items, but he wanted to at least have another way to reach the rest of the CSO team besides his phone.

Julie's car was gone, but no one had seen her leave. Victoria's own rental car was missing too, leaving Ben to deduce that Julie had done exactly what he was afraid she'd do: she'd gone with Victoria Reyes to Peru. At this point, Julie would be halfway to Anchorage. His fears were confirmed when he saw a note from Julie laying on the end table.

Ben, it began. *I know how this is going to make you feel. I'm sorry. I didn't want it to start like this, but I thought it was the only way. I hope you can forgive me, but I really hope you'll join me. — I love you, Jules.*

He held the note with a trembling hand. *This can't be real*, he thought. *This can't be happening.*

He stuffed the note into his pocket and threw the duffel bag over his shoulder. Reggie was waiting for him in the living room.

"Ready?" he asked.

Reggie nodded, wiggling his prosthetic arm. "Yes. And Archie left a few minutes ago. Has to take the rental car back and all that. Sorry, man. I had no idea —"

"It's fine," Ben said. "Not your fault."

Mrs. E entered the room. "I spoke with Julie's parents in the CSO wing. They are upset, but they understand that this is her job."

"*This* is not her *job*," Ben said. "Telling us where she's going and discussing it with us is her *job*."

"Harvey," Mrs. E said. "I understand. We are going after her, okay?"

"Yeah, brother," Reggie said. "She might be getting to Anchorage in fifteen minutes, but then she'll have to get her ticket, wait for TSA, all that fun stuff."

Mrs. E's eyes fell to the floor, and Ben noticed it immediately. "What do you know?"

She lifted her head up. Her face was at Ben's eye level. Back-to-back the woman was tall as he was, nearly as tall as Reggie. "I... uh..."

"Great," Ben said. "You're telling me she's *not* going to the airport?"

"No, she is. Just not —"

"Just not a commercial flight," Reggie said. "You got her a *private plane?*"

"Her *and* Victoria," Mrs. E said. "But our own tickets have already been purchased. Me, Archibald, you, and Reggie. Archie is flying out tomorrow, and he'll either meet up with us there or stay back in Iquitos and offer support from there."

She was going to continue, but must have seen the look on Ben's face. "Harvey, I —"

"*You* did this? You betrayed me — *all* of us!"

"Please, Harvey. Please understand that my husband and —"

Ben knew immediately. "*He* was behind this, wasn't he? That little speech of his, the one-on-one conversation I had with him. He was trying to talk me off the ledge. To get me to agree that this was all a good idea. But he already had plans. He already *knew* Julie was going, and he helped her do it."

"Harvey, I am truly —"

"Save it, E," Ben said. He turned and stomped out of the living room and out into the chilly morning. He made a quick pace toward his SUV, tossed the duffel across the console and onto the backseat, then started the engine before he'd even fully descended onto his seat.

Reggie was there in another second, and he pulled the door open and slid in.

"You're not packed," Ben said.

"Technically neither are you."

"I'm talking about —"

"I know, man," Reggie said. "And I figured it didn't matter. Mr. E has a private jet for them, ready to go. That means he's been planning. Maybe not for a long time, but long enough that I don't think we'll need to worry about packing."

"You think he's got *clothes* for us, too?"

"Ben, this is going to be a military-style invasion. Surgical. Precise. Tactical. He'll have full fatigues, in all our sizes, weapons, and a team."

"A *team*?"

"Remember what I was telling you about? The contacts I've got?"

"*You're* behind this, too? I can't believe —"

"Ben, relax. No, I'm not," Reggie said. "Honestly. I had no idea. But Mr. E knows my contacts. He knows how to get them onboard, and he's got plenty of his *own* contacts. I have no doubt he'll have a group of Special Forces ready and waiting in Peru."

"Great," Ben said. "Just great. We don't get time to plan anything out ourselves, to think through this."

"There's not a lot of time, Ben. You know Garza. He'll move as soon as he feels threatened. As soon as he's done with whatever it is he's been working on down there."

"I know, but it still doesn't give us time —"

"And, if I remember correctly, it's a *long* flight from Alaska to Peru. We'll have *plenty* of time to think through whatever you and I can come up and call it a plan."

Ben sighed, for the first time that morning taking a deep breath. He needed to do that more often — to just stop and *breathe*. Julie was gone, but he knew where she was and where she was heading. And this time she had the backing of her team. The CSO was on the offensive, planning to move against a known enemy who wouldn't know they were coming.

That enemy had bested them before, but now they would *also* have the help of another trained force — Special Forces, actual Green Berets, working with them.

He hoped.

CHAPTER 18

EDMUND

EDMUND SAT IN HIS CHAIR, knowing the shock and incredulity were still registered on his face. He was broadcasting uncertainty, insecurity. He did not like that feeling, nor did he appreciate another person causing him to feel vulnerable.

"Wait," He said.

Rebecca St. Clair had begun walking away, but she turned a few feet from the table and looked down at Father Canisius.

"I must say... I did not expect someone like you."

"A woman?"

"Someone so *confident*. It threw me off."

"I get that a lot," she said. "Although it is unfortunate there are not more people so *confident* in your line of work."

Canisius smiled, ignoring the slight, then continued. "I just felt as though I have been woefully underprepared for this interaction. And it is not for lack of trying — I was not briefed by my supervisors or subordinates, and the research I attempted to do on your company personally turned up next to nothing on your company."

"The Orland Group has been famously vague," St. Clair responded. "And that is on purpose, to protect our interests as well as our shareholders."

"Which tells me that the deal I am brokering here today requires a bit of finesse."

"A bit, yes," she said with that same smile that had first thrown him off.

"And your confidence, your entire persona, tells me that this deal is not entirely reliant upon your willingness to negotiate with *me*."

She walked back over and took a seat once again. "An astute judgement, Father. You are correct — this deal is all but finalized."

"Then I must ask, again — why send me to shake your hand? If the papers are all but signed already, and my being here has no purpose, then —"

"That's just it," she said, cutting him off. "Your being here *is* the purpose. The deal will be done, but having a man of your stature sends more of a message than what the deal alone could — and the message your presence sends is, believe it or not, one that will be received faster than the news of the deal."

Canisius was still very confused, but he tried not to show it. *A deal that requires a cardinal to fly halfway across the world, just for appearance? A negotiation that is already finished before I arrive?*

"Publicity," he said, almost under his breath. "They need my name — my face. This is for the publicity."

"Correct," she said.

"Then why not just tell me? Why keep this all a secret? If Orland Group needs to parade my face and name in public to help with branding, then —"

"Not Orland Group, Father," St. Clair said. "The publicity is needed for *your* side of the negotiation."

Father Canisius shook his head, still not understanding. "And you cannot tell me what it is, exactly, we are 'negotiating' for?"

"No," she said. "Not *exactly*."

His ears perked up. *Not exactly. Perhaps, then, subtly?* "Orland Group, from what I can gather based on the minimal information on your website and some of the information gleaned from a few other public deals, works with defense contractors?"

"We work with many contractors, in many different sectors."

"Yet one of your largest customers last year was the Australian military."

"Yes, we do business throughout the world."

He smiled. *She is not going to make this easy,* he thought. "Right. Well, we are in Peru. Ostensibly to present ourselves at this conference — a conference intended to promote security for parish environments and communities."

She nodded. "I am attending a gala in a few minutes, one put on by the conference hosts."

"So then this deal — an exchange of a lot of money for... something, is between a company that works with foreign militaries and governments and an organization that has long been interested in improving their own security."

"That is not inaccurate," she said. Father Canisius watched as she plucked her phone out of her clutch and checked the time. "I must be leaving, Father. I'm sorry we can't continue this discussion."

He stood, extending his arm to the side as if allowing her to leave. He had more questions, but for now there was too much to think about. Too many variables that required assumptions he wasn't prepared to make. He needed more information, but he wouldn't be getting it from this woman.

"Of course," he said. "I have kept you long enough. Please enjoy your evening."

She left him alone at the table, and the waiter appeared at his side. He ordered a Peruvian snapper entree the restaurant was world-renowned for — *pescado sudado* — as well as a glass of red wine, and he calmly sat and thought about the exchange while he waited for the food.

He considered what he knew. Orland Group was a conglomerate that was, essentially, a defense contractor. In one of the only articles he could find that disclosed any detail of the business' operations, he had discovered that Orland Group had brokered a deal between the Australian Navy and a supplier that promised them an operational railgun defense system for its fleet within three years.

In another press release, the details had been withheld but the Orland Group had again acted as broker, linking up an unnamed buyer with a weapons supplier in Prague.

He had no knowledge of defense contracts, military strategy, or weapons supply logistics, and he knew that his office back at the Vatican knew that as well.

Further, he had no idea what the Vatican — the Catholic Church, essentially — wanted or needed with weapons or defense of any sort. He was unaware of any looming threat to the Church, and he was absolutely positive that there was no *physical* threat nearby that would require any sort of military maneuvering. Certainly not any actual *prototypes* of anything related to defense.

It's not like the Catholic Church was in the business of buying tanks.

And he had *no idea* why whatever it was he was in the process of purchasing from the Orland Group had to cost multiple millions of dollars, and why — if it was supposed to be so secret — his organization had sent one of its most recognizable and visible cardinals.

It was an oxymoron: a secret sale between a defense contractor and the Catholic Church, and the two in charge of closing the deal were public figures.

He took a sip of wine as the waiter returned with his fish. Father Edmund Canisius was an inquisitive man, and he enjoyed puzzles. He had been given a chance to solve one, and he intended to do so.

The waiter asked if he needed anything more, and Father Canisius waved him away, eager to once again sit alone with his thoughts.

CHAPTER 19

GARZA

THE UNIT TO THE NORTH, to his left, opened fire first. Their rounds pinged off the suit's armor, sending sparks flying, but the suit reacted perfectly and sent a volley of paint rounds back toward the waiting soldiers. The soldiers, knowing now how the suit would respond, quickly took cover and Garza could see that no one had been hit.

The southern unit now fired, taking advantage of the opening. The suit hardly hesitated, and the subject inside turned the exoskeleton around on thick, alloy-strengthened legs while the upper portion of the suit redirected its volley of fire toward the new targets. Two men from that unit were hit, but they didn't go down. The paint rounds appeared to have hit their chests, but the soldiers were fighting through it.

The hailstorm of bullets flew in every direction, but Garza noticed that the units had moved toward the west a half-dozen paces, working to prevent crossfire and hitting one of their own teammates with the live rounds. The effect, however, was that the subject could now fire on both units simultaneously by moving itself back a few steps. It did, maneuvering the mechanical soldier it stood inside near the box from which it had emerged.

So far, the battle was a tie. For every round that hit the suit, another three were sent toward the soldiers. Garza saw two of the northern unit's men fall, another two men with bright paint splotched across their chests.

The chatter on the radio picked up in intensity as the soldiers realized the suit's defensive capabilities. *"... asshole's hard to kill..."*

"Copy that. Munitions rules?" another man asked.

"Use 'em if you got 'em, private."

Garza watched as one of the men on his right ducked behind a boulder, then leapfrogged his way toward the subject and the box. He was hit on his left arm, the yellow stain visible from the distance, but he recovered quickly and heaved a small object toward the box and the waiting exoskeleton.

The grenade detonated a few seconds later, and Garza was impressed by the young man's accuracy. Fire and dirt flew up around the suit, the metal box flying off in the opposite direction.

For a moment the firing stopped from both sides as the soldiers tried to make out what had happened. Smoke fell, and Garza saw the exoskeleton standing in place. The subject was staring straight ahead, a gash of blood across her forehead. Garza cocked his head, waiting.

"Shit!"

Suddenly the suit burst to life, the subject guiding the legs forward rapidly. The upper half spun as it ran, the shoulder-mounted rotary turret spraying rounds in volleys of two seconds each — north, then south, then north again.

Garza immediately saw what the subject had done and smiled. *Impressive,* he thought. It wasn't truly the *subject,* per se, but the *tech* controlling her from inside the mountain. Still, the move was precisely what Garza would have done in that situation.

By sprinting forward, the subject had placed the exoskeleton back within the angle of guaranteed crossfire — none of Garza's soldiers would take those odds; he had trained them not to. None of his men were going to act like brazen heroes unless he ordered it.

They were bunkered down, completely cut off from mounting a counterattack.

The suit kept firing, spinning around and hitting anyone willing to dare a look from behind their cover. Three more men "fell," their helmets coated with yellow paint. They would be the laughingstock of their units at the dinner table this evening.

Garza waited a few more seconds, knowing the suit's magazine would soon come to an end. They had re-engineered the Minigun's rounds to be lighter and smaller, but no weapon could fire forever. Between the rising heat and the decreasing amount of ammunition left in the chambers, the suit was nearing the end of its battlefield effectiveness.

One of the soldiers barked a question over the comm. *"What now, sir? If we engage, we'll probably lose our teams."*

Garza nodded. "Correct. But I want to see if you can get this thing on the ground."

"Copy that. All units, move to munitions. Three and Four, covering fire."

There were affirmations and clicks over the comm, and Garza crossed his arms. His men were more than prepared for this. They'd seen worse. If he had filled them in on the details of what they would be encountering out here today, they would have each packed a bit heavier.

But none of that mattered — Garza needed to know how much it would take to take down one of his creations.

Three grenades flew through the air in sync, each landing within two feet of the subject. The subject reacted swiftly, backing up and turning to move the opposite direction, but it was too late.

The three blasts, followed shortly by a fourth, sent the suit and its occupant into the air. It came down, hard, nicking a corner of the metal box. One of the suit's "arms" sheared off completely, the rotator cuff joint popping out. A fifth explosion took off one of the legs.

The suit did its best to compensate, and Garza saw it try to sit up and fire, but the weapons targeting system had been completely destroyed. The subject's head inside the suit was hanging, but the shoulder-mounted turret was still peppering out rounds, though none were hitting anywhere near the soldiers.

A final grenade was arced up and over the metal box, landing close enough to the exoskeleton that the machine fell on top of the metal explosive, just before it detonated.

The suit, blood from the subject, and yellow paint flew in every direction, mixing with the dirt and white smokescreen that was still mushrooming out from the area. Garza heard the tech in his ear. *"Subject 34 terminated. I'm compromised."*

"Affirmative," Garza said. "Teams, stand down. That's enough for today. Camera feeds will have results to each of your tablets this evening, if you want to review your performance. Technical, have the overall analysis sent to mine."

"Yessir."

BEN

THEY WERE GREETED at the airport by a man holding a sign with Ben's name on it. They had driven through the commercial entrance following Mrs. E in her own vehicle. They were guided to an airplane hangar, where they parked and walked toward the waiting jetliner.

"Seems like a waste," Ben muttered as he followed behind Mrs. E.

"What?" Reggie asked.

"Having two jets. Mr. E sprang for them? Why wouldn't he just *tell us* that Julie and Victoria were leaving, and we could have all gone together?"

"Right," Reggie said, grinning. "And you'd have been okay with that?"

Ben shook his head. "No. But I'm not okay with *this*, either."

Mrs. E turned around at the stairs. "And we did not have to pay for the jets," she said. "The other one was owned by the company, and was not being used for the next few days. This one —" she pointed upward — "is owned by the US Military."

"The military?"

"Yes, the Army, to be precise."

"And how'd you convince them to give you a fancy private jet?"

"It came with the team."

Ben frowned, looking up at the plane. "The team?"

"Ma'am," a man said. He had appeared in the doorway of the jet and peered down at them. He reached out a hand, and Mrs. E took it, even though she stood as tall as he did and her musculature was every bit as pronounced. Ben wondered which of them would win in a fistfight.

"Thank you," she said, blushing.

The man was dressed in Army fatigues, wearing a green beret. His right breast pocket had the name "Beale" patched on it.

"Captain Beale," he said. "Welcome aboard."

Ben climbed the staircase behind Reggie and Mrs. E and was floored when he saw inside. The entire jet had been gutted, the fancy leather seats the only remnants of the plane's previous condition. Wires ran the course of the fuselage on the floor and ceiling, and some of the windows had been blacked out, television screens and computer monitors placed in front of them instead.

"This... isn't what I was expecting," Ben said.

"We're not much for in-flight hospitality," another man said, this time from behind Ben. "Sergeant Jeffers, nice to meet you."

Ben turned and saw the largest person he'd ever seen in his life. The black man was easily six-five, and his chest and shoulders stretched from one side of the hallway to the other. Made of a singular pure muscle, his body was rectangular in shape, and Ben wondered if he were even able to move up and down the aisle or if he would be standing there the entire flight.

"It's a faster way to get around," Beale said. "Surgical, precise, and doesn't cause much trouble when we have to land in commercial airports. Sorry for the mess."

The 'mess' was, Ben now realized, tech gear and communications equipment, and it wasn't a mess at all. While the plane's interior itself had been decimated, the Army had replaced the luxury with utilitarian precision. There were stacks of laptops next to an open server rack, storage racks behind that against the port-side wall, and the overhead bins had been stripped out and replaced by more gear racks. Rifles and ammunition were stacked neatly in a corner opposite the door they'd come in on.

Beale slid sideways into an aisle and invited them aboard. "Jeffers and I came down from Elmendorf-Jefferson; we'll meet up with the others at Fort Carson, Colorado."

"How many?" Reggie asked. "Full A-team?"

"Split — Jeffers, myself, and four others are the operators. We'll do introductions and briefing there. I'm told we're in a hurry, though. Shall we?"

Ben and Reggie nodded, and Ben chose a window seat, one of the only ones available in that half of the plane. Mrs. E chose an aisle seat closer to the center of the plane, near what Ben assumed was the command station for the unit.

"This is all for you guys?" Reggie asked before sitting in the aisle seat next to Ben.

"We share it with a few other teams, but these days it's mostly us."

"Damn. Sometimes I wish I'd stayed in."

"You were 75th, yeah?" Jeffers asked.

Reggie nodded. "Sniper. Ranger School, all that jazz."

"Punitive discharge, too," Beale said. "I read your file."

Reggie nodded, his jaw set. Ben watched and listened from his seat. "Sometimes you get punished for doing the right thing. And files don't really tell the real story, do they?"

Beale sniffed and looked over Reggie's head. There was a long pause before he looked back at Ben and Reggie. "No, man. They don't. I get that; true story."

The jet began backing out of the hangar and Ben involuntarily buckled his belt. He'd always hated flying, but he'd gotten used to it lately, as having a cabin in Alaska but working in every corner of the globe was not a great pairing. He looked out at the passing commercial airliners and small prop planes. There were plenty more of the latter, which was common this time of year. Bushplanes and float-planes dominated the air for half the year, as hunters, trappers, explorers, and adventurists took to the skies.

"I thought you knew these guys," Ben said to Reggie as the plane began taxiing.

"Nope. They're Special Forces, though. Green Berets. Best in the business."

"So we're in good hands?"

Reggie shrugged. "There's always a bad apple somewhere, but these guys seem all right. They're smart, experienced, and they're used to working with civilians."

"That so?"

Jeffers had overheard the conversation and leaned over the seat. "Definitely so. We're 'warrior diplomats.' We go in and work with the ground forces. Mostly training and keeping the peace."

"Well," Ben said, "I'm not so sure there's going to be much 'peacekeeping' where we're going."

Jeffers smiled and looked out his own window. "That's what I was hoping. I'm tired of playing police officer."

CHAPTER 21

BEN

JULIE'S COMPUTER, sitting on Ben's lap, pinged with an incoming message. *Archibald Quinones,* the notification said. It was in her video conferencing app, and it meant their friend Archie had boarded his own plane and wanted to touch base.

He answered the call. "Archie," he said, gruffly.

Archie got right to the point. *"Ben, I hope you know that I urged Juliette to wait, to consult with you first."*

"Well, you know how hard-nosed she is about stuff. Whatever you told her last night set her off, and —"

"You were there, Harvey," Archie said. *"You heard it all yourself. Julie's decision was her own, and I do not condone it. But I also hope you know I am here for you. I am onboard my own flight, and I will be in Peru, wherever you need me. I will start as I always do, working on research and following these news stories, hoping there is something I may provide."*

Ben nodded, then took a deep breath. He noticed Reggie watching from the other seat. *He's on our team,* Ben thought. *And I do trust him.* "Sorry, Archie," he said. "I know. I didn't mean to accuse. And yeah, it'll be great to have you there with us. I hate that it's under these circumstances, but I'm glad you've got our backs."

"I do, and I mean it. You have enough help in the field with the soldiers you are with, so I will be setting up in an office, with a solid internet connection. My research will be at your disposal."

Jeffers was standing up in the aisle and when he walked by, Ben thought he saw a bit of a smirk on the man's face.

"Thank you, Archie. Speaking of, is there any news?"

"Actually, yes. There was a public relations notice posted to the website of a park very near the Chachapoyas Valley that stated that 'numerous bouts of gunfire' were heard from somewhere nearby. It was a warning that the discharging of a firearm in the park is illegal."

"Could have been Ravenshadow."

"Yes, perhaps, but I do not think there is anything more we can do to look into it. However, there is something else that might be related somehow. In Lima, next week, there will be a convention. The Conferencia Episcopal Peruana Internacional — the *Peruvian International Episcopal Conference. Held every year, it is a gathering of local and regional Catholic leaders to discuss innovations in church."*

Reggie laughed next to Ben. "Innovations? In church?"

Ben couldn't tell if Archie was offended, but the man's grayish-black eyebrows danced onscreen. *"Yes, Innovations. The Church has always hoped to be a beacon for the lost, and they recognize that the world will pass them by if they do nothing to acknowledge it."*

"All right," Ben said. "So it's a conference about innovation in church. What's that got to do with us or Ravenshadow?"

"Well," Archie said, *"and this is pure speculation, but this year's convention theme seems to be focused on innovations specifically relating to security. With the increase in public shootings around the world, especially in church settings, the conference has invited speakers and exhibitors who specialize in creating preventative measures, defenses, and security solutions for public gatherings."*

"Interesting, but —"

"And as I was reading through a list of some of these exhibitors and

speakers, I saw a bulletin post on their website claiming that one of the attendees would be none other than Father Edmund Canisius."

Reggie sighed. "Archie, come on, you know my 'current church leadership trivia' is outdated."

"He is a Jesuit official who works in the Vatican, for the Holy See as one of the administrators."

"And it's strange that he would be at this conference?"

"Very," Archie said. *"He is a high-ranking official in the Church, and no doubt has a long list of people below him who he would rather send. Besides that, the conference itself is hardly an international affair — it appears to pull in maybe 2,000 attendees every year, possibly less. And as I said, it is regional; most of the attendees are clergy and laypersons from local parishes and communities in Peru."*

"Got it," Ben said. "So there's a small-circuit local conference that's somehow attracted a high-profile bigwig from Rome. You think he's there to learn about security and defense against an active shooter?"

"I do not. I actually have no idea what his purpose would be for attending something like this, but it feels strange to me. Many of the men working for the Holy See at this level are simply figureheads — they have put in many years of service, and their reward is the appointment to a very honorable position. Their subordinates are the ones who run the system."

"So he wouldn't be there just to attend, unless he has a peculiar interest in security in the local Peruvian church."

"Precisely. So I will keep snooping around, but he has raised a red flag for me. I think there is more to this than meets the eye."

"We trust your instinct, Archie. He's a Jesuit, and we've got experience with what those guys are all about — no offense."

Archibald Quinones was a Jesuit as well. A member of the Catholic fraternal order, Archie had dedicated his life to the Church and its history. And the last time they were in Peru, they had stumbled upon an ancient and ongoing battle that was raging between the

Church — mainly a sect of Jesuits within the Catholic Church — and the Guild Rite. Both sides had wanted to recover the secret of the Church's true past, one side hoping to keep it a secret forever and the other hoping to expose it to the world.

Archie had no involvement in the Jesuit's betrayal of the Church, but he was a key asset nonetheless. He had taught history at the university level, and his sharp mind and infinite depth of knowledge of the church's past had proven itself time and time again.

"Thank you, Harvey. I will keep looking. I will send an email with any updates I have, but I suspect you and I will remain out of communication range when you touch down. Both of us have long flights ahead of us, so I wish you safe travels and restful sleep."

Ben wasn't sure about the 'restful sleep' part, knowing that his new wife was gone, heading directly toward their sworn enemy, and the fact that he was on a plane. But he wished Archie the same and closed the connection.

Reggie was already asleep and starting to snore.

CHAPTER 22

JULIE

JULIE AWOKE, scared, more tired than she'd been when she'd fallen asleep. She checked her phone's time.

She'd been asleep for nearly twelve hours. She and Victoria were about to land in Peru, where she would finally work up the nerve to call Ben. He needed to know the truth, that she had been nearly devastated when she'd decided to leave without him. But he also needed to understand that it hadn't even been a decision — at least not a conscious one. She had felt drawn to Peru, to Garza, and her nightmares about the man had only caused her mind to shut down any other possibilities.

I'm going to kill him.

She had awoken from sleep with that singular thought in her mind for days now, and she knew it was the truth. The *real* truth.

She didn't know exactly how they were going to accomplish this goal — two women in a foreign country searching for a man who was a trained killer and owned an army of other killers. They had no plan, no realistic goal, but Julie knew she needed to be there.

Victoria Reyes, Garza's estranged daughter, felt similar. She and Victoria had talked little during the flight, and Julie wondered if the professor of ancient history felt as ambivalent as she. They needed to be in Peru, but Julie hated leaving Ben and the others behind.

He'll come, she thought. *He'll get on the next flight out. Mr. E essentially promised me.*

Her brief conversation with Mr. E had ended in a state of 'agree to disagree.' Mr. E felt strongly that Julie should discuss the issue further with Ben and Reggie, come up with a plan of action, and then execute that strategy. Julie, however, felt that if there was anyone on the planet who could challenge her stubbornness, it was Ben. Mr. E had reluctantly agreed to organize the expenses and logistics for her and Victoria's trip to Peru, with the caveat that once they were in-country they were to wait for Ben and the others. She'd agreed immediately.

She felt she'd made the right decision. Ben, she knew, would have held out as long as possible, and by then it might be too late. Garza might have left the country by then, or at least moved his base of operations from the old temple complex in the Chachapoyas Valley.

But in her heart she also knew Ben was right. He was right to be scared, to be afraid of further confrontation with Garza and the Ravenshadow team. They'd dodged each other for nearly a year, and their brushes with the mercenary army had ended in disaster — and death — every time. It was no small miracle that she and her new husband were still alive.

But that miracle hadn't extended to the first leader of the CSO, their friend and mentor Joshua Jefferson. Garza had killed the man in cold blood, in the most brutal way possible. Julie had filled in Victoria shortly after they'd boarded the plane, explaining that her father had drugged Julie, forced her to face Jefferson with a loaded pistol in a converted gymnasium in Philadelphia, and then told her to pull the trigger.

And she'd done it.

She hadn't been in her right mind at the time, of course, but that hadn't helped her combat the nightmarish reality of what she'd done.

She remembered, through her dreams and flashbacks, Joshua's lifeless body crumpling to the ground, folding in on itself as if it were no longer flesh and bone but merely a set of rags. Her reaction to the dream — to the memory — was horror; at the time, her reaction had been cold, empty stupor.

When the drugs had worn off, she didn't remember anything of the previous twenty-four hours. Her mind was blank as to the events in the gym, and it had taken her subconscious nearly a year to process those same memories to the forefront of her consciousness. When she finally did, she'd discovered that Ben and the others had been silently waiting for that moment. They'd prepared for it. They'd had time to process through the grief, anger, pain, and understanding of what it all meant.

Julie, on the other hand, had not. She had had *no* time to process any of her new reality, and that infuriated her almost as much as what that reality was. They had been *waiting* for her to understand, but they hadn't given her the time to do that.

So she had taken matters into her own hands. They knew where Garza and Ravenshadow was, they knew he had plans, and they knew that he would move as soon as those plans had come to fruition. What they didn't know was what, exactly, those plans were.

The last time they'd met, Garza had revealed to them a piece of that plan: the creation of literal giants. Men who had been injected with a strain of yeast that caused rapid bone growth, then had their skeletal structures repeatedly — and brutally — broken and reset. The effect was a group of men so terrifyingly large that their own weight couldn't be supported. Their faces sunk, their skin stretched so tight that it simply gave up and had started to slide down their musculature. Garza himself had admitted that most of them wouldn't live past a year, but he had been working to perfect that process when they'd found him.

What was his long-term project, then? Julie wondered. *Was he working on more giants? Was that even a sustainable goal?* After all, while the 'giants' project had been an impressive — albeit gruesome — accomplishment, at some point Garza would run out of volunteers. Besides that, soldiers who could only fight for a few minutes at a time and died within a year would be of no use to any forward-thinking dictator.

She shrugged off the thought. *Doesn't matter. We'll find out what he's up to, and we'll stop him. I'll stop him.*

She felt her eyes beginning to water as she looked out the window. She was so far from home. So far from Ben. She had been so sure of herself yesterday, when she'd made the decision to leave without the CSO group. Now, she wished she could reach across the seat and squeeze her husband's hand.

He's coming, she told herself. *He'll be mad as hell, but he's definitely coming.*

CHAPTER 23

BEN

BEN WAS MAD AS HELL. *How could she just* leave *without us?* He'd spent the better part of the past sixteen hours in a cycle of sleeping, fuming, looking out the window, and then sleeping again. Reggie had somehow managed to stay soundly asleep the entire trip, and the two soldiers onboard sitting back in the comm section had been fiddling with their gear and tech whenever he'd turned to look at them.

He knew that no one on his team was conspiring against him. Reggie and Mr. E wanted what was best for both Julie and the CSO, and they all agreed — including Ben — that Garza and Ravenshadow needed to be stopped. But none of them were married to Julie, either. Ben had more of a connection to the woman he loved than anyone else, and therefore he had been more hesitant in launching an all-out attack on Garza.

But his lack of action had backfired, and now they were all flying to Peru in separate planes, hoping to meet up and make sense of things once on the ground.

The Ranger team had tripled in size when they'd landed at Fort Carson, going from just Jeffers and Beale to Jeffers, Beale, and four more men.

Ben hadn't gotten their names, but they'd promptly taken off and the six Rangers all sat together and dozed off within minutes. Ben had taken the hint and had tried to get some sleep for the long leg to Peru.

They were now on the ground, having just landed at an unmarked Peruvian Air Force installation near Iquitos, and they were heading toward the vehicles the Green Berets had organized with the Peruvian Air Force for their transportation.

When Ben saw them he had an immediate flashback.

"Don't like riding in style, Bennett?" Jeffers asked. Ben hadn't realized that he'd stopped short.

"No, uh, just brings back memories." These were the same style jeeps they'd rented last time they'd been in Peru.

"Right," Jeffers said. "Our brief said you guys, uh, *were engaged* down here. Crazy shit, man."

"Yeah," Ben said. "I guess that's one word for it."

"Anyway, these babies are loaded down with kit: 4x4, wench pulleys, the works. Modified to run on propane, too, in case things get dicey."

"And in case things get dicey somewhere where there's access to giant propane tanks," Reggie added.

Jeffers flashed him a glance that didn't take much work to interpret, but the man didn't say anything else. Ben smiled, knowing that if anyone here knew something about modifying vehicles to be a survivalist prepper's dream, it was Reggie. Gareth Red had been friends with Ben for a couple years, but before that he had owned some land in Brazil, where he ran a company teaching survivalism strategies and hosting backcountry expeditions for corporate and private defense groups.

He was a closet nerd, with an excellent sense of history and archeology, but his skillsets were really focused on everything related to staying alive, no matter the environment. So far, he'd been successful.

He waved his prosthetic arm up and wiggled it around, moving all five fingers in tandem, then flipping his hand over and repeating the gesture.

Ben nodded in approval. "Getting pretty good at that," he said.

Reggie shrugged, then reached out and used his artificial limb to grab the cage above the jeep. He swung in, then started to buckle his seatbelt. "It's not really something I've had to practice," he said.

"Really?"

"Really. It's myoelectric, so there are tons of little nodes that read the electronic impulses from my brain, which then send the signal to the microprocessors that move the limb. I just pop it in and get it set, then secure it around my shoulders, and I'm good to go."

Ben sat down in the backseat next to his friend. Reggie held up his fake hand and performed a perfect Spock wave, the Vulcan hand salute. His hand splayed apart between his middle and ring fingers. Then he added a flourish, bending each of his knuckles on each of his fingers one at a time, creating a sort of robotic dance.

"Nice," Ben said.

"Don't be jealous. The healing process is still going on. It hurts."

"Like hell?"

"Worse."

Ben laughed. "I bet. But still, pretty cool stuff. Mr. E really hooked you up, huh?"

Reggie nodded and winked at Ben. "This thing cost half a mil."

Ben almost spat. *"Half a million dollars?"*

The jeep started to move, driven by Jeffers while Beale checked something on his phone. From what they'd explained earlier, they were currently about half an hour from their designated rendezvous point, where they would hopefully meet up with Julie and Victoria.

Ben had tried to call her twice after they'd landed, but the ring had gone straight to voicemail.

"Half a million. Crazy, right? And that doesn't even include the insurance portion."

"We have insurance?"

"Actually, I have no idea. But I was in Mrs. E's room at the cabin, looking for the user manual, and I saw a bill on her desk."

"That thing has a *user manual?*" Ben asked.

"Well, when you're shaking hands with someone for the first time after putting it on, you don't want to turn their creamy palm into a hacky-sack."

"It's that strong?"

"Stronger," Reggie said, nodding. "Titanium used to be one of the strongest things we had, but recently some dorks at MIT figured out how to create a lattice-shaped structure out of graphene."

Ben looked at him blankly.

"That means it's ten times stronger than steel and about five times lighter. And they can effectively print it out with a 3D printer."

"Wow," Ben said. "I didn't know things had advanced that much."

Reggie nodded. "Yeah, it's crazy. I'm only just now starting to understand what it all means. But, at the very least, I'll be able to shake hands like a normal dude. And pull a trigger when I need to."

"Hopefully without breaking it off."

"Yeah, they installed a thrust guide that acts as a force multiplier. Zeroed out it's effectively the strength I had before. Turn it up to 10 and it crushes men's heads like they're a melon."

Ben raised an eyebrow.

"Well, you know. Something like that. I might be exaggerating a bit."

Ben laughed, and the jeep accelerated out onto the highway.

CHAPTER 24

BEN

BEN WAS NERVOUS. They had reached their rendezvous point, and the Green Beret team was already busy unloading the crates and duffel bags from the backs of the jeeps and carrying them into the one-story building. The building, a nondescript facility with broken windows and what appeared to have once been a gasoline pump out front, sat on a corner just outside of the small town they'd decided to stop in.

Ben checked his phone. He was sure Mr. E had equipped them with GSM-unlocked devices, but he still hadn't heard anything from Julie. He'd tried calling a few times in the air, and once on the ground, but he'd gotten nothing.

Is she mad?

She had sent a single text after they'd taken off from Fort Carson, telling Ben that she'd be at the briefing meeting. He'd responded by asking if she knew where it was, what time they would meet, and if she was okay.

He'd heard nothing in response.

So he was feeling a bit nervous. *Anxious? Scared?* He knew he had never been great with emotions, especially his own. He wanted to see her, to know she was fine, but at the same time he knew he was upset with her for leaving him hanging.

And for forcing us all to fly to Peru.

He followed Reggie into the dark interior of the worn-down gas station. There were still racks on the main floor, as well as a beat-up register stand, but there were no products anywhere in sight. The fluorescent light fixtures above his head had been smashed in, and the bulbs that weren't completely missing were broken.

Reggie passed through this area and turned left just after the register, where Ben caught sight of a swinging door. One of the Green Berets had just entered this secondary room, and he saw light bouncing throughout the store from this smaller chamber.

He entered and saw the antithesis of the rest of the gas station in this rectangular room: a clean, brightly lit interior, with non-broken chairs lined up in rows, all facing one of the short walls to Ben's right. A projector had been set up on a pair of milk crates and was beaming a blank white light onto the wall. Sergeant Beale was standing, his hands behind his back, next to the wall.

And in one of the chairs, staring at Ben, was Julie.

He ran over, and she stood, crying. "Ben," she said. "I'm — so... sorry."

"It's okay. I — I just wanted to make sure you were okay."

"I am. And I was. But I just... I don't know what came over me. All of this; I didn't mean for it to be —"

"Shh," he said. "Don't worry about it."

"You're not mad?"

"I... *was* mad." He tried to smile. "But I just needed to see you. To talk to you."

"I wasn't thinking straight," Julie said. "I should have at least mentioned it to you, or consulted the group, and —"

"You *did* do those things, Jules," Ben said. "And I was stubborn. We all knew this had to happen. Garza's *here*, Julie. You were right. He's here, and I don't think he'll stay here. Not for long."

"Yeah..."

Reggie walked over and gave Julie a hug. "Where's Victoria?"

Julie's eyes widened quickly, then her face fell.

"What?" Ben asked.

"She's... not here."

"She didn't come to Peru?"

"No, she did," Julie said. "But she got off the plane and took a taxi. Told me that she had business to take care of, and that she was sorry, and..."

"And you think she's going to find her father? To get to Garza?"

Julie nodded. "There's no other 'business' she could have here."

Sergeant Jeffers overheard this, and walked over to stand in the row directly in front of them. "That could be a problem, Ms. — sorry, Mrs. — Richardson."

"I — I know. But I couldn't stop her. I just was afraid to say anything before we talked in person."

Jeffers glanced at Beale, whose expression was entirely unreadable.

"It's okay," Ben said. "We just need to hurry. If Garza wants to use her as leverage, he will. She may be his daughter, but he's still the monster we know. He's unpredictable, and he'll do anything to maintain an edge."

"Besides," one of the other Green Berets said, "even if he doesn't *do* anything to her, he'll at least know we're here."

"True. He knows we were working together from the last time we came."

They'd met Victoria through a twist of fate. The history professor had been kidnapped by a dark organization that was related to Freemasonry, and they'd brought her to Peru to continue unraveling the plans of the Catholic Church. Garza's group had set up shop in the valley nearby, working from a different interpretation of the same information.

It had all been an unlucky coincidence that they'd ended up

together, but they'd forged a friendship with the woman that had lasted well past their terrifying encounter here.

"Let's get started then," Beale said. The group — five Green Berets and the four CSO teammates — all sat down and waited for Beale to begin. He started by retrieving a stack of papers from a case on the chair in front of him, and he took one packet off the stack and handed the rest to Jeffers, who began passing them out.

Ben received his and saw that the top page was nothing but a cover page, with little detail as to what was inside. The packet was four pages total, with a map and legend on page two and more information about the mission beyond that. He was about to flip through and begin reading when Beale called their attention to the front of the room.

CHAPTER 25

BEN

"INSIDE OF THIS PACKET, you'll find details of the mission. Locations, rendezvous points, timing. Everything's there, and I won't insult your intelligence by reading it all to you. But I will give you the overview and breakdown of essential mission parameters.

"First," he continued, "we are Green Berets. 'Force multipliers.' That means we *can* fight, and we can do it well. But if we're called in, it's because there is a diplomatic reason for us *not* to fight. That's why *you* all are here." He looked up and made eye contact with Ben and his team. "We want to equip *you* to do the task required. We're here for your support."

Ben nodded. *So far, so good.*

"Second, we do not know this Ravenshadow group. We've heard of them, but none of us have experience engaging them. Again, you do. That's why you're here. We provide support, you interact with Vicente Garza and his men."

Reggie frowned, and Ben looked at him as Beale continued.

"On page two you will see a map. This region, the Chachapoyas, is somewhat familiar to the CSO crew. Much of this valley is owned by the same order of Jesuits your friend, Archibald Quinones, is a part of, which works in our benefit as well. Therefore, the CSO will act as guides for us, though we will of course have GPS and satellite triangulation to help us navigate the dense jungle. Once we get there, we expect to find a large valley that stretches generally north to south, and some ancient structures dotting the landscape that were believed to have been built by the original inhabitants of the region."

He looked up and met Ben's eyes. Ben knew he wasn't going to add, *and we believe those original inhabitants were giants,* even though that's exactly what Ben and Reggie had put in their report. The 'giants,' they had discovered, were really just descendants of the ancient biblical tribe of Anakim — cousins of the Nephilim — and the same race of people that had given rise to the descendants of another famous biblical giant: Goliath.

Their history lesson of the area suggested that the original Chachapoyas, described by the Spanish conquistadors and the local Inca population as 'light-skinned and reclusive,' had come from somewhere in Europe, at some time after worldwide flooding had decimated their homeland. They sought refuge in the unknown lands to the west, ending up in South America.

And their relatives had been sprinkled throughout the postdiluvian world as well: the Aztecs had Quetzalcoatl, the 'fair-skinned, bearded man of the sea,' the Sumerians had Enki, and the Native Americans had their own versions of the flood legend and creation stories.

Ben and his team had found proof of these lost civilizations, both in Egypt and in Greece, and they had reason to believe that the reason the Chachapoyas had settled in Peru was to protect an ancient secret, one that had been nearly wiped out by the flood: their history, the history of the antediluvian world, kept in the ancient Hall of Records.

Beale, predictably, didn't care about any of that.

Ben looked at the page, and he saw a contour map showing the elevations and geologic features of the area nearby. He immediately recognized the valley, stretching from one end of the side of a massive mountain to the other. That mountain was ground zero — where Garza's team would be hiding.

"What I want to call your attention to, however, is this dark line that encircles the top half of the mountain at the center of your map. It's a river, and it's navigable. The mine that was built into the mountain used this river, as well as a natural spring emanating from the interior of the mountain, as its main water source."

"So it's an access point?"

"It could be," Beale said. "We won't know for sure until we're staring it in the face, but if this Ravenshadow group is as equipped and well-trained as we believe them to be, shooting out the front door and walking in doesn't seem to be in the cards."

"Right," Jeffers said. "So we need scuba gear."

"Already taken care of," one of the other men said.

Jeffers nodded, then looked up at the group. "Any questions so far?"

Reggie's hand shot up.

"Mr. Red."

"Yeah, uh, earlier you said *interact*. Not *engage*. I'm assuming that's purposeful, but —"

"It is absolutely purposeful. As I said, our job is not to *fight*. It is to reach a compromise and a conclusion agreeable to all parties that ensures the —"

"Bullshit," Ben said.

Beale looked visibly shocked. Apparently the soldier hadn't had much experience with his team interrupting him in the middle of a presentation. "You got something to say, Bennett?"

Ben stood up. "I didn't come down here to *make a compromise,* unless that compromise is you killing Garza instead of us."

"Mr. Bennett, I understand your frustration —"

"You don't understand *crap*. This guy — this *egomaniac* — he's not just a crazy psychopath who wants power. He's a crazy psychopath *with an army.*"

"We are planning to infiltrate their compound and take him by surprise, so we can have a one-on-one conversation with him that will —"

"He's not going to like that very much, I suspect," Ben said. "He tends to be of the "shoot first, ask questions later" sort of guy."

"Mr. Bennett," Beale said. "You *will not* interrupt me again."

"Or what?"

Beale raised an eyebrow, and Ben thought he just might have to fight off a well-trained Green Beret. *Probably not the best way to start the day.*

"Or we will be transferring control of this situation back to the Peruvian government and escorting you and your team home. In handcuffs."

"Got it," Ben said. "So you're advocating we all run in there with our assault rifles, *not* shooting at them, and hoping Garza will just sit down and have a chat with us?"

"No," Beale said. "I'm not advocating anything. I'm *mandating* it. This is *my* mission, and these are *my* rules. Further, I'm not at all suggesting that we will be armed."

"We won't?" Reggie asked.

"That is correct," Beale said. "*You* won't be armed. *My* men will be. If you turn to page three, you will see the load out for this mission. You and your team, Mr. Bennett, will be carrying communications equipment and tracking devices, as well as emergency kits, should we need them."

"And no guns," Ben said through clenched teeth.

"And no guns. I'm not in the business of arming civilians."

Jeffers shifted in his chair, and the other Green Beret who'd spoken earlier seemed to smirk for a split-second.

This is not *good,* Ben thought. *This is not good at all.*

CHAPTER 26

JULIE

THE LAST TWO days had been a whirlwind for Julie. Rather than catching plenty of sleep during the ridiculously long flights, she'd been awake, thinking about Ben. Wondering if she'd made the right call, and feeling as though she'd made a horrible mistake.

Victoria had duped her, using the CSO to fund her flight to Peru just so she could ditch them and run after her father. There was no question in Julie's mind that Victoria wanted vengeance, and she felt the same way, but the woman had proven to be a loose cannon.

And it had all felt like Julie's fault. She'd wanted to force the issue, to force action. The plan had worked, as she knew it would, and now the CSO team was in Peru, nearly ready to face off against their long-time opponent. But she had been disappointed and dismayed to find out that the Green Beret contingent was relegating her team to the back seat. They were civilians, and they were now going to be forced to act like it.

She wanted to take it all back, to make it all go away, but the issue remained: Vicente Garza was here, and he was alive. She knew she couldn't turn her back on that opportunity. She, like the man's own daughter, wanted vengeance for what he'd done to her.

She saw Joshua Jefferson's face in her mind. His handsome,

youthful face, dimples and all. His brown, medium-length hair falling over his right eye. He was talking, saying something she couldn't hear. She wanted to reach out and touch his hand, to grab it and pull him closer and tell him she was sorry.

But she couldn't bring back the dead.

And she wanted Garza to experience that exact feeling.

Ben had followed her out of the room, into the decimated gas station, then waited for the rest of the Green Berets and CSO teams to exit. They were on a five-minute break, both to use the disheveled restroom and to cool down, which seemed ironic, considering it was nearing one-hundred degrees outside.

She met his eyes, and she walked over, ready to talk. Before she could open her mouth to apologize again, Sergeant Jeffers walked over. Ben introduced them, and Jeffers smiled down at them from his massive, tall frame.

"Sorry for that."

"For what?" Ben asked.

"For Beale. He's a good soldier, and a great leader. Been with him for years, actually. He just gets a little hot, is all."

"Nothing to worry about," Ben said. "I wasn't really pissed at him, but with the situation. I know he's just doing his job. We're the odd-man out, I get it. He doesn't want to worry about us shooting you all in the backs."

"It's not that," Jeffers said.

Ben frowned.

"He said 'I won't arm civilians,' didn't he?"

"Something like that," Julie said.

"Right. So that means *he* won't arm you. The US Military won't have anything to do with it."

"But..."

"*But* that means he won't bat an eye if you were to, uh, somehow *procure* your own. We got about half a day before we hit the road toward Bad Guy Mountain, and I'm assuming not all of you need the sleep."

"Are you saying he won't care if we bring our own weapons?"

Jeffers sniffed, then looked both ways, as if he were about to offer a drug deal. "He's a good leader, like I said. A bit 'by the book,' if you ask me, but no one's asking me."

"He won't be upset?" Julie asked.

Jeffers laughed. "Oh, I'm not saying that at all. He'll be pretty pissed you didn't obey his orders. But guess what? You don't work for him."

"We still need his help. Your help."

"Yeah, I bet you do. Thing is, our mission is Garza, not keeping you folks out of trouble. And with your history — your background — and with guys like Red working with you, I know he trusts you all a hell of a lot more than he'd trust many other no-names in the force. So he feels the same way, really. *We* need *your* help just as much. His hands are tied, though. Mine aren't, so I'm telling you how it is."

Julie watched Ben as he considered it for a second. "You know anywhere we can get, uh, *stuff*?"

Jeffers took a step back and raised his arms, palm-up. "Whoa, whoa, what do I look like, an arms dealer?"

Ben smiled.

"I'm not telling you *how* to do it, I'm just telling you that you *should*. My opinion. Take it or leave it."

Julie smiled as well, and stuck out her hand for Jeffers to shake. "I think I can speak for all of us when I say we'll *definitely* take it. And I have a feeling our friend Gareth Red knows *someone* out here who's miscreant enough to hook us up for a few days."

Jeffers faked a hat-tip to the pair and turned on a heel, his feet pounding loudly as he left the store. Julie could feel the ground shake with each of his massive footfalls.

CHAPTER 27

BEN

THE JEEPS they'd hired had come with drivers, and now their convoy sped through the dense forest of the Chachapoyas region in Peru. Ben sat in the front seat next to the Peruvian driver, a man who called himself simply, "Nacho." Julie and Mrs. E were in the back, while Reggie had decided to travel in the jeep just in front of theirs with two of the Green Berets. The first jeep in the line held Beale, Jeffers, and another soldier, while the jeep at the back of the line carried gear.

Scuba equipment, weapons, and communications equipment had been piled high in the seats of the jeep, and the team had strapped everything in and tested it for shock before embarking on the three-hour trip. They would drive through a small town called Mendoza, heading deeper into the Peruvian Amazon, then turn southwest and head toward the mountain range and valley where they'd fought a month before.

Ben gripped the handle above his door as he looked out the window. Monkeys crowed into the misty air, the heavy humidity penetrating even the waterproof vinyl of the jeep's walls. He didn't recognize the road they were on, nor did he see any buildings or signs he knew, but it all seemed somehow familiar.

Now they were heading back to the hellscape, hoping to find Garza and his army and bring them to justice.

And this time, Ben knew, that justice would be coming in the form of a bullet to the head. He wasn't a killer — or at least he would never describe himself as one — but he had come to understand that there were problems that needed to be solved in the world, problems that could only be solved by rooting them out and destroying them.

Vicente Garza was one of those problems.

He tightened his other hand around the grip of a massive pistol Reggie had handed him earlier. During their downtime, Reggie, having lived in South America for years prior to meeting Ben and Julie, had called around to some of his friends who might have a lead in the area.

It didn't take him long to find a man who owned an army surplus store, and legally sold used Peruvian military weaponry that he had acquired over the years. But the story Reggie told Ben was that the man *also* collected the sorts of things that were a bit *harder* to find — more modern weapons, from Brazil to Venezuela. In the shipping and delivery industry, Reggie explained, every logistics technician calculates for a thing called "shrinkage," which is the uncanny ability of a certain percentage of a driver's delivery to mysteriously "walk off" and disappear.

The man Reggie went to meet was the type of man who often "found" these disappeared items. In translation: he had plenty of modern military weaponry available for sale.

So when Reggie had returned to the gas station before their departure with a duffel bag full of M16s, Glock handguns, and ammunition, Beale nearly lost his mind.

He shouted for a full minute at Reggie, who simply smiled back at him through the threats. Eventually Beale realized what had happened, understood that he had no ground to stand on, and fumed away. Ben, Julie, and Mrs. E waited patiently at the side of the room until Beale left, when Reggie walked over and showed Ben and Julie how to use the weaponry.

Ben wasn't sure if the episode would cause any lasting fallout between the soldiers and the civilians, but he knew Jeffers was right — the CSO was more help if they were armed and prepared for an engagement. They'd follow the soldiers' lead, but Ben wanted to be useful if things got out of hand.

Beale's voice sounded over the jeep's radio. *"Listen up, both teams. Let's go over the plan while we're still out of radio interception range. We've still got some details to iron out."*

Ben fiddled with the knob on the old stereo that they'd retrofitted. The cable hanging from the front of it crackled noisily with static electricity, then turned to a cleaner, louder signal. *"We've got the data back from our satellite scans. There has in fact been activity in the valley area over the past week, so we believe this is the correct location. Scans also show two fortified locations — likely some sort of bunkers or turrets — on the roads that lead in and out of the mountain. These mining roads have always been there, but the bunkers appear to be newer. So that means we're not going to chance a frontal or flanked approach from the roads."*

Another voice joined in. *"Sir, we don't have another way in — I thought we decided the best approach was via the river, until we can get close enough to look for some sort of access shaft?"*

"It was, but we just don't know what's down there. We thought the spring would be a shot, the one that starts in the mountain. It may have been expanded and used by the original miners as direct access to the river, for a trash chute or something, or it may be that the spring simply seeps out into the river. Meaning that's not a reliable way in."

All the soldiers had throat-mounted microphones that picked up their words without needing to manually start and end the transmission, but Beale had given one old-fashioned handheld radio to Ben's jeep. Ben grabbed the walkie-talkie and pressed the button on the side. "Bennet here. When we were in Antarctica I crawled through the vent and ducting system — this place has to breathe, right? So there have to be access shafts cut into the side of the mountain?"

Beale's voice returned. *"We checked, and there are. But they're too small for us, and we don't have any schematics — we're not sure which ones are still in use and which ones will just get us stuck inside a collapsed mineshaft."*

Ben shuddered just thinking about it.

"So I guess it's the river, then? Float down and hope we see a way in?" Ben asked.

"Affirmative. It's at least the only option that keeps us away from prying eyes. The Ravenshadow soldiers will be guarding the main entrances. Might be a few patrols around the perimeter, but the river cuts next to a cliff. It's pretty unnavigable landscape on the ground out there."

Jeffers' voice came over the feed. *"Boss, you said these guys have been down here for months?"*

"Likely even longer," Beale said. *"Over a year, probably."*

"Well," Jeffers said. *"If their army is as big a deal as the CSO guys make it seem, that's a lot of men to keep happy. Food, water, pot to piss in. You know where I'm going with this?"*

"You're thinking there is an access shaft they won't be guarding?"

"I'm thinking they've got to at least have a sewage dump line. Something more modern, but it could just be a channel that they're forcing water through. One that ends in a deep spot in the river."

Ben thought about it. Aside from the obvious environmental ignorance of building such a system, it *would* be the easiest way to remove the waste and debris from inside the mountain.

"Hold that thought," one of the soldiers said in reply. *"This right here..."* he seemed to be speaking directly with Beale, so Ben assumed it was one of the Green Berets with him in the front jeep. *"We thought it was just an anomaly from the visualization software. We used LIDAR and ground-penetrating radar, combined and superimposed on the topographical map of the mountain to build an image of*

the valley and surrounding area. Sometimes those interfaces don't always sync up and we get... imperfections. This one here..." his voice trailed off again, then came back, *"looks like it runs up from the river to the center of the base. It could be exactly that."*

"Or it could just be an imperfection."

"Yeah, true. But it really would be an easy shot to get in, and worst case, there's nothing there and we just have the drivers pick us up down-river and try again."

"Can't argue with that," Beale said. "Great. That's the plan. We drop in just north of the mountain, where the river's wide and calm. Our gear gives us a little over an hour to get in — we have to conserve the other half in case we need to make a water exit — and hopefully we can get where we need to go from there."

The soldiers signed off, and Ben looked back at Julie.

Hope this works, he thought. He knew he didn't need to say it aloud.

She was thinking the same thing.

CHAPTER 28

GARZA

GARZA'S MIND RARELY DRIFTED. As a stoic, he had practiced for years the techniques and training detailed by the Ancient Greek philosophers, and he had grown to control the thoughts that found their way into his mind. It was a skill he had needed numerous times on the battlefield, both in the corporate world and in the military.

But every so often his mind reached back for a memory that he thought had been locked away, a memory so deeply lodged in his archives that he wondered if his Stoic training couldn't even prevent it from reappearing at will.

He sat down, already feeling the exhaustion of his day's work taking a toll. He had been at it since five in the morning, a habit he'd picked up — and kept — since boot camp. He had done his morning walkthrough after eating breakfast with his men, then fielded a few training questions from his second-in-command, Morrison, and finally taken a call from his buyer, who was currently in the country.

But that was all normal day-to-day business. After lunch, he'd walked through his demonstration floor, examining the newest suits his scientists and engineers had built. He employed fifteen engineers, three chemists, two physicians, and a handful of other mechanics, technicians, and computer scientists. Together, the teams had churned out failed design after failed design, complaining about either low battery life, power output restraints, extreme stress on the human operators, or some combination of all three.

His weapons experts had struggled with fitting the rounds into their casings and then into a magazine that was able to fit within the Exos' shells, but they had eventually figured it out.

The first generation of Exosuits was a massive success, and he had allowed his men — in shifts, of course — to take extended four-day vacations to rest and recover for the next phase.

That next phase was the groundbreaking achievement. His magnum opus, the culmination of all the hard work he'd done studying and finding the perfect team of professionals. Moving his entire company to a country that wouldn't interfere with his work had taken more legal maneuvering than he'd cared to do, but the deal was done.

He was now the owner of the single best military exoskeleton suit of armor on the planet. His was going to change the world, but unlike his competitors, he wasn't interested in merely selling the new tech to the highest bidder. He had countless ways to make money and generate income, and at its core Ravenshadow was still a security company that could earn plenty of work overseas.

No, he wanted more. He wanted both the money for the tech *and* the control. Selling it outright was a recipe for disaster. It could end up in the hands of a dictator in a third-world country, or, even worse, in the hands of a corrupt *first*-world government's military.

Instead, he had worked a deal that was nearly as impressive as the tech itself. A four-way transaction between an ultimate buyer and him, the ultimate seller. But he'd also ensured that his part would be *broker* of that same deal, a way of both extracting more profit from the deal and in securing his bottom-line ownership of the tech. By explaining to the buyer that he was working with an exclusive broker who would own a liability license for half of the new tech, he could prevent the tech from being wholly resold as a proprietary item.

And giving this broker exclusive access to resell licenses to use the complete system, he prevented the technology from growing without him, or from getting into the wrong hands.

In short, of the two crucial components that made his tech work, he wanted to sell one half of it outright and license the other half.

And neither the seller nor the other parties involved needed to know that he was *both* the buyer *and* the broker in the deal. His legal exploits had made the confusion of these facts easy to pull off, and neither the buyer nor the third party who *thought* they were the broker knew the full details.

It was a massive, complicated mess, but in Garza's mind it was dead-simple. He wanted to retain the ability to control the tech. He wanted to ensure the future of his Exosuits would be governed by *him*, no matter who thought they had control of it.

All of this was on Garza's mind when he came to rest in the chair. But all of these things were things he'd *allowed* into his mind.

What he hadn't expected today was a thought of a different type: a memory. One that he apparently had no control over preventing.

His wife was there, as was his newborn daughter, Victoria. They were happy. *Very* happy. The kind of happy that almost causes pain. Perhaps even one of the last times he had felt that way.

He could feel the heartache crawling up from his stomach, the pain of remembrance, the pain of loss. In the memory, he looked down at Victoria. His daughter. His world.

He'd wanted so much for her, but he hadn't realized what it would cost. Losing his wife — Victoria's mother — had changed his outlook on life. He'd realized that while family was important, it had also been the cause of their loss. Without her mother, Victoria had drifted away.

Without his wife, Garza had allowed it to happen.

Without closeness of that nature, pain would never have been allowed to set in. If he had never taken these lives and intertwined them with his own, never committed to the journey of living life with loved ones, he never would have been set back.

He had focused his sights on something that could never leave him, something that wasn't human and couldn't cause him pain: his work.

He had turned away from Victoria after her mother had passed, turned his focus toward new beginnings, new achievements.

Victoria was there, in her mother's arms. The memory had a special place in his mind not because of the love that he felt, but because it was a good picture for how he envisioned both his wife and his only child: gone.

The memory wasn't a reminder of his time *with* his family, but of what he had been able to accomplish *without* them. It was a vivid reminder that the world would continue spinning no matter what. Best to spend it doing something that would leave a legacy.

CHAPTER 29

JULIE

JULIE GRIPPED Ben's hand tightly as they stood on the shore, waiting for the soldiers to hand out the scuba equipment. They'd trained together a few times, but hadn't gotten their certification yet. However, the basics and most of the early practice was second nature to both of them.

And since they would be in a river, they wouldn't be at much depth. Their trimix of nitrogen, helium, and oxygen was kept to a ratio that would benefit a shallow dive, as the only reason they'd need to be completely submerged would be to stay out of sight of any Ravenshadow patrols who might be looking down at the river from up above.

When Beale got to the two of them, he handed them each a pair of goggles and waited while two of his men brought over the tanks and began hooking them up. "I assume I don't need to give you a lesson in scuba, do I?" he asked.

Ben shook his head. "We're good. Done it a few times."

"Very well. All you need to know then is that we're using back-mounted BCDs, buoyancy control devices, so we're clear in front of us. More maneuverable that way, too. And there aren't any suits —

dry or wet — so be sure you bail out if you start getting cold; hypothermia isn't a joke, and we're not stopping to warm up."

They nodded.

"I guess… that's it. You know the drill. Don't get in our way. We need you to verify it's Ravenshadow when we're in, and help us get to Garza. That's it. It's not a sightseeing mission, and if something goes wrong with your tanks, you're off. Get out of the water and get back to civilization on your own."

"Don't worry," Julie said, starting to feel a bit annoyed at Beale's holier-than-thou attitude and pretentiousness. "We're not going to slow you down."

Beale examined her, then nodded once. "Oh," he said. "And don't forget. You've got a communicator that's waterproof, but there's no way to send or receive while we're underwater. Wait until we're back on dry land or out of the water, then flick it on. They're line-of-sight, and I'm the relay, so if you get more than fifty or so feet away from me you're incommunicado."

Julie and Ben nodded.

He turned and walked back to his group. Mrs. E, already wearing her tanks and flippers, waddled over. "These things are quite tight," she said.

"You're not the smallest of people, E," Ben answered. "Here, let me help." He reached behind her and fiddled with the straps of her tanks a bit. Then, when Julie saw that Beale was engaged in another conversation, Ben spoke again. "He's a real piece of work, huh?"

Mrs. E smiled. "He is a soldier. Not used to working with civilians, I predict."

"I thought they were supposed to be 'force multipliers,' or something like that," Ben said.

Reggie's voice joined in from behind them. "They are. They're just not used to having help. They want to swoop in and be the heroes. Either clean up the mess themselves or train the on-the-ground local troops how to do it."

"Well, he doesn't have to be a jerk about it," Ben muttered.

"He's not. He just wants to keep us all alive, and he's got a million things on his mind."

"It's not that," Julie said. "I mean, I get all that — that's how *we* feel, too. Victoria's in there, and I want to make sure we get her out safely. We all know the danger."

Reggie shrugged. "Yeah, he's not much of a people person, but I'd bet he's more than capable of getting the mission finished. Just trust him a little longer."

Julie sighed, checked her levels and equipment for malfunctions and problems, and, satisfied, walked over to the bin to pick out a set of flippers. She'd trained with Ben at a scuba school a few months ago, after their stint in The Bahamas, and they'd been snorkeling a few times. All of those times they'd been handed a set of heavy silicon flippers that never fit quite right.

The pair she grabbed from this bin, however, seemed to mold right to her bare feet, easing into the contours and shapes and forming a perfect seal around them. They were also smaller and lighter, and she knew they would allow her much more maneuverability, at the expense of a bit of power.

But they'd be traveling downstream, at least for this portion of the journey. The river was cumbersome and slow-moving, deep in some spots but in most places no more than eight to ten feet. They would be able to take advantage of the powerful yet slow current, allowing it to push them along without much strain. It would benefit their energy — and oxygen — stores, and give them more to tap into for the return journey upstream.

"Okay, let's move out," Beale said. His soldiers were busy camouflaging the equipment bins and jeeps, which they'd parked off the road far enough into the trees that they would be impossible to see.

Ben and Julie shuffled down to the shoreline, where Reggie and Mrs. E were already testing the water. Birds and monkeys scattered in a huff of activity and noise, all then turning back at a safe distance to eye the newcomers.

"It's warm," Reggie called back to them, smiling. "Nothing like a quick dip in a comfy river to start the day."

Julie wished she could borrow his optimism, but she knew their task was going to be monumental, if not impossible. They'd find Garza, but what then? Would there be time for the Green Berets to negotiate? Would Garza even allow it?

And where was Victoria? Had she already accomplished their mission, and they were now just running into a mess?

"Come on, Jules," Ben said, his voice redirecting her attention to the water, where he was standing, waist-deep. "It really is pretty warm."

"How's the bottom?" she asked. She'd always hated the feel of lakes and rivers — the squishy, mushy mess of plants and mud that festered in the darkness of the depths. She shuddered even as she said it.

"It's... a river. Pretty mucky, but we're not walking, we're swimming."

She nodded and stepped in, squeezing her eyes closed. *Why can't we be walking over a nice, sunny beach instead of slogging through an Amazonian tributary?* She wanted to get to the center of the stream as soon as possible, so she could start treading water.

"Anything we should worry about out here?" one of the soldiers asked.

Jeffers, who was already fitting his mask and regulator over his head, answered. "Nah, nothing besides piranha and crocs."

The other soldier's eyes widened. "S — seriously?"

Jeffers smiled, and Reggie answered. "No, piranha won't bother us, and all the big crocs are much lower — over in Brazil and the basin. Anaconda, too. They're all in the warmer, brackish water. Up here it's just monkeys and birds. Oh, and blood-sucking bugs. But in case we *do* see any of the bigger stuff, I've got a harpoon that'll fly through a brick wall."

The soldier shook his head, annoyed.

"Also them," Beale said. He flicked his eyes to the road, which they could barely see through the trees. Julie followed his gaze and saw that there were two vehicles — SUVs — moving slowly toward them. The road here bent in toward the river, and there would be a few seconds where they might be easily spotted. "Everyone, down. Underwater. Count out three minutes and resurface."

They all obliged, Julie having to rush putting on her regulator and mask and shoving her face beneath the water. She almost forgot that they were all armed as well, and her rifle nearly fell off her shoulder. She rolled onto her back and tightened the strap simultaneously, watching the bright surface of the water.

Trees and vines swayed above the surface, and she backed up toward the center of the river where Ben and the others waited, careful to stay underwater.

The water felt cool on her skin, though it was within the realm of what she'd describe as "warm," and it blocked out nearly all of the sound from around her. There was the swishing noise of Ben and Mrs. E to her right and left, messing with their digital controls and getting into position, and there was the sound of a monkey screeching from somewhere that sounded far away, and there was —

An engine.

Was it one of the SUVs? Had they been spotted?

She glanced toward the shoreline just as her vision was blocked by a huge, black shape.

CHAPTER 30

JULIE

BEALE.

Julie had nearly spat out her regulator and began shooting at the man. When he swam into her sightline, she had been focusing just beyond him at the edge of the water, where she thought she'd seen one of the SUVs.

He was motioning, using his fingers and eyes as a way to tell her what was about to happen.

The problem was that she had no idea what he meant.

Finally, with an annoyed flick of his wrist, he pointed downstream and nodded. Then he reached out and pulled Julie forward, then, as if she weighed nothing to him, tossed her that direction.

"Hey —" she tried to say, but the words through her regulator did nothing but come out as bubbles and muffled grunts.

Ben, Reggie, and Mrs. E were already in motion, and each of them had their rifles out and pointed the direction they were swimming. Deciding that she, too, wouldn't be taking any chances, Julie reached over her shoulder and pulled the rifle in front of her. Reggie had informed them that their weapons were essentially waterproof — though they wouldn't necessarily work well underwater — but the ammunition was not. If any moisture got inside the cartridges, the round would be ruined. However, he'd told them that it was highly unlikely with modern weaponry.

So their weapons were perfect for an amphibious assault, should it come to that. They could pop up and out of the water, firing almost immediately after their barrels emptied of water. Anyone on the shore would be taken by surprise, and it would hopefully be enough.

When she'd asked why he'd said *hopefully*, he explained that if they *didn't* eliminate their enemy with their first bursts of fire, they would be like sitting ducks — the difference being that ducks were a bit more adept on water than battle-clad humans.

She hoped it wouldn't come to that. If the SUVs *had* seen them, she hoped they'd be staying back at the place where they'd entered the water.

But if the SUVs were in fact part of Garza's crew, she knew they would be calling it in as soon as they found their stashed jeeps and gear. They would know to expect a breach, and that it would happen wherever the waterborne shaft led.

She shook off the thought and focused on the dark waters in front of her. The river here had narrowed but grown deeper, and the dark shadows of fish of all sizes danced in her vision, not allowing her to let down her guard.

She'd heard Reggie also explain what they could expect to find in this tributary rivers. She knew all too well what those beasts were, and she hoped he was right that the truly monstrous ones would stay in the warmer, murkier waters downstream.

Still... there was something unnerving about traversing a dark, cool river in the Peruvian Amazon. Creatures she probably never knew existed were watching her right now, some of them wondering how she might taste as a snack...

Ben was suddenly there, pulling her to the side. She allowed him to yank her sideways, and she narrowly missed banging her head on a sharp, protruding log that had been submerged directly in front of her. She wondered how he'd seen it, and only then realized that every other member of their crew was using their wrist-mounted dive light.

Feeling stupid, she flicked hers on, expecting to see a huge, hungry anaconda waiting directly in front of her.

But there was no waiting anaconda. Instead, the water around her exploded to life as bubbles and hissing streams of supersonic air flew through the water.

They're shooting at us, she realized. She felt the panic rising in her throat, and she tried to choke it down. *Calm down, breathe, swim.*

Apparently the Ravenshadow men *had* seen them, and rather than working their way back to their base and preparing the rest of Garza's army, they'd decided to take things into their own hands. Worse, Julie knew the men had likely already called in the breach and were simply trying to get a jump on eliminating the problem. They'd lost their element of surprise. If they were able to escape the attack now, they'd be met with a waiting Ravenshadow army.

She pulled herself ahead and around the sharp log, hoping that it might provide some sort of respite from the fight. Instead, she saw out of the corner of her eye the log exploding into a thousand pieces as it was nailed by rounds from the assault rifles. She considered bringing her own rifle up and trying to take out a couple of the enemy soldiers. She was a great shot, but she had to admit that coming up out of a murky river, wearing a scuba tank, mask, and regulator was not going to do her any favors.

Besides, she realized that she was the last in line, and the shots were landing just behind her. She remembered the topography of their entry point. The river buckled around and changed directions there, creating the small peninsula shape that the men were now shooting from. The area to the east and west of that peninsula, however, was completely impenetrable, the forest having grown to the edge of the river.

Unless the soldiers followed them into the river, all Julie and her group had to do was head downstream until they were sufficiently out of sight.

More shots landed in the water, one of the trails of air brushing against her arm. *Too close.* She swam faster, nearly bumping into the fins of whoever it was in front of her.

The team swam underwater, pumping hard, for another fifteen minutes. At that point, she saw that Reggie and Ben were treading water and had their heads out. Mrs. E and the Green Berets were all coming up as well, so Julie pulled back and allowed herself to rise to the surface. When her head broke, she ripped out her regulator and took a gasping breath of air. There was no difference between the air in their tanks and the air outside, but something about the restriction of the scuba gear while being shot at caused her to feel claustrophobic, constricted.

"You okay?" Ben asked.

She winced as his voice blasted into her ear, not realizing that her communicator was already on. She fiddled with the headset component for a second, trying to find the volume control. When she did, she pulled it down to about halfway and then looked up at her husband.

She nodded, breathing steady but large breaths of air, and she took in their surroundings. The rainforest had grown to the edge of the water here as well, and some of the trees and vegetation were even hanging out over the water. On her left, she saw that about twenty or thirty feet back a cliff rose from the treetops and shot majestically into the air. It had to be hundreds of feet tall, and Julie knew this was the side of the mountain that had been carved away by the slow, incessant flow of the massive river over the course of millennia.

"We're here," Beale said, calling out softly over the water from his spot twenty feet downstream.

"We are?" Reggie asked. "Seems quick."

"We had the current working for us," Jeffers said. "Not to mention a little kick in the ass when we got started."

"True that," one of the other Green Berets said. "Everyone okay?"

Nods all around, and Beale, satisfied, checked his dive computer and measured their progress. "Yeah, this should be it. We'll all take a peek, see if we can find the shaft. Jeffers, Lang, you two will be the first to enter. Check it out and report back."

Everyone affirmed, and Julie found herself plunging back underwater to look for the entrance to the tunnel that would hopefully lead them into the heart of a mountain, and the middle of an army ready and waiting to kill them.

She couldn't see much, even with the dive light, but it didn't matter. Within another five minutes one of the Green Berets, a man of asian descent named Lang, found the entrance. Beale called everyone together while Lang and Jeffers examined the shaft. It took another ten minutes, but they returned and filled in the rest of the team.

"Okay, good news," Lang said. "The tunnel's modern. Steel-reinforced, concrete, the works. It's definitely been put in recently."

"Perfect," Beale said. "Bad news?"

"It's long," Jeffers said. "We got about a hundred, hundred-fifty feet. It's dark, but everything points to it being pretty solid."

"That's... bad news?" Another Green Beret asked.

"No," Lang said. "The bad news is that there's a current — a strong one — and it was getting stronger the farther we swam."

"So?" Reggie asked.

"It means there's something *generating* the current. A fan, a compressor, something. It's pushing the water through to make sure whatever they're tossing down it gets all the way to the river."

"And you don't think we can swim through it?"

"Not in one piece, no," Jeffers said.

"But there's only one way to find out," Beale said. "Two by two, grab a swim buddy. Stow weapons, but have a sidearm ready. We don't know what we're getting ourselves into, but that hasn't ever slowed us down before. Let's go have a look at this thing."

"Got it."

"Roger that."

Julie felt Ben's presence in the water next to her. He was treading water casually, the BCD helping to keep him afloat. He nudged her forward, toward the entrance. "Diving buddy?" he asked.

She smiled. "I guess, if you're the best option I've got."

She was about to lean in to kiss his cheek when the forest behind them on the opposite shoreline came alive with noise of an engine.

"Shit," Beale said. "They found us."

"They knew where we were heading," Jeffers said. "Eyes up. We're about to be under attack."

Bullets began strafing the water even before Jeffers had finished speaking, and Julie ducked farther into the water. *We're sitting ducks out here,* she realized. *They've got us pinned between themselves and the cliff.*

"No," Beale shouted. "We can't mount a counterattack here. The shaft is our only way out. Go!"

She noticed a few Ravenshadow men in the trees on the opposite shoreline, but she also saw movement to her right. About fifty feet upstream, breaking through the trees, was *another* group of soldiers, all armed and looking for something to shoot at.

She felt Ben tugging at her soaked shirt, and she allowed him to pull her underwater and into the relative safety of the shaft.

Here goes nothing, she thought as more bullets impacted the water around her, their dull pinging sound drowned out by her own rapid breathing.

CHAPTER 31

GARZA

"SIR, we've got an update on the intruders."

Garza turned around and faced the soldier, though he already knew who it was. He would recognize the man's voice anywhere. Kurt Jacobsen. One of his lieutenants; the only man he employed who was older than Garza himself. They'd served together through two tours, and he had followed Kurt's progress after Garza had left the military to start Ravenshadow.

"Hey, Kurt," Garza said, immediately dismissing with the formalities. He was in no mood for anything formal at the moment. Usually the system, the structure, the formalities all kept him sane, kept him secure, but right now he wanted to tear his hair out and just blow it all up and move on.

"Sir, we caught them on a forest camera and have been tracking them via satellite. Their vehicles were hidden in the woods, empty, and one of our men saw them enter the river."

Garza frowned. "We're sure this wasn't just a group of tourists?"

Kurt Jacobsen shook his head. "They are not, sir. They were armed, assault rifles, and prepared for a dive. Dual tanks, regulators, the works."

"Okay." Garza paused, working the problem through his mind. He'd never had a problem thinking strategically — it had been why Ravenshadow was so successful, and how it had grown so quickly over the years. Most private defense contractors were focused on a single client at a time. Protect this, prevent that, or some combination of it.

Ravenshadow, on the other hand, had always been in Garza's mind an open playing field of possibility. Sure, they could protect a bank in a third-world country from a hostile corrupt government takeover, and vice versa: they were in the perfect position to *enact* a hostile takeover of a bank some government no longer wanted to compete with.

But Garza had always wanted more than just "get paid to scare." He had long been guided by the idea of creating something truly valuable in the world — something the world didn't realize it needed. *People don't know what they want until you show them,* he remembered a famous CEO once saying.

That *thing* Garza was certain the world needed was *order*. True order, the kind that ushered in not only peace and harmony and allowed the prosperous to continue prospering in their own way, but also allowed the most intelligent to seek solutions to problems, uninhibited by governmental oversight or corporate greed.

He wanted to show the world that with a bit of protection, with a certain amount of measured security, they could prosper without fear of retribution. They could produce beauty, fortune, world-changing science, without fear of it being stolen from them.

The tradeoff was simple, but necessary: Garza would be able to ensure their security, at a cost. They had to *trust* him. They had to *know* that their protection was in his hands. He'd founded Ravenshadow not as a private security company, but as the young, burgeoning police force of a brand-new nation, one that would grow to new heights of success at such a rapid pace the rest of the world would have no choice but to sit up and take notice.

It was a tall order, but Garza was up to the task. He ran Raven-shadow not as a top-down company, but as a democratic dictatorship — a sample size of the larger dream.

Kurt cleared his throat. "We believe, actually sir, that it is an American team."

Garza's head snapped around to his security feeds in the control room and observatory. He was standing behind a bank of monitors, each manned by a Ravenshadow crewmember.

"And why do you think that?" he asked.

"Well, sir, we looked up the registration of the jeeps. They're Peruvian through and through, but the trace on the credit card ends up at an IRS office in Salt Lake City, Utah."

"IRS?"

"Yes, sir," Kurt said. "And I know for a fact that the IRS is hardly efficient enough to rent jeeps in a foreign country."

Garza was waiting for the second half of the clause. *...Rent jeeps in a foreign country on such short notice,* or *rent jeeps in a foreign country without a mile of bureaucratic paper trail.*

It didn't come, and Kurt continued. "I was working with intelligence officers for a while before my retirement," he said. "One the of the cleanest — and fastest — ways to 'disappear' a credit card purchase like this one is to make it a real purchase, just on the bill of another US organization's line."

"You think this is a US military entity?" Garza asked.

"I do, sir. It reeks of Army, possibly SpecOps. If I had to guess, it's Sturdivant."

Sturdivant's name caused Garza to recoil. He licked his lips and stared at Kurt. He had shared his plans with no one else but his closest team of recruits and Kurt, so for Kurt to say the man's name in a closed room with other Ravenshadow employees was a serious offense.

"You'd better be right."

"I don't need to be, sir," Kurt said. "We'll be able to ID them soon enough, but the issue will be resolved long before that."

"Explain."

"Well, sir, if we're dealing with a US force that wants to infiltrate, they'll have done their homework. My guess is they have, and my guess is they've decided the only plausible entrance point is through the drainage system."

"The tunnel?" Garza asked. "We put in a massive fan pump; how would they get through? It's as wide as the tunnel."

When Garza had purchased the land and moved in, they had surprisingly little work to do to convert the place into a headquarters for his base of operations. They had widened a few tunnels and bracketed up power and water lines, and they had converted the old mine's spring-fed water shaft into a waste and drainage tunnel that could supply the entire base with running water and then dump the waste into the nearby river.

"True, but again, if that's *not* their plan, we've got nothing to worry about. If it is, disabling the fan in any way will throw an alert in the control station."

"And you said this would be taken care of long before we need to worry about it?"

"I did, and I mean it. I've already dispatched a unit to head downstream and intercept them. They may not reach it before this new team enters the tunnel, but we'll be there blocking off their exit point after they run into trouble at the pump."

"Good," Garza said. "But I want a backup. Send a few teams down through the original tunnels, and do your best to get them into the demonstration floor. No noise — this isn't permission to engage, understood?"

"Yes, sir."

Garza breathed. "Thanks Kurt." He reached out a hand and waited for Kurt to shake it. If they had become anything over the years, Garza had to admit it looked a lot like a friendship.

Kurt released his grip and turned, then left the room.

If he's on it, it will be taken care of, Garza thought. *Without a doubt.*

Whoever was infiltrating his base would meet up with Garza on the demonstration floor.

CHAPTER 32

BEN

THE TUNNEL WAS, indeed, dark. Their dive lights did little to illuminate their path, but thankfully there was nothing in the way to impede their forward progress.

Ben swam confidently, keeping the distance between Lang and the other Green Beret in front of him and Julie consistent. So far they'd held their own with the soldiers, but Ben knew they hadn't truly been tested yet. At the end of the day, they *were* still civilians.

But civilians who've been through more than most soldiers.

These guys were tough, but Ben knew his own crew had been pushed to the limit numerous times and come out the victors. The Ravenshadow attacks against them today had been spontaneous, but also unplanned and uncoordinated, so they'd been able to get away both times without fuss. Ben knew Garza, and he'd been up against the Ravenshadow men more than once.

They'd gotten lucky, twice. The geography of the river and forest around them had saved them once, and the existence of an underwater waste shaft had saved them the second time.

Ben knew that luck would run out.

Even now, he knew that Garza would be waiting. He might even have instructed his men to follow them into the tunnel — they could

159

be entering the shaft downstream at this very moment, and Ben had no interest in finding out how an underwater close-quarters fight with professional mercenaries would go down.

So they swam upstream. He felt the pressure of the current growing, pushing against his face and body, but he pulled himself forward. It wasn't too much to swim against, but he feared Jeffers and Lang were right: whatever it was pushing this much water was bound to be massive.

Another few minutes passed, and the current grew to a rate that began to feel oppressive. He wondered if they were still making forward progress, but it was impossible to tell. The distance between his arms and the man's fins in front of him had stayed constant, and the current's pressure made it *seem* like they were moving.

For all he knew, they were simply floating in space, not moving forward or backward in the tunnel.

He began to feel the claustrophobia of the constricting space, imagining the walls pushing in slowly. He wasn't prone to claustrophobia, but he knew that there was a point at which everyone began to feel uncomfortable.

Just when Ben thought they were going to have to give up and turn around, taking their chances with the Ravenshadow men, the soldiers in front of him reached up and pulled themselves out of the water. He felt himself being pulled up as well, the soldiers lifting him from under his arms. There was a ledge, about a foot wide, that they were sitting on.

Ben pulled himself up and out once his hands found the edge of the ledge, and he turned and helped Julie get out as well. Once they were both sitting, their backs against the wall of the tunnel, Ben looked around.

By the light of their dive lamps, he could see that the tunnel had widened considerably. They had entered some sort of antechamber that had ledges built along each wall, about a foot above the water line, no doubt for maintenance purposes.

And the object of that maintenance loomed over Ben to his left. An absolutely massive fan sat halfway out of the water, stretching from the very top of the mostly circular shaft to its floor underwater. The blades, made of some sort of reinforced steel, were half an inch thick and curved, a feature that Ben knew helped push the water in the proper direction.

There were six blades, evenly spaced out and spreading from the central hub of the fan. And they were spinning. The heavy machinery hummed as it turned, and the water roiled in front of the turbine.

"A propeller," Jeffers said. "Shit."

The blades were moving quickly, but not so fast that Ben couldn't see through the spaces between them as they cycled. The tunnel continued up ahead, but it seemed that the ledges they were sitting on continued on both sides of the shaft. He assumed they would lead directly to whatever maintenance exit door lay up ahead.

"Just like we thought, Lang said. He looked toward Beale, who was sitting out of the water on the other side of the shaft. "Any ideas?"

"Yeah," Beale said. "We turn around and get the hell out of here. Work our way up the cliff, maybe?"

Lang was shaking his head. "We have to get past this thing. There's got to be a shutoff switch or something."

"There won't be," Reggie said. "Not down here. That control will be farther up the tunnel, *inside* the base. It would be a pretty hefty security flaw if there was a way to shut it down from here."

"Well," Mrs. E said. "Can we blow it up?"

"No demolitions," Beale said. "We don't have anything small enough that would do the trick, and we can't risk the integrity of the tunnel. Could have a whole mountain falling on us."

Ben sighed, then looked at Julie. She shrugged.

"Okay, well for the time being, we're safe. Let's think about this a bit, and —"

The sound of gunfire erupted through the tunnel, reverberating around them. One round pinged off of one of the metal blades.

"Shit!" Jeffers said. "They're here."

He leaned forward, mounting his foot on the opposite ledge for leverage, and he started firing back.

The noise in the small space was deafening, and Ben immediately felt his ears begin to burn. He leaned out as well, trying to see what their options were.

The entrance to the tunnel was illuminated by the bright daylight filtering in from outside, and he saw the unmistakable shape of a man standing directly in front of it.

CHAPTER 33

BEN

"THEY'RE NOT COMING IN," Jeffers muttered between bursts.

Beale added. "I think they're just locking us down. Most likely cutting off our exit plan. They'll have another team coming in from the other side of the fan."

"Maybe they'll turn the fan off for us? To get shots at us from that side?"

Beale shook his head. "Maybe, but we can't wait that long. We're dead if we get stuck between them." He looked around. "Anyone got any bright ideas?"

"What about a gun?" Julie asked.

"Come again?"

"A rifle," she said, pulling hers out from over her shoulder. "Stick the barrel up on the ceiling where it's flat for a couple of feet, really close to the front of the fan, then let the butt swing in. It might work."

Beale was already in motion, with another Green Beret by his side. He reached out for Julie's rifle, and she handed it over. Ben was about to protest — he would rather they use their own weapons — but he didn't want to cause any more trouble than they were already in.

Beale and the soldier held the rifle steady, then lifted it up carefully and placed the tip of it against the flat part of the ceiling. They pushed it as far to the right as they could, where there would be the maximum amount of leverage against the blade as it spun in its counter-clockwise direction. When they were ready, Beale gave the order.

"Okay, slowly, just drop it in on three. But get ready to jump back if it starts chewing " He counted it out quickly, all while Jeffers and the Ravenshadow man at the other end of the tunnel exchanged shots, and then the two Green Berets softly nudged the rifle into place. Only a split-second passed before the first propeller blade impacted the assault rifle.

...at which point the rifle simply crumpled into two pieces, one of which sparked and flew into the other side of the tunnel beyond the blades.

Beale and the soldier fell back, cowering for a moment at the backlash. When the blades continued moving, now once again unimpeded, Beale turned to the rest of them. "That was a disaster," he said. "Any other great ideas?"

Ben felt the man's frustration, but he didn't like how he had directed his assault toward Julie. It may not have worked, but he didn't hear anyone else offering suggestions.

"I say we fight our way back out," the other Green Beret said. "Get to the river again and kill those assholes waiting for us."

"Those 'assholes' are well-trained," Beale said. "And they've got a clear shot at us. And heading downstream we'll be unable to maneuver."

"I got an idea, boss," another man said. Beale and everyone else turned to stare at him. He pulled out a small handheld weapon from a pack he had been wearing. "A harpoon gun," he said. "The propulsion is fast enough underwater that I can get it stuck in a rock on the bottom of the river. Out of water and this close? I bet I can sink it into the concrete. It's got a little umbrella thingy that'll hold it steady in there. Might be enough."

"Okay," Beale said. "But what about the other side? You can't just hold the thing."

"I've got that covered, too," he said.

"Go for it."

The Ravenshadow man and Jeffers had stopped firing at one another for the moment, both obviously feeling that it was a lost cause, and Ben was finally able to hear.

The soldier stretched his legs across the chasm between the ledges and aimed his harpoon at the wall on one side of the tunnel just beyond the fan's blades. He took a breath, steadied himself, then fired.

The harpoon shot between the blades, then mounted into the concrete, just as the man had said. He then flicked a switch, allowing the spool of steel fiber to release. It flew outward from the harpoon gun with a whizzing sound, then the man threw the entire gun into the *other* side of the propeller.

The gun bounced off one of the spinning blades, but then flew down into the water on the opposite side of the propeller. Ben watched it hit the water, then shoot back up and out of the water as the fan blades turned and pulled the line of steel wire tight. It re-spooled onto the propeller, the blades churning and grabbing the line until it was completely twisted and intertwined in it, and then there was no more line for it to pull.

And the fan abruptly snapped to a halt.

"Yes!" the man shouted.

Beale jumped into action. "Move, now. My team first. We don't know how long this thing will hold."

"Then why don't you let the *civilians* go first?" Reggie asked.

Ben frowned. *Yeah, what's up with this guy?*

"Because if it's going to fail, it'll fail early. I'd much rather one of us get caught in it.

"Right," Reggie said. "Better get going then. We'll hold back the Ravenshadow guys from this end."

Beale nodded and then slid between the blades. The rest of his men followed, one on each side, and Ben motioned for Julie to move ahead. Mrs. E had taken up a position guarding the entrance to the tunnel, but the Ravenshadow men still had yet to reappear.

"Go ahead," Ben said. "I'll be right behind you. The sooner we get inside, the sooner we find —"

Ben heard a snapping sound, and he flicked his eyes up. Beale met Ben's eyes, just as the propeller blades started once again to turn. He had pressed the release on the spear end of the harpoon gun, allowing the giant mechanism to spin freely.

And Ben suddenly knew everything. He had sensed it, but he hadn't wanted to *admit* it.

They'd been betrayed.

"Beale, what the —"

"I'm sorry, Bennett," Beale said, shouting over the rising sound of the fan's hum, even though his voice came through clearly in Ben's headset. "Things are more complicated than you think. And you — your team — you're a complication. Too risky."

Julie pulled away from Ben and spat through the blades. "You — you son of a —"

Julie's voice fell away as Ben caught her arm.

"Beale," Ben said. The leader of the Green Berets focused again on Ben. "Why? Why bring us all the way here?"

Beale hesitated, but then shrugged and offered a reply. "I told you the truth. We needed you. You got us here, but we can't risk getting slowed down."

"Ravenshadow is waiting for us out there!" Reggie shouted. "You're leaving us here to die, asshole."

"Just sit tight. Hopefully this is all over soon."

"'Sit tight'?" Julie scoffed. "What's that supposed to mean?"

Ben watched the faces of the other Green Berets. Lang, Jeffers, the men he'd gotten to know and trust a bit. Their expressions were unreadable. *They might know everything. Or they're just as in the dark about this as we are.*

It didn't matter. They were loyal to their captain, and they were going to follow his orders.

"I'm sorry, guys. Our goals no longer align. I can't risk it."

And with that, the Green Beret team turned and walked up the side ledges toward the Ravenshadow base, leaving the CSO team trapped between a massive propeller and a group of ruthless mercenaries.

CHAPTER 34

JULIE

JULIE SAT NEXT to Mrs. E on the ledge. The older woman's face was a mask, but Julie had known her long enough to know she was indignant. However, Julie wasn't sure what *exactly* was the source of her anger. She was likely upset about the betrayal, but Julie also wondered if part of it was the fact that none of them had suspected anything.

Perhaps she was angry with herself for not knowing better.

Still, Julie wasn't about to reach out and console her. They had a job to do, and at the moment that job was to stay alive, and potentially to fight their way out of the tunnel.

"We've got company," Reggie said.

His voice came through Julie's headset, but it was already beginning to crack and fade out. Beale's team was growing farther away every second, and if they lost communication with the Green Berets, they'd be completely in the dark.

He raised his voice and said it again, no doubt hearing the failing transmission.

"Ravenshadow?" Ben asked.

"Yeah. Two snorkels. Probably didn't have time to get suited up for a dive, but they're heading this way."

"Can you shoot them?" Ben asked. "It'll at least buy us some time."

Reggie responded by lifting his rifle and aiming toward the two thin cylinders that were slowly creeping toward them. He pulled the trigger. Julie watched as he fired, his shots slowly centering in the tunnel and finding their mark. He sent three bursts into the two divers, then waited.

Julie frowned. "They're... still moving."

"Yeah," Ben said. "It's like you didn't even touch them."

"I definitely hit them. More than once. What the —"

He fired again, this time aiming a bit lower. Julie saw all the rounds impact the water just in front of the snorkels, but when the water and mist settled, they were continuing to make their way up the tunnel shaft.

"Who the hell are these guys?" Ben asked. "Robots?"

"Try again," Julie said, her voice low. She was feeling the pangs of panic beginning to build in her chest, and she tried to ignore it. *There's something strange about these divers,* she thought.

Ben and Reggie raised their rifles and crammed close to one another on the ledge, Ben leaning outward just a bit and Reggie straddling both ledges with a foot on each. Mrs. E was watching, waiting, with Julie.

Both rifles kicked to life and they sent multiple bursts of gunfire toward the swimming shapes. They were still halfway to the entrance, but it seemed to Julie as though they may have begun to speed up.

Ben pulled one of his shots a bit to the right of the snorkel and suddenly the entire tunnel lit up in a flash of light.

A shockwave, followed almost immediately by the sound of a deafening blast, filled Julie's ears. She rocked sideways on the ledge, her head narrowly missing an impact with one of the fast-moving propeller blades. A surge of water pushed backward against the current, causing a torrent of whitewater that pressed upward for a few seconds, then receded.

Julie blinked a few times, and then leaned out to look down the tunnel.

"It's... gone. Both of them."

"Holy mother of God," Reggie said. "They weren't *divers*. They were *bombs*."

"How's that even possible?" Ben asked.

"Submersible-controlled demolition devices," he said. "Usually just MacGyver-ed together with whatever you've got on hand. These were radio-controlled, judging that snorkel-periscope thing. It was actually an antenna."

"They were *driving* them to us?" Julie asked.

"Must have been. Probably had a little radar scanner updating its position back in one of their cars. I've seen them made from grenades, RC boats, walkie-talkies — really, anything that's automated and blows up."

"These seem... a *bit* more advanced than that..." Ben said.

"Not really," Reggie said. "They're just semi-submersible RC boats that they've wired up a remote detonator. Like C4, or something that can be triggered from somewhere else. Your shot hit one of them, but the blast must have knocked out the other one, too. Probably factored in the integrity of the place, too — just enough to smear us all over the walls without damaging the fan or walls, or bringing the mountain down around us."

"Well, whatever they are, there's more," Julie said. She was watching the entrance to the tunnel shaft and saw two more tall, skinny shapes — what they had thought were snorkels — begin their ascent up the shaft.

"You've got to be kidding me," Ben said. "They can just drop in a couple at a time, let us take potshots at them, get our ammunition store depleted."

"And I don't even have a gun," Julie said. She was once again reminded about the soldiers' betrayal. Her list of people she needed to confront had just grown.

Ben raised his rifle and prepared to shoot at the newcomer submersibles, but Reggie pulled the barrel of his gun down.

"What's up?" Ben said.

"I think we're far enough from the Green Berets by now that we're out of radio distance."

"Which means?"

"Which means I think it's time to head into the base, see what we're missing out on."

Ben frowned. Julie was confused as well, until she saw what Reggie was doing.

CHAPTER 35

BEN

REGGIE HAD his right arm lifted into the air and he was gently waving it back and forth. "It's way stronger than these blades," he said. "And I think I can do what Julie was trying to do with the rifle."

"You think... it is safe?" Mrs. E asked.

"What's the worst that'll happen? I lose my arm?" He grinned, walking on the ledge toward the fan. He held his prosthetic arm up and then placed his closed fist against the flat part of the concrete ceiling. "I thought about it right away," he continued, "but I wanted to save it for... you know, something like this."

"Something like our getting betrayed and left for dead?" Julie asked.

"Yeah. I wasn't clear on the specifics, but I just had a feeling things wouldn't go as planned."

"Well I'm glad you did," Ben asked. "But if you lose your arm *again*, I'm never forgiving myself."

Reggie laughed. "This time it was my choice."

Without delay, he shoved his elbow out and into the rotating circle of blades. The impact was nearly immediate, and the clang of metal on metal rang out in the confined space.

But the trick worked. Reggie's prosthetic arm held in place, stopping the blades and opening gaps between which the team could climb.

"Go," Reggie said. "Hurry up. Those little bomb floaters are catching up."

Ben glanced backward and noticed that they were, in fact, moving faster than they had been previously. They would be at the propeller in less than a minute, and while the increasing current that had been pushing against them would have slowed their progress, for the time being, there *was* no current.

"Can you hold it?" Julie asked.

"We'll find out. Better get through quick," he answered with a grin.

Ben and Julie slid through the gap, then Mrs. E, and finally Reggie, contorting his body so he could step through. He rotated his elbow and shoulder as he did, ending up in the same spot on the opposite side of the fan.

When he finished, he looked back at the others. "Here goes nothing." He yanked his arm out from its position between the ceiling and the blade, and with a heavy thud it pulled loose. The propeller began to move once again, rotating faster and faster with each revolution until it was moving full speed.

This time, however, the team was on the *correct* side of it.

Or, rather, they were on the side they wanted to be on. Ben wasn't quite sure if being on this side of the fan put them in a better or worse predicament than they had been in before, but they were — so far — intact, in one piece, and together.

Let's hope it stays that way, he thought.

He turned to focus on the next leg of their mission. The ledges continued toward the interior of the mountain, and he now saw that the tunnel was on a slight tilt upward. There were two stairs on each side of the shaft, and then a long stretch of flat ledge, and then another two stairs. His dive light wasn't strong enough to see beyond that.

"Let's move," he said.

"You got it, boss," Reggie said. "What do we do if we see —"

"Treat everyone like the enemy, but if you see a Green Beret, at least give them the chance to explain themselves. Jeffers, for one, helped us. We'd be unarmed without his intervention. And Lang didn't seem to be so bad himself."

"Doesn't mean they didn't leave us behind too," Reggie muttered under his breath.

"No, it sure doesn't. But they're against Garza and Ravenshadow, too. For now, it's 'the enemy of our enemy' and all that. But if they start firing at us, they're toast."

Reggie and Julie nodded, and Mrs. E silently stared ahead. Reggie set off on his ledge, while Julie, unarmed, set off along the other one.

Mrs. E was about to start walking as well when Ben pulled at her elbow. "Hey," he said, quietly. "You okay?"

She sniffed, then looked back at him. "I am fine. I just — Ben, I am sorry. I led you into this trap, and I had my suspicions."

"Whoa, hey, this isn't your fault," Ben said. "No one could have predicted —"

"*I* could have," she shot back. "I *should* have. This never should have happened. Those men — the Green Berets. We should have sensed something was wrong."

Ben nodded, but was about to argue with her further, when he came to the realization that she was right. "Yeah, he said. "You are right. But we *all* should have seen it. It's just... there's something else. Something about the way..."

He stopped, then looked ahead at his teammate and wife, moving forward cautiously. *I need to work it out first*, he thought. Turning back to Mrs. E, he said softly: "Don't worry about it. I'm thinking about something, but I need to chew it around a bit. Let's just get out of this hell shaft, okay?"

She nodded, her face showing a complete lack of emotion, and then they started up the right-side ledge.

Ben wanted to keep talking to her, to keep his mind off what he thought might be a major shift in their understanding of this mission. But he knew she wouldn't budge; when Mrs. E was determined — in this case, to not talk — there was no way to change her mind. She was as stubborn as Ben, when she wanted to be.

But then again, this wasn't about her. Ben knew it — he hadn't been upset with her before she'd admitted to him that she took these events as her fault. He *couldn't* have been. The CSO was in his charge, and he had followed his own wife here to avenge the death of their friend.

None of this had made much sense from the beginning, and even up to the point where Beale and his group betrayed and abandoned them, it didn't stack up.

And that was just it. *It hadn't stacked up. Until now.*

Ben jogged behind the other three members of his group, then saw that Reggie had reached a closed door. Julie was right behind him, and when he caught up with them Reggie was facing him, awaiting his order to open the door.

"Wait," he said.

"For what?"

"I — I want to mention something."

Mrs. E flashed him a glance, but he continued anyway. "We all... *sensed* that something was off about the soldiers. Beale obviously didn't want us tagging along, but he let us anyway."

"Because we set this whole thing up."

Ben cocked his head sideways. "Right. But... did he?"

Julie frowned, stepping closer to her husband and placing her hand on his forearm. "What are you talking about? We called *them*, right? Reggie knew how to get in touch with them?"

Reggie's eyes widened and he lifted his arms, palms-up. "Whoa, hey. I didn't *know* them, I just knew some of the guys they used to work with. I had no idea —"

"Hey brother," Ben said. "No one's accusing you of anything.

But the truth is they betrayed us, *after* they let us help them get here. Why?"

"Why'd they let us help them?"

"Yeah, why not just refuse to let us come along at all?" Ben said.

Reggie cleared his throat. "They needed our help, they told us that. But..."

His voice drifted off.

"Yeah," Ben said. "That's my point. If they didn't want us along, they could have just not taken our call. But they *did*, and they *came*. That tells me, at least, that they *also* wanted to be here, but they didn't want *us* to be here."

Julie picked up his thread. "But they couldn't let us know that," she said. "They couldn't let us get here as well, and find out..."

"That they have other business here."

Ben finished the thought as if putting the cap on a conversation that had taken place only in his mind, with only his own thoughts. He was about to agree, to ask what it was exactly that 'other business' might be, when his headset wavered to life with a crackling noise, then a voice — Beale's — buzzed into his ear.

"*— stay alert —*" than a gunshot, then another. "*Go, go. Move out! Jeffers, get — body behind something. We can't — see us.*"

There was a half-minute pause, and Ben and the others waited, trying to decide if the attack was over. Whatever was happening inside the door was happening very close to them — otherwise the tiny communicators wouldn't have worked.

Snippets of an argument in broken, whispered voices. Whoever was talking wasn't as close to them as Beale was. Then Beale's voice came back on, more clearly. "*Sturdivant wants an update. Nothing more. From here on out, we're black ops, radio silent.*"

Another crackle, then the line went dead.

Ben looked up at the rest of his team. *This wasn't just a betrayal. This was much worse.*

CHAPTER 36
BEN

"LOOK," *Berndt said. "Your mom's upstairs right now, sitting with your dad. You've had two days to process all this, up close. She's had about ten minutes. She's gonna need some time to just get past the emotions of it and let the reality sink in, so give her a little bit. But not too much, all right? Don't make her wait too long. She's gonna need you, a lot. I don't know your mom, but my guess? If you run and hide from this, hide from that survivor's guilt you're feeling? That's gonna hurt her more than if all three of you were killed out in those mountains."*

Ben hadn't realized that he'd memorized those words. He hadn't thought of Dr. Berndt or that moment in the hospital, looking out that window, since it had all happened.

That had sort of been the point. He hadn't *wanted* to recall anything about the memory, so his mind had obliged and blocked it out.

But, as he had come to realize in about thirty-five years of life, the human mind's ability to retain and recall information with only the slightest nudge was nothing short of incredible.

So here he was, standing in a drainage tunnel outside of a moun-

179

tain filled with people who either wanted to kill him or just didn't care one way or another, and all he could think about was *why*.

Why had he just thought of *that?* What about his father's death — his feeling that it had been his fault — was important in this moment?

Julie must have seen it in his eyes. "What's up, Ben?" she asked.

They were waiting outside the door, hoping the Green Berets who had already moved inside were pushing into the base, moving farther away from them, so Ben's team could eventually enter without being immediately apprehended.

"I, uh... was just thinking."

"Yeah, I've seen that look before," Julie said. "You're thinking about your dad."

He shot a sharp glance at her, then tried to recover. *How did she just* know *that intuitively? Was it that obvious?*

"Yeah, brother," Reggie said. "You wear it on your face. Always have."

"What are you talking about?"

Even Mrs. E smiled and joined in. "You know, Ben, when I first met you, you had a look about you sometimes. I saw it and thought to myself, 'hmm, why is he so often thinking about his father?'"

"What?" Ben asked, stepping back. "No — no, that's not —"

Julie laughed. "Ben, it's fine. We're giving you a hard time. But we all know who you are, where you're coming from. There's a *reason* we're here, and that reason is *you*. And because you're *you*, there's a reason you're thinking about him right now."

He couldn't argue with that, so he stopped trying. "Okay," he said. "Fine. I was. I was thinking about him. When he died. How I... felt."

"How'd you feel?"

"Like it was my fault," he said quickly, as if mentioning it in passing would diminish its value. "But that's not really what I'm feeling now. It's more... it's about control."

"Control?"

"Yeah, like, I always used to think I ran away from my life because I wanted to be *in control*. And watching my dad get mauled by a grizzly was a decidedly *out* of control feeling."

"Yeah, I'd agree with that," Reggie said. He fiddled with his headset. Ben listened in on his own, trying to hear whether they were out of range yet or not. They had all figured out how to disable the microphone transmitter before they talked, to ensure their own conversations wouldn't be picked up.

"But then I started to realize that maybe it wasn't about *control*, really. Or, rather, that it's actually about not wanting to feel *out* of control."

"Can you explain that?" Mrs. E asked.

"Well, yeah, maybe. I think I don't really care about being *in* control — like, I don't *have* to be the guy in charge. But I *absolutely hate* feeling out of control."

"What's the difference?" Reggie asked.

"The difference is that coming here, trying to track down Garza, trying to accomplish that goal and getting out alive, and helping you guys stay alive — I don't have to be in control of all of it. I can control what I do, and what I think, and that's enough.

"But when I'm betrayed, left for dead, and trapped between two enemies, I feel out of control. I don't need to be *in* control, but I don't want *that*."

"That makes sense," Julie said. "But... what do we do with it? What does it mean?"

"Yeah, man," Reggie said. "It's real deep and stuff, but... what the hell are you talking about?"

Ben shook his head. "I know, I know. It sounds crazy. Insane that it matters, but it does. All my life I thought I was the guy who needed to be in control, at least of my immediate surroundings. But I think I'm realizing that I don't care about that. I just *cannot* feel out of control, or that my situation is beyond something I can affect."

Reggie and the others looked at him blankly, as if he hadn't even tried to answer the question. *I'm not explaining this very well,* he said. He pinched the area above his nose, then took a breath.

After a few more seconds, he summed up his thoughts. "Look, here's what you guys need to know: I'm dealing with some stuff, and it's made me a bad leader. Getting married, then Julie running off to fight a battle knowing that we'd all follow. Then... all of this. It's been a lot. But here's what I promise: no matter how *out of control* we feel, how off that equilibrium we are, I've built my life around making sure I get back to that equilibrium.

"So... what does that mean?" Julie asked.

Ben sighed. "It means I want to get out of this base, alive, more than I've ever wanted anything in my life."

"Yeah, but that means —"

"It means I want to kill Garza more than ever."

PART THREE

ACT 3

CHAPTER 37

BEN

THE INSIDE of the base appeared to be, at first glance, nothing but a mine. Ben had to duck as soon as he'd entered, as the ceiling of the hallway they found themselves in upon opening the tunnel door fell to a low height. The air tasted like sulphur, old dust, and the stale salty breath of a cave.

He took a few steps forward, trusting his dive light to illuminate enough of the hallway to reveal anything noteworthy. The others followed behind him, and Reggie, last in line, closed the door behind him. There were shallow puddles on the floor, the imperfections in the mine shaft collecting the slow drips of water from humidity into small pools. He sidestepped these as he traveled along, moving with one arm in front of him, the other on the wall next to him.

It was cold inside the shaft, cooler than even the drainage tunnel they had been in previously, and it felt to Ben as though he were spelunking in an ancient cavern system. The walls had obviously been cut by human hands — the rough streaks that had taken out chunks of the black rock were still visible, and he even saw boring holes in certain spots, areas where the rock had been tested for whatever precious metals the miners had been searching.

He wasn't sure how long the mine had been here, but Beale's

team's dossier had indicated that the mine had been active up until the late 70s. Ben was no expert in engineering or mining, but by his estimate that put the mine into the 'modern' category. This was no ancient, hand-cut mine. He wondered why it had been abandoned in the first place: perhaps the mine had been too expensive to operate, or it had been depleted?

When they were all in the hallway, Ben walked to the opposite side of it, finding another door. This one was similar to the one they'd entered through, but it was smaller, due to the lower height of the ceiling. He opened it slowly, careful to avoid any unnecessary noise. When it was open fully, he stepped through.

Into a hallway that was, unlike the cramped space he'd just emerged from, wide and tall. LED lights had been mounted every ten feet, near the ceiling, and that ceiling was studded with lines of cabling and electronic wiring.

When the rest of the team entered the more modern hallway, their communicators clicked back to life with a quick crackle. Ben didn't hear any chatter over the airwaves, which meant that they were likely in range of Beale's broadcaster, but the Green Berets were not currently speaking. Still, Ben held up a hand and told the others to wait for a moment, to ensure they were safe to move forward.

Forward, in this case, meant one of two directions — left, which seemed to offer miles of empty, long hallway, or right — which offered a t-intersection a few hundred feet down.

"Anyone have any idea which way they went?"

He saw Julie shake her head, and Reggie responded. "Negative. But they engaged with some Ravenshadow guards here. They may have headed that way."

He chose to head to the left. First, it seemed like heading *away* from the center of the mountain would keep them on the perimeter of the interior base. It could provide them with an emergency exit point, or at least a place to hide if things went south. Second, he thought he could see a door about fifty feet down.

No one argued. He pointed that direction and then began to move. In his mind, he ran through the plan: *find somewhere to hide, then make a plan.*

It wasn't much, but he knew he didn't want to be caught in the middle of this hallway between the Green Berets and Garza's men.

He jogged toward the door and considered their options. The cabling on the ceiling, power and lighting and what he assumed was CAT-6e — ethernet — cables meant that the Ravenshadow crew had run communications all the way here, from wherever their "headquarters" inside the mountain was to whatever these outposts on the extremities were. In other words, it meant that they were connected, and there was not likely a place they'd be able to hide that the Ravenshadow soldiers wouldn't be able to find them.

One thing at a time, he thought. *One problem at a time.*

The major problem he had to deal with was that he had no idea where he was, where Garza was, or where Beale and his men were. He needed to find Garza, but there were too many other unknowns waiting for him inside this base.

The problem *preventing* him from tackling that goal was that he was here with his wife and friends, and keeping them alive was far more important than finding and rooting out Garza.

It was the predicament he'd found himself in more than once before, and he had yet to figure out a way to solve it: by going it alone, he would just about guarantee his failure, but by allowing them to help, he put them in danger.

Relax, he tried to tell himself, *they're adults. They've chosen to come along, and they knew the risks.*

The door was unlocked, and Ben looked through its rectangular window as he opened it.

The others were right behind him as he entered.

"Stairs," he said.

"Well, up or down?" Reggie asked, closing the door silently behind him. They were standing on the landing of the stairwell, and

Ben saw at least two floors above and below them — both paths were dark, lit only by a single bulb mounted above each of the landings, casting an ominous golden glow that spilled out onto each set of stairs.

"Up," Ben said, without hesitation.

"You sure?" Julie asked.

He looked at his wife. He wanted to reach out and hug her, to pretend that this was all a dream, a horrible nightmare that they'd both found themselves in, and that they were really on a vacation to celebrate their marriage.

But instead he saw her, saw the strong, confident woman he'd loved for so long, and knew that his decisions here were not only supported by her and the others — they were strengthened by their presence.

"I've never been sure of stuff like this," he said. "But it's about time I start being sure of it."

They looked at each other for a long moment, until Reggie broke the silence. "Well," he said. "I guess that's a good enough reason for me."

CHAPTER 38

JULIE

JULIE, Mrs. E, and Reggie followed Ben up two flights of stairs until they reached the top of the staircase. If this was the highest point of the mountain's base, they'd reached it. Ben stopped, waiting by the door.

Julie reached Ben, placing her hand on his shoulder. "Let's do this," she whispered.

He nodded, then pushed the door open. Like the one below, this door was unlocked. Either the Ravenshadow group didn't know they were inside, or they were not concerned about the intruders.

It was the latter option that terrified Julie. *They could all be waiting for us,* she thought. *Just letting us walk in and getting us corralled into a single spot so they can —*

"Jules!" Reggie's voice broke into her thoughts. "Come on!"

She started jogging, realizing she was the last one to step over the threshold. The others were inside, their guns drawn and pointing down the hallway.

And it was a hallway, only... different. Rather than the cut-stone mine shafts they'd walked through, and the modern industrial concrete-and-metal staircase they'd ascended, this hallway was differ-ent. It appeared as though Julie had walked back in time. The stone was the same stone that had built the rest of the mountain, but its surfaces were curved and smooth rather than cut, as if they were natural.

The rectangular shape of the hallway itself seemed man-made, but just barely. The right angles at the corners weren't absolutely perfect; the slight bends and bows in the walls dipped and thrust outward in irregular ways. The entire shaft held the appearance of a funhouse that had been erected 3,000 years ago.

"Weird," she whispered as she stepped forward. "It seems... old. Older than the rest of this place."

"Yeah," Reggie said. "Probably one of the first shafts that was cut by the miners."

"You think?" Ben asked. "Beale's guys said the Peruvians started mining around 200 years ago. This seems older than that."

"Like, *Atlantis* old?" Reggie asked, with a mocking tone.

"It wouldn't have to be that old," Julie said. "I mean, not necessarily as old as Atlantis. We found evidence of the Hall of Records in Egypt, and we had reason to believe it had been moved. And the last time we were here..."

She didn't finish the sentence. She felt silly — *all* of them remembered the last time they had been here. The time they had nearly been killed, wiped out by literal giants, gunned down by the Ravenshadow private army, or blasted by the Guild Rite's tank.

The memory caused her to shudder, but then she recalled the *real* reason they were here: Vicente Garza.

No matter what hell she had been through, she would push forward until Garza was dead. Finding the Hall of Records was more in line with the CSO's stated goal, and unraveling the true history of the ancient world was certainly exciting, but Julie simply couldn't focus on any other goal than ridding the world of the scourge that was Garza and his personal army.

She looked at the walls with interest, but the examination would have to wait.

"Doesn't matter," she said. "Garza's here, somewhere. Let's find him."

Ben and Mrs. E nodded in agreement, and Reggie turned back to the route. "Looks like it dead-ends about thirty feet up. This may be an ancient tunnel, but Ravenshadow uses it. There's light and power conduits on the ceiling."

Julie looked up and saw that Reggie was right. Furthermore, the two conduits ran alongside one another toward the dead-end and then turned sharply to the right.

"There's a door there, I bet," she said. She took off at a jog, and found soon enough that she was correct. The ancient hallway terminated, but on the right wall there was a more modern rectangular doorway cut through the stone. She slowed and peered around the corner.

"It's another room," she said. "Modern."

"Empty?"

"Yeah." She stepped inside the room and spun around, allowing her small dive light to prove that they were alone. She noticed a light switch on the wall near the door, and flicked it on. The room was immediately bathed in an orange glow.

And she immediately understood what it was. Rows of computer servers, sleek and black, sat in 19-inch racks beneath slanted desks on two sides of the square room. The desk itself was outfitted with multi-panel video displays, ranging in size from a mere few inches to more standardized widescreen HD monitors.

A video controller joystick sat next to a recessed rolling ball, similar to the one found in old arcade games, and those were both affixed to one of the desks that sat in front of a four-panel monitoring console on the wall. She'd seen desks just like these back in college, in the broadcasting suite for the campus news station, as well as in the video production studios near the computer information systems department she spent most of her time in.

"It's a video production setup," she said. "I can hear the hum of the processors, so it's on and working, even though the screens aren't on at the moment."

"Must be some sort of observation room," Ben said. "Maybe a security control room?"

"I don't know," Reggie said. "Seems a little *un*secure for a security station. That would likely be behind closed and locked doors in the center of the base, not at the end of a hallway at the top of the mountain."

"Reggie and Julie are right," Mrs. E said. "Whatever they are doing here is for observation and recording purposes, but I do not think it is related to security. These video production suites are usually set apart from wherever the main event is, for isolation and control purposes. That is why there are no windows, either."

"Any way to find out what they're observing?" Ben asked. "I mean, without letting them know we're here."

Julie's headset crackled. She'd forgotten she was still wearing it. She still had the microphone turned off, so they were in no danger of Beale's crew hearing them, but it did mean that they were close by.

The others heard it, too, as each of them reached up and fiddled with their over-ear clips.

"To answer your question," Julie said. "Yeah, I think I can get some of the monitors on, at least." She walked over to the largest of them and started looking around the desk. The desktop was bare, but there were single drawers directly underneath, above the server racks. "The monitors are probably all on, they're just asleep. I need a —"

"A mouse?" Reggie held up a wireless computer mouse, then handed it to Julie. "Do the honors, Jules. You're the computer expert, after all."

She laughed. "Yeah, right. My comp-sci degree and systems management experience at the CDC all led to this moment. Of turning on a bluetooth mouse and letting it connect to a computer."

She flicked the on switch on the bottom of the mouse and then set it on the desk. Within ten seconds a red LED light on the mouse lit up, and a computer monitor on the desk in front of Reggie turned on

Ben smiled. "Well, for what it's worth, I wouldn't have thought of that."

The computers must have been linked, because as soon as the first computer monitor turned on, others around the room began flickering to life as well.

Julie was about to examine the desktop icons on the screen in front of her when her eyes were drawn to the multi-panel display to her right.

Her eyes tried focusing on the image on the screen, until she realized that it was a video feed that was still buffering. The image started blurry, then slowly came into focus.

She frowned, squinting at it until it was clear.

Then her jaw dropped.

CHAPTER 39

BEN

BEN STRODE over to Julie's side and peered up at the computer screen. Julie had been able to drag the video file to another monitor that was mounted on the wall above the desktop. It was one of the larger monitors, and the four of them were easily able to see the HD, full-color video feed.

Ben's clothes were nearly dry from their scuba trip through the river, and he shook off the leg of his pants, dropping a few drips of water on the stone floor as he stared at the computer display.

Onscreen, Ben saw that the camera feed was showing them the inside of a large space. The floor and back wall of the space were identical to those of the room they were currently in — beige stone, scraped out of the core of the mountain by either the original mining crews or by contractors hired by Ravenshadow when they took over the mine.

But that was where the similarities ended.

The space they were looking at was absolutely massive. Ben estimated its size to be at least as deep as a football field was long — three hundred or so feet, and he couldn't see the left and right walls, as the room was simply too large to fit within the frame of the camera.

He thought it might have been a trick, an illusion played on his eyes by the camera and display, except for another feature of the room that gave him some sense of scale.

In the center of the stone-walled warehouse, dozens of rows of biped-like machines stood next to one another, shoulder to shoulder, facing the left-hand side of the screen. It reminded him of a scene from one of the Star Wars movies, the rows of thousands of stormtroopers standing at attention, preparing for battle.

Except these weren't fictional film characters. He was looking at an *army* of machines, each shaped like a human soldier, with wide, broad shoulders and a rounded back that he assumed held whatever power source the machine used, and thin, short legs with knee-shaped joints that he knew would be hydraulically powered.

"What the..." Reggie whispered.

"It's some sort of army," Ben said. "Of machines."

"Exoskeletons," Reggie replied. "Gotta be hundreds of them down there."

"You think they... work?" Julie asked.

Reggie shrugged, and Ben didn't answer. *Knowing Garza, they probably do.*

His eyes were pulled to the left side of the screen as they detected movement. Small, shapeless forms — shadows — appeared on some large crates and wooden shipping boxes that had been piled in stacks on the edge of the floor.

"What is that?" Mrs. E said, pointing at the shadows.

Where the shadows had been a second ago, they were now gone.

Julie frowned, but Ben nodded. "Yeah, I saw it too — there!" he poked at the screen, and just next to one of the boxes, he saw it.

A foot.

More accurately, a *boot*. A soldier's boot.

"Beale's team," Reggie said. "Looks like they found the payload right away. Almost like they knew exactly where to look."

"Judging by their conversation earlier, I'd say they *do* know exactly where they're going. Or at least what they're looking for."

Ben recalled their words from the comms when they'd first entered the mountain base.

Sturdivant wants an update.

"'Sturdivant wants an update,'" he recited. "That was your old boss, right?"

"He was a lieutenant colonel back then, XO of our brigade. Now he's probably a colonel, or brigadier general."

"Which means?"

"Which means he's in charge. Of a lot of stuff."

"Strategic sort of stuff?"

Reggie nodded. "Yeah, covert stuff, the things higher-up generals don't want to mess with, or stuff the US government might want to wash their hands of. They'll send it down the chain to a guy who's got the grit and experience to know how to handle diplomatic situations with the delicateness needed."

"Diplomatic situations like checking in on a top-secret military development in a foreign country without getting caught?"

"Yeah," Reggie said. "Stuff like that."

"But I do not understand why they must be here in secret," Mrs. E said. "If they are somehow working with Garza..."

"That's just it," Julie said. "They must *not* be. That's the whole ruse — the reason they wanted to go with us. It upholds the illusion of anonymity. Plausible deniability. They're here checking in on Garza's work, but they're probably trying to be *seen* by him or his men."

"Well it's too late for that," Reggie said. "I'm pretty sure those Ravenshadow guys weren't just shooting their guns and sending little submarine bombs into their tunnel just for fun."

"No," Ben said. "They definitely weren't. They saw us, but they might just assume it's *us*. As in the CSO, plus a few hired guns. No reason for them to suspect there's an active covert US military operation breaching their walls, too."

"So bringing us was a way to keep up the ruse," Julie said. "So they can blame it on us, get in, get out, and get back to Sturdivant with their information on what Ravenshadow's doing down here."

"Makes sense," Reggie said. "Sounds like the type of stuff the Rangers and Green Berets do. They're trained to fight, but their specialty is stuff like this. Infiltration, covert maneuvering, and extraction of information. And judging by their special little espionage jet we got to ride in, they're pretty good at what they do, and get a lot of really cool toys because of it."

"Okay, that tells us *why* they're here, but it doesn't tell us the more important thing: *what* is Garza working on? Last we saw, he was creating giants by injecting them with yeast and breaking their bones."

Ben shuddered at the memory. It had happened to Reggie, as well as to his girlfriend, Sarah. They'd been kidnapped by Garza and taken to Peru, where Garza's doctors had injected them with a strain of *albicans* yeast that caused rapid bone regrowth.

It was how Reggie had lost his arm.

"Seems to me like he's abandoned that project," Reggie said, staring at the screen. "Those aren't exactly giant-sized suits. But they're definitely meant to be filled by someone. You think he's got his soldiers training in them?"

"I don't see why he'd waste them like that. They're already well-trained, most of them from military backgrounds and perfectly happy in their own skin."

"It's just a lot of suits to fill."

Then Ben heard a high-pitched sound. A single buzzing note, nearly inaudible.

"You hear that?"

"I do," Julie said.

"I cannot hear anything," Mrs. E said. "What is it?"

"A really high-pitched sound," Ben said. "And typically higher-pitched sounds are the first we lose as we age."

"Are you calling me old?" Mrs. E asked, smiling.

Ben put his hands up. "I'm just saying that I can hear it. That's all."

Julie and Reggie grinned, but Julie nodded as she spoke up. "I can definitely hear it. It's probably from down there, and we're hearing bleed from it traveling all the way up here."

"What is it?"

"Well, check out the screen."

Ben did, and he saw movement again, this time on the *right* side of the screen. The exoskeleton suits there began to move, slowly at first. He saw one of their arms rotate, then another. He stared at the screen, then pushed his face closer.

"Oh, my God," he said. "They're *already* inside."

"Who?"

"The people — whoever they are — they're already *in* the suits. All of them are full. Each one of them is *manned.* That sound we're hearing must be the sound of all of them activating."

"Whoa," Reggie said. "That's more than a little unnerving. It's like they were in a coma. Totally asleep. We should have noticed it, but they weren't even moving a little bit."

Ben felt his blood run cold. *This is not good.* Just when he was about to voice his concern, a voice exploded through hidden speakers in the room.

"Hello, Captain Beale. It's been a while."

"That's Garza," Julie said.

"I want to personally welcome you to the Ravenshadow headquarters, and into my latest project."

CHAPTER 40

BEN

BEN WAS STILL STARING at the screen when Garza's exoskeletons began moving. The wave started on the right side of the screen, then moved to the left. Eventually, all of the robots were moving in perfect sync, as if being controlled by something externally, rather than by the individuals wearing the suits themselves.

They jostled and shifted in perfect formation, eventually tightening their rows and then taking a single step forward. They stopped, waiting.

Garza's voice continued through the speakers. Ben could see one of them, a small three-inch circle recessed into the top of the slanted portion of the desk to his left.

"These are my newest invention," Garza continued. *"Although I have to give you — the US Army — most of the credit. You were the original purveyors of the tech. The HULC and the XOS 1 and 2 — they were created for your use, although neither Lockheed Martin nor Sarcos could ever figure out the power maintenance requirements."*

Onscreen, a single man stepped out from behind the crates.

Beale.

Through his headpiece, Ben heard his voice. *"What do you want, Garza?"*

"What do I want?" Garza replied. *"I am not the one trespassing onto private property, bringing weapons into my facility."*

"We're just here to check in with our —"

"A phone call would have sufficed."

"What are you building here, Garza? This isn't what Sturdivant —"

"Sturdivant is not my employer, Captain Beale. He is merely a middleman. He has a list of requirements, no doubt a list you are carrying as we speak, and rest assured, I will check off every box on that list."

"But we need to assess the technology and the support system, and report back with —"

"You will do nothing of the sort."

There was a pause, and Ben could barely see Beale's mouth moving on the screen.

"They switched channels," Reggie whispered. "That's not good."

"It is a private communication," Mrs. E added. "Which means Beale is discussing something with his own men."

"Like I said — not good."

Beale's voice switched back to their channel.

"Garza, we can finish this one-on-one, in your office. Have your suits stand down and we'll —"

"You are not here to give me orders," Garza interrupted. *"Nor are you here to negotiate. You are here to steal my tech."*

"Garza we're not —"

"I didn't move my entire business to Peru to simply be once again infiltrated by an illegal force," Garza said. *"I don't appreciate the implications. I'll tell you what. I'll let your team leave, and we won't speak of this again."*

Another pause, and then another voice came through Ben's headset. *"Door's locked, boss."*

Beale spoke to Garza. *"You locked the door behind us?"*

"There is another exit on the opposite side of the demonstration floor." Garza said. *"But I thought you came here for a demonstration?"*

"Garza…"

"I will let you leave," Garza continued. *"If you make it through my demonstration."*

"What the —"

A few others on the channel — Beale's other men, still hiding behind the crates and boxes — cursed. Ben heard the distinct sound of the men arming their rifles.

"I'll make this easy. You have exactly ten seconds to get to the opposite side of the floor. I will activate a single Exo for the demonstration, so as not to damage any of my other prototypes."

The CSO group watched the screens, each of their faces full of shock. Ben couldn't believe what he'd just heard.

"You think he'll go through with it?" Reggie asked.

"It's Vicente Garza," Julie said, her voice full of rage. "He answers to no one. This is pure arrogance, and I have no doubt —"

Her sentence was cut off by the sound of a klaxon ringing through their headsets, then the sound of a computerized female voice, counting down the seconds.

"10…"

"9…"

"Shit!" Beale's men began chattering, none of them bothering to switch channels. Ben and his team could hear everything.

"Head to the sides, flank them," Jeffers said. *"We don't know which one of these assholes will be activated."*

On screen, Beale's six-man team split in half, three men heading to the top of the screen and three heading to the bottom. The bottom three disappeared from view, but Ben could clearly see the three soldiers on the top half of the screen running, sprinting flat-out alongside the stone wall.

"Six…"

"Five…"

"Should we attack? Take out the people inside the suits?" a man asked.

"Negative," Beale said. *"Conserve ammo, get to cover where those boxes are on the other side."*

Ben couldn't see the boxes, but he assumed there were crates and boxes stacked alongside the far wall, just as there were on the left-hand side of the computer monitor.

"Three..."

"Two..."

"Shit! Beale, we're not going to make —"

"Shut up and get behind something!"

Jeffers' voice again. *"Get ready, boys. Aim for the legs. The head's shielded, but if we can drop it to the ground —"*

"One..."

Another klaxon sounded, and Ben saw Julie put her hand over her mouth. He sucked in a sharp breath of air.

Surely Garza isn't going to...

One of the exoskeletons — Exos, as Garza had called them — in the center of the group of machines came to life. Ben could barely see the dark-skinned, black-haired person inside of it. It turned completely around with a fluid, three-step motion, then began marching toward the opposite wall.

"The door's still open, guys," one of Beale's soldiers said. *"It's about fifty more feet, and we can —"*

A flash of light filled the screen, before the camera had time to adjust the exposure settings. A second later, Ben heard a loud *rat-tat-tat* sound in his ears, and then he saw that the Exo had fired from a weapon he hadn't seen before.

"It's on his shoulder," Reggie said. "Some sort of machine gun, like a mini turret."

The weapon rattled again, and Ben saw the tiny sparks of tracer rounds dancing out from the Exo. The light from the rounds stuttered across the screen, no doubt the refresh settings on the display and camera unable to keep up with the high-speed bullets.

He heard the result of the fire through the soldiers' own microphones. One man screamed, another just grunted, a sickening, wet sound of gurgling blood and air.

Another round of one-way fire, and two more men screamed.

"Shit!" Jeffers said. *"Lang is down. Sir, we need —"*

Another round of fire and Jeffers' voice cut out.

There were a few more blasts from the shoulder-mounted turret, and Ben thought he heard a couple shots of return fire from whoever was left of Beale's crew, then there was silence.

It was palpable. Ben looked around the room. Mrs. E's expression was stoic, but he could sense the energy inside her, the fire behind her eyes. Reggie was livid, his body gently shaking.

Julie's face was an abstract artwork of emotion. Anger, rage, sadness, confusion. Perhaps even satisfaction, the amazement of not being with Beale's group when it had happened.

"Are... you guys okay?"

Heads shook. Julie looked at him. He wanted her to tell him — to tell all of them — to turn around, to head back down the stairs and get their scuba gear and leave the way they came.

He wanted this to end, to get out, to run home and sit by his fireplace and not worry about exoskeletons or corrupt soldiers or Garza.

But then there was a pinprick of realization. A tiny, microscopic revelation that began as a seed, then quickly germinated into a fullfledged feeling. He knew it was the truth, and he had been trying to hide it within himself.

He wanted it to *not* be true, but he knew Julie was feeling the same thing. They all were.

They were just waiting for him to give the order.

She opened her mouth, and spoke her truth. *His* truth.

"We have to keep going," she said. "We have to stop him."

Ben nodded, then waited for the others to agree. They did so without hesitation.

"Okay," he said. "Okay. Let's go. The stairs will take us down to that level; we can find the warehouse and get our bearings. We don't know where Garza is, but he's not going to leave the base until he knows Beale's crew is dead. Let's take advantage of the element of surprise while he doesn't know we're —"

Ben was cut off by the sound of the speakers cackling through the air once again.

He heard his name, and his blood immediately cooled.

"*Hello, Harvey Bennett,*" Garza said. "*I didn't want you to miss the demonstration, either. I'm glad you were able to find our observation deck. Hopefully you were able to get a feed?*"

The statement ended as though it were a question, but Garza's voice continued. "*Now that we're finished with Beale, I think it's prudent to finish what we've started — you and me. How does that sound, Ben?*"

Ben's fists clenched and his knuckles whitened. *He knows we're here.*

"*Very interesting strategy, I might add. Using our waste and circulation tunnel? Very good stuff. I have to ask, though: what the hell is your plan now?*"

Ben closed his eyes and bowed his head. *That is a good question. What the hell is the plan now?*

CHAPTER 41

GARZA

"SIR?"

Garza's back was to the door, his eyes on the computer screen on his desk, where he had been watching the events play out on the demonstration floor. He threw his right hand up and waved for the soldier to enter. Vicente Garza was in his private quarters, which to him barely passed as a room — no windows, no closets, and he didn't have a personal restroom. The room had been cut into the stone, much like the other spaces on the mine's main operations floor.

"Come in," he added, his voice straining to add an air of annoyance.

The soldier's boots clicked quickly on the floor, and he sensed the young man on his left side.

"What is it?"

"The, uh, intruders. They're still in the warehouse, but we believe they're dead."

Garza nodded. "Keep them there. And keep the Exo powered up. Any movement will be detected, and Beale's crew will be thoroughly out of the picture."

"Yessir."

"And the other intruders?"

The kid paused, then abruptly launched into a recited security protocol. "We first detected the second group about four minutes after the first, and we've been tracking them since. They're still in the top floor observation deck, but we believe they'll make a move for the stairs, coming down the way they arrived."

"That's likely the only option they think they have. Are they armed?"

"We... uh, we don't know, sir."

"Well, find out."

Garza leaned back in his computer chair and ran two hands through his salt-and-pepper hair. He felt as though he'd aged fifteen years in the past five. Lately, he'd even felt that his aging speed had tripled.

He felt distracted, on edge, and jittery. He'd only had two cups of coffee — one less than his usual — but he had a feeling he knew exactly why he was feeling this way.

"I know this man. Harvey Bennett. And his team. The Civilian Special Operations. They've been interfering with our work for a couple of years now, and it's about time we handled it the way we should have back in Philadelphia."

"Yessir."

The soldier stood like a sentinel next to Garza. He was undoubtedly the kid who'd been ordered to keep Garza happy, the kid tasked with the unfortunate job of delivering whatever bad news his team had dug up.

It annoyed Garza that his men — trained killers, used to taking orders, most from a military background — were afraid of him. But he wasn't the sort of man to sulk over things like that. He hadn't started Ravenshadow to test his leadership and charisma. He wanted his men to appreciate him, but their loyalty to him ranked far higher on his list than their love for him.

"Son, what's your name?"

There was a time in the early days when he'd known all of his men. He knew most of them by name, on paper, but he hardly recognized many of them now. His organization had doubled in size over the past two years, and he had nearly killed himself trying to maintain his rigorous standards for training and development.

Now, Ravenshadow Group, LLC. boasted nearly three-hundred men, all either in the process of training through his 'gauntlet' of onboarding exercises or ranked among his active paramilitary troops. Half of those men were still stateside, working on some of Garza's existing contracts.

The rest, including this young man, were here.

"My name is Private Miller, sir."

"Very well, Miller. Thank you for your report. If that is all, then I —"

"Actually, sir," Miller said, his voice faltering. "There's... something else."

Garza cocked an eyebrow.

"Your, uh, buyer. The deal — in town?"

Garza nodded, silently urging the young soldier to spit it out. 'In town,' in this case, meant 'Lima.' While Lima was an hour-and-a-half flight from the nearest airport, it was the only other city in Peru that had any meaning to Garza, and therefore Ravenshadow. His men had all passed through Lima before landing in the region, so it had effectively been christened their 'town.'

"What about it?"

"There's been... a setback."

Garza stiffened. His timetable was extremely tight. Delivery of his product needed to occur at precisely the right time or the deal would fall through. Any delay on either side would mean disaster.

And any disaster would cost Garza a *lot* of money.

"What kind of setback, Miller?"

"Well, sir, the buyer has been... asking questions."

Garza shook his head. *Idiots. I knew they should have handled this whole process differently.* He despised politics, and only played the game when there was a major benefit to him. Even then, he wasn't very good at it. This entire deal hinged on the other parties playing the politics game, and playing it well enough that the world would turn a blind eye to Garza and Ravenshadow.

The risk was great, but the reward was potentially the greatest.

Garza was rather risk-averse, but in this case, he'd placed his bet.

"What are they asking?"

"I, uh, am not entirely sure of the details of the transaction, sir," Miller said. "Obviously. But I'm told they are hesitating."

"To close the deal? The deal is all but done, we just needed an in-person meeting."

"Right," Miller said. "They're just... getting cold feet."

"Did they know about Beale's team?"

Miller looked visibly shocked. "No, sir — of course not. *We* had no idea they were here until an hour ago."

"Okay, fine." Garza stood up, signaling that this meeting was over. Miller would have no more information that would be useful to him. The deal would close, with or without the 'hesitant' party. It was unfortunate, and it would change the nature of the political fallout that would be involved, but the deal would close. "Tell your team to activate. My orders. Three units on active patrol, the rest business as usual, but on high alert."

"Yessir."

"The CSO team is *not* as civilian as their name implies, Miller. I expect you to take that information back to your team as well."

Miller frowned, and Garza could almost hear his thoughts. *But there's only four of them. And they have no military training as a unit.*

"Miller," he said, his voice dropping a few notes. "I mean it. This team is fully capable of taking out a quarter of our forces if they're not prepared. They will not leave this mountain alive, but I intend to lose as few Ravenshadow men as possible."

Miller nodded. "Yes, sir. I understand, sir."

Miller didn't wait to be dismissed. He turned on a heel and left the room. Garza waited until he heard the soldier's boots down the hallway, then he turned back to his computer.

CHAPTER 42

BEN

"WE NEED to get out of here," Ben said. "Now."

Reggie nodded, but Mrs. E and Julie seemed to be in a trance.

"Jules," he said again. "Come on."

Ben started walking toward the door when Julie stopped him. "Ben," she said. "Wait."

"We can't afford to wait," Reggie said. "We need to get out —"

"Get out *how*?" Julie shot back. "We're not getting out the way we came in — there will be Ravenshadow guys *crawling* over that entrance tunnel by now. And there's no way we're getting through that 'demonstration floor,' or whatever Garza called it."

"So what are you suggesting?"

"I'm suggesting you two guard the door, at least for a minute. Let me and Mrs. E see if we can get into the computer system."

Ben sighed, but Julie didn't wait for a response. *She knows what she's doing,* he told himself. He walked to the door with Reggie, then dared a look down the hallway. *Empty.*

"How long you think it'll take?" Reggie asked Julie.

"To get through whatever encryption they have? No idea. But it's not like we're in danger of alerting them to our presence. We're well past that."

"Yeah," Ben said, "which is why we need to *get out of here*. We're sitting ducks in here, and —"

"Shut up and let me work," she replied.

Ben watched the two women work as he and Reggie stood just inside the doorway of the stone-walled room. He felt the pressure of anxiety flooded his systems; the adrenaline building yet having nowhere to go. He'd tried to train himself to push those feelings away, but he knew they were chemical reactions — there was little he could do to bend them to his will besides exercising them out.

"Seems like they've got their deeper systems locked down tight," Ben heard Julie saying to Mrs. E as the pair flicked around the computer station. "Password-protected, even retinal scan for some of these folders."

"There," he heard Mrs. E say. "We do not need a password for that file."

Julie double-clicked on something and an enormous grid flashed onto the screens above the station. An image of a labyrinthine tunnel system, an artist's rendition, appeared.

"It's a map," Julie said. "Of this place."

She clicked again and the image shifted, seeming to fall sideways in 3D space and then collapse in on itself. "Looks like these are the levels," she said. "The warehouse — demonstration floor — must be here, right in the middle. The old mine shafts cut through the spaces along the outer walls, but most of Garza's newer excavation and construction is focused toward that central space."

Ben and Reggie walked back over. Ben wanted to get a good look at things, to try to memorize the spaces and corridors. It was a tall order, but he hoped the four of them together could get a realistic impression of the interior of the mountain.

Especially its exit points.

"See any way out?" he asked.

Julie flicked the image back to the top-down view they'd seen before, and Ben now saw that there were four separate levels that made up the Ravenshadow base. The warehouse where they'd seen Beale's team massacred took up a central space in the top three of them. The lowest level, labeled only by the letter "X," stretched past the sides of the map and off the screen. Julie clicked on the level just above that, labeled "Level 1," and then pointed to two long rectangular passageways that branched off from the central area.

"Here," she said. "One that heads west and another that shoots up to the north."

"Yeah," Reggie added. "That's all I'm seeing, too. Damn."

"There has to be something else," Ben said.

"Why?" Reggie asked in response. "It's hard enough building a mine, and Garza's not really the hospitable type. He doesn't want company, and when he does he probably wants to keep them where he can see them."

"Right," Julie said. "He'll want to be able to control the entrances and exits, so having only two — or three, if you include the way we came in — is much more manageable."

"Okay," Ben said. "Fine. Only two real exits. They'll be guarded, and there's no way we can fight our way through."

"Especially not against whatever those Exosuit things are," Reggie said.

"So what do we do?" Mrs. E asked.

"The same thing we always planned on doing," Julie said. She enlarged a section of the map by using the scroll wheel on the mouse. Ben saw that the area she'd enlarged, filled with square-shaped rooms and spaces, was labeled with the letter O. "Offices. This is where Garza will be."

"We're still going through with the plan?" Reggie asked.

She shot him a glance that told Ben everything he needed to know.

"Why wouldn't we?" she said. "If we take out Garza, then everything — including getting the hell out of here alive — gets easier."

Ben nodded. "She's got a point. His army will still be pissed and likely put up a fight, but without their leader in place, their organization will crumble."

"Okay," Reggie said, slapping the magazine of his assault rifle. "Let's get to it. Down two flights of stairs and we're dumped out into the offices? Nothing to it."

Mrs. E and Julie stood and walked over to join Reggie and Ben near the door.

Nothing to it, Ben thought. *If only it were that easy.*

He turned to leave, then stopped short at the doorway.

He realized he and Reggie hadn't been guarding the door.

"What the..."

"What is it?" Julie asked.

"Not *what*. *Who*."

He turned to the side, revealing the person standing at the door.

Victoria Reyes.

EDMUND

FATHER EDMUND CANISIUS slammed the phone's receiver down. *This is an outrage,* he thought.

He stood and paced the room, talking to himself. "All flights are full?" he said to no one. "Not even a flight to another city."

The conference was going to be over in a day, and it appeared that everyone was planning to leave town at exactly the same time. He hadn't previously booked an outbound flight due to the nature of his work here. Namely, because he had *no idea* what that work was truly supposed to be.

He took a few breaths to calm himself down. *Do not overreact, Edmund. There has simply been a misunderstanding.*

He knew he was still frustrated at his peers and superiors at the Vatican — they had sent him on this fruitless quest to do... something. In a foreign country where he did not know anyone, and to close a deal for which he did not understand the deliverables. Sure, his side was providing the funding, but he was still unsure of what the Orland Group was to provide.

Rebecca St. Clair had been cryptic, but nice enough. She was a polished bureaucrat, a trained executive, a role for which acting skill would be a notable plus. So it was highly possible that she had simply been playing with him, working against his emotions and confusion to extract something from him.

But... what?

He couldn't figure out what game was being played — in what game of chess he was acting as the pawn. He knew he was one, he just didn't know the other pieces. Was St. Clair the Queen? Or the King?

Or was she one of the *players*?

The call with the front desk of the hotel offered little to calm his nerves. The woman's voice, while soothing, was laced with exhaustion, and he knew he was only exacerbating things by asking over and over again whether she could book him a flight back to Rome. It was an antiquated way of doing things, but Edmund knew of no other way. His assistants usually did that sort of thing back home, and he was simply given the itinerary.

It was becoming more and more clear to him that he was here in Peru because he had ruffled someone's feathers in the Vatican. It was not an uncommon thing, but to force him to travel around the world, tasked with signing a deal that was all but finished, without the means to seek help from anyone around him, was another thing altogether.

He had upset someone, but he wasn't sure who. Nor did he know what exactly he had done. Was he here to make a mockery of himself? To expose to the world just how little *of* the world he understood? He was a man of the cloth, and he took his faith seriously, but he couldn't understand what God would be asking of him in this moment.

He turned to the phone once again, and reached for the number he had hastily scribbled onto a notecard a few days ago.

He picked up the phone, waited for the dial tone, and then dialed the number. He didn't expect anyone to answer, but he heard the connection by the third ring.

"Hello, this is Rebecca St. Clair."

"Hello, uh — Ms. St. Clair? This is Father —"

"Edmund!" the woman on the other end seemed positively joyous to be hearing from him. *She is like a politician,* he thought. *Trying to make me feel good.*

"Yes, hello," he continued. "I was, uh, wondering if you received the transaction?"

"Indeed, Father. Thank you. All is well."

"Wonderful. In that case, I was hoping we might be able to wrap up this —"

"We need to sign the papers, Father. Remember? The contract is not yet signed, and we are scheduled to meet in another day."

He knew. Tomorrow evening, to be precise. At the same restaurant they'd met previously. But he didn't know *why* they had to wait so long. *Can we not simply sign the contract and then be done with it?*

"I know you are interested to get back to the Vatican," Rebecca said. *"And I apologize for the fanfare and charade, but it is crucial that we adhere to the timeline."*

Father Canisius mustered up a small bit of courage from somewhere inside. "Why?"

It came out blunt, and, he guessed, rather rude.

"Well, Father, because that is what our stakeholders and investors have requested."

He nodded to himself. *A blunt response to a blunt question.* It didn't answer anything, really, and they both knew it.

"And I am glad you called — you must have received the updated instructions from your superiors?"

Canisius frowned. *Updated instructions?* And who were these *superiors*? He worked with an office of cardinals and bishops, as well as assistants and program directors from the layman sector. Someone was pulling the strings — *his* strings — and it did not sit well with him.

He cleared his throat, attempting to feign knowledge of what exactly she was talking about. He wished, in that moment, that he was as savvy with technology as he was with scripture. He should have had some way to check emails, be it on a cellular phone or a laptop. As it was, he had planned to get to the hotel's business center on the way to dinner to log in and check in with his Vatican office, but he hadn't done that yet.

"I, uh, apologize," he finally said. "I have not."

There was a pause on the other end, and he heard the muffled sound of St. Clair speaking with someone else.

"I believe it is my turn to apologize, Father," she said. *"I was informed earlier this morning that your presence will be requested at the time of purchase."*

"I do not even know what it is we are purchasing."

"Of course," she said. *"Yet that is what the updated itinerary states. The parties have personally requested your presence."*

He squeezed the area above his nose. *So much for catching an early flight home.* "And just where is this transaction going to take place?"

He hadn't intended to sound so irritated, but he knew it was no secret that he was frustrated. St. Clair might not be playing him, but someone was. And whomever it might be — whomever was calling the shots back in the Vatican — was going to have a long conversation with Edmund when he returned.

"I apologize, but I must be going. All the information you need is in the itinerary update, and I am told you have been emailed personally with the request."

He thanked St. Clair and hung up the phone.

He needed to clear his mind, to try and make sense of this. Someone wanted him to be in Peru, but did not want him to know *why* he was there. He didn't like the feeling of being a pawn in someone else's game, nor did he care for the implications that he was disposable.

He decided to take a walk. He could log into the hotel's computer on his way out, and perhaps the itinerary email would give him more information. He wasn't sure he would be able to *do* anything with that information, but it was information nonetheless.

CHAPTER 44

JULIE

JULIE RUSHED FORWARD and embraced Victoria. "Oh, my God," she said. "I thought you — I didn't know you were still alive."

Victoria stood straight, not embracing Julie. When Julie released her, the woman seemed to relax a bit and exhale, though her eyes seemed to be looking straight through her.

Weird.

"Follow me," Victoria said.

Julie turned to Ben and waited for his reaction. Her husband didn't move at first, and Julie wondered if he'd even heard her. Julie was about to nudge Ben when he turned to her. "What do you think?" he asked.

Before she could respond, Reggie jumped in. "Do you know a way down? Besides the stairs? Somewhere there won't be a bunch of your dad's army men crawling around?"

Victoria nodded.

"Great — let's move."

"Reggie," Julie said, her voice wavering.

But he was already gone. Victoria led Reggie and Mrs. E out of the room, to the right.

Julie grabbed Ben's arm before they left. "Ben," she whispered. "Something's not right."

"Yeah," he said. "We're in an ancient mine, being chased by mutant machines, and —"

"No," she said. "I'm not talking about that. I'm talking about *her*. Victoria."

Ben frowned. "What do you mean?"

"She's... not right. Something about her seems off."

Ben paused for a second, then looked down at Julie. "She's our best option, Jules. At least for now. Let's try to see what she knows — she's been here longer than we have."

"That's exactly my —"

Ben pulled Julie out of the room and in the direction they'd seen Victoria and the others moving. Julie had assumed the hallway ended there, in the dark and shadowy corner of the mountain base, but she noticed that Victoria was pressing her hand up against the wall, and the wall itself appeared to be moving.

It danced and swayed, and then Victoria stepped *through* it. Reggie and Mrs. E followed closely behind.

"What the hell?" Ben said. "How did she —"

"It's a curtain," Julie said. "We must have missed it."

Julie stepped forward and pressed her own hand against it. Sure enough, what she'd thought was a wall of stone was nothing more than a heavy piece of burlap fabric, the same grayish color as the rest of the walls. In the low light spilling out from the communications and video room they'd just exited, the fabric faux wall was identical to the others.

"Trippy," Ben said as he stepped through next to Julie.

They found themselves in another hallway, this one darker than the one they'd just exited, but Victoria had retrieved a flashlight from her pocket and was pointing it down the tunnel. Julie saw that the stone here was like the entrance tunnel they'd ascended, the one that had connected the drainage shaft to the rest of Garza's base.

The stone seemed weathered, and it had a lighter, more brown color. She wanted to examine it with her dive light, but Victoria was leading them quickly down the slightly descending passageway toward what appeared to be an intersection.

"I didn't see any of this on the map," Ben whispered.

Julie shook her head. "Me, neither. I think it's part of the original mine."

"Yeah, what did they mine here, anyway?"

"No idea. Beale's guys said they weren't sure — there aren't any official records of what *type* of mine this was, but judging by the others in the area they figured it was silver or copper."

"Hmm. Yeah, I just don't see any 'mine'-y stuff, like tracks. Or mine carts."

"Or trolls or dwarves," Julie said, chuckling. "It's not like we're mine experts, Ben. Just because we don't see any stereotypical mining apparatus doesn't mean there wasn't ever any of that stuff here."

"True," he said. "But I feel like we'd *know* if we were in a mine, you know?"

"Maybe. Anyway, these walls are like those other ones we saw. Like a different type of stone or something."

"Older," Ben said. "*Way* older. We're in one of the original shafts. The rock could even be of a different composition, or it had more or less contact with natural subterranean water, so there's a completely different style of deposits here."

"Whatever it is, it *feels* different. And that brings me back to Victoria. She's just... off."

"She's been acting strange since our wedding."

Julie thought about this for a moment as the group hustled along the shaft. "Yeah, that's fair. But it seems like we're missing something else."

"We're *always* missing something else," Ben said. "At least, it feels like that. We're always getting in over our heads with stuff like this, and end up having to play catch-up."

"At least we're alive."

Victoria turned and entered a room to the right — one that had a door crudely mounted on it. To her credit, Julie thought she saw the woman looking both directions before entering, no doubt looking for any of the Ravenshadow men who might be patrolling these forgotten corridors.

She ushered Reggie, Mrs. E, and Ben into the room, all of whom had their guns drawn and at the ready, waiting for any sign of a Ravenshadow ambush. Julie had a sidearm, but it was still holstered at her waist. As she passed her friend, Julie flashed the dive light into her eyes.

"Are you okay, Victoria?" Julie asked.

Victoria seemed confused. Her eyes flitted left and right very quickly, very slightly, but they didn't seem affected by the light shining into them. Even her very demeanor was an oxymoron. She appeared to be off-balance a bit, like a stone statue on uneven ground. Her hands were steady, matching her eyes, but they were almost *too* steady.

"Victoria," she said again. "Are you —"

Victoria pushed Julie a bit into the room, then slammed the door shut.

"What —"

"Oh, for the love of God," she heard Reggie shout from behind her.

I knew it, she thought. *I* knew *it.*

Julie grasped for a handle, but realized that the door's inside didn't have one. Her hands slid against the rough surface of the shoddy wooden door, trying to find purchase.

"Push it back open!" Reggie yelled. He and Mrs. E rushed forward.

Julie heard a sound she immediately recognized. *A lock.*

"Victoria!" she shouted.

But instead of a response, she heard another sound. A deeper, *heavier* sound. It sounded like metal-on-metal.

Or...

Metal on stone.

"She's dragging something in front of the door!" Julie shouted. "Hurry!"

Ben and Mrs. E looked around the room, using their lights to look for something to use to push the door back open. Julie knew they wouldn't find anything. She and Reggie started kicking at the door haphazardly until Reggie pulled her gently away.

"We need to take turns. Aim for the center of the door, just off the side of where the handle should be. That's the structural part, and if we can kick through that, we —"

She didn't let him finish. She reared back and slammed her boot, still a bit soggy from their dive, into the bulk of the door. It didn't move.

The sound of metal dragging outside came to an end, and Julie could almost sense the weight of whatever object had been placed in front of the door.

Sure enough, her second kick seemed to land on pure stone. It felt like kicking a boulder; the impact of her boot — even Reggie's, when he tried — hardly resonated through the room. Their kicks were nothing but dull thuds, the heavy rubber soles nothing against the massive friction of the obstacle.

"We're locked in," Reggie said. "Shit!"

"She tricked us," Ben said, his voice low and his breathing heavy. "You were right, Julie."

But Julie was barely listening. She was now pacing the room in the darkness, trying to put the pieces together.

She had some theories previously, just inklings of ideas, but she hadn't been able to formulate a cohesive hypothesis.

Until now.

Her mind raced — what she knew of Victoria, what she remembered from their past encounters, her own memories.

And what she knew of Victoria's father.

"It wasn't Victoria," she finally said.

Everyone stopped talking and turned to face her. "What are you talking about, Jules?" Reggie asked. "I *saw* her — she's right outside -"

"No, no. I know it's *her*. But *she's* not the one who did this."

"She's not?"

"I'm starting to figure out what exactly is going on around here. And no, it wasn't Victoria at all."

She turned a full circle, meeting everyone's eyes.

"It was her father."

CHAPTER 45

BEN

"WHAT ARE YOU TALKING ABOUT, JULES?" Ben asked. He had been watching Julie pace for over a minute, but he had moved to the side of the locked door, where he was now standing, leaning against the cool stone wall.

He was seething. Livid, even. Mad at himself, for not listening to Julie when she'd told him there was something going on with Victoria. Angry with Reggie and Mrs. E for blindly following her, and upset with Victoria for... whatever it was that was happening.

"I'm saying her father made her do this."

"Garza got to her?" Reggie asked. "You think he somehow *convinced* her to betray us? And then lead us here to wait for his men to kill us?"

Julie shook her head. All three of their dive lights were on and pointed at Julie, and while her face was lit with an orange glow, it did little to illuminate the room around them. They'd examined the room thoroughly and found nothing. No benches or chairs, no electricity or lightswitches, no more of the fabric faux walls.

The room was cold, dark, and oppressive. In Ben's mind, it was a perfect reflection of their captor.

"No," She said, her voice lower. "Think about it. Remember Philadelphia? His experimentation with that drug?"

"Scopolamine," Reggie said. "The 'date-rape drug.' Nasty stuff."

Ben suddenly realized what Julie was implying. "He would have had to perfect it — back then, it was little more than a 'zombie' drug. Knocked people out, even though they were effectively sleepwalking."

"And sleep *killing*," Julie said. He heard her breath catch in her throat, and he didn't need to be reminded of the nightmare she was referring to.

Before their first trip to Peru a couple months ago, Julie had shared with Ben that she had been having terrible nightmares.

Unfortunately, as Ben and the others knew, the nightmare was no simple manifestation of her subconscious. It was a *memory*, one they all took part in.

He remembered the event as if it had been yesterday. The loss of their leader and good friend, Joshua Jefferson.

His mind fell back into the scene, fighting against his own judgement.

Julie.

He wanted to call out to her, to see if his words had returned. He opened his mouth and felt the dizziness grow once again.

Julie.

She was there, the man called The Hawk standing next to her. He had just shoved a needle into her arm...

Ben tensed up, also curious about what drug Vicente Garza had put inside her. What would it do? How long would it last?

And, most importantly, what were the side effects?

Ben tried to shake away the memory, one of the top-three worst events he'd ever witnessed.

Julie's head fell backwards, her eyes open wide. She began to mumble, loudly, and Ben could hear it from his position against the back wall.

The soldier in front of him didn't move, didn't divert his eyes from Ben.

Julie's head snapped forward again, and she looked right at Ben.

He recognized the look now. The slightly drunken appearance, the dazed expression of dead eyes.

Victoria had the same look, he realized. It was far more subtle — Victoria had been able to look around, to respond to their questions, albeit in a stilted, forced sort of way.

The memory continued.

He watched her face, trying to determine if the woman he loved knew who he was in that moment. If she could see him. Her eyes flitted back and forth once, quickly taking in the rest of the room. At this point there was no one behind Julie. She sat in the center of the gymnasium, her back to the opposite doors, and all the Ravenshadow men as well as The Hawk and Daris Johansson were standing or sitting in a wide arc around Julie.

He, Reggie, Joshua, and Derrick were all standing with their backs to the wall in front of Julie, but they each had a soldier, weapon drawn, guarding them.

Julie's face scanned Ben's, but there was no reaction. She was blank, empty.

"Ms. Richardson," The Hawk said. His voice had changed. No longer was he the confident leader, the intimidating figure of power for his men. His voice was calm, almost gentle, and as he addressed Julie, Ben wondered if the man's voice was part of the test — perhaps the tone of the man's voice affected Julie in some way.

She turned to look at The Hawk.

"Hello again, Ms. Richardson. I'm glad we could talk in front of the rest of these people. Ms. Richardson, do you see these people?"

The Hawk made a point of drawing a wide half-circle with his open palm, showing Julie the room.

"I do," Julie said.

Ben's heart raced. He hadn't heard Julie's voice since...

Since before the phone call.

He'd heard her scream, cry out, beg, but he hadn't heard her in so long. Her normal, day-to-day voice.

He was hearing it now.

Whatever was affecting Julie was causing her to be completely collected, at ease. She felt no strife, no pain, and she had no care in the world for the four men — four friends — standing by at gunpoint.

Whatever agent had affected Julie then was affecting Victoria now. And Ben knew it didn't end there. He fought to make sense of the drug, to recall what he knew about it.

"Ms. Richardson, please take this weapon."

Julie reached up and took the weapon.

"Ms. Richardson, you know how to handle this weapon, correct?"

She nodded. "I do."

"Good."

The Hawk walked forward a few paces, toward Ben's wall.

"Ms. Richardson, please follow me.

Julie stood up and trailed behind The Hawk. When Garza had reached the side of the gym Ben was standing on, he stopped. He moved sideways over to the soldier standing in front of Joshua, then stopped again. Julie followed, now standing next to Garza.

"Ms. Richardson, who is this man?"

"Joshua Jefferson."

"And do you know him well."

"Reasonably well. We're friends."

"I see. And how long have you know Mr. Jefferson?"

Julie thought for a moment. "Probably six, seven months."

"And do you like this man?"

She nodded. "I like him. He's a good friend, and a good leader."

His heart sank.

Ben didn't want to remember the rest of it. The nightmare that had turned out to be *very* real. It had ended in the worst way possible.

His mind, however, had other plans.

"Ms. Richardson, please shoot Joshua Jefferson in the head."

Julie immediately complied, her arm coming up quickly. She aimed, and Ben saw Reggie lurch forward, catching his soldier off guard. Julie was now behind Reggie and the soldier, and Ben couldn't see her or Joshua.

But he heard the gunshot.

CHAPTER 46

BEN

BEN SHUDDERED. The nightmare was there, forever lodged in his subconscious, ready to make an appearance just when he thought he was safe. He was a man accustomed to torment, to personal demons and dark pasts, but he had worked hard — for a long time — to compress those demons into a finite space within a dark corner of his mind.

In his inability to purge them completely, Ben had created a prison-like vault for them. A place they could live and exist and occupy nothing dangerous, but he insisted on controlling their access to the rest of his mind.

His system was, clearly, not perfect.

Julie stepped forward. "Ben," she said. "Are you okay?"

He swallowed, a hard lump that took longer than normal to go down. He felt like he wanted to cry, but he sniffed in a sharp smack of air and looked down into her eyes. *Whatever demons I'm facing, she's facing them even more.*

She had pulled the trigger.

"Ben, he drugged me," Julie said. "And I think he did the same thing to Victoria. To his own daughter."

Reggie nodded. "He's been testing it. Ever since we stumbled into his gymnasium lab in Philly. He's been *perfecting* it."

"And those Exo things," Ben said. "Remember how we didn't even know there were people inside of them until they started moving?"

"They were in a trance," Mrs. E said. "This 'zombie' state you mention, it seems to be medically induced, as you say, but how then is Garza controlling them?"

"It's not pure scopolamine," Reggie said. "Unlike that, which is an antiemetic in smaller doses and simply knocks you unconscious in larger quantities, Garza's figured out some other chemical or chemicals to combine with it. In Philly it was just the borrachero, which is the plant scopolamine comes from. It's native to Peru, but I'm thinking that what he's been extracting isn't *just* the borrachero."

"Definitely not," Julie said. "And it's absolutely been run through his labs. Nothing in nature can cause that sort of stupor and *then* be used to ply someone to do what you want."

"And only what *he* wants," Ben said. "She wouldn't listen to *us*."

"That's true," Reggie said. "And that's a big deal. There's something deeper going on with it for it to be 'activated,' or whatever is happening, by just Garza's voice."

"Is it his voice?"

Reggie pondered it for a moment. "No idea. I just can't think of what else it *could* be. I mean that's the only thing unique to Garza, right? None of us sound like him."

Ben shook his head. "But to create a designer drug that responds to that *exact* timber and vocal frequency? Reggie, you and I have a deep enough voice that it would fool that drug into thinking we're Garza, at least a bit. It should have confused Victoria somewhat."

Reggie nodded. "Yeah, true. Still, it's weird. I've never seen anything like it."

"Weird is an understatement. We need to keep our eyes up. Since he brought us here, he probably doesn't just want to kill us or he'd have done it already. That means there's a good chance we're next in line to be his mind control guinea pigs."

"Sounds fun," Reggie said, waving his prosthetic arm in the air. "I've actually benefited from his experiments in the past..."

Julie shot him an ugly glance. "Not funny."

Reggie shrugged. "A little funny. Anyway, what's the plan *now*? I have a feeling we're not going to have much time before —"

The giant metal scraping sound returned, and all four of the team members were silenced.

"They're here," Reggie said. He stepped backwards, disappearing into the shadows next to the door. Ben and Julie closed in next to one another, Ben putting his arm around his new wife. Each of them were holding their rifles, but there seemed to be a shared understanding that they wouldn't attack the intruders.

It could be Victoria, Ben thought. *Maybe the injection wore off, and she's coming to help us.*

He didn't voice this to Julie, but he could almost sense that she felt the same way. Julie's breaths were steady, slow and even. She was focused. Nervous, but expectant. He hoped it would prove fruitful — that he was right about it being Victoria on the other side of the door.

He was wrong.

Two Ravenshadow men appeared in the doorway, both holding nasty-looking modern assault rifles, some kind Ben didn't recognize. They had attached flashlights, and the wash from the lights pierced through Ben's eyes, blinding him.

He immediately threw his hands in the air, allowing his assault rifle to fall by his side, still harnessed over his shoulder. It swung back, out the way. Julie did the same, and the first of the men entered the room.

"Get on the ground!" he shouted.

The second man stood in the doorway, but Ben saw that his eyes were on Reggie. The two soldiers were locked in a silent fight, neither wanting to make the first move for fear of getting their partners killed. Reggie finally gave in and put his arms up, too.

Ben and Julie slowly retreated to their knees, their hands still in the air. Ben could feel the cold, unforgiving stone floor through his pant legs. His knees were already sore, and he hoped the Ravenshadow soldiers would make quick work of whatever it was they had been ordered to do.

"Remove your weapon," the man said. His rifle's barrel was pointed directly at Ben's face. Ben knew he wasn't going to shoot him, but it was still a bit unnerving. He slowly began working the strap of his rifle up and over his shoulder. Out of the corner of his eye he watched the standoff between Reggie and the soldier in the doorway. He wondered if his best friend had any tricks up his sleeve.

They had been in the middle of discussing a possible plan when the Ravenshadow men barged in, so Ben wasn't entirely sure where Reggie thought they had left things. He knew Reggie wasn't the type of man to just wait around for Ben's orders, but Ben also knew he wouldn't risk the lives of his friends.

As it turned out, Reggie didn't need a plan at all. Before Ben knew what was happening, he heard a low-pitched growl emanating from the space *behind* the door, in the far corner of the room. A massive shadow lurched and crawled over the ceiling, followed by an even darker, more ominous shape.

Mrs. E.

CHAPTER 47

EDMUND

AN HOUR EARLIER, he had returned from his walk, stopped in at the hotel's business center, and logged into his Vatican email account. He had never been great with computers, but even he surprised himself with the speed with which he was able to connect. *I must be getting younger*, he thought, coyly.

When he saw the email — return address somehow obfuscated into an unrecognizable sender — he had nearly gasped out loud. He had no doubt the email had been sent from the company that was brokering the deal between St. Clair and the Orland Group.

It was written in English, but English was a language he had much practice with. It took him mere seconds longer to read the note than it would have had it been written in his native Spanish.

Father Canisius, we appreciate your willingness to jump through so many hoops, and for the same reason I must apologize. You have no doubt grasped the delicacy of the situation, if not the full reasons for it. I assure you, however, keeping these matters and our dealings out of sight of the public eye are of the utmost importance to all parties involved.

I hope you will grant me one final request in this transaction. I understand you have been meeting with Ms. St. Clair, and she tells me you are prepared to finalize the deal and get home. I must ask that this final phase be conducted in person, yet out of sight of prying eyes.

Canisius was not terribly excited about the proposition of meeting the seller and the broker in person, but he shouldn't have been surprised. Throughout his years working for the Vatican, he had been privy to many deals like this one — deals that the Church felt would come across as a bit unsavory to the general public. He knew the Church had worldly needs as well as anyone, and therefore he had signed off on meeting requests that would begin the acquisition process for weaponry for Vatican police officers and the Swiss Guard that operated in their precinct.

In another unlikely purchase, the Vatican had purchased a telescope at the observatory on Mount Graham, in Arizona. While no one doubted the Church's interest in the study of heaven and the celestial bodies in it, this was the same church that persecuted and executed people for their belief that the stars were, in fact, other suns.

So Canisius' feelings of his time in Peru had been one of muted acceptance. He didn't *want* to be here, but he was finally understanding *why* he was. This deal was one that would mark the beginning of a new era for the Vatican, and one that would push the Vatican back into relevance. He had hoped and prayed for that very thing for most of his nearly seventy years of life.

If his superiors back home wanted him to be here, he decided he needed to be here. He was done second-guessing them. If the deal was to be conducted with the utmost secrecy, for whatever reason, then all the better they had chosen him. He was a well-known cardinal, but he was a professional, and he was not swayed by politics or press.

He was about to log off when he noticed that another email had hit his account a while earlier. He frowned as he read the sender's name.

Brother Archibald Quinones.

He did not recognize the name, but then again just because he was a Jesuit did not mean he should know every one of the other 16,000 Jesuits in their order.

He did not receive any mail from the general public, as his email address was strictly for work only, and he had never shared the address with anyone else. Still, it did not seem like a fake sender, or a junk message. He opened the email.

Father Canisius, I have been trying to reach you for some time, the email began. Canisius settled back into the chair in the hotel's business center. He continued reading.

My name is Archibald Quinones, and I work with an American group you may have heard of called the Civilian Special Operations.

Canisius nearly jumped. *The CSO?* he thought. *The same group that illegally infiltrated the Vatican earlier this year and nearly cost us a fortune in security reassignments?*

The email was short, to the point: Quinones wanted Canisius to call him, as soon as he got the email. The man had left a phone number and told Canisius that he, too, was in Peru, though he did not specify where.

Canisius knew there was a payphone nearby, but he wasn't sure he had any coins, and certainly not any in Peruvian denominations. Besides, he wasn't even sure payphones were connected to anything anymore — they might be standing around as some sort of nostalgic decoration; he'd seen stranger avant garde art exhibits back in Rome.

He wrote down the phone number on an index card he found in a stack next to the computer station, and then he returned to the front desk, where he tracked down the concierge and asked what he thought was a simple question.

"Excuse me — do you happen to have a cellular phone I can borrow?"

"Like... for how long?" the young woman asked.

"I am not sure. I also need a cab — a taxi — may I get that here?"

The woman smiled, then reached into her pocket. She pulled out a phone and opened it to the dial pad, then looked back up at Canisius. "I can dial it for you."

"Oh," he said. "I — am sorry. I was hoping I could borrow it for a short trip. There's... somewhere I must be."

The woman seemed to dislike this response, but to her credit she continued the smile. "I'm sorry, I really can't let you take it." Her eyes lit up. "But we sell phones in the gift shop! You may purchase a set number of minutes, that should be more than enough for an outbound call."

Canisius followed her pointing finger and saw the gift shop, just beyond a set of double doors. He thanked her, asked about the taxi once again, then walked to the store.

After purchasing what the cashier described as a "burner" phone, he returned to the lobby to wait for the car the woman had ordered, then turned on the phone, saw that there was a decent charge, and dialed the number.

It rang three times before a man's deep, powerful voice answered.

"This is Archibald Quinones."

CHAPTER 48

JULIE

JULIE HAD TOTALLY FORGOTTEN about Mrs. E, and it seemed as though everyone else in the room had, as well. The large woman was now barreling toward her and Ben, and she was moving *fast*.

Mrs. E was large, but she had honed her stature into a solid mass of muscle and functional strength through years of hand-to-hand combat training, including becoming a master in Krav Maga.

Julie ducked out of the way, but there was no reason to. The Ravenshadow soldier stood between them and Mrs. E, and it was into this man that the massive woman flew, her head tucked and aimed at the guy's chest.

The impact this close to Julie's ears was almost deafening. She heard — and *felt* — the sickening crunch as the man's sternum collapsed, and Ben had barely enough time to duck out of the way before the man came crashing up and over him. Mrs. E was still in motion, her truck-thick legs pumping with more power than speed, and the man tripped over Ben's extended boot and sailed over his head and into the rear wall.

Another crunching sound ended the man's life, but Mrs. E wasn't finished. She brought the butt of her rifle down onto the man's head and sealed the deal.

On the other side of the room, in the doorway, Reggie had also made his move. He punched up with his artificial limb and sent the other soldier's rifle clattering toward the ceiling. He followed that swing with a solid left hook with his *real* hand, which was certainly not made of metal alloy but was nonetheless hard as a rock.

The Ravenshadow man at the door grunted in pain but, to his credit, raised his arms to stave off another attack.

Reggie was faster. He had his prosthetic lifted, his upper arm out and his elbow and forearm parallel to the ground, and he simply *smashed* the man's face as if it were a melon. Julie watched the scene in disbelief, as if she were watching some disturbing science fiction movie.

But it was real life, and that life, for both Ravenshadow men, was now over.

Julie stood up slowly, waiting for the rest of the group to react, and waiting for any signs of life from the two downed soldiers.

Nothing.

Reggie grinned, twisting the wrist of his prosthetic around and examining it. "Damn," he said. "Not a scratch."

"*That's* what you're worried about?"

"Hey, it's like a brand-new truck," he retorted. "You want to be the first person to scratch it, not some random Ravenshadow asshole."

Mrs. E was wiping her pant legs as if she'd simply fallen in the dirt, and then stood to her full over-six-foot height and shook herself off.

"Well, you'll probably have plenty more opportunities to test it out," Ben said, groaning as he rose to his feet as well. "There are lots more of these dudes, and they're not going to waste any time shooting at us if they catch us out there."

"Fair point," Reggie said. "It's ironic."

"What is?" Julie asked.

"We worked so hard to get in here," he said. "And it was easy. The challenge is going to be getting back out."

"Yeah, that's true. Especially since Garza knows we're here." Julie stopped herself then thought a moment. "You think there are more of these secret passageways?"

"The curtain, you mean? That piece of fabric that led to this room?"

"Yeah, exactly. It's part of the older mine system, not a newer Ravenshadow development. And, unless I'm mistaken, it wasn't on the map."

"It definitely wasn't," Ben said. "And yeah, there are probably more of them. Maybe they thought the tunnels were unstable or something. Didn't want to risk a cave-in?"

"Maybe," Reggie said. "Or, maybe this was Garza's plan all along."

"To *trap* us in here?"

"He knew we were coming, right? How else would he have sent men *right* where we went into the river, and then basically let us through the waste shaft? He acted surprised on the intercom, but this is Vicente Garza we're talking about. The Hawk."

"And he's been *watching* us like a hawk since we got here."

"And the whole thing with Victoria," Ben said. "It was all planned. Staged, as if he had orchestrated all of it. We played right into his hand."

"So Beale was in on it, too?" Julie asked.

"No way," Reggie said. "They were crooked, but they weren't on the same team as Garza. He was surprised they were there, too. Expected *us*, maybe, but not them. That's why he killed them all."

"In a way that was meant to demonstrate his power," Mrs. E added. "And I believe it worked."

"I believe that, too," Ben said. "Those... *things*... the exosuits? They're unbelievable. All controlled by a human operator —

someone under Garza's spell. He could take out an entire army with them."

Julie nodded. "Which means we can't get anywhere near them. One shot from those turrets and we're toast."

"More like Swiss cheese," Reggie said.

"So we need to find another way out," Ben said. "But the map we saw showed tunnels and hallways that all basically lead to that demonstration floor, where the machines were. This place is crawling with Ravenshadow men, too."

"So let's hope there's another set of these tunnels, then?" Julie asked.

"Yeah, and let's hope they lead somewhere besides back to the monsters."

They were interrupted by the sound of voices echoing into the room from outside in the hallway. Men's voices, low and clearly discussing how they were going to breach the room.

"They're here," Ben said. "Julie, grab that guy's weapon. The rest of you guys, get into a corner. We want to fight our way out, but we don't want to hit each other."

Julie did, and the weight of the rifle gave her a moment of relief. She no longer felt naked, vulnerable.

She was armed once again, and she was going to fight her way out of this hell.

CHAPTER 49

BEN

THE EXOS HAD STARTED to move. Ben knew that because he could hear the faint sound of the high-pitched whine as the machines moved throughout the base. The sound was more like a piercing, shrill *poke* — a physical sensation — than it was a sound. It made sense to Ben, since he knew that sound was literally a *pressure* wave. The Exos made noise as they powered up, and it was enough noise that they essentially broadcasted their location as they moved.

Not exactly stealth, Ben thought. Perhaps that was why Garza was still working on them? Why Beale — and his boss, Sturdivant — wanted an update? Maybe Garza couldn't figure out how to get the whining noise out of the Exos' modus operandi. While Ben hardly thought the Exos were meant as stealth infiltrators — their lumbering, monstrous machine bodies thundered around, preventing any hope of moving incognito — Ben knew that a high-pitched sound at that decibel level would travel *massive* distances, alerting any enemies to their locations long before they were in firing range.

One of the Exos had marched down the hall and past the CSO group, narrowly missing them. They'd hidden by sliding to the floor, lying flat and hoping that the Exo was merely patrolling, not actively pursuing them. They'd gotten away without being spotted. Apparently the suits were incapable of determining enemy locations without a decent amount of light, and the onboard human host was incapable of using its own senses for that purpose.

Ben had watched it closely as it passed, taking it in, memorizing what he could. The sleek aluminum braces around the vertical leg shafts shone against the dim light cast by its own flashlight, mounted on the opposite shoulder as the thing's turret. Ben saw a battery pack the size of its torso strapped to the alloy frame, where there were also a few canisters that he assumed held some sort of hydraulic equipment or ammunition.

The thing's feet were diamond-shaped pads, split down the middle horizontally, allowing the "toes" to bend. The arms were mounted on ball-socket swivels, and he saw that they had claw-shaped grips on the ends, extensions that could be used to grab rocks, branches, and other objects.

And he had no doubt the thing knew fifty ways to kill a man. They didn't even need weapons, Ben realized as it passed. They could simply walk *through* a human, smashing it into the dirt around its feet. The vice-grip hands could likely crush a human skull without much trouble. In all, it was a tank on two legs, capable of running them down and killing them without burning any extra battery life.

Ben's group had run down the hallway after leaving the stone chamber Victoria had locked them in, opposite the direction from which they'd come. They'd decided that running *toward* where they thought the center of the base was would lead them to another exit.

It was a risk, but Ben knew it was time to act. They were pinned down here, inside Ravenshadow headquarters. Garza knew they were here, and the longer they spent inside the base the better chance they'd all spend eternity here.

And Ben wasn't a fan of that option.

Beale's group had experienced that fate, and it hadn't ended well.

But Ben *also* wanted to continue their mission. While Beale had betrayed them, Ben intended to redeem their deaths. He added theirs to his tally of reasons to seek vengeance.

It had all started with Joshua Jefferson, and by extension Julie, and she had led them all here. But Garza had killed and kidnapped many others along the way, and there were likely countless more they would never even know about.

Garza and his men were a scourge, a virus, one that Ben hoped to eradicate. Beale's team of professional soldiers had failed, but they had gone into the battle with different expectations. Ben wouldn't make the same mistake. Garza was prepared to kill them. All of them. And Ben wouldn't miss the chance to take a shot at him.

He knew the others felt the same as well.

Reggie, leading the group through the maze of tunnels, stopped at another t-intersection.

"Which way?" Ben asked.

"I think we should go right," Reggie responded. "But that's not why I stopped."

Ben slowed to a halt and stood next to his friend. "What's up? You hear something?"

Reggie shook his head. "No, thank god. Those monster robot things are loud, thankfully. So we won't miss them coming. The Ravenshadow men will be running as well, so we should be able to pick them off when we hear them." Reggie turned and felt the wall, then spoke again. "Remember the briefing? Beale said this place was a mine."

"Yeah," Ben said. "The locals mined it a hundred years ago."

"They *said* the locals mined it. And I looked it up — that's what the general consensus says, anyway. That this mountain was some sort of mine, cut into the rock over a hundred or two-hundred years ago."

"What's the point?" Ben asked. He was feeling impatient, knowing that around any corner might be an exit — or a group of

Exos ready to kill them. He wanted to get out. He wanted to go home.

"The point is that I don't think this place was *ever* a mine."

"You don't?" Julie asked.

"I don't. These walls — they were cut, but then *smoothed*."

"Could have been water, over thousands of years."

"Then it was *definitely* not a mine," Reggie said. "If water had any part of it, it would have had to have started long before civilized people took to mining."

Julie seemed to be just as impatient as Ben. "Okay, then —"

She stopped herself, then looked at Ben and Reggie, then Mrs. E. "You don't think..."

"It has to be, Julie. We *knew* they were here."

Ben nodded. *The original descendants. The Chachapoyas. The 'fair-skinned' tribe who had simply appeared in the jungle, their civilization complete and in existence in an instant.*

"They were here," Reggie continued. "We saw their temples and their writing." Ben thought back to the Chachapoyas valley, just on the other side of this mountain, where they had encountered the gigantic soldiers Garza had been trying to build and the Guild Rite, the ancient fraternal order that had ties to Freemasonry. "They were *in* this mountain. After they fled their previous home, they settled here."

"Those temples outside," Ben said. "You think they were just that? Temples?"

"I do. It makes sense now — they didn't *live* there. They *worshipped* there."

"Because they lived *here*," Julie said, finishing his thought.

"Exactly. Look around — this place was never a mine. Sure, it has long, straight tunnels and shafts, but there are *rooms*, large spaces cut into the walls that are ordered and organized. Not like a mine."

"Like a city," Ben said.

"Like a city." Reggie brushed his hand along the wall. "The Peruvian locals around here invented stories and myths about this place, about the inhabitants, and they simply assumed it was a mine. That their predecessors built it."

"They would not have known that their predecessors *did* build it," Mrs. E said. "But that it was not built a single generation before them, but *many* generations before them."

"Yes," Reggie said. "It's the only thing that makes sense. When Ravenshadow came in here, it was out of necessity. Garza needed a place to work, a place away from prying eyes."

"And since we now know Beale was here to snoop, they probably wanted a place that couldn't be seen from above, either. By satellite."

"Reggie," Julie asked. "Are you saying what I think you are? That this isn't just the lost city of the Chachapoyas, but also their *original* goal? The entire reason they came here?"

Reggie nodded solemnly. "I am suggesting that. I believe this place was the home of the descendants we've been chasing. The lost civilization of Atlantis. The survivors fled from their homes on their island nation after the catastrophe 11,000 years ago. They spread around the globe, building monuments to their gods and teaching the uncivilized world about farming, agriculture, philosophy.

"They built the pyramids, and the original sculpture that eventually became the Great Sphinx. Then they moved again — likely driven out by warring factions."

"And they ended up here."

"Yes," he said. "They ended up *right here*. But that's not all — they would have taken their collection of records with them. They would have brought them to protect them, and this would have been the perfect place to store them — just like Garza, they would have wanted to keep them out of sight of prying eyes, of enemies who would take advantage of them.

"I believe that somewhere inside this mountain is the lost Atlantean Hall of Records."

CHAPTER 50

EDMUND

"HELLO, MR. QUINONES," Canisius began.

"Please, call me Archie," the voice returned in perfect Spanish.

Canisius felt relieved, and immediately felt more at home. "Very well, Archie. I hope I did not catch you at a bad time." He wasn't sure what he was supposed to say, and he wasn't sure that what he'd said was even appropriate. *Too late.*

"Nonsense, I appreciate your taking the time to reach out. I hope you are well, and I hope you will forgive my breach of privacy, but I have a matter to attend to that I believe is of the utmost importance."

"And what matter is that?"

"As I mentioned in my email, I do some work with the Civilian Special Operations. They are currently here in Peru, investigating a company whom we believe to be involved in the murder and kidnapping of innocent civilians."

Canisius sucked in a breath. He had never been part of anything like this, and he certainly had no idea how to handle it, or how to respond. "I — I am sorry to hear that."

"Rest assured, I am not accusing you of anything, Father. I merely want your help."

Canisius waited.

"I know you are in Peru for the convention, though it seems a bit strange as to why your office would send such a high-ranking cardinal."

"And I thought I was not being accused of anything, Archie?"

"No, of course. I am merely wondering if you were in Peru for another reason altogether. A reason that involves the buying and selling of assets?"

How did he know? Edmund Canisius felt the blood inside him run cold. *No,* he thought. *He can't know. There is no way to know — both the buyer and the broker have been completely silent about this matter.*

He relaxed a bit. Archie's words hadn't revealed anything suspect, though they had been close to the mark.

"I can confirm that I have additional business to handle while I'm here."

"Very well. Please understand that I am not trying to uncover the details of that deal. But I am afraid that there may be more at stake than a simple transaction."

"Can you be more specific?" Canisius asked.

"Are you aware of the recent history of your office's dealings in the area?"

"I... cannot say that I am."

"The Guild Rite, an ancient sect similar to Freemasonry, and a sect within the Jesuit Order, recently fought over control over land near the Chachapoyas region of Peru."

"That is... certainly new information to me," Canisius said, now growing even more confused. "But I cannot understand what that has to do with —"

"The deal you are participating in involves some of the same groups that were interested in the land in that area. We — the CSO — are interested in preventing one of those groups from completing that deal."

"Well, then it seems as though our interests are misaligned, Archie. I am *very* interested in completing this deal — whatever it may be — and getting back home."

"I am sure you are," Archie said. *"But again, I am afraid there is more at stake here than our own comfort. I truly understand your predicament, but I cannot express enough the —"*

"You cannot understand my 'predicament,' Archie, because *I* do not understand it. I have been here for days, waiting around for meetings that are laced in cryptic vagaries, messages that always carry an air of urgency, and living in perpetual anxiety and confusion as to what exactly this is all about.

"I was sent here by my office to close a deal I know nothing about, for reasons I cannot even begin to comprehend."

There was a pause. *"Yes, I see,"* Archie finally said. *"I do apologize. Please, I am not trying to waste your time. On the contrary, I strongly believe that by putting our heads together we can make sense of some of this."*

Father Canisius was still irritated, but Archie's words had piqued his interest. "I would like some sense, if only a little."

"Very well. I have told you just about everything, but I will tell you one more thing, in the hope that you will reciprocate with something I might be able to use to help my own team."

"And what is this thing?"

"I do not believe the Catholic Church — your employer — is interested in whatever it is that is being purchased. In fact, I believe the price they will pay will be substantially less than what the actual cost of the asset will be."

Canisius thought about this for a moment longer. "That is your opinion, Archie, but you have not given me any details. Why should I believe you — and why should any of it change what I am doing here?"

"I do not want to change anything. I believe your role here must be completed as they have requested. But I think the Church is covering up something they would like to keep hidden."

This statement felt like a personal attack, and Canisius steeled himself and took a breath before answering. *"Just what is it they are trying to cover up?"*

Archie sighed. *"That is where I must leave things. If I told you what I know, you would not believe me."*

"Then we are done here." *I will not be made a fool,* he thought. *And I will not disclose information I do not even have.*

Canisius pulled the phone away from his ear and was about to hang up when he heard Archie's voice once again through the tiny speaker.

"This deal — do you have reason to believe is for some sort of defense technology?"

Father Edmund Canisius looked up at the clouds passing overhead. He took a deep breath.

I cannot continue this way. He wanted to come clean, to tell everything. The trouble was that he knew *nothing.* Nothing of importance.

"Yes. I do believe that, Archie."

"As I suspected. And one of the parties to the deal, by chance, a company called the Orland Group?"

Canisius swallowed. *This is about to get considerably more complicated.*

CHAPTER 51

JULIE

JULIE'S MIND WAS RACING. It was torn in two — one side of it wanting to escape as soon as possible, to get away from Garza and the strange mechanical-human hybrids that had taken out Beale's force without so much as a second thought. The other side of it wanted revenge even more than it had before. She wanted to kill Garza, to see him die a slow, horrible death, a death only he deserved.

And she wanted to save Victoria. She'd been drugged, by the same sort of chemical that Garza had used on Julie in Philadelphia.

And there were others, too. She remembered what Archie had told Ben and Reggie about the local tribe that had been murdered. The Ravenshadow men, obviously hoping to keep their presence and work here unknown, had wiped out an entire village of men, women, and children.

Never in Julie's life had she felt so strongly the drive toward vengeance. It coursed through her blood, pushed her forward, flooded her mind. It pushed the sanity away — the safe side that wanted to flee stood no chance.

They ran toward another doorway at the end of the hall, this one on the opposite side of the base. Julie guessed it was a corner that marked the edge of Garza's additions to the original space. She tried to recall the picture of the map they'd found. If she was correct in her assumption, the two hallways they'd just run through lined the upper level of the base, marking the border around the larger, central room where the Exos had been.

Had been.

They had already seen one of the exoskeleton soldiers, and she knew there were more. Garza was playing his cards close to his chest — he obviously knew where they were, as he had hailed them in the communications room they'd been in first. He'd either seen them come in, or he had seen that they'd turned on some of the monitors.

The fact that he hadn't sent his entire army of Ravenshadow soldiers and Exos to their location meant that he was playing it safe. Either he had fewer men than they thought, or he was simply not worried about them.

It wasn't like Garza to underestimate them, so Julie had to assume there was another reason he hadn't already sent in an over-whelming force to wipe them out. *Maybe Beale's group scared him,* she thought. Perhaps he was worried Beale's team was just an advance force, one that meant there were more US soldiers on the way?

She didn't dwell on it. Reggie threw the heavy door open — again, it was unlocked — and they ran down the stairs. There was no reason for stealth; their boots pounded against the metal frame with resounding *thuds,* loud enough that anyone listening in would be able to hear them coming from at least two levels down.

They reached the bottom floor — the floor they'd decided would be their best bet at finding an alternative exit. She hoped they were right. If the Hall of Records was here somewhere, the original creators of this mountain city would have cut multiple entrances and exits. She'd seen it in Egypt, as well as in other places of historic inter-est. Anything as grand as a Hall of Records would be the *first* reason they would build inside the mountain. The city would be a secondary concern. And the city would have been created for the inhabitants, while the Hall of Records would have been erected for only the most worthy of individuals.

In other words, it would have been a secret. Only the elite would know about it, and how to find it. That meant there would be a way into the Hall of Records, as well as a way out, that bypassed all of the city. Garza had adopted the same space the original city had taken up, so they were hoping there would be another space — and another exit — one still hidden somewhere behind these walls.

When Reggie and Mrs. E reached the landing at the bottom of the stairs, they paused for Ben and Julie to catch up. If they were going to be spotted, it would be here, as they entered the hallway on the floor they believed was the primary level for Garza's men.

Reggie tried the handle. It was unlocked. He slid it down, gently pressing until it clicked with a nearly inaudible sound. Then he pushed the door open a crack, simultaneously swinging his rifle up and out the newly formed hole.

He paused there. Julie knew the drill from his training. *Lead with what shoots, not with what gets shot at.* In other words, stick your gun out of the hole *before* you stick your head out.

The idea was that if anyone were going to shoot, they'd do it as soon as they saw the crack in the door. And since anyone shooting *back* at them was guaranteed to be an enemy, there was no harm in returning blind fire.

But no one fired, and Reggie popped the door another crack. Julie listened, leaning toward the opening. Ben and Mrs. E stood back now, but both were gripping their assault rifles tightly, preparing for an onslaught.

When none came, Reggie slid out and into the hallway. Julie could hear him whispering as he did. "It's a corner, so we've got two fronts to watch out for. And it's not as dark here but it ain't bright either; light fixtures are florescents, spaced every fifty or so."

She nodded as Ben pushed her forward. It was well known that she was the best shot in the group besides Reggie, who had served as an Army sniper before his discharge. She practiced as much as Ben and the others, but she'd taken to it quickly and, according to Reggie, was a natural.

She enjoyed the praise, but it was times like these that she wished she wasn't quite as good with a gun. Entering the hall where she knew there were plenty of enemy forces, as well-trained as she was, looking to put a bullet through her skull.

Reggie took the right side of the door, Julie fell to the left. She looked down her hallway, not even bothering to look to the right. Reggie would have it covered, and it would only be a few seconds before Ben and Mrs. E had entered the hallway as well.

Mrs. E caught the door behind her and slid it shut silently.

Now what? Julie wondered. While she was great with a weapon, she left it to Reggie to decide which direction they should head.

"I think that's the demonstration floor, where Beale and his guys were cornered," Reggie said, pointing at the wall directly opposite their corner.

That was Julie's impression as well — the corner in front of her formed two edges of the large open space where the Exos lived.

"Let's go this way," he continued, pointing down his hallway. "There's not really any hard information suggesting it, but it seems like the base was laid out in a left-to-right format, so this way would be heading toward the 'front.'"

At the same instant Reggie finished speaking, Julie heard the distinct sound of another Exo crunching toward them from the other hallway. It had just begun rounding the corner, and she felt the vibrations of each step beneath her feet.

"Also, let's not get in front of that thing," Reggie said.

"Works for me," Ben said.

"Same," Mrs. E said. They set off, walking next to one another, and Ben and Julie followed closely behind.

CHAPTER 52
JULIE

THE HALLWAY they were jogging through was larger, and it was clear to Julie that this was, in fact, the Ravenshadow base's main level. Rooms and side chambers had been cut into the stone tunnel's walls, the entirety of the place sculpted out of the interior of the mountain base. The Ravenshadow men and their contractors had likely only done a few things: added electricity and water access from the mountain's spring, set up the furniture, cut the stairwells and mounted the doors.

Everything else seemed original. Julie saw that these walls, while not as smooth and well-formed as the smaller tunnel shaft they'd found earlier, had been cut by hand, with the precision and care of a master craftsman.

While Garza's soldiers were quite good at what they did, she knew none of them would have had the training or patience to pull off a feat like this. To completely cut out the interior of a mountain and convert it into a working and livable city was beyond even what Vicente Garza could do.

"It's incredible," she whispered to herself. Ever since they'd agreed that this place had to be the original home of the Chachapoyas, descended from the ancient antediluvian Atlanteans, the signs began appearing in front of her, as if her subconscious had finally registered them. The walls, smoothly cut, met the ceilings and floors with a beveled edge. The hallways seemed to be of the same dimensions as those they'd found in Egypt, and the individual chambers and rooms the same style as those they'd seen beneath the Sphinx at Giza.

It was, without a doubt, a structure related to the lost Atlantean race. But did that mean Garza had found the Hall of Records? Had he cleared it out? Sold it off?

It was impossible to tell without knowing exactly where the actual Hall of Records was — and unfortunately they had more pressing matters at hand, like getting out of the place alive. If they could, they'd find Victoria and her father, but Julie was beginning to think those goals would have to be tossed aside.

They'd walked into a trap, and they'd nearly been killed because of it. Had Beale's team not betrayed them and left them for dead, they would actually *be* dead.

Reggie held up a hand, and Julie and the others halted. They'd reached the opposite end of the hallway, and Reggie was about to turn left when he stopped.

"Got a few Ravenshadow boys," he whispered.

"Can we take them?" Ben asked.

"Sure," Reggie said. "Four on three. But it's the two Exos behind them I'm a little worried about."

Julie didn't need to see them for herself. As soon as Reggie said the words she began to hear the telltale high-pitched noise of the Exos. She immediately turned around and glanced the other direction. "The one that was coming from the other way is also still behind us. I can hear it, and it's getting louder."

"We're going to be sandwiched in between them," Reggie said. "And that's not a fight I want to be a part of."

"There was a door about halfway back," Julie said. "A big one.

All the other doors have been unlocked, so maybe this one is, too. But —"

"Let's roll," Reggie said, cutting her off.

She was about to argue but decided against it. *Better than fighting three of them on two fronts.*

Maybe.

Reggie led the way once again, and she found herself running behind the massive man, inadvertently ducking behind his tall frame. She knew it would do no good if the Exo rounded the hallway before they could get inside. The machine's shoulder-mounted machine gun would slice Reggie to ribbons — and she would face the same fate about three milliseconds after.

Reggie reached the door just as the Exo turned the corner. It began firing before it had even finished turning, and Julie felt the impacts of the slugs smacking into the ancient walls on the opposite side of the hallway. She ducked, as did Ben and Mrs. E.

When she looked up again she was facing the opposite direction, and she now saw the other two Exos and their Ravenshadow escorts at the other end of the hallway. They were raising their weapons to fire, and she closed her eyes, waiting for the first rounds to hit.

"Julie, move!"

Ben's voice pierced through her mind, and she bolted into action once again. She grabbed at her rifle, pulling it up and preparing to aim...

"Julie, *go!*" She met eyes with Ben, just as the first shots from the other two Exos and the soldiers hit. They peppered the wall above her head.

Not enough time.

She realized what Ben was telling her. *Get away from here. Not enough time to fight back.*

They needed to get inside.

The soldiers pressed forward, perfectly syncing their attacks and reloading so there was a constant barrage of fire. The Exos fought similarly, their turret guns blasting away pieces of stone and wall, obliterating it into sand that blistered Julie's exposed skin.

It would be only another second and...

The soldiers had stopped moving. They were still firing, but they were still *missing*.

She crawled on her hands and knees the rest of the way. Not enough time to focus on the Ravenshadow men and their machine suits.

The door she'd noticed was recessed about six inches into the wall. Not enough to completely conceal them, but enough that she felt a bit more safe than she did waiting in the center of the hallway.

The Exo standing alone on its side of the hallway was firing at full speed now, and the noise was deafening. It was still hitting the wall directly opposite the CSO team, and it didn't seem to be working to readjust its aim.

Ben pushed past her, and Mrs. E fell in line behind him. Reggie was moving to push the door open.

The firing stopped abruptly, but she turned and sprang through the open door anyway, entering the dark, open chamber. She immediately knew she was in a much larger space, as her palms smacked against the stone floor and echoed throughout the pitch-black space.

She stood, sensing the others standing around her. Reggie was last through the door, moving his mouth as if trying to pop his ears.

"Damn that was *loud*," he said.

"Reggie," Julie said. "They weren't shooting at us."

'Like hell they weren't!" Reggie said, nearly yelling. "They almost got us, and if those Exos were any closer —"

"She's right," Ben said. "They weren't firing *at* us. They were *corralling* us."

"They were what?"

"They were herding us, like cattle."

The look on Reggie's face said more than he could have with words. Julie knew the truth, and now he did, too.

She'd been hesitant to enter this room, because she knew what it was.

They all knew what it was.

In an instant the lights flicked on. Julie's eyes were stunned, but quickly recovered. Her worst fears were realized.

In front of her stood stacks of wooden crates and boxes, and just beyond that she saw the headless tops of rows of Exosuits, standing at attention. There were a few rows missing, and the Exos in the row that stood just beyond were empty, their human operators nowhere to be found.

"Oh, shit," Reggie said.

"Yeah," Ben said. "I was going to say that."

Julie heard a popping sound, like a cork being ejected from a bottle of champagne, and then she heard the rising, high-pitched sound hitting her ears. This time it wasn't in the distance. This time it hit her, hard, as if it were a wave of water, slamming into her and the team in full-force.

They were on the demonstration floor, and Julie had a feeling there was about to be another demonstration.

CHAPTER 53

BEN

THE DOOR behind them slammed shut, and immediately the sounds of gunfire from the three Exos and the three soldiers ceased.

Ben's eyes watered as he stood on the cold stone demonstration floor, likely a reaction to the sudden change in pressure from entering the massive warehouse-like space. His clothes were dry now, but he thought he could still feel the river, the dampness of the water dripping off his skin. It was a combination of sweat and humidity, the leftover clamminess of having been sopping wet only an hour before.

He shifted on his feet, looking around. It was the demonstration floor, the place he'd seen from the upstairs observation room. He knew this was where the Ranger force had been cut down, and he knew this was going to be the endgame for his team, as well.

They had been corralled in here, cows led to slaughter.

Ben felt the humidity rise in the room once again, as if someone were ratcheting up the level by blasting water vapor inside. It was a strange sensation — the rest of the mountain base had been bone-dry, save for the small connecting tunnel they'd been in after exiting the drainage water chute.

He sniffed, trying to place what it was that was different about this room.

"Ben," Reggie whispered. "Over here."

Ben flicked his eyes over to where his friend was standing behind a stack of wooden crates. The boxes stretched nearly halfway to the ceiling, which was far enough above their heads in the darkened space that Ben could hardly see it.

"What is it?" he asked.

"We're..." Reggie's voice trailed off.

Ben walked over to where he was standing and noticed Julie and Mrs. E cowering behind another stack of crates near Reggie.

"We're right where they were," Julie said softly.

Ben suddenly refocused, as if his mind had been blocking out the reality of their situation. He looked down at the floor, near where he had been standing. A pair of legs stretched out from behind a crate, lifeless and set atop a pool of dark liquid.

About twenty feet away he saw the head and arms of another soldier, but couldn't see his face enough to know who it was, as it was contorted and veiled behind a shiny black substance. Perhaps Lang. He leaned out a bit and saw that his head and arms connected to his torso, but that torso was connected to... nothing.

The man had been chewed in half by the gunfire from the Exo.

The single *Exo that had been activated.*

Ben wiped some sweat from his brow, then turned to the others. "Keep your voices down. We're almost definitely being monitored. This is some sort of game to Garza."

"Doesn't seem that fun," Reggie shot back.

"He wants to test these things. The Exos. They're what Beale's team came here for. What their boss, Sturdivant, wants to get his hands on."

"Well I'm sure he'll be happy to know that they work *just fine*, in that case," Reggie said.

"Not yet," Julie said, staring at the massacred bodies lying in disarray around them. "They're too noisy. That high-pitched screeching sound we keep hearing before the Exos arrive."

"Yeah, true," Ben said. "Maybe that's why Garza hasn't sold them to the highest bidder yet. And why Sturdivant was getting antsy."

"Well, that's all nice to know," Reggie said. "But how do we get out of this little 'demonstration?'"

Ben looked around. "I have no idea. But they absolutely funneled us in here. Garza has been playing with us this whole time. Toying, guiding us here. You all saw those things. Any *single* one of them could have cut us in half." He immediately regretted his choice of words as he took another look at Lang. *Doesn't make it untrue,* he thought. "Why not kill us before? When we were holed up in that room?"

"Because he needs us for a demonstration."

"But *why*?" Julie said. "We've already seen that they work. Garza knows that. Why bother with us, specifically? If we're just food for his meat grinder, why waste all this time and energy getting us down here again?"

Ben heard a cough. All four of the team members crouched behind the nearest crate they could find. Ben stepped out slowly, moving in the direction of the cough with his gun drawn.

He considered whispering, asking the person to name themselves, but decided against it. Whoever they were, they already knew Ben and the others were there. They'd coughed, which wasn't exactly the stealthiest sound to make.

He rounded a corner behind another crate and looked down just as the person coughed again. The man's lung expunged a horrific gurgling sound, then a wheezing, then drew a nearly silent, sharp breath.

"Jeffers," Ben whispered. He knelt down. "Are you —"

He stopped himself before finishing the question. This man was clearly dying, and it was a miracle he hadn't already perished. There was a hole in his neck, toward the side but close enough to the center that Ben wondered how it hadn't severed his carotid artery. Another hole, probably one that went completely through him, was in the center of Jeffers' stomach. He had his huge hands covering the hole, but blood was easily seeping up around his fingers. The man's black hands had been turned a darker shade, the liquid only showing maroon when it interacted with the dim, glinting light.

"Hey, hey," Ben said, placing his hand on the man's shoulder. "Don't move, don't talk. It's okay. We're —"

What? Going to get you out of here? Save your life? Ben pondered how to end the question, then spoke again. "We're stuck in here, too."

More accurate.

Jeffers tried to force a grin, but instead coughed again. Blood splattered outward all the way across the space to another nearby crate. The others joined Ben, and they crouched around Jeffers on all sides. Mrs. E began checking the man's legs for more wounds but stopped when Reggie placed a hand on her arm. He shook his head, ever so slightly.

Jeffers' mouth cracked open a bit and a single word spilled out. "St — Sturdi..."

"Sturdivant," Ben said. "Your boss, right?"

Jeffers nodded.

"He wants to know what Garza's been working on? The Exos?"

Again, a nod.

"He's going to buy them?"

Jeffers paused, then shook his head. "No."

Ben and Julie frowned. Reggie stared down at the man who had been on their side, then on the team that had betrayed them. Ben wondered what he was thinking. Reggie had served in the same military as this man, had gone through the same Ranger training. He'd come out a much different soldier than Jeffers. Much different loyalties.

"Sturdivant doesn't want to buy these things?"

"No," Jeffers said again. He grunted. "Different buyer."

"What does Sturdivant want? Why did he send you here?"

Jeffers shook his head again, just a bit. "Too... late."

"Help us, Jeffers," Ben said. He wanted to add, *because you're going to die here no matter what.* He didn't. "Help us figure out what your boss wants so we can end this."

Again. "Too late."

"*What's* too late?" Reggie asked.

"Everything... all too late. He — he'll bring it all down. On top of us."

Ben's blood ran cold. *He'll bring it all down on top of us? What the hell does that even mean?* "Are you saying... Sturdivant doesn't care anymore? That all this — all of these *things* — are not his concern?"

"Exactly," Jeffers said. "Exactly. ...no longer... concern."

"Why? How?" Ben knew they were all struggling to understand. To make sense of it. To figure out why Sturdivant sent in an elite team of soldiers to check in on an investment, then —

"It's a failsafe," Reggie said.

"A what?"

Jeffers nodded, once, small enough that Ben nearly missed it.

"A failsafe. A dead-man's switch. When the mission failed, Beale signaled Strudivant somehow. RF that got out to a relay, maybe, then shot a 'fail' message up to a satellite."

"So there was something connected to Beale's pulse that was blocking that signal?" Julie asked. "And when he died, the pulse stopped, so the signal got through?"

"That's how they do it in movies, sure," Reggie said. But things are much simpler than that. This was a team, not just one guy. So..." Reggie reached forward and grabbed Jeffers' wrist, pulling it sideways and then rotating it.

The man's hand fell from his stomach, releasing a sticky river of blood. Reggie placed his hand back on the wound but rubbed his shirt against Jeffers' watch. Ben leaned in.

Numbers flashed on the watch face.

Counting down.

Ben saw four sections of two numerals, each separated by a colon. *Hours, minutes, seconds, milliseconds.* A typical clock display.

The numbers at the far left were zeroes.

47 minutes, thirty-nine seconds.

"It's a countdown," Reggie said. "That's the failsafe. Jeffers — or any one of them, before they died — sent the 'fail' signal when they got cut down. If it got out, and Sturdivant received it, he'll know his team is eliminated."

"Can we send a message that says 'never mind… false alarm?" Ben asked, already knowing the answer.

Reggie shook his head. "No. These guys weren't Rangers. Or at least not *just* Rangers. Their plane, their whole MO, everything. They were an elite force, likely one that's been working together *since* their Ranger days. Sturdivant probably bought them wholesale, reassigning them to a classified sector that he could shuffle away with enough paperwork."

Ben shook his head. "So what does that mean?"

"Exactly what he said," Reggie responded, looking Ben in the eyes. "Sturdivant's team is gone. His mission failed. He's got only one option left, and he's absolutely going to use it."

Ben looked up, then at Mrs. E, who was staring straight down at Jeffers. She was the first one to speak. "He is going to bring it all down on top of us."

CHAPTER 54
JULIE

THE COUNTDOWN ON JEFFERS' watch pulsed in Julie's vision. It was all she could see. Her peripheral vision had died away, and she couldn't avert her eyes.

Forty-seven minutes, she thought. *Until everything literally comes crashing down.*

She watched Reggie removed the watch from Jeffers' wrist and place it on his own, just above Reggie's diver's watch.

"What now, boss?" Reggie asked. His voice was calm, steady, and hinted at humor, as if they weren't just standing in the middle of a death-filled warehouse at the heart of an enemy base. "We've got just over 47 minutes to figure out what to do — I suggest we get started?"

"It's not the Exos," Ben said.

Julie looked at her husband. "What?"

"Jeffers said that. Sturdivant didn't send them here to check in on the status of the exoskeleton suits, remember?"

Jeffers coughed gently, but didn't respond. Julie knew he was fading away. She'd seen enough death to know that there was no coming back from an injury like this one. She was amazed at Jeffers' ability to hang on. He was a massive man in perfect shape, but even he wasn't going to live through this one. She felt a pang of regret as she looked down at him.

He was a good man, no matter what team he'd been on. Julie felt she had a decent comprehension of character, and she'd pegged Jeffers as one of the good ones.

We're all just trying to do what's right, she told herself. *We're all just trying to survive.*

"So what does he want?" Mrs. E asked. Her words were stilted, a slight hint of the Russian accent slipping back into her voice. Julie knew the woman was stressed, rattled. Mrs. E would keep her cool, but their nerves were all starting to falter.

"I don't know," Ben said. "But it's the missing piece. We figure that out, we —"

His voice was interrupted by the high-pitched whine, a gentle tone at first, then growing harsher in her ears as it rose in volume.

"Shit!" Reggie said. "They're waking up!"

Julie spun around to face the machine monsters on the demonstration floor. She couldn't help but notice the crate she was hiding behind at the moment had a few holes in it. *All the way* through it. Her hiding spot was no more than that — it wouldn't offer her any protection whatsoever.

She swallowed a lump in her throat and felt her body beginning to melt into an automatic mode of adrenaline and dopamine. She reached for her weapon, pulled it up and around, and aimed at...

The suits in the first row were empty. She hadn't noticed it before, but the people who she'd seen inside the Exos from upstairs were not in these suits. There was a whole row of them that stood on the floor, empty, waiting.

"They're... empty," she said.

"And they're not moving," Reggie added. "That means they're coming from behind us! Everyone get your weapons up on the doors — get ready!"

A voice interrupted their preparations.

"Hello again, CSO team."

The high-pitched whine rose to a higher volume level.

Julie felt her mind seized, her thoughts halted, her throat constricting. It was as if she had been bolted to place on the demonstration floor, suddenly shocked into a stunned inability to move.

She tried forcing her foot forward. It worked, but not well. Her foot came up a few inches, halted, then slammed itself back down. It landed only a few millimeters in front of where it had been before. The exertion needed to pull it off was incredible, and she felt herself involuntarily taking a deep breath.

The rest of her team stood stock-still as well, locked in place by the invisible force. It gripped them, had taken them all at precisely the same time. None were moving, and even Ben's eyes — the only of them facing her — were staring straight back at her unflinchingly.

What the hell is happening?

Her ability to think came back. Her body was still affixed in place, but her brain began churning into overdrive, calculating where she was and what had happened and how it could help get her out and —

Memories.

Her brain had also drudged up memories, as if it were a supercomputer riffing through millions of files all at once to find the one that might serve as a reminder as to what was happening here.

Specifically it found *one* memory, one she hadn't realized she still had. She knew exactly where she was, what she was doing.

Holding a pistol.

Aiming the pistol.

Her mind recalled the events leading up that from the perspective of an unreliable narrator. She couldn't be entirely sure the events were correct, but there was one — right at the beginning of the memory — that she understood.

Her body was fixed in place, unmoving. Couldn't move it, and she tried.

She remembered how she'd gotten to the point of holding the gun. Aiming it at her friend's head.

The injection. The thing he stuck you with. The thing Garza stuck you with.

The chemical.

She was paralyzed, just as she'd been in Philadelphia, in Raven-shadow's gym. Couldn't move, couldn't react, couldn't do anything but stare straight ahead. Her mind was racing, but it was unable to come up with a solution.

The good news was that it was also unable to panic. She stared straight ahead, thinking quickly but moving slower than she ever had. She tried again, this time moving a hand, but a thousand pinpricks of paralysis stifled her. It felt like her arm had fallen asleep, but over her entire body. A painful situation when she tried to move, a more bearable one if she stayed as still as possible.

He did it again was her next thought. *He somehow injected us with —*

No.

Not an injection.

Julie thought hard, tried to understand what had happened. She would have known it if they'd been injected with something. It had to be enough of the chemical compound that it would render their entire bodies useless, but one of them would have noticed long before.

"If you're wondering," the voice said again, the voice of Garza, piped in from high above through invisible speakers. *"It was in the air. It's like a gas chamber. Easy enough to maintain, and we can focus the vapor toward the bottom of the room, preserving the strength of the chemical."*

Of course, she thought. As soon as they'd entered the demonstration room — been *led into* the demonstration room — she'd felt a slight change in the air. More humid, a little cooler, as if they were walking through a light cloud.

She hadn't thought much about it, but the others had noticed it, too. Ben's brow had been covered with droplets of moisture, and Mrs. E had been constantly rubbing her palms against her pant legs.

It was humidity, she realized. *It wasn't* water *vapor.* Garza had injected her in Philadelphia with some chemical compound, one based on the drug scopolamine, and he'd figured out how to release it through an airborne vehicle.

A much cleaner, more efficient method, to be sure.

And a way to get the chemical into *a lot* of people at the same time.

Her mind wandered to the people inside the Exos. They weren't Ravenshadow men.

The village.

There had been a mysterious disappearance of the inhabitants of a nearby village. Every man, woman, and child had simply vanished.

She knew what had happened. As if a lightbulb had flicked on, she had the answers they'd been wondering about.

Garza hadn't *needed* to put his own soldiers in the suits. He hadn't needed to train them to control the Exos at all.

He had found an entirely different workforce, and it was one he no longer had to train.

"I hope you are excited about the next demonstration," Garza continued. *"I, for one, cannot wait. This technology has taken me countless hours of experimentation, and a lot of money. But I have to tell you — without you all, this never would have been possible. Juliette, your help in Philadelphia directly led to this demonstration. This final demonstration."*

Julie wanted to scream, to cry, to run, to do *anything at all*. Instead, she stood riveted to the floor, forced to do nothing but listen to Garza's words and the oddly soothing sound of the high-pitched whining noise.

"Now, let's begin. CSO team, please turn and face the center of the room."

Julie felt her legs moving, her feet shifting. In a few seconds, she was facing the middle of the room, the rows of Exos staring blankly and lifelessly back at her.

"Very good. Now, CSO team, please walk toward the first row of Exos."

Julie did as she was told.

"Please step around to the back of the nearest Exo you find and pull the large blue handle. The battery hatch will swing open, revealing a small ladder."

Julie's arms began working, her hands immediately finding the hatch lever and pulling it up. The interior of the Exo was larger than she'd expected, and she saw a few buttons and display screens at chest-level on the front-end of the suit.

"Finally, CSO team, will you please climb the ladder and enter the suit. The hatch will close behind you automatically.

"Oh, and get comfortable — this will be the last place you'll ever see."

PART FOUR
ACT 4

CHAPTER 55
EDMUND

I DO HOPE *this all ends soon,* Edmund thought. He was in the backseat of a car heading out of town. An "Uber," the concierge had called it. A strange name for a taxicab service, but Father Canisius was not about to complain when the concierge had offered to set it all up. She'd even offered to pay for it and put the amount on his hotel tab.

He had gotten into the Uber and given the location to the driver, and then settled into the backseat, a weight lifted off his shoulders. *I am here because God wills it,* he told himself. *Have a little faith, Edmund. You are the right man for this job.*

It didn't matter that he didn't know what that job was — it didn't matter that he was confused, frustrated, tired. It didn't matter that this newcomer, Archibald Quinones, seemed to know more about the whole thing than he. None of that mattered. *What little trial to go through compared to that of Job.*

This was nothing. He could handle it.

Best of all, he had a feeling he was about to get answers. St. Clair had sounded a bit surprised as well when he'd spoken with her on the phone. He assumed that receiving the email from the broker, whoever they were, had been as unexpected to her as it had been to him. She, being the utmost professional, had barely shown whatever surprise she had experienced.

Archie's call had been more troubling. Here was a third group — or fourth, or fifth, he wasn't even able to keep track — interested in the deal he was currently in the middle of. Archie had known it was Orland Group, and he had known that the assets being transferred were some sort of defense technology.

It was strange, the Catholic Church involved in the brokering of a deal for arms and munitions, if that's what it was. But Canisius didn't know — for all he knew of technology, it could be a simple computer system.

That's it, he thought. *It must be.* Archie and his CSO team had been involved in the break-in at the Vatican, which had led to a complete overhaul of personnel and systems training for the security staff. *Orland Group* must be selling us a new computer system, one that will help with this sort of thing in the future.

It was a harmless purchase, but having the key players' identities public knowledge would be off-putting at best, and harmful to his organization at worst. The Pope would be under massive scrutiny — purchasing defense systems from a defense conglomerate? The questions would be never-ending, and the cost to hold the press at bay would be mountainous.

Still, there would be talk. Rumors would abound, and they would be especially difficult to deny considering they would be based in truth.

That must be it. They needed Canisius because he was about as removed from anything related to organizational computer systems and defense security as anyone, yet he was high enough in the organization that his seal of approval would be taken at value.

He had figured it out. Satisfied, he allowed his thoughts to drift a bit, even allowed himself to relax in the car.

He leaned back in the seat, feeling exhaustion and surprise and excitement all at once, hoping again that this would be over soon. He dreamt of his own bed in the Vatican, in his home. He closed his eyes. How far he'd come, touring the countries of South America as a young priest, working his way up the ladder of the Catholic Church, until God had called him to Rome.

This place, once much closer to his home, no longer felt familiar. He had grown accustomed to the crowds of Rome, the streets and avenues of Italy, the bustling life of Rome. He had grown apart from this place, and he was surprised he didn't miss it much.

He had fallen asleep apparently, as a bit later the driver slowed to a stop and turned around in the seat, speaking to him in soothing tones in rapid-fire Spanish.

"Sir," he said. "We are here. We have arrived."

Edmund looked around. *Where are we?* He hadn't bothered to check the location on a map program when he was at the computer, and he didn't have a phone to double-check now.

Turning around fully, he saw through the windows that they were in a thick forest, dark shades of greens and browns all around. It looked like the Amazon — a far cry from where they had been in the city. Stones and boulders had been scattered to the sides to clear the unpaved road, and up in front of the driver that road had widened into a parking lot-sized open area.

Just beyond that, behind a massive concrete wall that had to be nearly fifty feet tall, stretched an even more massive structure, this one not manmade.

They were at the base of a mountain, one that seemed to rise straight up on all sides, a spire guarding the surrounding area. A watchtower, overlooking the entire country.

Canisius frowned and asked in Spanish where they were.

"The mountain," the driver said, shrugging. He lifted a piece of paper — the same one Edmund had given him upon entering the vehicle. "You have given me this location, and the concierge at the hotel has as well."

Edmund saw two men jogging toward the car, both carrying rifles in their hands.

Edmund looked back at the driver. "No," he said, swallowing, "it seems that this is the correct location. Thank you."

He reached into a pocket for his wallet, but saw that the driver was clicking and swiping at something on his phone's screen, and then he saw the total amount, and a "paid" sticker digitally super-imposed.

Technology, he thought. *How far we've come.* He smiled inwardly. *How far* everyone else *has come.* He knew he hadn't advanced beyond being able to check email, as long as it was on a computer that had a large, obvious icon on the desktop he couldn't double-click.

The two men, wearing black body armor over black pants and boots, reached the car. One on each side, immediately stepping to the back doors. Both were opened simultaneously, and Edmund pulled himself out.

The man on his side of the vehicle reached a hand out and held onto Edmund's arm. His grip was tight, unmoving, and Edmund saw that the man was very young — possibly in his early twenties.

"My name is Quinones," the kid said. "Welcome to Raven-shadow. Please, this way. Our director is waiting."

CHAPTER 56

BEN

BEN COULDN'T BELIEVE what had happened. How they had been led into the demonstration room, given a minute to allow the chemical to enter their systems and completely envelope them, then activated.

Coming here, they had planned for a fight — a traditional exchange of gunfire — and had prepared for a tough slog, an uphill battle. They hadn't expected an army of Ravenshadow men *and* an army of mech suit walking tanks.

But they *really* hadn't expected to go down without a fight altogether. To be simply "activated" and told what to do by a distant operator. To be funneled into the very suits they had been so mystified by upon seeing them.

Unfortunately it had all become clear to Ben *after* he'd been locked into place on the demonstration room floor. It had all come crashing down on him as Garza spoke. The missing villagers. The empty row of Exos. The battle in the hallway, where the Exos and the Ravenshadow men had been *purposefully* missing them, instead forcing them into this room.

And the chemical. Sturdivant hadn't wanted the *suits*. It was very likely he didn't even *know* about them. The military leader had wanted to check in on Garza's progress with the *chemical*. The scopolamine-like compound that Garza had first used in Philadelphia. The compound that was based on a plant *native to Peru*.

He'd fled the United States to flee men like Sturdivant, men who wanted to profit from Garza's tech. In the United States Garza would have had a tough legal battle wresting control of his invention from the hands of the government suits, but not here. In Peru he had nearly unlimited access to both the resources — unassuming villagers, the borrachero plant, cheap unused land — *and* a government that could be easily bought.

Sturdivant had known enough about the chemical and Garza's goals that he had gotten jealous, had wanted to keep Garza under his thumb. Ben knew men like him, and he also knew that men like Sturdivant were likely the reason men like Garza weren't allowed to roam free.

It was a battle between the greater of two evils, and so far Garza had won.

Ben half-stood, half-sat in the center of his Exo suit, analyzing and thinking and trying in vain to get his limbs to move. The sound of the high-pitched note seemed less harsh now, likely an effect of the chemical's dulling of Ben's senses. But he felt sharp, as if he *thought* he could react as quickly as normal, but *couldn't* when actually trying.

It was similar to having had too much alcohol. He felt as though his thoughts and expressions weren't inhibited, yet his voice and movements simply didn't work. It was like being drunk without the headache and without any of the outward signals.

In a word, it was incredible. Ben wasn't pleased to be on this side of the testing wall, but he had to admit that Garza was sitting on a goldmine. Selling this tech would ensure Garza an unlimited supply of Ravenshadow troops, likely a lifetime cashflow as well. There wasn't a government on the planet that wouldn't give their entire GDP forever to get their hands on it.

Why convince citizens to keep in line when you can simply *drug* them into obedience?

So that was the endgame, but who, realistically, would be the buyer? Ben wanted to know everything, but first he needed to figure out how to live through whatever was about to happen.

And, of course, he needed to figure it out in less than forty-five minutes.

Garza's voice tore through the air. *"CSO team, please activate your Exo by pressing the red button near your right hand."*

Ben did, and the Exo hummed to life. The legs of the machine stiffened, Ben's own legs pressed a bit tighter by the kevlar padding in the interior of the suit. The arms, where they connected to the torso of the suit, rotated and came to a ready position slightly bent at the elbows, the "hands" resting just a bit in front of the shoulder.

Ben also noticed that the high-pitched sound wasn't the sound of the Exo after all. The machine had been completely lifeless, dead to the world save for the locking mechanism that had automatically activated after he'd entered.

That meant the sound was coming from somewhere else.

Then Ben heard it. There were small speakers inside the suit to his right and left, and when he'd activated it they had turned on as well, and the sound — the whine that he'd been hearing — emanated even more loudly through those speakers.

So it was *coming from the suit.* He couldn't frown, as that was a physical exertion he had no control over, but in his mind he tried piecing it together. The team had heard the Exos coming before they could see them, which implied that the piercing high-pitch was indeed emanating from the suits, but these suits had been deactivated *before* Ben and the others had entered, and the noise had clearly still been audible.

Did that mean there were a lot more of the Exos, still activated, nearby?

No. Ben knew the shrill pitch had been coming from some larger source, similar to the source Garza's own voice had come from.

He's piping it in, Ben realized. The sound they had all been hearing — the one they'd associated with the Exos — had also been amplified and played through the main speakers of the demonstration room.

Before *we got into the suits,* Ben thought. *That means the sound actually helped* activate *the suits.*

It didn't make sense. The Exos were powered by sound? Why would Garza go through the trouble of building speakers into each of the suits that, when powered on, re-amplified and broadcast the same high-pitched signal if it *didn't* have something to do with the Exos?

"Thank you, CSO team. Now, please turn and walk toward opposite corners of the room."

Ben found himself complying before he even realized he was. He turned in the Exo suit, finding it rather simple to control — two joystick-like handles controlled the direction and speed, while tensing the muscles in his thighs pressed against the kevlar-covered legs of the suit, which helped with nuance and maneuverability. It was intuitive — like playing a modern first-person-shooter video game. No matter what the game was, the controls were generally the same: the triggers would fire or launch certain weapons, the joystick knobs would move and turn the player.

The combination of the drug, the intuitiveness of the controls, the suit's own capability and maneuverability — it all clicked into place when Ben moved. He understood what was happening.

Garza's project wasn't the *suits* — the Exos. It wasn't the incredible drug that somehow took away all the voluntary functions and disallowed physical movement in its hosts.

It was *both.*

It was the *combination* of the two. The ultimate in military weaponry; the most advanced weapon ever created: not a human, not a machine, but a bit of both.

And best of all, it was completely and utterly *controllable*. A commander at the helm of an army of Exos and their occupants would be the commander of a real-life version of a top-down tactical real-time strategy game. They could literally speak their orders into a microphone and their will would be drawn out on the battlefield. The soldiers themselves — the human factor — would be diminished to the role of driver.

Any fear, trepidation, or hesitation would be nonexistent. No disobedience. No undermining or questioning of authority.

A perfect workforce. A perfect army.

Ben knew there were downsides, of course — humans were still an integral part of any modern-day army because armies needed to adapt on the fly, to be able to maintain some sort of individuality. But the upsides were huge — a force of walking tanks, maneuverable and responsive, would be a deciding factor in just about any battle.

And he had a feeling he was going to be testing that very premise.

"Thank you, team. Now that the four of you are in one of each of the four corners of the room, I would like to call your attention to the other Exos on the demonstration floor."

Ben's eyes flicked up and he did, indeed, see the twenty-odd Exos standing erect, silent, in front of him.

"There are twenty-six more units. Each of them has an operator, and each of them will be activated soon. They are the previous model of Exosuits, which will be replaced by your own. However, the demonstration videos our buyers have requested for these proofs-of-concept unfortunately require us to prove the capability of any and all possible battle scenarios. They have informed us that computer-generated models or enhancements will not suffice, and are willing to pay twice for a new, rebuilt force.

"As such, it is your job, CSO team, to eliminate as many of these enemy operants as possible until you yourselves have been eliminated."

Ben wanted to swallow. To gulp in terror. He could do neither. He could do absolutely nothing but listen to Garza's words. And react to them.

"You may engage."

CHAPTER 57

JULIE

JULIE LISTENED on in abject terror. The whining sound had been replayed through tiny speakers in the interior of the Exosuit, but she could still hear Garza's voice perfectly through the larger speakers situated up near the ceiling.

"You may engage."

She was looking diagonally across the room, standing inside her Exo in what she believed was the southeast corner of the room. Ben was in the southwest, Mrs. E across from her in the northwest, and Reggie and his Exo were to her right in the northeast corner. Directly in front of her stood the remainder of the thirty Exos — the twenty-six suited villagers that had been abducted from their homes and turned into Garza's personal science experiment.

And they were beginning to move.

The Exos in the center of the room turned in a precisely coordinated motion, those closest to Julie rotating around and facing her, the other three quadrants of Exos turning to face Ben, Mrs. E, and Reggie, respectively.

Shit.

Garza had said that his buyer wanted proof that these machines worked — but also video proof that they could fight with *each other.*

It was probably a wise move; if Garza was able to create these monstrosities, surely other governments or private defense contractors were working through the same problems.

A mech-on-mech battle would not only soon be possible, it was almost guaranteed. The buyer was simply covering their bases, doing their due diligence.

And Garza had told them that the twenty-six Exos they were facing were the older model — the ones Julie and the others were in were the newer edition.

Hopefully, she thought, that meant their suits were better soldiers and fighters. Each of the CSO members would be facing nearly seven-to-one odds.

She felt her arms moving naturally over the controls. Her right wrists rotated a bit and the entire top half of the Exo's torso shifted, rotating in kind. Her left wrist flicked back and the shoulder-mounted turret on her right side flew into position.

The Exos staring her down had similar weaponry, but she could see that their turrets were a bit smaller, while the packs on their backs — the batteries, she figured — were larger. That meant they were heavier, and possibly less maneuverable, as well as less powerful.

If only I could figure out how to use that to my advantage. Her hands and arms were reacting as if she still had control over them, but when she tried to remove them from the controls she felt the same prickling paralysis overtake them. It was as though the machine were a part of her, and she was allowed to control it, and only it.

"You have been given a hefty dose of the scopolamine compound my scientists have been working on for over a year," Garza's voice said. It was now coming through only her speakers, and she assumed that meant Garza wanted to talk with only to her and her team, not the other Exos. *"That chemical has been activated, but I've reduced the level of exposure to allow you basic motor functions within the suit."*

Activated? Julie wondered. *I thought the chemical was what caused the paralysis?* How had it been dormant, and then —

She realized what had happened. They had been dosed with Garza's compound as soon as they'd entered the demonstration floor. The airborne chemical had been in the room the whole time, and they'd all been breathing it in, letting it percolate.

Garza was watching us the whole time we were talking to Jeffers, she realized. *Making sure we didn't leave. Making sure we were in there long enough for the chemical to get into our systems.*

And then when he spoke...

The high-pitched whine had been there the whole time, she remembered, but it had *risen* in volume just as Garza had finished talking.

That sound must have somehow activated the chemical. It was a trigger, a sound-based switch that turned on the chemical. She'd heard of a new medical field called non-invasive neuromodulation, where doctors and scientists were working together to use sound waves to control — rather than damage — certain highly focused neurons so that they can't fire. Controlling these brain waves would hypothetically help prevent the pain of migraines and potentially reverse some of the damage caused by Alzheimer's disease or Parkinson's.

Garza must have stumbled onto some sort of balance between the chemical compound they'd ingested *and* the sound waves — that perhaps instead of controlling her brain's neurons, the sound was controlling that chemical instead.

She'd been under the spell of Garza's scopolamine-based treatment once before, but he had needed to inject it directly into her system through a syringe, and then she had been completely unable to move without his coercion. Now, she was moving a bit, able to use her hands and arms at her will, as long as she was still following his general instructions.

It was fascinating — the man must have been able to block the certain area of their brains that connected her freely formed thoughts from acting out physically. Her body was no longer responsive to *her* thoughts, but those of Garza. Her body still required stimulus, voluntary direction, but it was unable to receive it from Julie.

Garza's voice broke through once again. *"You'll notice that the previous generation of Exos are maneuvering toward you. They are programmed with a basic, adolescent-level AI, so a direction like 'engage' means one thing: walk forward until they decide they are within striking distance.*

"Their operators are also on a much higher dosage of the drug, so their response time and reactionary procedures have been greatly diminished. The newer suits you are in not only come with a far more advanced AI, they allow you to guide your Exo through involuntary reactions — in other words, they let you react much more quickly to threats."

As if on cue, the Exo closest to Julie raised its arm and blasted a cannon round toward her.

THE HEAVY SLUG whizzed past the place where her Exo's head would have been — mere inches above her own — and slammed into the stone wall behind her. Chips of rock and dust flew into the back of the Exo's suit, the metallic pinging sound reverberating through the inside.

But before she realized what was happening Julie was in motion. Something deep inside her, on an instinctual level, sprang into action. She — through the Exo suit's heightened response time — jumped sideways and *rolled* toward a group of crates. She hardly felt as though she was upside-down during the roll, and the Exo recovered perfectly, coming to a rest in a crouched position.

Then she lifted the left handle and the Exo fired a return blast from its own arm, striking the lesser Exo directly in the chest. The Exo fell backwards, but it didn't appear to be damaged.

This is absolutely ridiculous, Julie thought. *I'm inside a mech suit fighting with other mechs.*

Fighting for my life.

"Well done, Mrs. Bennett. I knew you would get the hang of it before everyone else. After all, this isn't your first experience with the chemical compound."

Julie felt rage, but it was unable to manifest itself in any way. She simply stared blankly at the opposing Exo, which had now recovered and continued its march toward her.

She saw the eyes of the person inside, deep and blank and staring back at her. She wondered, for a moment, what they were thinking. Garza said they were more affected by the chemical, but she had no idea if that meant their involuntary control and ability to think had been hampered.

But it didn't matter. She could think and wonder all she wanted, but she too was under a spell. She rose, the Exo moving smoothly and effortlessly, and she flicked her wrist up and heard the gentle whirring sound of the turret on her shoulder spinning up. Another flick of her wrist and hundreds of rounds seemed to leave the turret at once.

Each of the rounds was much smaller than the cannon blast she'd fired before, but there were so many more of them that the damage was incredible. A few dozen found the armor plating on the Exo's chest that had been damaged before, and the impacts bore tiny holes through the suit.

Something inside the suit malfunctioned, and Julie saw the operator's eyes seemingly widen and contract again, as if the chemical had accidentally let out a brief moment of surprise. The suit sparked and smoked, and the Exo's left leg collapsed in under itself. That brought its own turret, which had just started firing back at her, around and through the top of the stack of crates Julie's was hiding behind.

It may have been a smaller turret with less power, but the Exo's weapon splintered the crate into a thousand pieces, and sawdust and debris rained down on Julie's exposed head. The Exo continued falling, eventually coming to a stop on its side.

...Just as another Exo pushed forward and its massive flat, diamond-shaped foot crunched down on the Exo and its occupant. The second Exo continued moving as the first lay dying, sparks and smoke billowing out from the compressed hole where the occupant's intact head had previously been.

Julie wanted to react, to wince or cry out in surprise, but instead she calmly rotated and bent her wrists so that her suit was now facing the second intruder. She fired three cannon rounds in as quick succession as the suit would allow, taking down the second Exo with ease.

I'm killing people, she thought. Then, immediately after, *I'm following orders that I can't argue with. Even if I tried.*

"Very good, Julie. It appears as though you all *are capable of piloting these machines. Reggie is onto his third Exo, and Mrs. E and Ben have also taken down one each."*

Julie tried to move her Exo to see the others but she had inadvertently pinned herself down between two stacks of crates and the southern wall. She couldn't see any of the rest of her team, but she heard the destruction and chaos from each of the three other corners.

She hoped they were faring well, but again she was unable to act on any other instinct than to protect herself and her Exo.

She rotated her torso to face the next two attackers, coming from a bit off-center on her left and right side. She wanted to try neutralizing the threats simultaneously, to see if she could target one with her cannon and the other with her turret.

A fast calculation and a flick of her wrists later, meanwhile stressing and applying pressure to the legs of the Exosuit from inside, and she had her answer.

The two Exos fell into a heap, adding more carnage to the wreckage that lay in front of her.

"Very impressive, Mrs. Bennett," Garza's voice said. *"But you've been facing one and two Exos at once. Let's make this a bit more fun, shall we?*

His voice came back over the main speakers in the demonstration floor. *"All remaining Exos, please converge on your targets at once. Spare no ammunition."*

THE LOOK OF DISMAY, of utter failure, on the man's face told Vicente Garza everything he needed to know. *I've already won,* he thought. *And I haven't even played my trump card.*

The man looked visibly sick. His face had paled upon entering the observation room, upon seeing beyond Garza into the massive, dimly lit demonstration floor. Upon seeing the Exos.

The stunned Father Edmund Canisius, flanked by two Ravenshadow soldiers, stood in awed silence after entering the room. Garza had given the command for the Exos to engage in their bloody display, all while being video recorded and observed by the seven men in the observation room.

Garza had allowed Canisius to simply watch on, to let him consider the repercussions of what he was seeing, to consider *why* Garza had invited him here.

Forced him here was probably a more accurate statement.

Garza sipped his coffee, watching in admiration as his creations battled each other. It was a shame to lose so many fully working prototypes, even if they were first- and second-generation. His first generation of Exos was nearly twice as advanced as the next closest thing that had been produced in the world defense community.

His second generation suits, the one the CSO team was wearing, was close to ten times more advanced. Faster, lighter, more powerful, better equipped — just about every metric that would matter to the end user had been drastically improved. The sum total of the advancements made his second generation Exos the closest thing to a one-man army the world had ever seen.

And his team was already drafting plans for the third generation. They had worked to reduce the battery load, using more air intake modules around the suit to cool it, and they had been working with graphite sections that would make the suit much stronger and lighter — and therefore faster.

He wanted the third generation Exo to be able to run, duck, and crawl, just like a human soldier. The AI would be the same, but if the advancements he expected were on track, by the time he had a fourth- and fifth-generation model, the suit would be able to not only react to the operator's instructions within a split-second, it would be able to *anticipate* their instructions.

He wanted a suit that linked operator and machine as if it were one organism. He knew they were close already, but there were still problems with preventing the user from having access to their own voluntary functions. He wanted a true symbiotic relationship — an exoskeleton enclosure that not only worked with its operator, but *thrived* with it.

Garza couldn't help but smile. Everything was coming together. Everything was moving forward exactly as planned, with the exception of Beale's Green Beret force's intrusion.

But they had been handled, and he hadn't even wasted a single suit or operator on the job.

The CSO team had snuck in with them, faring slightly better than the Green Berets, but as Garza could now see, their eventual fate would be no different than Beale's.

A fitting end for such a strong-willed team. Fighting as a team. Dying as a team. All in the name of scientific advancement.

He wished he could have faced Harvey Bennett and his new wife Juliette once more, but he wasn't the type of man to take needless chances. He had needed to record a video for his buyer, a final documentation of proof that he had what he said he had.

What better way to do that than to use the CSO crew as the operators in his latest generation of tech? What better way to prove to his buyer that their expectations would be met and exceeded?

"Wh — what are we watching?"

Garza turned and faced Canisius, taking another sip of coffee before responding. "This, Father, is what your organization is purchasing."

"There is *no way* the Catholic Church or the Vatican has *any need* for something... of... such —"

"Such *what?*" Garza asked. "Destruction? Such overwhelming *power?*"

Canisius swallowed, then looked side to side. There were two chairs nearby, but the soldiers standing just inches away from him tightened up. *Good,* Garza thought. *If you sit down, you may miss something.*

"This is irresponsible. It's *sinful.* So much unnecessary killing has already plagued this world, and —"

"*And* how much of that killing has been done at the hands of the Church? How much of that killing has been *perpetuated* by the Church? By *your* church, Father Canisius."

There was a flash of rage on Canisius' face, but the man swallowed it back, staring defiantly at Garza.

"I urge you to look, to see what your organization has purchased, Father. This display is being recorded, of course, but —"

"My organization has *nothing* to do with this."

"Ah, that is where you are wrong."

"They would *never* purchase something like this. No matter the potential benefits they may have been sold. These are *death machines,* and... *what?* You expect me to believe that they want *machines?* For what? To replace the guardsmen? To stand at the foot of the Basilica?"

Garza smiled. *Good. Get more worked up. Begin to* feel *it again, Father. Just like I've felt it.*

"No," Garza said. "No, not at all." He laughed. "I see the confusion. Of course. I haven't been entirely forthcoming with you. I apologize."

He snapped his fingers, and one of the seated Ravenshadow men stood and nodded.

"Get Victoria," he said. The man immediately turned and left the room.

CHAPTER 60

BEN

BEN HEARD Garza's voice as he maneuvered his own Exo around in the corner of the room. He was amazed at how easy his suit was to control, but he knew Garza was capable of such miraculous feats — there was nothing technologically possible that was out of reach to the man. He had unlimited funding, and it was clear why: he had been able to produce something no other government or corporation could. The Exos weren't perfect, but they were as close as anything that had come to market. He knew that was why the buyer wanted them — they were close to perfect. Ravenshadow had figured out that it wasn't just a well-trained soldier *or* a fancy, technologically advanced exoskeleton suit that would be the difference.

It was both — or, rather, it was a suit and a soldier that didn't *need* to be trained.

The three suits in front of him advanced, their short, dark-skinned operators staring as blankly back at him as he knew he looked. They all raised their weapons — the arm-mounted cannons — and fired.

He felt his Exosuit performing before he'd realized he'd issued the command. He ran sideways, his torso still facing them, and fired with his turret. The lighter rounds tore hundreds of tiny holes through the advancing Exos, dropping one of them and halting the forward motion of the other two.

It took them a second longer to adapt and change their focus of fire, and Ben took full advantage of it. He stepped forward, moving out from the relative safety of the heavy crate and fired again, this time adding his cannon to the mix. The blasts hit the center Exo full-on, throwing it onto its back. Another one that had been focusing its attention on Mrs. E tripped over it, stumbling, but then turned to face Ben.

Crap, he thought. *One down, one more takes its place.*

His actions never faltered. He accepted the addition of the newcomer, fired a cannon shot to prevent it from getting overzealous, and then once again turned to face the third Exo in the previous wave.

But that Exo had maneuvered to Ben's flank, and he felt the impact of its cannon round before he registered that it was still firing on him. His own instincts, or his Exo's built-in artificial intelligence — he wasn't sure — turned the turret gun and launched a barrage of tiny bullets toward it.

The new advancing Exo fired at the same time. Rounds from both Exos' cannons hit Ben's side and chest, and he faltered. He grunted, then the Exo he was standing in fell to its knees. He struggled with the controls, suddenly feeling as though they were foreign. He was no longer in sync with the machine as he had been, and he wondered if there was a way to —

There.

He pressed his feet downward in the suit, trying to simulate the motion of standing up. The Exo reacted immediately, and he felt the hydraulic lifts in the legs pressing upward. The Exo stood, then fell again. Ben's left leg screamed out in pain — the suit had been hit on its left leg, and when it fell back again Ben's leg had been caught inside.

He couldn't tell if it had been crushed or badly bruised, but he had no time to worry about it. Nor did he have any way of reacting if it had been injured. His body simply moved on, as if it had marked down the loss and worked to readjust its strategy.

The problem was that Ben had no idea *what* that strategy should be — he was nearly on his side on the ground, his Exo unable to stand. He was firing back at the advancing Exos, but now two more had joined the fray. They were working to spread out, to make Ben's attack on more than one of them at once impossible. The Exos' torsos could rotate quickly, but they had a limit.

Ben threw his wrists side to side and up and down, working the controls as naturally as he'd been born with them in his hands. He moved the Exo's weaponry side to side, firing when he knew there was an open shot. The AI worked as well to diminish the threat, accepting control of the weapon Ben was currently not using, and together man and machine fought to stay alive.

But without the ability to move, Ben knew it was an impossible task. There were more and more Exos joining in every second, and he wondered if perhaps they were joining the fight because one or more of his teammates had been annihilated. *Had Mrs. E fallen?* The woman was a hell of a *fighter*, but Ben had no idea how comfortable she felt behind the controls of a fighting *machine*.

She was also the hardiest of them all — she could survive anything. Reggie had once called her the 'cockroach of the CSO,' a term she hadn't seemed to enjoy.

Maybe Reggie or Julie had been killed? Maybe the Exos had overcome their position, firing on and relentlessly pressing forward until they, like Ben, had been reduced to a pile of guns and metal, and then...

No. He refused to allow himself to think that. If his thoughts were the last thing he had control over, he'd use them constructively, right up until the very end.

In that case, he thought, *let's figure out how to get the hell out of these things.*

He knew the suit was their best protection, but it was also their best chance at death. The Exos had been ordered to fight *each other*, the operators inside simply along for the ride, unable to remove themselves from the machines. He didn't know if they would start firing at him directly if he were somehow able to get himself out of his suit, but he figured it was a chance worth taking.

But how to do it?

The CSO team, as well as the other Exo operators on the demonstration floor, were all under the spell of Garza's chemical compound. He knew there was nothing he could do to break it, not on his own.

But...

There *had* to be a way. He knew it. He'd been in enough sticky situations to know for a fact that there was *something* he could do to extricate himself. Something he could do to break the spell, to turn off the...

That's it. He didn't need to get the *chemical* out of his body. He needed to *turn off* what was controlling it.

And he had just realized that the chemical — and his mind, because of it — was being controlled by the sound. The high-pitched noise.

CHAPTER 61

BEN

WHEREVER THEY HAD BEEN, the high-pitched noise had signaled the arrival of enemy Exos. The singular pitch, nearly inaudible to them, had been a pinprick in his eardrum the entire time they'd been on the demonstration floor, and Garza had made it a point to never let the sound die out — even allowing it to continue being piped in through the speakers *while* he talked over it.

The sound was activating the chemical, which was controlling his mind enough to prevent him from acting on his own volition.

He didn't know how it worked, nor did he care. He now had a mission.

And if there was anything he knew about *himself*, it was that he would take his stubbornness to the grave. When he had a goal, a mission he could see, clearly, he wouldn't stop until he accomplished it. He *couldn't* stop.

And his mission was clear: figure out how to turn off the sound.

The problem, however, was still ever-present in his field of view. His eyes were barely above the top edge of the suit, but since he was lying diagonal to the floor, lower than his attackers, he could see them all.

There were six of them, and they were still pressing forward. He couldn't move his head or eyes to see behind him, but he knew the back wall of the demonstration floor was only feet behind him. Crates were stacked high to his left, most of them shredded. If he pushed, he could clear them and break free, only to find that he'd lost a few precious seconds to the machines trying to outmaneuver him.

To his right the path was clear.

That was his goal, now: *get there.*

After that, he didn't know.

He tried to will the Exo to understand the plan, to explain to it that it didn't *need* both legs to move. It took a second and a half — an unbelievably long time in the realm of human thought and artificial intelligence, but it worked.

The Exo complied, dropping its left "arm" to the ground and pulling itself forward. Ben could feel the scraping of the broken left leg as it dragged behind, but he kept on moving. The right arm cannon was still firing, the shoulder-mounted turret doing its job to stave off immediate death. Thanks his Exo's superior firepower and speed with its weaponry, the onslaught was stifled enough for Ben to move the machine toward the right, around the next stack of crates.

But the Exo was too slow. The damage had been done, and without one of its legs to move, the suit was helpless to the next attack.

It came in the form of seven rounds of cannon fire, blisteringly fast, all centered around the Exos back.

The battery housing was hit immediately, a cap or metal cover on the top of it flying off and nearly taking Ben's head off with it.

The other rounds peppered the back of the suit, taking out enough components that even Ben's gentle prodding and urging couldn't convince the Exo to push itself back up. A gear rolled away from the suit, now lying flat on its stomach.

Ben knew the end was coming. He wasn't sure how well he would hold up against the barrage, but he knew there was no metal that couldn't be pierced — the enemy Exos would break through, no matter what. It was only a matter of time.

A few seconds, perhaps? Maybe a minute? The Exo was down, but the others weren't stopping. The cannons blasted different bits off the suit. The entire right leg, the foot of the left, a few more gears and a long line full of dark fluid.

Ben sighed. *This is the end.* He moved his right hand off the controls and tried to push himself up and away from the front of the suit. He could now feel the weight of the suit on him, as if...

Wait a minute. He had just *moved.* He had moved his hand, and he'd lifted himself up off the suit's front.

What the hell?

He frowned, again noticing that the thought had translated into an action. An action *he* had initiated.

He smiled. *No idea what's going on, but I'm taking advantage of it.*

He pulled himself forward — out of the top of the suit — and toward the two crates lying in front of him and to his left. There was another dead Exo there, too, a sign that he might have a bit more protection than just a few thin planks of wood.

He reached the downed Exo and noticed that the other Exos were still firing at his *old* suit. *Good,* he thought. *They must be working to eliminate the* Exos, *not necessarily the* humans *inside.* His theory had so far proven true, but he didn't want to wait around to test it out.

He crawled forward a few more inches, and suddenly his mind lost connection with his body.

Once again, he was completely immobile.

CHAPTER 62

BEN

WHAT'S GOING ON? Ben wondered. *How was I able to move?*

He realized that the droning whine had faded in volume. He hadn't noticed it at the time, but it had in fact had an effect: when the high-pitched tone was gone, he was able to move.

As he'd felt himself locking back up, his motion stymied, he'd heard the sound creep back into his mind, filling the void it had previously left.

Now he was lying on the floor, just out of reach of his Exo suit. Not that he could reach for it anyway, if he wanted to. He could lift his head, and he was thankful that he had been looking sideways, focusing on the advancing enemy Exos, as he'd frozen up again. His hands lay motionless at his sides, one of his legs was bent and the other was straight.

Is this the position I'm going to die in? he thought. *Will I be crushed or trampled to death? Or will the Exos just ignore me for Garza to kill after?*

He wondered how much time was left on Jeffers' watch. It had to be less than thirty minutes by now. And what would happen when it reached zero? Jeffers had told them Sturdivant planned to "bring it all down on top of them," but what *exactly* did that mean?

Didn't matter now, Ben figured. He was laying like a half-dead snake on the stone floor, hearing the sounds of the battle raging around him. The Exos behind him banged away at his fallen suit, apparently not satisfied with its operator escaping and leaving the suit useless on the ground. They wanted to seal the deal.

He heard another explosion as a component from a nearby Exo exploded, and he felt the vibrations through his body as it landed inches away from his head.

Add: death by flaming debris missile to the list of possibilities, he thought.

Out of the corner of his eye he saw another two cannon rounds smack against his fallen Exo, pushing it toward him. The shoulder-mounted turret of his suit crashed against his leg, bending it inwards and upward. Ben couldn't feel it, but it didn't seem to have done any damage.

And then... he moved it. His leg bent, and unbent, his other leg straightening out, now fully extended. He tested his arms, then hands, and found that they too could move. His head was still riveted in place, as if the topmost quarter of his body had been rendered inert.

He pulled himself backwards with his hands and feet, sliding slowly toward his downed Exo. The chemical abruptly released its hold on his head, and he worked his jaw open and closed a few times, working out the kinks and sleepiness.

Okay, he thought. *Time to figure this out.*

As before, the sound piped in from the speakers up above had been mostly silenced, only the slight pressure of the noise evident in the back of his mind. He strained his ears but couldn't hear the pitch above the racket of the fight.

The fight!

He had almost forgotten about his comrades, and he took a precious second to glance left and right, looking for his team members. He saw Julie and Mrs. E fighting, working side-to-side against their respective walls, each fighting off a handful of slower, heavier Exos.

He couldn't see Reggie, but he didn't have time to check, and he knew it wasn't worth the risk. The last time he'd been freed from the grip of the scopolamine chemical compound he'd been within proximity of his suit. When he'd crawled away, the rigor mortis effect had immediately set in.

The effect had something to do with his proximity to the Exo suit — *his* Exo suit. But what? He couldn't figure out why his suit — previously his own private prison — was now the thing that allowed him his freedom.

Unless...

Ben shifted around, now facing the "head" of the fallen exosuit, examining its damage. Only *after* it had been hit, nearly destroyed, had it "turned off" Garza's noise.

He examined everything he could see from this vantage point. He was no engineer or mechanic, and even then these were far more technically advanced than anything he had inspected before. He didn't even know what he was looking for, but he figured he'd know when he saw it.

His eyes traced the outline of the Exo, down to the backside of it that faced the wall. Where the arms connected — one now completely missing — where the battery had been attached...

There.

A panel that used to cover a section of the Exo's upper-right torso, just beneath the shoulder area on the back of it, had gone missing. There were blast marks around the rectangular section, giving Ben a clue as to what had happened. He reached a hand inside and pulled out a mess of wiring and cables, careful to not unplug any of them.

The Exos that had been attacking his downed suit had lost interest, apparently satisfied that the suit was effectively disabled. Ben also assumed that Garza couldn't see him at the moment — if he had,

Ben had no doubt the other Exos in the room would suddenly have received new orders, and Ben's life would have ended a few seconds later.

For the moment, Ben was alive and no one was the wiser. He hoped he could keep it that way. He moved aside bound and zip tied collection of cables and found a small, rectangular object, hanging from the top side of the interior of the Exo.

He pulled it out. He knew exactly what it was, as it was one of the few things in a vehicle he *did* know something about.

An amplifier.

The tiny device was perhaps half the size of the units he'd seen before. He had installed one into his ancient hand-me-down Corolla in high school, his first car. His father had purchased the car from a work friend, and he'd given Ben the rundown on how to maintain the old vehicle. Changing spark plugs, oil, and refilling washer fluid was about all Ben remembered.

But he *did* know a thing or two about car stereo systems. Mainly that he'd wanted one, and he'd saved up his money from part-time jobs until he had enough to purchase a massive subwoofer for the Corolla's trunk. He had then discovered that his new sub needed an amplifier to power the massive speaker, so, frustrated, he saved up another three months' worth of income and purchased a cheap amp from a big-box electronics store.

One of the many little knobs and switches on the amp was labeled "phase." It was a bipolar switch and had two settings: 0 degrees and 180 degrees.

That was what he was looking at now — a tiny amplifier with a knob for volume, a knob for pan, a knob and some numbers for something called "crossover," — and a phase switch.

He didn't dare flick the phase switch, but he examined the device and ran the hypothesis through his head. He wished he'd paid more attention in school, when his physics class had gotten a brief over-view of acoustics.

But he knew the basics: sound is a pressure wave, literally a physical "wave" that travels through the air. The louder the sound, the "higher" the wave moves above and beneath the baseline axis. The lower the pitch, the longer the distance between the peaks and valleys, and the opposite was true for the higher the pitch.

And *phase* was a concept that implied two or more sounds ringing at once — when each of the waveforms lined up with one another, those sounds were said to be "in phase." They were essentially copies of the same sound, played at exactly the same time.

But when two sounds were "out of phase," their waveforms were exact opposites of one another: when one waveform went up, the other went down.

The result? He vaguely remembered his physics teacher, a product of 80s dance music and a wannabe keyboardist, playing two sine waves on two identical keyboards, one of which was phased to be opposite the other:

When the teacher played the two notes, there was no sound at all.

In car audio, sometimes a speaker would be wired incorrectly, or the polarity was somehow reversed, and the effect would be that another speaker playing the exact same music would be "out of phase" with the others — causing a detriment to the sound quality.

Ben considered all of that as he stared down at the amplifier in his hand. He knew it had to be the answer: all the pieces lined up.

A single, sine wave-like sound, had been piped in through speakers both from above *and* from the two speakers inside the Exo suit. Since the sound needed to be amplified, the Ravenshadow engineers had simply purchased inexpensive amps that had been designed for small car audio systems, and they by default shipped with a phase switch.

When Ben's Exo had been destroyed piece by piece, one of the impacts had jostled the amplifier free and hit the phase switch, causing the speakers inside the suit — the ones that were still sending their signal — to reverse their polarity.

The speakers' reversed phase sound was perfectly opposite of the sound from the other speakers in the room, and when Ben was close enough to the Exo's speakers, they cancelled out the high-pitched noise.

It was a beautiful accident, and it had freed Ben.

The only problem was that he needed to figure out how to use it to free everyone else.

CHAPTER 63

JULIE

JULIE'S EXO had maneuvered nearly all the way along the wall, and she could see Ben in the distance, hiding behind a fallen Exo.

It took her another second to realize that he was *outside* his suit.

How did he get out? she wondered. *Did he get thrown?*

And then, she couldn't help herself: *he must be dead.*

She wanted to *feel* that truth, to decide for herself if it were real, but the chemical wouldn't let her. It didn't block her thoughts, but it blocked their ability to control her motor functions.

She watched Ben as her hands and wrists controlled the Exo. It was second nature now, and she found that because the suit's AI was nearly capable of controlling the suit on its own, she could free her mind to think about other things. A few blasts from her turret, followed by a couple cannon rounds, took out another Exo advancing from in front and to her left.

All the while she watched Ben.

No, she saw, *he's not dead.* He was very much alive, and he seemed to be fine. But how was he moving? She could see that he was messing with something behind the suit, his feet and legs just visible from behind a crate.

How did he get out?

She watched as her Exo fought, and in a few seconds she saw Ben pull something up from behind the suit. It was too small for her to see it clearly, but it looked like some sort of small box. She watched as Ben moved something on its surface, like a knob or switch. He was looking up and around, watching the other Exos.

Suddenly one of the Exos closest to Ben shifted unnaturally, jumping to the side and spinning around halfway. She was intrigued by the motion, and a few seconds later she saw the operator — a thin, middle-aged woman. She stared directly at Julie, and then she blinked.

Oh my God, Julie thought. *He figured out how to get us out.*

The woman blinked again, then moved her head from side to side as if testing the theory that she might now be free, and then she did something amazing.

The woman turned around inside the Exo suit and simply *got out.* She threw the back hatch open and stepped out, then descended the small ladder and landed on her feet. The woman stood there for a few seconds, swaying, but then found her strength and began running.

Julie saw her target destination. There was a single small door near the center of the long wall, painted to match the stone surrounding it. Only the handle and a faint outline of the frame made it visible, but the woman was heading directly toward it.

Except she never made it.

Julie watched in horror as the woman simply *froze* in mid step. She slowed to a halt, as if she'd just ran into a vat of rapidly setting concrete. Her feet stopped working, and her hands and arms simply melted back to her sides and then came to a stop.

What's happening? The woman had left her Exosuit and began to run, and then when she'd gotten far enough away she'd once again come under the spell of Garza's drug.

Ben was still kneeling behind his own suit, controlling the tiny device.

Was that it? Julie wondered. *Is he somehow controlling her?*

No — that didn't make sense. It had to be simpler. Ben was next to his suit, and he was able to move freely. The woman had been able to move as well, *as long as she was near her suit.*

It was a proximity thing, Julie realized. Ben had somehow figured out how to nullify the sound Garza was piping into the room and into their suits, and he'd been able to do the same for the woman. When the woman had left the area around her own suit, she had left the circle of protection.

Julie's mind raced. She knew she couldn't get closer to Ben on her own — that would be a direct violation of her commands — but she saw a coupled Exos near the woman's suit, each looking in opposite directions, perhaps searching for a new target.

I'll be your target, she thought. She didn't have to do much — her Exo seemed to accept the new coordinates as soon as she touched the controls, and she turned and pointed them toward the center of the room.

Ben saw her coming. He waved, just a quick flip of his wrist, but it was enough for Julie to know he saw her. *He knows I'm coming,* she thought. *But he's trying to stay hidden.*

That meant he would be taking a huge risk coming to her — he would not only reveal himself to Garza, who was almost without a doubt still watching on from up above somewhere, but Ben would also risk leaving the safety of his suit's perimeter.

She shifted left, moving closer to Ben's fallen Exo. It was a move that ensured she'd be protected from view by some crates, but it was also a smart strategic move to be out of direct fire from all sides, so the Exo allowed it. It took half a minute to get there, as they had to dodge the fallen suits and wreckage from the battle, as well as step over or through damaged crates, but she made it. She was ten feet away from Ben when he started running over.

"Move closer!" he yelled. She did.

She was now about eight feet away, and the effect was instantaneous.

CHAPTER 64

GARZA

GARZA WAITED PATIENTLY as the destruction continued. He added a few comments using the microphone in the booth, commending Julie on her performance. He could only see two of the CSO team members from his perch in the booth, but he knew the others would be on the recording, which he planned to preview and help edit before sending it to the buyer.

Victoria appeared in the doorway a minute later.

"Ah, Victoria," he said. "Please, enter."

She walked in. Her eyes barely moved, but he knew she noticed Father Canisius in the corner of the room. She walked to the center of the room, staring straight ahead at Garza.

"Please Victoria, turn and greet our guest."

She turned to her left. "Hello," she said. Her voice was soft, meek.

"Father Canisius," Garza continued. "I told you I have not been entirely truthful with you. I understand your trip to Peru has been rather frustrating. You are confused about your reason for being here?"

"I... was. And then I decided that the Church was interested in purchasing technology, only that technology was being sold by a known arms dealer. Legal or not, it would cast a disparaging glow on the Church's character. By having someone of my stature within the organization attend the proceedings, it would prove to both sides the validity. And yet no one watching on in the international community would accuse someone like me of knowing anything about technology."

Canisius attempted a shy smile, but it disappeared almost as soon as it reached his cheeks.

"That is... an astute observation, Father. And yet it is woefully wrong."

Canisius' eyes fell.

"There is, in fact, a deal that is being finalized. And there is, in fact, going to be an exchange of money — a lot of money — and assets, between your church and my company. However, that money will not be for the purchase of the *machines* you see here. Not *just* the machines."

Canisius frowned. "And what, then, will we be purchasing?"

Garza sipped his coffee, then waved a hand around, motioning toward Victoria. "This."

"Th — this woman?"

Garza smiled again. "The *drug* that is inside this woman." He turned and faced Victoria. "Please, Victoria. Take my coffee and set it on the desk."

Immediately Victoria complied.

"Thank you. As you can see, she does exactly what she is told."

Canisius didn't look convinced. Behind Garza explosions from the Exos' cannons and turret fire peppered the air, reaching his ears through the bulletproof glass.

"Father Canisius, I know that proving something like this is a bit difficult to do, but I also assume you are not the sort of man who would be interested in testing the willingness of this woman to comply to a request — any request — you may have?"

He didn't move. Garza nodded at him and continued. "In that

case, look again into the demonstration floor. You will see that each of the suits has an operator inside it, both working the controls and acting as the suit's central nervous system."

Canisius did.

"How do you think we convinced each of those operators to enter their suit?"

Again, Canisius watched on.

"Finding able operators is the easy part. Finding *willing* operators is another story entirely. In my quest to find some solution to the problem of soldier insubordination, I stumbled upon a chemical extracted from a plant native to this country. It grows in abundance here, and only here.

"From that chemical, I created a compound that does exactly what you are seeing in Victoria, and what you are seeing in these men and women on the demonstration floor."

"You created a *mind-control* drug?"

"In a sense, yes," Garza said. "And *that* is the technology my buyer is interested in."

"What could the Church *possibly* want with a mind-control drug?" Canisius asked.

"Choose your words wisely, Father, or you may start to sound ironic." Garza sniffed. "Anyway, to be honest with you — the church *doesn't* want the drug. In fact, the only thing they are interested in is giving me money."

"Giving you — what for?"

"Because if they have a reason to spend money in the region, they have plausible deniability when it comes to cleaning up the mess they made a few months ago. Just beyond this mountain, in the Chachapoyas Valley."

Of course. Archie had mentioned this, and Father Canisius knew it made the most sense. *The Church needed to cover up their dealings here, to make it impossible to trace the events of a few months ago back to them.*

"If they give *me* money, they've opened a believable chain of transactions that can ultimately end with their getting off the hook. And they can turn around and sell my tech to the *real* buyer, both earning them more money *and* getting my tech to the people who wanted it most all along."

"And... who is the buyer?"

"Father, don't be naive."

Canisius looked surprised, then defeated. "The United States."

"Of *course*," Garza said. "They have been hounding me all along for it. Hell, even *after* setting up this deal and promising updates, someone from the Army set up a sting operation to check on my progress. While it took hardly any time or effort to quash the infiltration, it greatly *annoyed* me. I am, after all, a businessman. And I don't take kindly to veiled threats of usurpation."

Canisius shook his head, ignoring the carnage taking place right on the other side of the glass. "But, I still don't understand. Why am *I* here? If this is simply a deal you intend to make with the United States, why allow the Church to be a middleman at all? Why force them to send someone like me out here to play a pawn in your game?"

Garza leaned his head back, eyeing Canisius like a crow might eye a worm. "And finally, Father, we get to the *real* topic at hand. Finally asking the *real* questions."

He paced across the room, then turned and came back to stand next to Victoria, whom he examined as she stared straight ahead, unmoving.

"Father Canisius, it has been many years, but I am still surprised you don't recognize us."

THE SOUND suddenly lowered to a nearly inaudible level. She could almost feel the single note still reverberating out of her Exo's speakers, but it was faint.

Better, the sound was no longer strong enough to activate the chemical in her brain.

She felt her whole body shift back to life, a sort of "melting" feeling, and she shook her head and blinked a few times. She suddenly felt her legs turning to mush, but she locked her knees and waited until the Exo came to a halt. She could still control it, but it felt more like they were two separate beings now — her reactions were just a bit muddled, her control of the machine just a little slower.

She didn't wait around. She turned around in the suit and unlatched the rear door, then jumped out of the Exo and landed five feet down onto the ground.

Ben was there. She hugged him, but he brushed her off.

"What's wrong?" she asked.

"Huh? Oh, sorry — not enough time."

Time.

She'd completely forgotten. As if this mess with the walking tanks wasn't enough, Sturdivant was going to do *something* devastating to the entire base, in... *what was it? Twenty-five or thirty minutes?* She didn't know — Reggie was wearing Jeffers' watch.

But if they didn't release Reggie and Mrs. E from the grip of the scopolamine compound, it wouldn't matter how much time was left. They'd be dead either way.

She watched Ben work. He was using the butt of his rifle, banging the back of the Exo suit as hard as he could.

"What is it?" Julie asked. "How you were able to get out?"

"I got lucky," Ben said, once again smacking the rifle against the shoulder section of the machine. "But it's inside this thing. Here, help me."

Ben hit the corner of a rectangular sheet of metal, and the side of it dented inward, giving her a small handhold. She walked over and helped Ben by pulling the rectangular sheet of metal, wrenching it sideways as it broke from its top rivets, then coming off completely.

"It's a weak spot on the armor," Ben said," meant to allow easy access to some of the internals." He paused, climbed the ladder of Julie's Exo and leaned over to the new hole in the suit. He reached in, moving his arm up and toward the inside of the Exo's shoulder. "It's a little amplifier. It's got a reverse phase polarity switch. Used to have one on my car amp, but I never knew what it did."

He pulled the device out, which was still hooked up to a few cables — one for power, and two for the two speakers, Julie figured.

"See?" Ben said, flipping the switch.

The high-pitched sound immediately went away. Julie looked up at Ben. "Apparently it's for turning off mind-control chemicals when you're fighting giant exoskeleton battle mechs."

"Yeah," Ben said. "Apparently so. Who would've thought they'd need those in Corollas?"

Julie smiled, then frowned. "How much time?"

"Probably getting close to twenty-five minutes left," Ben said. "Which doesn't give us much time at all."

"But we have a plan," Julie said. "Right?"

"Sort of."

"Is it 'run around and try to reverse the polarity of all the Exos between us and Reggie and Mrs. E?"

"Sort of."

"Do tell."

"Well, it's that, but I wasn't just thinking about Reggie and Mrs. E."

Julie cocked an eyebrow.

"Way I see it, there are a lot of innocent people in here — not just the four of us — and we might need some help getting out of the base. They might be able to give us a hand."

Julie looked up. There was a tower of crates that had somehow survived the battle protecting them from Garza's view. She had seen the observation deck — a bulletproof glass-encased box hovering halfway up the wall on the opposite side of the room — and she assumed that would be where Garza was.

There were no other cameras in the room, so as long as they worked to stay out of sight from the observation deck, Garza wouldn't be able to see them.

She hoped.

"Okay, sounds good," she said. "Want to tell me what you did, so we can split up?"

Ben showed her. "It's literally as simple as flipping a switch. But what it does is reverse the polarity of the *exact same sound* through the speakers, which is how it really works — it essentially cancels out the sound from the overhead speakers."

"Like noise-cancelling headphones," Julie said. "That's exactly what they do — they produce a sound that's exactly the same as the incoming noise floor, then they reverse the polarity and send that new signal into the headphones as well, cancelling each other out, and voila. No noise."

Ben stared at her.

"What?" she asked. "I was a computer geek before I met you."

"You're *still* a geek, Jules. Anyway, as I figured out earlier, it's proximity based. The volume can only go up so high, so we'll have to crank each Exo's amp and then get to the next one. Hopefully we can leapfrog around, eight or ten feet or so at a time, eventually getting everyone out."

"The culmination of all these reverse-polarity sounds should eventually reach equilibrium with the volume coming from the overhead speakers," Julie said. "Meaning we won't have to do *all* of them. Just enough to create a loud enough reverse signal."

"Like I said, geek."

She smiled. "Let's roll — I really don't want to find out what it is Sturdivant's got planned for this place."

"I don't want to find out either, geek."

He leaned in and kissed her, and then pulled away. As she was turning to leave, he called over his shoulder.

"Oh, and if you get yourself killed I'll kill you."

"Noted."

CHAPTER 66

EDMUND

FATHER EDMUND CANISIUS stared blankly at the younger woman standing next to the man — the leader of this group called Raven-shadow. He was unable to process what it was the man wanted from him. Why he had called him here, ordered him to be a part of this... *massacre*.

Down below in what the man had called the "demonstration floor," a handful of mechanized robots slung bullets at one another, firing upon one another with a hellish fury that made his blood run cold. Never in his life had he been privy to anything remotely like this, and the sheer violence of it all was causing him to stumble over his words.

"I... uh — no, I apologize, I... do not think I know you."

He looked from the man, to the woman, to the demonstration floor. A robot — an "Exo," the man had called it — shot another one from the opposite side of the room, catching it in the back. A faint splatter of blood flew forward out the *front* side of the Exo, and Canisius knew immediately what had happened.

"Another one failed, Garza," one of the seated men said, not even glancing up from his display. He tapped something on the display screen and swiped it to the left. "Looks like Soldier 231," the man continued. "Fatal wound just below the cranial cavity. Shot fired from..."

Garza. Canisius listened to the conversation between the leader — Garza, apparently — and his soldiers.

He paused.

"What is it?" Garza asked, turning his attention to the man at the workstation. "A problem?"

"Well, I — I'm not sure, sir. The shot seemed to have come from Soldier 192."

"And?"

"And Soldier 192 is across the room. And they're wearing a first-gen Exo, sir. Both of them."

Garza frowned and Canisius tried to read his expression. *Is this bad news? Good? Has something changed?*

And, *who is this Garza person, and why does he think I should know him?*

"Was it accidental friendly fire?"

"Unlikely, sir," another technician said. This man was also swiping on his screen, pulling his fingers apart to enlarge a video image. The technician played the video again, first full-speed, then in reverse at half-speed. Canisius couldn't see exactly what was onscreen, but he knew it was a replay of the kill that had just been made.

The man continued. "All of the second-gen suits are still active, and they are all near the west wall, except for suit 4, which is lying dead on the southern wall."

"And the shot came *from* a first-gen and *hit* a first-gen, and it was on purpose?"

"Yes, sir. It appears so."

Garza sniffed again, then chewed his lip. "Find out why. Do we have cameras on the south wall?"

"Not the entire wall, sir. That's the dead spot directly underneath us."

"Fine. Get cameras on the second-gen suits and the remainder of the CSO team. I want to know what they're doing, and why one of the first-gens hit its comrade."

The men nodded and furiously began swiping and clicking at their touchscreen monitors.

Canisius turned back to Garza. "Garza," the man said. "That is your name?"

Garza nodded, then faced Canisius fully. He took a step forward. Victoria stayed silent, standing like a sentinel in the center of the room, staring at everything and nothing at the same time.

"Yes, that is my name. Garza. *Vicente* Garza. I was born in Arizona, but my parents were from Mexico. My men call me 'The Hawk.' Do you know why?" Garza's head fell sideways a bit, as if examining Canisius. *Sizing him up.*

Like he was prey, and Garza was a hawk.

"I — I do not."

"Throughout my career I have seen professionals like me fail because their men were not truly accepting of their leader's ability to get a job done. They didn't *trust* them. They didn't truly *believe* in them.

"Over the course of *my* career, however, I have come to the conclusion that it is *never, no matter what,* acceptable to miss an opportunity to make a point. My men have come to trust me for that, and when I make those points they are further willing to trust me.

"A hawk is the same — they *never* miss an opportunity. They are *opportunistic* creatures, yet they are cunning as well. They plan, but they will sidestep that plan in order to take advantage of a situation. They take every opportunity to capture their prey."

Canisius sucked in a breath. He may have been naive, but he

wasn't an idiot. He knew his position here, even if he didn't understand *why*.

I'm the prey. Garza is the Hawk.

But he didn't know *why*.

"Who are you?" Canisius asked.

Garza smiled then returned to stand next to Victoria. He put his arm around her, and in that moment Canisius recognized the similarities.

Father and daughter, he thought. He could see it now — there was no doubt.

"This is my daughter, Victoria," Garza said. "Victoria *Reyes* now, though she is no longer married. She is highly intelligent, and is a professor of ancient history and religion.

"And, you might have guessed, we have both met you before. In fact, we were all in the same room once."

Canisius frowned. *What is he talking about?* His mind raced through the years, trying to uncover any hint of his interaction with this man and his daughter. He couldn't recall how or why they would have met, or how Canisius could have angered him so much that he would have gone through all this trouble to lure him here.

What's the connection? Canisius wondered. *Vicente Garza. Victoria Garza Reyes. From the United States, but his parents were born in —*

Canisius bit his lip. *Oh, Lord, no. No, that cannot be —* he stopped. *It has to be.*

"Mexico," he whispered.

"Yes," Garza nodded.

"You were in Mexico. Your whole family —" he stopped short.

"That's right, Father. My *whole* family. Me, my daughter, and my wife."

Canisius swallowed.

"And *you* were there, too. *You* were part of the deal. The doctor and the businessman, and the local church."

"No, I —"

"The local parish that sent a young priest to administer rites to a grieving family."

"That's not —"

"You accepted the position and the role, and you pocketed the money. *My* money."

"Garza, I swear to you that —"

"*Enough!*" Garza yelled. "Enough. It's lies — always lies. Everything you stand for — everything the *church* stands for. *Lies.*"

Canisius stepped forward. "Garza, it was a long time ago. I was young, and I swear to you — my hand on my heart, to the Lord God himself, I had nothing —"

"It *was* a long time ago, Canisius," Garza said, slipping into a more informal style of berating. "But wounds take a long time to heal. Sometimes a *lifetime.* And I *know* you were involved. I did the digging. I did my research. As I said, I *never* refuse the opportunity when it arises."

Canisius felt sick. More blasts from cannons and weapons from outside the glass reached his ears, but they were faint next to the pounding of his own heart.

I was young, he told himself. *I was taking orders. I had no idea it would lead to this.*

"How much money did they give you? How much of *my* money?"

"I — there was — "

"*How much?*"

Garza screamed and flung his coffee cup directly at Canisius' head. There was no dodging the bullet of a throw, and at Canisius' age the best he could hope for was to simply turn his head at the last moment.

Still, the liquid inside — still somehow blisteringly hot — splashed across Canisius' eyes and he screamed in pain. His skin felt as if it were melting, and that was before the heat actually set in.

He groaned, collapsing, and whimpered as the searing-hot liquid spilled over his neck and chest. He smelled the nutty roasted beans as well as the singed flesh of his lips and cheeks. He gripped his face with his hands, rocking back and forth on the floor.

He noticed a shadow standing over him.

Garza. The Hawk.

"You betrayed your god, Canisius. All those years ago you established what sort of person *you* are. You have been lying to yourself — and everyone else — ever since."

"No..." Canisius croaked.

"Yes," Garza said. "I brought you here because I had the *opportunity* to. I saw the opening, and I took it. I needed the Church to finish the deal. When I discovered that *you* were in a top role there, I began working toward this moment."

Canisius' heart sank. Somehow the pain of realizing the great lengths Garza had gone to for Canisius to be here hurt worse than the coffee.

"I am called The Hawk because I take advantage of opportunities, but also because I am *very* good at planning out my attack."

He turned and walked over to Victoria, and Canisius saw through blurry eyes as he handed her something.

"Victoria," Garza began. "Please step closer to Father Canisius."

No, Canisius thought. He started panting. Sweat and spittle combined collected on his lips and he tried to wipe it away. It didn't work, and tears — his own — were added to the mix.

"Sir," one of the men said. "We've got a problem."

Garza ignored him.

"*Sir.*"

"Not now!" Garza snapped.

As Garza turned to address his soldier Canisius saw, finally, what it was he had handed his daughter. A massive pistol, the largest Canisius had ever seen. It looked heavy in Victoria's hands, but she held it confidently.

"I wanted to prove to you how effective the drug could be. But it is also possible that it doesn't work at all, and my daughter would like to avenge the death of her mother. The *murder* of her mother.

"Victoria, please execute this man."

THE CLEARNESS in Garza's mind had returned. He was no longer conflicted, no longer out of control. He no longer had the unsteady feeling of being out of touch with his own inner demons.

He took in a deep, long breath, watching the flowing trail of blood behind Father Canisius' head. Victoria stood over him, the gun in her hand smoking. She too was stoic, calm, but he knew it was for a completely different reason.

"Sir," the soldier said again. He was standing now, looking down at his tablet. He shoved the tablet to Garza, who flinched and almost pushed it away.

But something onscreen caught his eye. The man tapped the play button on the screen and the video began. In the far corner of the screen, in what would be the southeast corner of the room, Garza saw a flash of color, a shadow. The shape of a human.

"Is that —"

"It's one of the operators, sir," the man said. "One of the CSO team members."

Garza was completely caught off-guard. "But... how?"

The man shook his head, the other soldier, a young technician, answered. "We're running it back, trying to see if we've got cameras picking it up. But they're in the dead zone, where there's no —"

"Then *get* into the dead zone!" Garza snapped. "Why in the *hell* is someone out of their suit?"

"Sir, again, we aren't able —

"Get *inside,* then. Where are the nearest units?"

"We've got two on-duty patrols on that level, and one —"

"Send them in."

"Sir?"

"*Send them in!*" Garza did nothing to hide his rage. Somehow, one of the CSO team members had figured out how to disable the high-pitched signal they were sending through the speakers. Or they had somehow overcome the scopolamine compound. Or...

No, he thought. *There's simply no way they could have done it.*

The two techs were scurrying around, and the Ravenshadow soldiers who had escorted Canisius into the room were standing by, waiting for their orders.

"You two," Garza said, "get down there and call up another two units. Get them from the second level if you need to, but get them ready for engagement."

The two soldiers nodded and hustled out of the room.

Garza continued watching the looped video, trying to make out exactly what it was he was seeing. He saw an arm and a leg, clearly, but the person's head was indistinguishable. A first-gen Exo turned and fired at a point near the person, but the explosion only caused them to duck back behind a crate, out of sight.

"Can we reconfigure the Exos and their operators to fire at the human targets instead of at other suits?"

"We... tried, sir. We're not sure what's going on down there, but it's like none of them are responding."

"Get me another feed," he barked. He walked over to the bank of computer monitors and watched as the tech manipulated one of the feeds until Garza saw a wide, single-camera shot of the entire demonstration floor, save for a space ten or fifteen feet deep along the side walls.

"There!" the tech said. Garza followed his finger and saw a man walking in sync behind a second-gen Exo.

"Is this live?"

"Yessir."

"That's Harvey Bennett," Garza said. "And who's in that second-gen?"

The tech paused, then flicked through something on his tablet. "I believe that's the woman they were with."

"Mrs. E," Garza said.

"Is she…"

"She's controlling it," Garza said. "That Exo is no longer under my control."

Testing his theory, he grabbed the microphone that had been mounted onto a gooseneck microphone stand and affixed to the desk. He flipped the broadcaster's switch at its base.

"Mrs. E," he said, hearing the reverberation of the sound of his voice as it was amplified just beyond the glass. "Please stop."

The Exo continued moving.

"Mrs. E," he said again. "You will stop, immediately. Turn your Exo around and face —"

He stopped as he saw the Exo comply with his command.

"Maybe I was wrong," he whispered to himself.

Mrs. E's Exo spun and faced the glass bubble Garza and his men were in. For a slight moment there was a delay as everything seemed to come to a halt. He frowned.

Is she really…

And then his world exploded.

The bulletproof glass had been installed in the booth after a mishap with an early version of the control drug, and Garza hadn't bothered to have it tested. He knew it was sturdy enough to prevent the first-gen Exos' turret weapons from piercing, but he didn't know how the more advanced second-gen units would fare.

And they had never tested the glass against the newer arm-mounted cannons.

Both, unfortunately, had been fired directly into Garza's face.

A section of the glass simply ceased to exist after the first twenty or thirty rounds hit, and one of the cannon blasts from her Exo's arm flew through the open wound.

It took off the tech's head and Garza fell backwards with the young man, both hitting the floor on their backs, both coming to rest next to one another, only Garza able to respond. He gasped at the headless corpse as the entire contents of the man's bloodstream began draining onto the floor.

The shots pounded on, taking out a line of glass and shredding the desk and computer consoles. Somewhere, high above and beyond his ears, Garza faintly heard the sound of the ringing noise, the pitch that activated the chemical in the compound.

How the hell?

The noise was still active, but somehow the CSO team had been able to switch it off.

Still Mrs. E's Exo threw slugs into the room. Many landed in the stone ceiling, doing no harm, yet raining down splinters of rock chips and clouds of dust. The entire room's visibility dropped to a few inches, and Garza waved his arms wildly around as he tried to see.

He pulled himself up to the mangled remains of a chair, daring a look over and into the demonstration floor.

What he saw terrified him.

CHAPTER 68

BEN

THE CSO TEAM had been seventy-five percent freed. Ben was approaching Reggie's Exosuit now, getting ready to duck and jump behind him to peel back his panel and flip the polarity switch. He had discovered on Mrs. E's suit that it was easier to open the back hatch of the Exos, jump onto the ladder, and do the work while the Exo was still active — the machine couldn't do anything to flip Ben off of it, nor could the person inside while they were under the spell of the compound.

Julie had been doing the same thing on the opposite side of the room, freeing as many of the operators from their first-gen suits as possible. The operators in the suits were staying inside, likely opting for the relative safety of the machines than the dangerous demonstration floor. Even the woman they'd freed earlier had fled back to her machine.

Those first-gen Exos were still moving, now under the control of their operators instead of Garza, and from Ben's view it seemed that there were only a handful of working Exos that still needed to be freed. Unfortunately, he also saw nearly fifteen downed machines, their operators in varying states of injury. Some, he knew, wouldn't make it out of this room alive.

He freed Reggie and the tall man immediately spun around and faced Ben, a huge grin on his face.

"Ben! These things are *amazing*!"

Ben frowned.

"I mean, uh, thanks for flicking the switch off, or whatever you did."

Ben told him.

"So, like, noise-cancelling headphones?"

"That's exactly what Julie said. You're both nerds," Ben said.

"It's not like it's really crazy technology, Ben. You should read more."

"Shut up and help us. We're mounting an attack."

Reggie looked over his shoulder. "Yeah, I can see that. Mrs. E's tearing it up."

"She is, but if Garza was in there he's going to be trying to get out before the whole thing goes up. That means we've got to get out of here and find him."

"Agreed. So, uh, how do we do that?"

"Julie's guiding the other Exos to Mrs. E, where they'll focus on knocking out that control booth up there. You and I are going to suit up and focus on the doors — they're massive, but if we can make a dent in them we might be able to get them to open."

"Or we'll just lock them up and prevent them from ever opening again."

"Yeah," Ben said. "Or that."

Reggie shrugged. "Eh, whatever. Good a plan as any, I guess. And at least I get to manually operate this beast finally." He held up his artificial arm and hand. "This thing is even more incredible than I thought — the built-in tech is *fast*. I didn't even have to really think, and my hand was moving. Aiming is second-nature, too."

Ben smiled. He had always appreciated Reggie's ability to stay calm — even nonchalant — in any situation, no matter what. He knew it was due to Reggie's long-time practice of controlling his own emotions, his training to push back certain things in his past that he had no business allowing to roam free.

It helped Ben calm down, too, watching his friend. *If he's calm, I can be calm.*

And he knew that calmness was going to be a major asset to him in the next few minutes.

"How much time do we have, by the way?" he asked.

"Oh, right — forgot about that." Reggie checked the watch he'd taken from Jeffers. "Looks like just over ten minutes."

Ben's mouth fell open. "Shit, Reggie. That's not enough time."

Again, Reggie shrugged. "What are you doing trying to butter me up, then? Get off my ass and let's get this show on the road."

Ben did. He jumped to the floor and slammed the back hatch closed, then ran over to Mrs. E. He yelled up to her between blasts from her cannon. "Reggie's good! That's all of us."

She nodded, never taking her eyes off the smoking booth on the opposite wall. She had continued sending rounds into the broken studio but had slowed considerably, allowing time for the dust and smoke to settle so she could see into the ruins.

"See him in there?"

She shook her head. "Negative," she said. "He poked his head up earlier, but I either took him out then or he's gone."

Ben knew which option was more likely. "Stay vigilant, and keep your eyes on the booth. It's the only other open access point we know about besides the two large doors on the sides and the small one in back, and we've got them all covered."

She nodded. "Trust me, he — or anyone — pops their head up, I blast them."

Ben was about to turn and run to a new Exosuit when the door at the side of the room began to open.

"GET TO THE DOORS!" Ben yelled. He had already started to run, well aware that he was not in any sort of protective suit. He was an easy target for anyone on the other side of the door, and there would be nothing standing between him and the end of a Ravenshadow rifle.

The door had opened halfway, but rounds already began bursting through the gap. Ben ducked and rolled sideways, landing in a heap amid the top half of a downed Exo. He dragged the torso portion slightly to the side, near a pile of crates that had been demolished, and created a makeshift shelter.

The first bursts of rounds finished, and the room fell into silence.

Ben watched as three Ravenshadow men entered, each taking a different path — left, middle, right. They flicked their rifles around, looking for something to target and shoot at. Ben saw the man's face closest to him, and saw his eyes widen, then constrict again as he took in the sight in front of him.

He spoke into his wrist, waited, then nodded.

Three more Ravenshadow men entered the room. It was clear by the expressions on their faces that they were confused. The remaining Exos that were in fighting condition were all standing at attention against the back wall, two lines descending away from Mrs. E on either side. Reggie and his Exo stood at the far end, while Julie's stood on the side closest to Ben.

Ben heard the man near him speak to his fellow soldiers.

"What the —"

Before he could finish, Reggie flicked his controls and his Exo came back to life, his torso flying around and his cannon immediately finding its target.

The man standing near Ben stood, shocked, as the cannon round blew a hole *through* his chest. He stood silently for a second, blinking, then fell into a heap.

The other soldiers reacted far too late. They lifted up their weapons, but the Exos standing near Mrs. E turned and rained hell on them.

It was over in about ten seconds, all six of the Ravenshadow men lying dead on the cold stone floor. Ben watched, waiting for more, but nothing came. He turned to Mrs. E and the rest of his team, as well as the other operators in their Exo suits.

"Does anyone speak English?"

A small man next to Reggie raised his arm.

Ben walked over to him and faced the Exo and the man inside. "My name is Harvey Bennett. My team, like your people, were forced into this room. We never intended to hurt any of you. Do you understand?"

The man nodded.

"We are going to stay and fight the rest of these men, but we are running out of time. Can you tell your people that?"

The man nodded again. The other Exos were beginning to gather around Ben and the man as they spoke. Ben knew there would be more Ravenshadow men, and he knew that they really were running out of time. Whatever Sturdivant had planned for them, it was going to happen in less than ten minutes.

"You need to get out of here, then," Ben said. "Please, if you stay here, you will die. We all will."

As he finished the sentence, another two groups of Ravenshadow men rushed in.

"No," the man said to Ben. "We stay. We fight them."

The soldiers starting firing on the Exos, and Ben threw himself behind Reggie, then climbed up his back.

"Hey buddy," Reggie said. "Welcome back."

"Yeah, feels great to be here."

"What's the plan?" Reggie asked. He looked at Ben.

"Kill the bad guys, get out that door, find Garza, kill him, figure out how to get out of here, get out before the clock runs out."

"Right. Any idea *how* we do that?"

Ben pointed at the wave of Ravenshadow men still spilling into the room. He pointed toward them.

"One step at a time," he said. "Get through that first."

"You got it, buddy."

Reggie pushed his control forward and the Exo began marching toward the door. The others followed suit, but it seemed as though having an entire army of ten Exos would be unnecessary.

Reggie, Julie, and Mrs. E had cut down the Ravenshadow men before they'd even finished entering the room.

"Okay," Reggie said, laughing. "Now what?"

"Step two: walk through that door."

Reggie was already moving. His Exo was in the center of the room, and the line of Exos streamed out behind him, one after the other, a chain of robots marching toward their freedom.

Ben waved at Julie, who was nearest the door. He wanted her to go through, to get out of this hell first, but she seemed to be happy waiting for the others to exit first.

Reggie was twenty feet from the door when it happened.

Ben felt the tingling sensation at the same time he noticed the pitch change — it grew louder, stronger. Once again it filled his head, once again it took him over.

He froze.

Reggie and his suit did as well.

All along the line the Exos froze in place, their operators locked back inside their own bodies.

Oh, no, Ben thought. *No, not again.*

He was looking straight ahead, but Reggie had his hand up on the edge of the Exo's frame, not on its controller. His wrist was tilted, giving Ben a perfect view of his watch.

7:54.

7:53.

While Ben and his team was frozen, time was not. It ticked away, the brutal seconds mocking Ben and Reggie, alerting them every moment to their fate.

At the edge of Ben's vision Ben saw movement. Someone was walking into the room.

Garza.

He stepped over the bodies of his fallen men, twelve in all. Ben knew it was nothing to him — hardly a loss.

But Garza would be upset for a far deeper reason.

Ben had played him. Ben had figured out his ruse, figured out a way around it.

And he was here now to return the favor.

Garza walked up to Ben and Reggie. Ben was still locked onto the back of Reggie's suit, but Garza had a clear view of both of their heads.

"Hello, gentlemen. Harvey, Gareth."

He walked a full circle around them, inspecting. Ben knew he'd see the open panel. He wondered if he would be able to put things together.

"My men figured it out," Garza said, his hands in his pockets. "The polarity of the signal. The amplifiers installed within my suits have phase switches, don't they? And you figured out how to reverse it.

"The only problem with that strategy is that you haven't *eliminated* the signal chain. The sound is still *there*, isn't it?"

Ben heard the sound ringing in his ears, still coming from far away from the ceiling-mounted speakers.

"The thing about reversing the polarity to cancel out a signal is that you need *two* signals — one with a waveform that's been fully phase-switched away from the other.

"But what happens when you *remove* one of those waveforms, Harvey? What happens when I simply *stop broadcasting* the signal through the suits?"

He turned and looked up at the speakers. "There's still *a* signal, and it's plenty loud enough. Clearly."

He walked up to the Exo, looked up at the two men, and smiled. "I'm proud of you, though. It's about time you took the *opportunity* to figure something out, Harvey. Luck comes to those who earn it, right?

"It took you this long to realize: you can't beat men like me until you *think* like men like me. You never wanted to go there, Harvey. You never wanted to admit to yourself that you *could* think like me. That you could scrape the depths of your soul to figure out how to beat someone."

Ben wanted to break him in half, to snap his neck and be done with it.

But he couldn't.

And the seconds we're still ticking off the watch.

6:38.

6:37.

6:36.

CHAPTER 70

JULIE

JULIE FELT her body stiffen up, the sense of her entire body falling asleep hitting her all at once. The pain of the tiny pinpricks of excited nerves, then the nothingness of feeling afloat in space, yet rigidly connected to the ground simultaneously. She wouldn't ever get used to this feeling, and she never wanted to.

Somehow Garza had triggered the signal once again, but she wasn't close enough to Ben and Reggie to hear his explanation, if he'd given one.

Now she was about five paces away from the open door, still inside her Exosuit. The others were stacked in a waving line behind Ben and Reggie's, all waiting their turn to exit.

All frozen, all unable to reach the exit standing directly in front of them.

She wondered how much time was left. It had to be less than ten minutes. How would they make it? Even if they somehow freed themselves, how could they make it up to the next level to the base's exit, *and* get clear of whatever it was Sturdivant was going to do?

She assumed it would be some sort of bunker-buster bomb — smaller than a nuclear warhead, which would no doubt cause much more political mayhem than physical — but also something that could pierce the mountain's craggy exterior and root out whatever was inside.

Or, more likely, simply collapse it in on itself, killing everyone inside.

Sturdivant would then be prepared to kill anyone trying to leave by blockading the exits to the Ravenshadow base.

In short, they were screwed. Fewer than ten minutes wasn't enough time to do anything but speculate on their fate, and since there was literally nothing she could anyway, she speculated.

Garza's voice grew in volume, and Julie couldn't shake the idea that the man sounded rattled. She'd never heard him like this before — enraged, maniacal, possibly even scared? She strained to hear what he was saying.

"It took you this long to realize: you can't beat men like me until you *think* like men like me. You never wanted to go there, Harvey."

Garza got even closer to the two men he was addressing, but his voice still rose.

"You never wanted to admit to yourself that you *could* think like me. That you could scrape the depths of your soul to figure out how to beat someone."

And then, to Julie's horror, Garza pulled out a pistol.

"It's about time I finished what we started in Philadelphia. Back then you were chasing me, and I was too busy to worry about you. A hawk catches its prey when there is a good opportunity to do so, and I never found it worth my time to bother with your little group.

"But now — *now,* Harvey — look around, with whatever your peripheral vision allows, and see what I've been able to accomplish. See that even though your work brought you here, to fight me and to prevent this, see that I've been able to *still* accomplish every aspect of what I set out to achieve.

"Know this, Harvey, in your last seconds of life: know that you failed. Not a failure of physical accomplishment, nor one of desire or teamwork or any other morally righteous failure, but a failure of *character*.

"You failed, Harvey, because you are *not enough*. You simply cannot bring yourself to do what it takes to defeat someone like me. You are simply not equipped to deal with the harsh reality of life: that you must take every opportunity, when it is presented to you."

Garza lifted the pistol and held it up the side of Ben's head.

"Know that you tried, Harvey, and that's not for nothing. But success comes to those who can handle it; to those who aren't afraid of what it brings. Or what it might cost."

Julie felt the scream building inside her, the rage and fear and fury and overwhelming grief building to a point that she wondered if it would even be enough to bypass the chemical that was holding her back.

Unfortunately it wasn't. She was still locked in place, unable to move, and unable to take her eyes off of Garza and her husband, and the gun that was being held to his head.

"I wish there was a way to let you have a last word or two, Harvey," Garza said. "I always did appreciate your little quips."

He took a deep breath, and even from her distance Julie could see him gently squeezing the trigger. The pistol was against Ben's temple, pressed hard against it.

Garza pulled the trigger.

Julie felt the shock of it from where she was. It was like a wall of sound, entering and leaving her body in the same instant, a pressure wave of epic proportions hitting her and pushing her back.

She felt as though she were falling backwards, her mind tumbling through open space, her limbs flailing helplessly as she watched her husband fall.

BUT BEN DIDN'T *FALL.*

He *moved.*

Julie realized then that the pressure wave had been exactly that — but it was the *absence* of pressure that had caused the effect. It was the *feeling* of sound, but it was actually sound leaving the space around her that had caused it.

The noise, the high-pitched whine that had once again driven them into their captive state, left. The sound had disappeared.

She had been straining against it, wiling it to move, to release its hold on her, and in the instant it did leave she had burst forward, pushing against the controls of her Exo and immediately causing it to lurch forward.

Ben and Reggie had apparently done the same thing. In the instant Garza had pulled the trigger, the noise had disappeared, and Ben had simultaneously fallen away, no doubt also trying to press against his noise-induced prison.

When Garza fired the pistol, Ben had jerked to the right, moving out of the way of the round and catching himself — and Garza — by surprise.

Reggie had reacted exactly as Julie had, by nearly falling on the front of his Exo and unknowingly pushing it forward. In the first second of their newfound freedom, Ben dodged the bullet while Reggie drove his Exo directly into Garza.

Garza stumbled backward and fell, his back to the stone floor, and he scrambled away from the marching Exo.

"Kill him!" Julie yelled. She was still finding her balance, working desperately to regain control of herself and her Exo.

She watched Garza regain his composure, wipe the sweat off his face with a sleeve of his shirt, then stand and begin running toward the open door.

"Kill him!" she yelled again.

She knew the others were feeling the same — a slightly drugged state consciousness that would wear off in a few more seconds.

But it wouldn't be enough time.

Garza was nearly at the door. He would disappear into the base, once again slipping through their fingers.

She looked over at Ben and Reggie, her eyes seeing double as they tried to keep up with the motion of her head.

No...

She knew they wouldn't make it. She knew they wouldn't be fully freed in time, and it would be to Garza's advantage.

This time, she did scream. Of all the physical manifestations of strength she was trying to regain, her ability to scream had been the first to return. She put everything she had into it, screaming and pushing against the controls and screaming more and finally —

Pulling the trigger.

She had him in her sights. The cannon fired.

The blast of it shook her to her core. The Exo nudged backward as the round exited the chamber and flew toward Garza's back.

He was out the door now, turning...

And the round hit the wall next to him.

It blasted a chunk of stone off the wall, creating a crater of dusty rock and debris, but she saw Garza through the cloud of dust. Saw that he was unscathed.

She had missed.

She heard his boots, falling against the stone floor as he continued around the corner.

She felt the tears welling up, and knew that they would be falling freely in a few seconds.

Garza was now completely gone, completely free.

Julie let the tears come. Everything she had been feeling fell out through her eyes — the rage, the confusion, chaos, sadness — all of it.

She heard a gunshot. It echoed through the corridor and into the large room.

Julie craned her neck to see, just as the bits of dust and rock finally settled to the floor just beyond the doorway.

Garza was there.

Stumbling, walking backwards.

What the hell?

He had a hand out, palm-up, in front of him. Holding something off, trying to persuade it to stop.

He backed up a few more steps, now fully back in Julie's sights.

She wiped her eyes. Placed her hands back on the controls. She had a clear shot. One press of the trigger, one flick of her wrist, and it would be over.

She wondered how many minutes were left before Sturdivant made his move.

Garza turned to face her. She gasped.

He had a long bloody line down the side of his face. His ear was in shambles, wrecked by a —

Another gunshot. This time Garza was hit in the side, puncturing a spot just between two ribs.

He made a strange gurgling noise, part high-pitched squeak and part groan. Julie watched on, mesmerized.

He stumbled again and fell, landing heavily on his shoulder and side. He spat a chunk of something, something red. More blood fell out behind it. He blinked twice, three times, staring at Julie and the others.

And then...

Victoria appeared. She was standing over him — standing over her father — holding a pistol. She stepped up next to him, right above his head, and aimed down.

She looked at Julie, met her eyes, then nodded.

And pulled the trigger.

This time the gunshot was deafening. Julie's ears felt the pain of the searing blow as the wave concussed through the chamber. The pistol must have been Garza's — the huge, 50-caliber Desert Eagle she'd seen him carry.

Julie opened her eyes and saw Victoria standing there, sobbing.

Suddenly Ben and Reggie were by her side. Ben reached out and jumped over to Julie's Exo. He placed his hands on her shoulders, gently pressing against them.

"Jules," he whispered. "Julie, we need to go."

Julie nodded, then stepped backwards, allowing Ben to pull her along and guide her out of the Exo.

Reggie and Mrs. E, followed by the remainder of the villagers — eleven in all — were there. They were all standing nearby, just inside the doorway, staring.

Staring at the man who had started all of this.

Staring at the daughter who had finished it.

"Come on, Jules," Ben whispered again. "We may not have much time before —"

The ground beneath Julie's feet shook and buckled, and she felt herself thrown into Ben's arms.

"It's happening!" Reggie shouted. "Time's up!"

She didn't know what to do, but it didn't matter.

Above her, the ceiling cracked and boulders of stone began tumbling a hundred feet straight down.

Onto their heads.

CHAPTER 72

BEN

BEN LUNGED FORWARD, taking Julie with him.

Get to the door.

He didn't know why that direction seemed necessary, seemed correct. He just knew.

He pushed his wife toward the exit and into the hallway. Reggie was at his side, Mrs. E shortly behind. They ran, taking the final ten feet of space on the demonstration floor before the doorway in three huge strides.

Pieces of rock were already hitting them, and they were growing bigger. He had seen the ceiling give, seemingly cracking in half and immediately pouring thousands of missiles of rock chips down onto them.

A head-sized rock caught Reggie's shoulder, but he hardly flinched. It looked like it had been moving fast enough to break a bone, but Ben hoped the strap holding Reggie's prosthetic had taken some of the impact. Still, it was likely to have dislocated it.

They made it to the edge of the doorway, and then into the hallway. They collapsed onto the floor, each laying out on the stone next to the disfigured, bleeding corpse of Vicente Garza.

The boulders continued tumbling down, and Ben pushed them

farther into the hallway. One especially massive one crushed the others in the entrance, effectively closing down access to the demonstration floor. A final volley of rocks and boulders sealed the shaft, a few of the smaller ones spilling out and nearly reaching the CSO group.

But it didn't matter. They were safe.

For now. Ben didn't know what Sturdivant had done, but his best guess was that he'd somehow sealed off the entrances and exits to the mountain base using explosives.

"Saddamizers," Reggie said. "Bunker Busters. We developed them in the 90s for Desert Storm. We called them Saddamizers."

"Sturdivant hit us with those?"

"The exits, sure. They're not nuclear, so they'll be impossible to detect more than a few miles away, but they'll be more than big enough to smash the doorways and shafts that lead out of here."

"So, we're hosed?" Ben asked.

"Yeah, we've been hosed since we got here," Reggie answered. "So the way I see it, we're actually *lucky* we're still alive."

"Well, don't count your blessings," Julie said. "There are still Ravenshadow goons around here somewhere, unless they all ran out when things in there got heated."

Things in there... Ben couldn't believe what they had just been through. He looked up to find Victoria staring at him.

"Thank you," he said.

She nodded, then wiped a tear. Her hands were shaking. She had placed the weapon down next to her dead father.

"You saved our lives," Ben said. He turned to the villagers — only half had made it through the doorway before the entire thing collapsed. "Most of us, anyway."

"I — I had to do it," she said. "After what he did. What he *made* me do. I... I couldn't help but —"

She began to sob uncontrollably, and Julie stood and walked over to the woman. She consoled her, wrapped her arm around her. She whispered to her as Ben and the others watched on.

They stood there for a moment, silently taking in the devastation, loss, and annihilation that one man had ravaged upon the world. They were stuck here, stuck inside a small mountain base with all of their possible exits destroyed.

Unless...

Ben looked up at the others. "You think Sturdivant knew about the drainage tunnel?"

Reggie smiled. Mrs. E answered him. "I believe it is worth checking. It could be an easy way out."

Ben had, over time, come to adopt the mantra of *there is no easy way out,* but he decided to keep that to himself this time.

"I'm in," Julie said. She looked from Victoria to Ben and then back again, as if questioning.

Victoria nodded as she spoke. "If... if you'll have me, you're my best shot at getting out of here alive. I know — I know I caused all of this, and —"

"Nonsense," Reggie said. "You know Ben causes more trouble for us than anyone else." He winked at Ben, who just shook his head. "Anyway, yeah — I think all of us should stick together. There still may be some of those Ravenshadow guys around."

"Agreed," Mrs. E said. "They will be looking for their commander. But until they find him dead, they will treat us as enemies."

Reggie sighed. "Too bad we don't have any of those Exos left over. We wouldn't have any trouble getting through here with them."

Ben looked at the rubble spilling into the hallway from the demonstration floor. The Exos and half of their operators were lost forever, sealed beneath a tomb of stone. There was nothing to do for them now except get out, get free, and tell the world what had happened here.

They could easily get the attention of the world press — Ben and his group had already been in the headlines a few times, for small adventures and takedowns of criminals around the world. Their status was far from celebrity, but they had enough clout to at least bring Garza's estate to justice.

He just hoped none of it would fall to Victoria. Ben wanted nothing more than to smear Garza's name, point to him alone for the abduction and murder of at least one entire Peruvian village, as well as the international war crimes, including killing Sturdivant's Green Berets.

But first, of course, they had to get out.

The drainage tunnel was their best bet, but even then it would be a long shot — the missiles that had taken out the main entrances and exits had caused enough destruction to lead to a complete cave-in of the largest central room, the demonstration floor. What would be the chances that the water-filled tunnel had been left undamaged?

They were about to find out. But first, they needed a bit more protection.

"Garza took all our rifles," Ben said. "We've got the Desert Eagle — Reggie, take that."

"Should we look for weapons?"

"No," Ben said. "Our best bet is to let Reggie take point —"

"— human bait," Reggie said. "Got it."

"—let him take point so he can *kill* anyone we come across."

"So we can steal their weapons," Julie said.

"Right," Reggie added. "Human bait. Whatever man, I thought we were friends."

Ben smiled, but still shook his head. How one man could remain so resilient and nonchalant in times of stress was beyond him, but he vowed to become more like his best friend.

"Okay," Ben said. "Let's roll. Reggie, lead the way."

THEY RAN for ten minutes without interruption, all without seeing another living soul.

Ravenshadow must have cleared out before the first bomb hit, Julie thought. *While they were getting blasted in the observation room.*

When the team had reached the stairs, Julie paused.

"Wait," she said. "There's... water. Coming from near the door."

They all looked down. In the dim light the water sparkled as it sloshed through the tiny gap between the door and the stone frame around it. She wondered where it was coming from, and — more importantly — if there was more of it.

Reggie opened the door, and the trickle of water turned into a slightly larger stream. Still not much, but it worried her.

"Let's hope that's just from a broken pipe or something from a higher floor," Ben said.

No one spoke as they ascended the stairs. The water continued pouring down, and Julie saw that it was originating from somewhere high above. They climbed the stairs to the second of the three floors — the floor they came in through — and when they reached the doorway Reggie paused once again.

"It's picking up," he said. "The water level."

Julie saw that he was right. The water coming from above them was now pouring down in a single sheet against the wall. Drips were hitting her face, the humidity in the stairwell was already starting to rise.

Ben turend to Victoria. "Did your father show you around this place?"

She shook her head. "He barely spoke to me," she said. Her voice was still shaking, still full of trepidation. "The only thing I heard about this place was that they didn't think it was a mine at all. None of them saw any mining equipment, and my father could never find any official blueprints or area maps that mention it."

Julie knew why — this place *wasn't* a mine, nor had it ever been one.

"There obviously weren't staircases here before," Victoria said. "My father added them when they moved in. But the shafts were already here."

Julie was surprised to hear that. The shafts were large, perfectly sized for the metal staircases that now filled them, so it was strange that they hadn't been originally meant for staircases. It was all further proof that this place had once been a sort of underground city rather than a mine, inhabited by the descendants of the Atlanteans.

But what were these shafts for? she wondered. *If this* was *a city at one point, how did they get from one level to the next? Ropes?*

It seemed like having stairs or ladders would have been ideal, but it was clear that there had never been any stairs in these shafts.

The water came in more heavily as Reggie opened the door to the second floor. The stairwells on each level were lit with a single, dim light fixture mounted above each door, and Julie looked up to the floor above them. It was obvious now that the water was pouring in from the top level, from somewhere beyond the door that led to the third floor. It seemed as though the only thing keeping a solid wall of water from falling over them now was the door itself.

"We need to get out quick," Reggie said, stepping through the doorway.

He didn't bother to look for any opponents — it was clear now that the Ravenshadow base had been cleared, or the men were dead. Julie hadn't seen much more evidence of Sturdivant's earthquake that had caused the ceiling to collapse in the demonstration floor, but it was also true that they had stayed along the southern side of the base. The entrances Sturdivant would have targeted were on the north and west sides, according to Beale's reconnaissance.

It was very possible that they were in fact sealed inside a tomb of stone. Julie ignored the feeling, pushing it away as a problem to be dealt with later.

They ran along the same hallway they'd run through before, this time heading toward the smaller offshoot shaft that would lead to the drainage tunnel. But even before they got to the entrance to the shaft Julie could see there was a problem.

"It's blocked," Ben said.

The tunnel had collapsed in on itself, and bits of stone had tumbled out into the hallway. Water was gushing around it, heading down the hallway in the opposite direction, pooling in the corners. And even from here, Julie could see that it was getting higher.

"Shit," Reggie said. "Our scuba gear is on the other side of that shaft."

"Even without the gear, our *way out* is on the other side of that shaft," Julie said.

"We must find another way," Mrs. E said. "But we would have seen any other obvious exits."

Julie turned to find Victoria speaking in hushed tones with some of the Peruvian villagers. They conversed for a moment then looked back at the CSO group.

"They say there are other ways out," Victoria said. "But none of them know where."

"Great," Reggie said. "So... there aren't any ways out of here that we *know* about. Any of them want to take a guess?"

"They say there are air shafts, for ventilation, that locals have found accidentally over the years. Many are blocked by debris and stones, but some may be accessible."

"Ask them if they're large enough for us to fit in," Julie asked.

Victoria asked, and the Peruvian man she was speaking with eyed Ben.

"He says *they* can fit into the shafts."

Julie stepped toward him. "It's better than nothing," she said. "Let's find one of them, see if someone can fit into it, and they can call for help once they're out."

Victoria translated along. But when she looked back at Julie, she knew there was something wrong. "That's just it," Victoria said. "I haven't *seen* any of those shafts, and neither have they."

"But... you said they exist."

"That's what they told me, but they haven't ever seen any from *inside* the mountain. Their village knew of two, but there was only twenty or thirty feet of length before the shafts were stopped up with rocks and debris."

"And they were human-made?" Ben asked.

Victoria asked the man.

"Absolutely," she said after a moment. "They explained that the shafts were square-shaped, with perfectly straight walls, chiseled out of the stone itself. They were part of the myth and lore of the region; a way for the 'keepers of the mine' to access the outside world."

"Okay," Reggie said. "We need to find one of these little shafts. Let's get back to the stairs, head up a level."

"Agreed," Ben said. "If there are any, they'll be at the top level."

Julie found herself once again following along, once again wondering if they would actually be able to find an exit, and once again wondering how she'd gotten them into this whole mess.

They reached the stairwell — once again — and began climbing. Julie noticed the water level rising, and the pace of the water was increasing.

CHAPTER 74

BEN

AT THE TOP level of the base, Ben looked around for anything that might hint at potential freedom. Unfortunately the place was exactly the same as they'd left it — the long, straight hallway dumping into the small video booth at the end of the hall, and the smaller, older shaft covered by a curtain next to it. He tried to see if there were anything else that seemed out of place, but the lights were beginning to flicker. Two bulbs near him had already gone out, either from the original explosion and earthquake or due to a short from the flowing water.

There was no water collecting on the floor up here, but Ben saw it trickling from the ceiling and pouring down the walls. He hadn't noticed the tiny cracks in the ceiling before, but it was almost as if the ceiling blocks were somehow hovering, not actually connected to the walls. It was a feat of engineering, but it was one he'd seen before.

Ever since they'd determined that this place had originally belonged to the Atlanteans and Chachapoyas, the details began revealing themselves. The size of the shafts was similar to those of the tunnels they'd found in Egypt, and the design, build quality, and workmanship was exactly the same as well.

"Want to go to the video room again?" Reggie asked, still holding the Desert Eagle.

Ben shook his head. "I have no idea. There's nothing up here. It's the same as we left —"

Ben's feet fell out from underneath him. He felt his knee overextend a bit as he landed hard on it, but he regained his balance. Julie and Reggie crashed to the ground in front of him, while Mrs. E bounced off the wall behind her.

"The hell was that?" Reggie asked.

"Aftershock," Ben answered. "The mountain's shifting."

"You don't think Sturdivant hit us again, do you?" Julie asked.

"No need," Ben said. "The exits were most likely blocked off during the first explosion, and he's probably got men on the ground to take out anyone who's made it beyond that."

"In other words," Reggie said. "The mountain's coming down on top of us."

"Just like Jeffers said."

To answer, the water surged and picked up, pushed along from a space beyond Ben's vision. It curled and ebbed against his boots, first at the ankle, then up to his calves.

"Water's coming in fast, now," Reggie said. "We need to figure this out *now*, guys."

Ben was thinking the same thing. They were on the top level of the base, and where there had been no standing water on the floors before there was now a river.

And that river was rising — fast.

Two of the Peruvians, a man and a woman, began breathing rapidly. Ben turned to face them when Victoria translated.

"They cannot swim," she said. "They are scared."

"We're all scared," he replied. "But they're going to have to learn to swim, and stat."

"Over there," Mrs. E said. "It looks like the water is coming from that tunnel."

It was the tunnel they'd been led through by Victoria, the one that had been obscured by the curtain. They trudged toward it.

"Why did your father hide this tunnel behind the curtain?" Ben asked.

"He only meant to make it more difficult to find the interrogation room," she answered. Ben sensed a hint of regret in her voice. "You all weren't the first he used it on."

Ben nodded. "Besides connecting this side of the top level with the stairs on the other end, does it go anywhere?"

She shook her head. "Not that I know of."

"It's graded," Reggie said. "The water's coming this way because it's slightly downhill from the origin point."

As he spoke, the water in the tunnel reached Ben's knees. It was beginning to froth and foam up, miniature whitewater rapids around their legs.

"Let's get up there," Ben said. "We don't have a better option. The lower levels will be even more flooded than this one."

No one spoke as they sloshed forward. Ben waited for the four villagers to hike past, taking up a point at the back of the line, just in case someone slipped. He wasn't about to let anyone else die on his watch.

The three men and one woman from the group of villagers were surprisingly strong as a group. Their feet were solid on the stone floor, though it was growing more slippery by the second. They held hands and pulled each other along, one step at a time.

By the time the water was at Ben's waist, they'd reached the end of the narrow shaft. He could barely see the source of the water in the dying light. It spilled out from a small, rectangular slit in the ceiling, one that disappeared upward into the rock.

"Have you seen this before?" Ben yelled. The water was crashing out of the hole with a fury, and he knew they had only minutes before it would completely consume this shaft.

"No," she said. "But I wasn't privy to much of it. He only showed me a few of the main rooms before he…"

Before he took over her mind, Ben thought, finishing the sentence for her. *Before he took his own daughter's mind and turned it into his slave.*

Ben turned to the rest of the group and shouted over the din of the pouring water. "Best guess, we've got a minute before this whole place is an underwater tomb. That means we can't head back the way we came — it's already underwater.

"And we have nowhere else to go, unless it's up."

"But that means —"

"That means we have to wait until the water's done pouring into this shaft, then swim up into it."

"And we'll be holding our breaths the whole time."

Ben nodded. "And we'll have to hold our breath."

One of the Peruvian men in their group spoke to Victoria. She tuned to Ben. "How do we know there's open air up there?"

Ben looked around, just as the water level rose to his shoulders. The current had slowed, so he found it relatively easy to keep his balance. The Peruvian woman, a whole head shorter than Ben, was treading water and holding onto the shoulders of the man next to her.

"Guys — we don't. We don't know anything. We're just hoping now, that's all. This little ventilation shaft — whatever it is — might be our only way out."

He paused, looked around his team and the villagers they'd picked up along the way, wondering if this would be the last time he saw them.

"Or it might be the end."

CHAPTER 75

BEN

THE WATER HAD REACHED Ben's eyes. The Peruvian men and woman were treading water, their lips pursed and pointed upward as their heads barely breached the surface. Julie was treading water as well, but Reggie and Mrs. E were still able to touch the ground.

"Julie, you go first with two of the villagers," Ben shouted. "Then Mrs. E and the other two. You two are their lifelines — got it?"

Julie and Mrs. E nodded. "Keep them in front of you, and push them if you need to. Remember, Reggie and I are last, so we'll be holding our breaths the longest."

Julie swam over to Ben.

"Ben," she said, softly, speaking into his ear so the others couldn't hear. "Let me go last. I can hold my breath —"

"No."

He didn't argue, he didn't even look at her.

"Ben..."

He grabbed her hand underwater, pulling her closer. "I love you, Jules. I'm not arguing. Get these people out, and wait for me."

She nodded. It looked like there was a tear falling down her face, but their faces were all covered with splashes of water.

"Thirty seconds!" Reggie yelled. Victoria translated, asked the villagers if they needed any other instructions. They shook their heads.

Suddenly the water was at the ceiling. Ben pushed his lungs free, expelling all the air from them, then sucked in the deepest breath he was able. Next to him Julie and Reggie did the same.

Before he'd even pulled his head completely underwater Mrs. E was pushing forward, nearly throwing the first two villagers into the rectangular ventilation shaft. She violently kicked and shoved the three of them up against the slowing current.

In a few seconds she was gone, and Julie was in her place, working the two remaining villagers into position. She swam with them, having an easier time of it as the water had finally stopped pushing against them and these two villagers were capable of pulling themselves along.

And then Reggie went.

Ben's breath was still in his lungs, but it was beginning to poison him. He felt the burning sting of the air souring, his body beginning to fight back against it, willing him to open his mouth, and then —

It was his turn.

Reggie's feet were in his face, but Ben wasn't about to wait another second. He kicked with everything he had, using energy that meant it was directly working against his ability to hold his breath. He pulled with his arms, the rectangular slit not wide enough for him to move forward with his arms fully extended, while continuing to kick with his legs.

He made progress, but it was too slow.

His lungs were about to burst, the involuntary desire to breathe growing as strong as his voluntary ability to prevent it. It was a balancing act, but it was one he would eventually lose. The human body was incapable of preventing its most basic needs, and breathing ranked high on the list of things that were required.

There was no light.

The darkness of the shaft penetrated his soul, and the water consuming him caused him to feel as though he were weightless, lying at a diagonal in the center of a black hole. He focused on the walls, focused on the smooth, hand-cut stone blocks, the gaps between them nearly unnoticeable.

But it still wasn't enough.

The darkness deepened somehow, his throat and mind constricting, and he knew he wouldn't make it.

He reached forward, knowing that if he could just feel Reggie's boot, grab his friends ankle for just a moment, it would be enough. He would find a bit more strength and stamina there.

But there was no boot. There was no ankle to grab hold of; Reggie was gone.

CHAPTER 76

BEN

BEN WAS ALONE NOW, floating in his black hole, fighting the slip into unconsciousness.

He'd read somewhere that death by drowning was one of the better ways to go — your mind experiences a state of euphoria, of an elated sense of self. The problem was that he'd also read that the moments *before* death — the period during which the body tries desperately to stay alive — is severely uncomfortable. The body sucks in gasps of water, screams as it realizes there is no air with which it can breathe, and then struggles in vain to get to the surface.

Ben was experiencing this now. Bubbles escaped the corners of his mouth, his lips barely strong enough to keep in the last of the life-giving air. He also knew that life-giving air was now mostly carbon dioxide, and it was this that his body was trying to expel.

He flailed, feeling the helplessness and terror set in.

I'm not going to make it.

Ben fought, hard, against the darkness, but he no longer knew which way was up. The walls seemed to disappear, taunting him as he strained to reach them.

He let out another burst of carbon dioxide. The bubbles tickled his face, his nose. He wanted to scream, and so he did.

The last gasp of air left his mouth and was immediately replaced by water. Cold, sweet death. It fell into him, covering his throat and his lungs and his mind. Water everywhere, and yet he continued screaming and struggling and fighting until...

Everything stopped.

Everything fell silent.

His mind felt the elation. The true euphoria of near-death setting in. He saw lights — gold, silver, greens and blues — dancing across his vision. Were his eyes even open?

He remembered something, something that seemed distant now. *Swim toward the light*, he thought. *Was that just a saying? Something he should actually do?*

He decided not to. Everything was perfect in here, everything calm and still and perfect. He liked it. This was true bliss, and yet he knew the end had come. Was this, then, a transition? Something that would lead to something else? Or was this *it?*

Was this all it was at the end?

He didn't know. Didn't care. His mind was racing along, but it was no longer his own. He was in control of nothing, and finally, he didn't care.

He let himself be pulled along by death, allowed himself the sweet satisfaction on not having to worry anymore — about anything.

Ben smiled. Or thought he did. He didn't know, nor did he care. *This is it*, he thought. *My final thought. And my final wish.*

No. There was more. He was still in the black hole, in the tunnel of lights, but now there was something else. *Julie.* He felt her lips, felt her caress.

My wife. He was dreaming of her, reaching out to her.

Julie. He wanted to say her name. He wanted to grab her hand, to pull her in close and kiss her back, but he couldn't do a thing.

Death had set in, and he was now merely a spectator to his own end. To whatever transition there was. He believed there was something else, something more, but he had the realization that if there were something else, it was taking a long time to get here.

He felt himself swallow, then — something lunged out of him and some of the lights disappeared. The blues and greens were gone, the golds and silvers still there. The darkness still covered all of it.

He thought he could feel his body again, a gentle tingling sensation as it moved and shook. He felt Julie's lips, soft and warm, a *real* feeling.

They were gone, and then they returned once again.

Julie.

He tried saying it aloud. Forced everything he had to form the words.

"Julie."

It was a whisper, but he knew he'd heard it. *Sound.* It had been real.

"Julie — lips."

And then his eyes opened. There was gold, and silver, the lights he'd seen. Blues and greens shifted into the form of humans and water and whatever sat behind them.

And there, right in front of his face, were lips.

He felt something pushing against him, against his chest and lungs. He could breathe, but it hurt.

He blinked, allowing the lips to come into focus.

They belonged to Reggie.

He was laying on his back on the stone floor, the water seeping out of him and around him. He was cold. Reggie smiled back down at him as he stopped compressing his chest.

"Man," Reggie said. "I *knew* you had a thing for me."

JULIE WAS CRYING, but also trying to watch Reggie work. It was a constant battle between wiping away tears and trying to stop shaking. Victoria was holding her, and the four villagers were standing behind them. The woman had her hands on Julie's shoulders.

Mrs. E, for her part, was kneeling next to Reggie, ready to take over the CPR as soon as Reggie needed a break. Julie couldn't see clearly through her own tears, but it seemed as though the other two members of her group — the closest friends she had in the world — were also struggling to keep it together.

And then, with a sputtering splash of water that began inside Ben's mouth and ended on Reggie's face, Ben came back to life.

"Julie — lips."

"I knew you always had a thing for me," Reggie said, wiping his face with a sleeve.

She smiled.

Reggie laughed, then spoke quietly to Ben. She moved over to her husband and kissed him, but Reggie gently pulled her back.

"You might want to stand back, Jules," he said. "There's usually another —"

On cue, Ben rolled to his side and coughed out another bucketful of water, mixed with vomit and spit and bile. It splashed her knees, but she didn't move. She went back in for another kiss.

"Ben," she said. "I love you. I love you. I thought —"

"I was — I was dead," Ben said.

"Yeah, because you're an idiot," Reggie said. "You were three inches from the surface, but you kept sinking back under. I had to stick my whole upper body into the hole to grab you, or you would've sunk back to the other shaft."

"Th — thanks, man."

"Eh, don't worry about." He held up his right arm. "You'd better hope this thing is waterproof, though. Or it's gonna cost you another one."

Ben smiled. Julie hugged him.

"What happened?" Ben asked. "Where are we?"

"Well, we all got out and waited. We never saw you come up completely, but Reggie ducked back in and found your arms."

"You might... have a bit of a bruise," Reggie said. "You were a bit slippery."

Julie saw Ben rubbing the area of his wrist where Reggie had clamped his prosthetic arm around it.

"And to answer your second question," Julie continued. "I think we found out where those ventilation shafts end up."

Julie looked around once again at the space they'd ended up in. The shafts that hadn't been filled in over the course of centuries sent pinpricks of light down to the center of the chamber. The space was shaped like the upper half of a diamond, a six-sided pyramid. The room had been carved into the interior of the mountain's peak, and each of the shafts that were visible seemed to end on a different face of the mountain.

It was miraculous — they'd found a hidden room inside the mountain, one that had been filled completely with water, thanks to a natural spring that trickled water down one wall.

"Whoa," Ben said. "This is... something else."

"It's the hidden chamber," Julie said. "The Hall of Records."

"It was totally filled in with water," Reggie said. "When Sturdivant bombed the exits, it caused instability up here and something broke. The water fell to the lower levels."

Ben slowly sat up. "Why was it filled with water?" Ben asked.

"Come here," Julie said. She helped him stand, then guided him a few feet to his right. "Look around."

She followed his gaze, watching his expression as he realized where they were. While the overall shape of the room was that of a diamond, the floor they were standing on was circular. About fifteen feet in diameter, they were standing on a circular crop of stone. Outside of that circular rock, a ring of six inch-deep water encircled them, followed by two more rings of stone and water.

Scattered amongst the concentric circles, on the stone rings, were etchings and carved writings. They looked familiar, and Julie knew Ben recognized the writing as the same that they had discovered in the temples in the valley just outside this mountain.

"It's... Atlantis," Ben said softly. "Their city was built in concentric circles, allowing them protection from invaders."

"Exactly," Julie said. "It's a replica of their original world. Their entire history is probably here, written in stone."

"Something that water wouldn't destroy."

"Something no one would find, unless they knew exactly where to look."

"Their goal was to reseed the world with their knowledge. After the flood, they spread out to every corner of the globe and taught civilization. They gave us farming, art, and laws."

"And they recorded it all here. In their Hall of Records."

"Julie — guys — this is incredible. This is one of the biggest finds of the century... of *all time.*"

Julie smiled. "Well, it was your idea."

Ben shrugged. "I just really didn't want to die."

"And neither did they. It's *why* they built this place. They were fugitives from their homeland, but they refused to go quietly. They helped kickstart the world once again, knowing that if they were ever needed again it would be because of a major catastrophe."

Ben looked up at the ceiling, deep in thought.

"What's up?" Julie asked.

"It's just... why put your secret Hall of Records *above* your city, then fill it with water? Doesn't it seem a bit... masochistic?"

Reggie walked over. "Or symbolic."

"How so?"

"Think about it — these guys were chased from their homeland by a cataclysmic wall of water, which completely drowned their original city. We saw that in Santorini. They moved to Egypt, but there was always unrest and uneasiness there, and they were eventually chased from there, too.

"Then they finally found a home here, in the Chachapoyas Valley of Peru. The 'light-skinned natives,' the Spanish called them. The Spanish were always on the search for gold and silver, and treasures, and essentially destroyed the Inca for it."

"But *this* was the treasure the whole time," Ben said. "The *record* of their life. What they used as their library, to spread their culture again. They reached the Egyptians, the Vikings, the Native Americans, and the Inca, Aztecs, and Maya here."

"So it's *symbolic* that the only time they'd need to access this vault of information is if and when something cataclysmic happened. Or, in other words, they set this up *as* the cataclysm."

"They would flood their home to access the Hall of Records once again," Ben finished.

"And then move somewhere else, and start over."

"Exactly. They were always oppressed. The misunderstood 'daughters of Cain' from scripture, the race that led to giants, the first murders, and eventually the flood itself. They were said to be descended from Cain, bred with fallen angels. Certainly not a favored people in God's eyes."

"Right," Julie said. "I remember that. They strayed from God's commands and sought other knowledge, much like Eve in the Garden of Eden. That eventually led to their understanding of mathematics and engineering, which gave them a leg up on the rest of civilization."

It all made sense to her. The Daughters of Cain, as they were sometimes referred to, were seen as the original group of rebels that included the nephilim, the race of giants from which the storied Goliath descended. Their cousins were thought to be the titans that wrestled with the Greek gods of antiquity, the race of half-god, half-human giants that ruled the antediluvian world.

The Atlanteans.

"But... how does it all work?"

"I've been thinking about it," Reggie said. "And the mechanism would be relatively simple for them. They were engineering geniuses, remember? They could have a door that would open only if there was enough pressure on the other side of it."

"Like water pressure," Julie said.

"Exactly. Have just enough pressure up here from the thousands of tons of water, and all they'd need to do is redirect that drainage tunnel — the water from it, anyway — up here for a minute or two, and it would push the whole thing over. The scales would tip, and the door would open, releasing the rest of the water.

"It would flood their homes, but it would reveal their Hall of Records."

"And if they didn't survive for whatever reason, their Hall of Records would still be here, literally written in stone."

Reggie nodded.

"That's all great and stuff," Ben said. "But how the hell do we get out of here?"

"That's the best part," Reggie said, pointing. Julie followed his finger and saw that one of the rectangular ventilation shafts had what looked like a ladder etched into the wall beneath it. "I think all that water would have no trouble opening a *second* door — one that allows people into the Hall of Records."

"Or, in our case," Mrs. E said, joining them. "Letting us *out*."

AFTERWORD

If you liked this book (or even if you hated it...) write a review or rate it. You might not think it makes a difference, but it does.

Besides *actual* currency (money), the currency of today's writing world is *reviews*. Reviews, good or bad, tell other people that an author is worth reading.

As an "indie" author, I need all the help I can get. I'm hoping that since you made it this far into my book, you have some sort of opinion on it.

Would you mind sharing that opinion? It only takes a second.

Nick Thacker

ALSO BY NICK THACKER

Mason Dixon Thrillers

Mark for Blood (Book 1)

Death Mark (Book 2)

Mark My Words (Book 3)

Harvey Bennett Mysteries

The Enigma Strain (Book 1)

The Amazon Code (Book 2)

The Ice Chasm (Book 3)

The Jefferson Legacy (Book 4)

The Paradise Key (Book 5)

The Aryan Agenda (Book 6)

The Book of Bones (Book 7)

The Cain Conspiracy (Book 8)

Harvey Bennett Mysteries - Books 1-3

Harvey Bennett Mysteries - Books 4-6

Jo Bennett Mysteries

Temple of the Snake (written with David Berens)

Tomb of the Queen (written with Kristi Belcamino)

Harvey Bennett Prequels

The Icarus Effect (written with MP MacDougall)

The Severed Pines (written with Jim Heskett)

The Lethal Bones (written with Jim Heskett)

Gareth Red Thrillers

Seeing Red

Chasing Red (written with Kevin Ikenberry)

The Lucid

The Lucid: Episode One (written with Kevin Tumlinson)

The Lucid: Episode Two (written with Kevin Tumlinson)

The Lucid: Episode Three (written with Kevin Tumlinson

Standalone Thrillers

The Atlantis Stone

The Depths

Relics: A Post-Apocalyptic Technothriller

Killer Thrillers (3-Book Box Set)

Short Stories

I, Sergeant

Instinct

The Gray Picture of Dorian

Uncanny Divide (written with Kevin Tumlinson and Will Flora)

ABOUT THE AUTHOR

Nick Thacker is a thriller author from Texas who lives in Colorado and Hawaii, because Colorado has mountains, microbreweries, and fantastic weather, and Hawaii also has mountains, microbreweries, and fantastic weather. In his free time, he enjoys reading in a hammock on the beach, skiing, drinking whiskey, and hanging out with his beautiful wife, tortoise, two dogs, and two daughters.

In addition to his fiction work, Nick is the founder and lead of Sonata & Scribe, the only music studio focused on producing "soundtracks" for books and series. Find out more at SonataAndScribe.com.

For more information, visit Nick online:
www.nickthacker.com
nick@nickthacker.com

facebook.com/AuthorNickThacker
twitter.com/NickThacker
instagram.com/thenickthacker